SPIDER 2-3

SPIDER 2-3

Robert Vallier spent much of his life in music management, covering international touring, recording and theatre production. He created the *Into Space!* series of lectures and books (which he published) for his close friend the late Sir Patrick Moore. He raised his 3 children as a single parent. Robert holds a private pilot's licence. He was responsible for sending over 5½ tons of books to needy schools in South Africa as catalogued working libraries. They continue today to enhance the lives of over 12,000 children annually. He shares his love of flying by taking handicapped and sick children and their parents up into the air in fun charity flights, bringing some much-needed respite to the families.

Spider 2-3 is his first novel.

www.robertvallier.com

ROBERT VALLIER

SPIDER 2-3

Jaguar Publishing Inc

Jaguar Publishing Inc
265 South 9th Street, Suite 4
Philadelphia, PA 19107
USA

ISBN: 978-0-9908811-4-8

www.Spider2-3.com

Copyright © Robert Vallier 2015

Robert Vallier
asserts the moral right to be identified
as the author of this work.

This Edition first published by Jaguar Publishing Inc *Publishers* 2015.
Reprinted 2016.

All Rights Reserved. No part of this publication may be reproduced, stored in a retrieval system or transmitted, in any form or by any means, electronic, mechanical, photocopying, recording or otherwise, including information storage and retrieval systems, without the prior permission of the Publishers.

The information in this book is distributed on an 'as is' basis, without warranty. Although every precaution has been taken in the preparation of this work, neither the author nor the publisher shall have any liability to any person or entity with respect to any loss or damage caused or alleged to be caused directly or indirectly by the information contained in this book.

Trademarked names appear throughout this book. Rather than use a trademark symbol with every occurrence of a trademarked name, names are used in an editorial fashion, with no intention of infringement of the respective owner's trademark. The use of registered names, trademarks, etc. in this publication does not imply even in the absence of a specific statement, that such names are exempt from the relevant laws and regulations and therefore free for general use.

Neither the author nor the publisher make any representation, express or implied, with regard to the accuracy of the information contained in this book and cannot accept any legal responsibility or liability for any errors or omissions that may be made.

This is a work of fiction. Names, characters, places, and incidents either are the product of the author's imagination or are used fictitiously, and any resemblance to actual persons, living or dead, events, or locales is entirely coincidental.

Cover Design: Damonza

For Rosemary and Diana

CONTENTS

	Acknowledgements	*iii*

PART ONE: THE BEGINNING

1	Berlin. The Present	3
2	St Lucia. 3 Weeks Later	6
3	Moscow	13

PART TWO: SIXTY-FOUR SQUARES

4	London	29
5	Awaking	43
6	Breaking	56
7	Afterwards	70
8	Hospital	75
9	The Fifth Rubric	79
10	The Plan	93
11	Preparing	104
12	The Twelve Apostles	126

PART THREE: ACQUISITIONS

13	Theft One	141
14	Out-Foxed	151
15	Delivery One	165
16	Sochi	170
17	Theft Two	178
18	Tracking	196
19	Reflections	211
20	The Trail	223

PART FOUR: USE OF ASSETS

21	Into Zimbabwe	239
22	Kawala	257
23	Back Home	282
24	Hermes	291
25	Target	304
26	Countering	312
27	Arrival	323
28	Surveillance	337
29	The Last Day	350

PART FIVE: THE END OF THE BEGINNING

30	Soar Again	379
31	Sorting Out	395
32	Falling Down	404
33	Onto The Stage	410

	Author's Note	*431*

ACKNOWLEDGEMENTS

Many have helped me along the journey.

My thanks to Rosemary, Diana, Becky, Shelley Reid, James Crabbe, Ian Hoare, Pam Tabor, Cameron Muir, Gavin Rajah, Richard Wainwright, Barry King, Mace Neufeld, David Barnes, Rufus Thompson, Mike Hollister, Mark and Jamie Richardson and last but certainly not least Sue Constantino.

Each has given kindly and generously of their own time and thought, and to each I am most grateful.

Finally, my thanks also to my editor Martin Fletcher, for new light.

Robert Vallier

www.robertvallier.com

PART ONE

THE BEGINNING

1

BERLIN
THE PRESENT

THE ELEVATOR DOORS opened. The night receptionist looked up from her keyboard and glanced at the man. She noticed the light brown coat, the dark shoes, the grey hair. No-one important. She put away her empty smile.

It would be the last smile he'd ever see.

The man walked briskly, the bushy white eyebrows drawn together beneath lines of worry, his darting brown eyes sharpened by months of danger.

He pushed through the revolving doors and stepped out into the Kurfürstendamm, and cursed as there were no cabs in sight. He didn't have that far to go. He pulled his coat closer around him as the cold air hit, and turned left to walk up the street.

The central reservation split three traffic lanes either side and was filled with cars parked up for the night. The pavement was wide, with rows of square advertising kiosks and mature trees along the kerb that splayed a graceful umbrella of spring foliage. Although Berlin at night was far from deserted there were fewer pedestrians at 2am midweek and those were lovers or prostitutes or drunks who were not interested in him.

He broke into a run.

His legs were tired and his chest heaved from too much smoking for too many years. He crossed one street, and then another, but at Uhlandstrasse a grey Mercedes screeched to a halt as he ran out in front of it.

Two men a hundred yards behind him turned in the direction of the sound, and started a gentle run towards it.

The man from the hotel went further up the Kurfürstendamm. He stopped on the corner of the Café Kranzler to catch some breath, leaning against one of the ornate black lampposts, putting his hands down onto his knees. He was gasping, sweating profusely. He didn't feel the cold any more.

He ran on. Now he could see the Kaiser Wilhelm Church, the ruin from the Second World War. He crossed the next street, dodging the cars, at the C&A store. A vision flashed into his mind of when he was a young boy shopping with his mother; he saw her loving face, her soft eyes that had started to carry wrinkles but that laughed happily still. That was a different world.

Another couple of hundred yards and he was there, a landmark of imperialistic power destroyed in battle. One side of the light brown stonework had been ripped off by a bomb that had blown the rest of the Church to pieces and taken all of the glass from the huge circle windows and archways with it. What remained eerily bore craters from hundreds of bullet and shrapnel hits. He followed the curve of the building round and ran up the first couple of steps. He leant back against the wall, panting for breath. He was early, he knew, but that was ok.

He saw the feet of the other man first. He looked up and his breathing halted in a gasp. It was the eyes that scared him most. The other man was six feet tall easily, younger than he, strong, fit. He had to get away, and with all his strength he brought his clenched fist up, smashing it into the man's face. He ran up the steps along the side of the Church, and straight into the second man who had gone around the other side. An easy punch into the solar plexus and the man from the hotel was completely disabled.

The two men picked him up and carried him, one arm each, to the entrance between the two pairs of white statues and slammed his back against the heavy wooden door. The one with the bruised jaw pulled a knife from his hip pocket, flicked it open and plunged the gleaming six inch blade into the man's chest. He grinned, while the older man looked up at him in amazed disbelief, feeling his strength ebb away as his cut heart stopped, the lips twisting and trembling in shock. The eyes began to empty of life, and his lungs exhaled for the last time.

He was dead before he hit the ground.

One of the younger men knelt and quickly rummaged in his pockets, while the other stood guard. There were a few couples walking hand in hand, a tramp on the other side of the street sifting through waste baskets, two women kissing, cars going back and forth. Nobody stopped, or looked, or called out.

His companion found what he wanted. The two men walked back into the Kurfürstendamm and disappeared into the night.

Berlin. For Dr Philip Keppof, the city of death.

2
ST LUCIA
THREE WEEKS LATER

JIM PEREGRINE GAZED out over the Caribbean sea. The blue waters lapped gently on the beach thirty yards away and massaged the sides of two rowing boats resting lopsided in the shallow water. The sun was already warm and the sky a beautiful light blue that met the sea at the horizon without a single cloud spoiling the view. To the right, the beach curved gently for five hundred yards until low cliffs cut into the water; to the left, more beach and sand led to a rock-laden promontory eclipsing the small restaurant and huts round the other side all topped with the Island's corrugated roofing. The local fishermen were already out, and he wondered what would be on the menu that evening.

The bungalow beach house was constructed on wooden stilts that protected it from the waters of a high tide, and a little imagination and local rum justified its legend of *The Smiling Face*. Two windows either side of the front door nose, white spindles under a ruby bannister lip and a tongue of steps down to the beach; it was a happy home, owned by a local family that rented it out from time to time.

JP sat down on the steps and leaned back on his elbows to enjoy the sun. His short-sleeved shirt was open and his shorts hugged his contours, their small length leaving most of his thighs uncovered. The sun had lightened his black hair over the last few days, and was deepening his tan by the second.

Stella came out of the door holding two cups of coffee and JP put his head back further, looking at her upside down.

"You look good from every angle, did you know that?" he quipped, as he watched her slowly walk in her heels and bikini.

"Yes, I know darling," she said with a smile. "Are you going to look at me all day, or are you going to have some of this coffee?"

"It's a tough choice," he said, "I'm not sure yet."

"Well while you're thinking what to do, would you come and take one of these cups off me?" She held the cups at her waist, her legs slightly apart. She liked to tease him.

"I think I can do that," he said, and stood to rescue a cup. He looked down at her and smiled, kissed her lightly on the lips and said, "Thank you."

She smiled back, "You're welcome."

The coffee was creamy and strong, and the aroma carried nicely through the air. They sat on the top step, close so their arms and legs touched often. Sometimes she tilted her head and rested it against his arm; she couldn't quite reach his shoulder, he was too tall.

This was a paradise, thought JP. He turned to look at Stella. Twenty-six, bright, cultured, oozing sexuality; a natural beauty whose blazing golden hair and generous curves would always turn heads. Her soft elegant cheeks yielded to a slight blush when she laughed and blonde eyebrows and long eyelashes danced over sparkling emerald eyes.

Stella had always embraced her beauty modestly, as a gift from nature, and taken it in her stride.

Her father, Sebastian Fincrest, had created a profitable munitions company in South Africa. It grew to financial greatness in the difficult years of Apartheid, during which he quietly worked to bring political change, and successfully embraced the democratic era with a variety of on-going government contracts.

He had wooed and won the hand of a new Miss South Africa, a beauty from Pretoria, and it was natural to Seb Fincrest that their two children should inherit the family fortune. The level-headed Stella was schooled in South Africa and the University of Cape Town, then added business management at Harvard, where she graduated summa cum laude. She moved into a senior management position in the family business, and her brother into politics. The Fincrest heiress was never far from the gossip columns and media outlets of South Africa, who followed every move of their 'Scintillating Stella' as a celebrity, and it was clear she was being groomed to take over the business upon her father's retirement in five or six years.

Men had been after her since a young age, but she steered a sensible path. She knew what she wanted in a man, but hadn't found it yet.

Or had she?

Stella thought of the man she was sitting next to, and of the days they had spent together. They had been fun, fine days.

Stella broke the silence.

"That was the last of the cream and the coffee, by the way," she said, straightening her head away from his arm, "so you can go hunting today to bring us some more."

"Right," said JP, "I'll get my spear and machete."

She giggled.

"Or, I could just take a walk down to the store."

"Do you always take the easy way out?"

"Yes," he said. "Always."

JP's eyes followed her hair gathered round her shoulder. Stella held his gaze.

The coffee would have to wait.

JP lifted her up. She put her arms around his neck as he carried her, and kissed him; one of her shoes fell off and clattered down onto the sand. He stepped over the empty coffee cups on the top step and crossed the veranda into the beach house, kicking the front door closed behind him. He walked over to the bed with her.

≈

"I've had a wonderful few days, Jimmy," she said as she nestled her head against his chest, twirling its hairs around her fingers, the brightly-painted red nails teasing him. "It's strange, to have known each other, what, almost three years, and never to have… got together like this."

"I know. We shouldn't have wasted so much time apart," JP replied.

"Didn't you know I liked you?"

"Liked me? No, I thought you loathed me. Just another muscle-laden athletic guy, and you had so many in your life of course…"

"Oh stop," she giggled. "It doesn't matter, we're together now," she said, putting her arm around his chest and squeezing. "It still feels as though we've been with each other ages, and everything is just good with you."

They lay together quietly. She glanced up at him. He was a magnificent specimen of a man, and, she reflected, probably the kindest one she had ever met.

"It's time for me to do that hunting. I'll walk over to the store and see what I can find."

"Ok," she said, "I'll jump into the shower while you're gone." It was past 11am and the sand, sea and the rest of St Lucia were beckoning.

He stood up. Stella loved the shape and look of him as well as the way he was physically with her. It was more than that though, she knew. They had connected in a closeness she had not been able to find with anyone else.

JP emerged from the washroom in a sleeveless shirt and shorts.

"Don't go to sleep now," he joked, "I guess you've got about an hour or one and a quarter tops, and then I'll be back."

"No don't worry," she replied, stretching her legs out.

"Hmmm, well I'm not convinced." he said as he turned away, "but I'm ready to believe anything."

JP heard her laugh as he went through the doorway and down the steps, but then stopped to pick up her shoe from the sand. He was back inside. He stood at the base of the bed, the shoe dangling from a finger.

"I think this belongs to you, ma'am."

"You brute," she said, "you ripped my clothes off and scattered my belongings all over the place."

"I know." He placed it down. "And the real danger is - it might happen again..."

She pulled the sheet over her head, then brought the top down to uncover her eyes, pinning it around her face.

"Whenever you want, boy," she said, and gave him a sensual wink with her right eye.

"I'll see you later," said JP with a grin.

JP took off his sandals and carried them. The soft sand was a brilliant white and warm, and he walked slowly on the beach line so the lapping water could rush over his feet. A few brightly coloured shells speckled his path, and sometimes a crab moved from the waters up to the coconut trees at the beach edge. The trees were at all angles, some upright, some beginning almost horizontally and then turning skywards, each inviting him to sit beneath them and contemplate love, life or nothing at all. Behind were closely packed banana trees laden with fruit, and fifty yards beyond that lay the dirt-track access road. Every now and again a cormorant dived into the sea to catch one of the myriad brightly coloured fish swimming amongst the coral.

JP reached the end of the cove and passed round the point.

The man lying in the small boat nestling around the rocks of the opposite peninsula stopped peering through his anti-glare non-reflective binoculars resting on the rim of the boat. He told his companion to bring in his fishing line. He turned on the electric motor, and the boat sped silently inland towards the beach house.

JP sauntered to the stilted shack, pushed open the door and went inside. He chatted and joked with the owners, Gracie and Thomas. Stella and he had easily become friends with the two locals, buying supplies from them as they needed and in the evenings enjoying local dishes in their restaurant prepared under Gracie's skilled hands, and dancing to the vibrant sounds of Thomas's creole, sometime calypso, band.

JP got the coffee and the cooled cream, and began to wander slowly back. Everyone in St Lucia seemed to be so happy, always laughing and smiling. It must be the effects of the combination of beach, sun and scenery, he thought.

It wasn't until he was within thirty yards of the beach house that he noticed. The two cups and saucers were on the ground, the broken pieces scattered. JP's heart skipped a beat. He dropped the bag, ran the rest of the short distance and flung open the door to the house, calling out Stella's name.

The bed was made, the shower wet; at the little dressing table her perfume, lipstick and makeup bag were strewn on the floor, the stool had been knocked over and the side light lay smashed. He searched the other two rooms and the kitchen; he dashed outside and looked up and down the beach; he ran round to the back of the house.

Nothing.

He returned to the beach house. He walked to the bed, a sick feeling in his stomach, and sat down.

JP took a deep breath. He reached inside his pocket and brought out his small mobile phone, tapped the glass screen and sent the text.

It read, *'It's started. They've got her.'*

3
MOSCOW

WHATEVER THE SEASON, Moscow was always a cold city. It had its ballet, its pretty onion domes that topped ageless pre-revolution buildings, and ushanka hats protecting the ears of a people that were still watched by their own. It was a coldness that had passed down the ages.

The view from the Kempinski Hotel was impressive. Bars of sunlight pierced the blanket of grey cloud and blazed like spotlights onto a panorama of stepped concrete towers, brightly-coloured old roofs and the shining glass of new high rises divided by the snaking Moscow River. Across lay the mighty Kremlin and to the north-east the Lubyanka Building, the former home of the KGB, complete with its prison and torture chambers. Over the Red Square peered the tops of St Basil's Cathedral, a creation under Ivan the Terrible. It was a stark view, thought Barakah Malekka, and seemed to fit the harsh reality of what most people perceived to be Russia.

Communism? Capitalism? Malekka couldn't care less, and in his mind he spat at them both, their hypocrisy, their false loyalties. Only money mattered. With money comes the power to dominate and subjugate, and the millions of little people serve your will because they have no other way. A dictatorship is ruled by such power, by killing and terrorising. A democracy is ruled by those elected via media bought with the same power. Money.

Malekka had come to Moscow to initiate a special sequence of events on which he had been working for over four years. He had taken a room in the Kempinski for convenience and location, not a suite as he usually would have, since that might draw unwanted attention. Money talked nowadays in Moscow more than ever before.

It was time.

Malekka tightened his silk tie, then lifted the matching handkerchief a little higher in his breast pocket. He liked three-piece suits; they seemed to fall well from his tall slim frame and, although his many homes contained over four hundred, like most wealthy men he was very specific in his preference for a certain style and cut. Those from Henry Poole at Savile Row were amongst his favourites. He looked at himself in the full-length mirror on the front of the wardrobe, and nodded approvingly. The mid-grey with gentle blue stripes was finished well by the exquisite black Italian brogues.

He put on a coat, left his room and strolled over to the two waiting men who recently had spent some time in Berlin. As the elevator doors slid open, Aarif Haddad, the younger of Malekka's two devoted servants and bodyguards, stepped aside to let his master and Tarek Raboud enter first.

"Thank you, Aarif," said Malekka. When the doors opened at the lobby, the three exited as strangers.

Haddad moved out into the street first. His short clipped beard was an acceptable gesture to Islam for an Arabic Muslim, and a strong physique gave an efficient lithe ability that had proved its value to Malekka on several occasions. He lit a cigarette and casually looked around.

Malekka strolled to the Reception. Raboud leafed through the newspapers at the hotel shop waiting, his six foot two of lean muscle in a smart tie-less suit an imposing figure. Above the wide neck sat a round head with a crew cut of dark hair, and a squashed nose caused by a breakage some years ago in the military rested meanly between sharp alert eyes.

Malekka passed through the doors held open for him by the doorman and walked out into the cold Moscow air. He took the stairway up the side of the Bolshoy Moskvoretsky Bridge and began to walk across the River, instantly mixing with the throngs of Muscovites, followed by his two men a few yards behind. The green lampposts at the edges of the busy road looked old and dated, with their arms hanging out dangling the power cable for the trams. To his left, running adjacent to the River opposite, was one of the Kremlin walls, a dull-red elongated monolith capped periodically by small turrets with larger ones at each corner; the golden tops of the cathedrals within gleamed in the sunlight and the Grand Kremlin Palace itself stood ominous and imposing.

At the bridge end the traffic curved right. Malekka crossed left, went up to St Basil's Cathedral and into the Red Square, overlooked by the north-east wall of the Kremlin. He walked quickly, passing Lenin's Tomb and exiting the Square on the far side. Haddad and Raboud followed discreetly, ever keeping a watchful protective eye on their master.

≈

A little before, General Evgeny Kutuzov Vashinsky rose from his deep leather chair behind the large mahogany desk at the Lubyanka Building and told his secretary that he was going out. As Deputy Director of the ever-growing FSB, the Federal Security Service of the Russian Federation, the surviving child of the KGB, Vashinsky's office occupied an entire front corner on the top floor. It was staffed by three captains of the army, one lieutenant and three female administrative staff, as well as his private secretary. Only the Director, General Alexander Bortnikov, had a larger office and more personal staff, located at the end of the corridor on the opposite corner of the huge building. The two were close enough; and distant enough too. Time and experience had shown that distance was sometimes more useful to the Director. That same fact would now be particularly helpful to the Deputy Director.

When in uniform Vashinsky imposed a firm strictness on his staff, demanding full army routine with sharp salutes. At fifty-five, Vashinsky felt his title earned him that right and he exercised it with some relish. However, today Vashinsky arrived in a suit, and his staff knew he would be out and their day easier. The suit was generously tailored. It needed to be. Vashinsky stood six foot three in size thirteen shoes, and carried a rotund midriff that still put the middle button of the jacket under pressure. Powerful arms swayed from broad shoulders and a short thick neck, but somehow the proportions didn't balance and appeared to have been thrown together hurriedly from spare parts during their creation. It hadn't always been so, though. As a young twenty year old soldier in the initial Soviet deployment in Afghanistan in 1979, he had been a tall, handsome and extremely fit young man.

Vashinsky exited the elevator on the lower ground level where his personal driver, Sergey Baskov, came to attention and held the car's rear door open.

"Thank you, Sergey," said Vashinsky as he stepped into the spacious limousine and sat down on the deep leather seats. The backwards-slanting broad cap with its gold and blue braids rested exactly level over Sergeant Baskov's forehead. His young blue eyes shone with life. He walked smartly to the other side of the car and got in.

"Sergey, I want to go to this address," said the General, handing a piece of paper through the open panel divider. "Do you know it?"

Baskov glanced at the paper. "Yes, sir," he said. "We may hit traffic though, would you like me to obtain an escort?"

"No. We'll just drive and you get me there as quickly as you can. But discreetly. Don't break any speed limits or do anything to get us noticed."

"Yes, sir."

Vashinsky took back the address paper and returned it to his pocket. The Zil's 7.7 litre engine roared into life and the car purred off quietly into Lubyanka Square. The black and silver chrome lines of the car were lovely to look at, thought Vashinsky, and the space and comfort inside were far superior to some of the cars his compatriots liked to use - the fancy Mercedes S-Class or the BMW 7-series. Pah! Western nonsense. They were too tight for him. And anyway, what's wrong with a Russian car, especially when it's a Zil?

≈

Malekka and his men took the first taxi at the Hotel Metropol. They travelled west across several Moscow ring roads and finally stopped before the MKAD ring close to the Strogino Metro, at a short parade of dirty-fronted shops that obviously hadn't seen a window cleaner for months. Malekka doubled back fifty yards to a small shabby café and went inside.

The door caught against a brass bell. The café was

thick with smoke. A waiter in a stained white apron continued to dry glasses in front of rows of spirit bottles and tobacco shelving; the sole occupant at the bar remained immersed in his newspaper and cigarette. A television was making a noise somewhere in a corner.

Malekka walked through to the small rear alcove where a lone man sat at the corner table. They shook hands with just the hint of a smile, and Malekka took the chair at Vashinsky's right with his back at the wall and a view down the café. He placed his gold-rimmed cell phone on the table. The next few minutes would decide whether he would need to use it.

Vashinsky pulled out a Black Russian Sobranie and thoughtfully lit the cigarette. The two men leaned forwards with their elbows on the table.

"I think it is best that we speak in English," said Vashinsky softly.

Malekka nodded in agreement.

"The item is ready to be moved."

"Excellent," said Malekka. "Have there been any repercussions as a result of our friend's involvement?"

"None at all my side," said Vashinsky. "You dealt with him of course?"

The waiter came and took their order, and the two men stayed silent until he was out of earshot.

"Some colleagues of mine did, yes," said Malekka. "If he was on his way to meet someone, that certainly did not occur. The issue is dealt with." Malekka paused, then added, "Have you found out what he was doing in Berlin?"

"No. We have heard nothing. If he was meeting anyone, it seems it was not the Americans, or the British, or any of the other Western countries. I can find nothing, and trace nothing. The right action was taken; he has had zero impact or effect. The matter is finished."

"Are there any other problems, anything at all that should concern us?"

"No. And I am certain that there won't be any. Before was an extraordinary involvement, and I do not foresee any more."

"You didn't foresee the first one," said Malekka. The clumsy ape, he thought. His monolithic bureaucracy almost ruined everything.

The waiter was back. "Here we are, gentlemen. One tea, and one Turkish coffee." With an exaggerated flourish the man delivered the drinks, bowed slightly and walked off.

Vashinsky thoughtfully dropped a couple of sugar cubes and lemon slices into his tea, gave a stir and lifted the ornate podstakannik and glass to his mouth. His greying hair and rather chubby red face were very affable on first sight, but behind the glasses a pair of dark-brown steely piercing eyes never seemed to blink, and gave away nothing. He stared coldly at Malekka.

"There are many people through whose hands this has quietly and unknowingly had to pass," said Vashinsky, speaking the words slowly and deliberately. He sipped again at his tea. "There was always a possibility that someone might spot something. You knew that. The difficult work is done; now it should be clear."

Malekka had held his stare, and now looked away. There was no point in recriminations. It must move forwards and be made to work. His men had silenced Keppof in Berlin, and the trail there was now dead. Literally. He had had to find out if there was going to be a problem, something in the way, someone else that needed attention, and was relieved to hear that Vashinsky had nothing.

Which was just as well, thought Malekka, as everything was already in place eight thousand miles away and in flow. Unless he made a phone call to abort. He inwardly breathed a sigh of relief.

"All is in place and ready," continued Vashinsky. "Now it is for you to take the next step."

He opened his wallet and slid a small folded piece of paper across the table. Malekka glanced discreetly at the numbers and then placed the paper carefully inside the plush leather of his own wallet.

He sipped some coffee, wincing at the coarseness of the blend. The heavy caffeine content was unmistakable though; he could almost feel the energy surge as he swallowed. He took a paper napkin and dabbed his mouth. Malekka decided.

He nodded to Vashinsky.

"Very well. I will arrange the first this afternoon."

The two men sat back in their chairs and smiled at each other.

Malekka raised his cup. "Na zdorovie, comrade."

"Salut," replied Vashinsky.

The cup and glass clinked quietly in the corner of the café.

Malekka picked up his cell phone, and slipped it back into his inside jacket pocket.

He wasn't going to need it.

"However," said Vashinsky, "there is one thing that you should be reminded of. The item is without one essential part. It always has been. You know that."

"Yes," said Malekka, "I know."

"For me to obtain that part was always going to be impossible. And without it, the item will not do quite what you need it to do. What I provide will, itself, be in perfect working order. But it will not function fully and properly without the other part. And there is only one place outside Russia where you can get it."

Malekka smiled blandly. "Don't worry yourself

about that, comrade." He said the word with a little force, since a deal was being done between them that was worthy of the highest merits of Capitalism. "We already have that in hand."

Vashinsky stubbed out the remnants of his cigarette, and raised an eyebrow. I wonder what he's got planned, he said to himself.

"So. When I see the first, I will issue the orders. And you arrange the second within twenty-four hours of when you arrive back and see the merchandise."

"Yes," said Malekka, "that is our agreement." He paused for a while, and then added, "I do not think we shall meet again. So - I wish you well, comrade. What will you do?"

Vashinsky looked up at Malekka, and smiled. Of course, there was no answer. Malekka smiled back, with warmth. For a moment, they were two soldiers standing shoulder to shoulder.

Vashinsky pulled out a few Rubles and put them on the table, just as Malekka had begun to reach for his wallet. "No, let me do this."

"Thank you." Malekka paused, and then added, "Good luck, my friend."

"Good luck to you too," returned Vashinsky. He held out his hand, and Malekka took it, each feeling the firm grip of the other.

Malekka walked towards the door of the café, nodding to the waiter as he went past the bar. His two men were waiting at the agreed place. Haddad promptly hailed down a car to be a 'Chastniki', which is the Moscow way; there are few official taxis in the City.

As they were ferried back towards the centre of Moscow by a driver who was delighted to have picked up such a useful fare Malekka put his head back and thoughtfully closed his eyes.

Vashinsky took out another cigarette. There was no hint of a smile on his face any more. The momentary warmth between the two men had vanished almost as quickly as it had arrived, replaced with the familiar cold and expressionless façade that a world-class poker player would have difficulty penetrating. He was allowing time for Malekka to leave the vicinity, and reflected over the implications of their earlier discussion.

There was only one other person who knew the plan, and Vashinsky wanted to keep it that way. His close friend Colonel Anatoly Linchuk, in the Spetsnaz, the elite special forces unit of the military. The Spetsnaz is so secret that most of the time nobody knows what they are doing. They mix in with regular army units, whose uniforms they wear, and their identification is carefully protected. Anatoly is completely loyal to him, Vashinsky knew. Over the years there had been times when each had trusted the other with his life. The leak couldn't possibly have come from him.

However, someone, somehow, had come across a fragment of information about a planned asset movement and considered that it was unusual enough to send a report in, which - fortunately - had come straight to his own desk. His response would normally have been to send it on to Bortnikov, but he had instead taken different steps resulting in the elimination of the man who had submitted the report. It had been signed simply as P. Keppof. Vashinsky had not taken direct action himself, in case it raised more queries within the department; instead he had decided to send a coded message to Malekka by special envoy, first via Finland then Sweden, for them to deal with the problem.

Vashinsky would have to make very certain there were no more clever reports or smart people doing their job well and picking up the unusual. No-one, nothing at all, to link him with Malekka or even the remotest fragment of what had started to unfold.

His ability to monitor such matters, and arrange the movement of the asset in the first place, was he knew the very reason why Malekka had approached him. Malekka was a very clever, dangerous man. It had been the usual thing - during a visit to the Middle-East he had been introduced to Malekka at one of his wonderful houses, with its resident harem, alcohol, drugs, opulent surroundings, wonderful food, and a supremely comfortable style of living that he now found he wanted. Vashinsky's love of Mother Russia had been strong throughout his life, and still was, but times were changing and people now were able to embrace the old enemy Capitalism quite freely and enjoy its great benefits.

However, at his age and in the military, he was not going to be able to do that. He could not make a fortune like the young people, idiots, can do today, and be one of them within Russia.

So what had been the point of his earlier years? The fight against the West, against the evil capitalists, for Communism. The conclusion was obvious. They were wasted years.

To say that some disillusionment and resentment had set into General Vashinsky was an understatement.

So now he was taking steps to change his life dramatically and obtain some capitalistic monies of his own. It was time to leave the confines of the Lubyanka, and of Russia herself, and enjoy his life in a way he had never been able to do before.

The fact that over three million people were going to

die in the process didn't worry Vashinsky one little bit.

≈

Once back in his room Malekka issued the instructions to proceed to his colleagues in Iran. The action had been arranged well in advance, carefully taking time zones into account and ensuring high-ranking personnel around the world would be alert to carry out instructions within their normal work routine, but immediately. For which they would be well compensated. Only Malekka's final confirmation was now required, to initiate the sequence.

Within twenty minutes, the sum of half a billion US dollars left the Central Bank of Iran in five equal separate wire transfers to banks in Saudi Arabia, Pakistan, Afghanistan, Turkey and Uzbekistan. Within the hour, those banks each forwarded $100m in wire transfers to banks in Angola, Nigeria, Bulgaria, Turkey and Algeria and they in turn sent the funds on to banks in Nicaragua, Brazil, Poland, Germany and Panama. Deposits of $100m each reached five of the six hundred banks in the Cayman Islands. By the end of the day, those last five would each wire $100m to Clariden Leu AG Bank in Zurich, Switzerland, depositing the combined total of half a billion US dollars into the numbered account of General Evgeny Kutuzov Vashinsky.

Malekka sat in his comfortable room at the Kempinski, and thoughtfully closed the lid of his laptop. He smiled to himself, and prepared to leave for the airport.

≈

Sergeant Sergey Baskov had enjoyed his work today.

He parked the Zil close to the Strogino Metro, its domed sausage-like glass structure stretching a hundred metres along the sidewalk. The General walked off quickly to meet his people; Sergey read his book, as permitted, but kept a watchful eye open for the General's return. He drove them back to the Lubyanka, the General departed and he took the car round to the service area. The Zil gleamed, ready for the next excursion.

At 6pm Moscow time, just slightly before Stella Fincrest was being snatched eight thousand miles away in St Lucia, Sergey came off duty. He walked down Theatre Drive, thinking of his girlfriend. He had been with Anna for two years and they were very close, and in fact he was going to ask her to marry him. The world had become an entirely different place to Sergey since she had been around; a happy, wonderful, colourful place full of opportunity and excitement - typical symptoms of a man in love, so his friends had said. His army colleagues teased him, but they were really just a little jealous. He knew Anna's love for him was deep and serious; she had told him often enough. Tonight would hold the right moment for the question. Dinner at his apartment, with soft light and gentle music.

He walked past the Bolshoi Theatre set back a couple of hundred metres from the street, the white eight-pillared colonnade of its front magnificent and grand, gleaming in the early evening sunlight. Yes, I will ask her tonight.

He entered the Teatralnaya Station of the Metro to take his usual train on the Zamoskvoretskaya Line. However, this evening he was oblivious to the Station's lovely décor; even the usual sardine-like squash of the Moscow rush-hour, with hundreds of other people descending to the trains thirty metres below, didn't trouble him.

Sergey stood at the platform edge and together with those either side and the eight rows of people behind waited for the train. He would be home within thirty minutes. He could hear the train approaching. The noise increased. He looked up to the right, saw its lights getting close to the end of the tunnel, ready to charge out to collect people and take them home. I wonder if these other people are happy or sad, said Sergey to himself. He thought of Anna once more, and smiled.

The last thing that Sergeant Sergey Baskov felt was the hand that pushed him hard in the middle of his back, sending him flying forwards just at the moment the train was all but in front of him. His arms came up instinctively in a desperate effort to protect himself, but he had no chance. His head smashed against the front of the train and he knew only instant blackness; his body rotated in its fall as the emergency brakes were applied by the shocked driver and the screeching train began to slow more. When his frame reached the tracks, first Sergey's feet were severed and then his head was crushed like a melon by the far wheels. His torso rolled underneath and the central steel buckets of the motors and electrical systems snapped it into two pieces at its waist, rolling the two halves forwards and sideways and giving momentum that bounced them up to the undercarriage of the train and down to the ground and then back up again, cutting them to pieces and forcing parts under the other wheels of the train, which sliced off strips of flesh and limbs as it rolled mercilessly forwards.

The train finally ground to a halt, and the screams from the horrified passengers filled the air.

Moscow. For Sergeant Sergey Baskov, the city of death.

PART TWO

SIXTY-FOUR SQUARES

4
LONDON

JIM PEREGRINE EXITED the cab at Buckingham Palace Road outside the Grosvenor Hotel in London.

He passed through the centre of the three arches into the hotel, acknowledged the concierge's smile with a discreet nod and continued across the lobby. He exited into the large Victoria Station precinct, where he was quickly lost in the crowds of people rushing to or from trains, milling around or buying tickets.

Sunlight permeated through the myriad of glass panels of the steel and wrought iron framework roof. The old Victorian strength contrasted with the flashing neon signs, garish advertisements and tall columns of electronic departure boards spread out below. JP walked a long confident stride, his thick dark hair brushed back cavalierly above the bronzed face and bold determined eyes, his six foot three frame in a smart pin-stripe cutting a *figure fringant*. He headed for the escalators across to the right. As the ridged steps rose JP dropped down to re-tie his shoelaces and be less visible. He was certain that he was not being followed, but then old habits die hard. He continued through the mall, greeted by the smell of cooked foods and fashion store perfumes, and out to the taxi rank at Belgrave Road. He took the first cab and told the driver to head for Regent Street.

Since Stella had disappeared JP's mind and heart had been in turmoil. He was meant to play out the scene of a devastated man whose lover had been kidnapped, but to his surprise realised that actually it was no act; he was far more concerned, in fact distraught. Those emotions were fighting the strong practical approach that he knew he had to maintain.

After sending the text he immediately called the police. The people who took her would expect that, and indeed may have been watching to check that his reaction to Stella's disappearance was both genuine and serious. For a small Caribbean island, the police had swung into action pretty quickly and made some impressive early moves. At the end of an intensive period of activity by the island police, involving the Chief of Police, the British High Commissioner and seventy-five local policemen and women, they had discovered precisely nothing. It was as though Stella had disappeared into thin air.

The police were certain she must be on the island still and assured JP contact by the kidnappers would be soon, for in such cases the kidnappers only ever wanted money and the sooner the better. After all what else could they be after, they said?

JP knew better.

In discussion with the Chief of Police, JP pointed out that when the kidnappers make contact it would be with Stella's family in South Africa and so he should leave the island immediately to be with them. The Police agreed - *if there had actually been a kidnapping.* So far there was only a missing person, and so they were understandably reluctant to let JP off the island; what if the woman turned up dead? There would be a murder investigation and the prime suspect would then be JP himself. However, in short order the British High Commissioner vouched for JP personally to the Police (somewhat surprisingly they had thought) and JP was permitted to leave the island. He immediately bought a ticket to South Africa and took the next available flight, which was the next day, to Miami, the main hub for international flights for St Lucia. Once in Miami and unbeknown to anyone in St Lucia except the High Commissioner, instead of boarding the connecting flight to Cape Town JP changed his ticket and flew straight to London.

"What part of Regent Street, guv'nor?" called out the taxi driver as he turned off from Piccadilly Circus. He had an intercom system to talk with his passengers, but like many cabbies still preferred the old method.

"Just at the corner of New Burlington Street please."

"Right you are, sir."

Thirty seconds later the taxi came to a stop. JP handed over some money and stepped out in front of the Samsonite shop. He walked up Regent Street at a brisk pace amidst the heavy grey stone buildings with their ornate iron balconies.

He turned left into Hanover Street and paused to look at the Molton Brown shop, using its double aspect corner windows for one final check he was alone. Satisfied, he turned and walked down the Street towards Hanover Square. Opposite a pair of red telephone kiosks was a small shop selling souvenirs and postcards. JP opened the door to *Cards Galore*, and walked inside.

The shop was packed with racks displaying its wares, from teacups with the Queen's face to dishcloths of the British Isles, and multi-size postcards that carried every possible scene of London. Behind a small counter an elderly grey-haired man in a shirt and tie and well-worn ruby cardigan sat reading a magazine. JP browsed nonchalantly until the other customer in the shop had selected what she wanted and left. Then JP walked over.

"Hello Beefie, you old rogue," JP said in a low voice.

"How are you?"

"Hello sir," he smiled back warmly, "I'm good. Go on through."

"Thanks."

Beefie pressed a small buzzer under the ledge of the counter. JP pulled aside the curtained entrance to the back room and walked through, carefully sliding the velvet back along the rail. On the far side of the small room a camera cast its eye over him and a buzzer sounded, releasing a thick steel-plated door. JP pushed it open and stepped inside, hearing the door lock again firmly behind him.

A short corridor sloped to the floor of a comfortable drawing room resembling one of London's more famous clubs. Two red leather Chesterfields and green-shaded standard lamps at either end faced each other across a low coffee table. A mahogany conference table and twelve high-backed chairs were on the other side of the room. A deep red paper decorated the walls and a crystal chandelier hung from the high ceiling. On the right a large viewing screen was paired with a second at the conference table, both displaying the view outside the entrance door. A couple of computers on desk-like tables provided the electronic information and data support for the room. A picture of The Queen hung between a pair of wall lights.

Three people sat at the conference table. Charles Melton rose and strode over. He was the same height as JP, older and one of his closest friends. Thick dark wavy hair parted left overhung a high intelligent forehead and a strong face with smiling brown eyes. The jacket of his charcoal suit covered a powerful chest.

"Hello Jimmy."

"Hello Charles," said JP as the two crunched hands. The warm grins were brief, quickly overrun by the sombre atmosphere in the room.

"Do you know my boss, Sir Alastair Crewe?" Melton extended his arm in invitation. "Sir Alastair, Jim Peregrine."

JP held out his hand and took that of the head of MI6. Sir Alistair was a shorter man, with a jovial face despite its deep furrows under the long thick hair that flowed straight back. He had a natural air of authority, immediate and inescapable. His dark steady eyes bore into JP inquisitively, quickly examining, analysing, and then the eyelids closed down once like a camera shutter taking a picture. JP knew he had been filed away in Sir Alistair's famous photographic memory.

"Hello, Sir Alastair."

"How do you do, Mr Peregrine. I'm pleased to meet you at last." He turned towards the third person at the table. "Lieutenant Jane Chapman, may I present Mr Jim Peregrine." The woman didn't stand but turned as JP walked round the table. He took her outstretched hand and said, "How do you do, Lieutenant."

"Mr Peregrine," she responded, smiling and giving him a firm but unmistakably feminine handshake. Charles Melton had told him quite a bit about his extremely capable twenty-something right-hand. She was in uniform, her auburn hair tied in a high-bun above a round soft face and slender sensual neck. She exuded confidence and competence.

"Please, everyone, sit," said Sir Alastair, who resumed his own place at the top of the table and indicated JP to his left opposite the other two. Sir Alastair spoke first.

"Mr Peregrine, I must say I find it somewhat dryly amusing that you resign from the SAS after an exceptionally brilliant albeit brief career, decline to accept the invitation from your old boss, Major Melton there, to come and work at MI6, and then six months later, now as a civilian, you bring him the most fantastic story of dangerous happenings around the globe that we ourselves would have been hard pushed to concoct as fiction. And, a proposed course of action to deal with it that is staggeringly imaginative, dangerous and brutal but which now seems to be bearing fruit exactly as you predicted."

"Well, sir, now that you put it that way, I do agree that there is a somewhat ironic twist to the whole situation," replied JP with a slight smile.

"I have of course read the file, and as you know I sanctioned your plan at the outset with Major Melton after some lengthy and deep discussions with him, but I was interested to hear directly from you and decide where we go from here."

Sir Alastair Crewe may have been approaching his sixtieth birthday and his hair may have turned white over the passing years but his mind remained ruthlessly sharp. His rank of colonel, retired, meant that he was well used to considering plans, issuing orders and expecting their prompt implementation, and he neither tolerated fools lightly nor wasted time. The fact that he had left the confines of the green and white concrete building of the MI6 Headquarters at the Albert Embankment some three miles away to conduct this covert meeting was indicative of the weight of the international intelligence and military establishments now gathering.

"Tell me first of Dr Keppof and of his unfortunate demise."

"Well," said JP, taking a deep breath as he quickly thought out a cogent summary, "I first met him when I was a student at Cambridge in 2002. I was reading Mathematics and he had a four-week period of guest lecturing there. He was born in Moscow in 1953, his father was a teacher and his mother a dress maker. He was extremely talented academically. After his basic schooling, he won a place at the Moscow State University Faculty of Mechanics and Mathematics, where he studied between 1972 to 1975. He did his Masters at the Moscow Institute of Physics and Technology in '75 to '76, then went to the Bauman Moscow State Technical University '76 to '77 to study engineering."

He paused slightly, and then continued.

"Keppof was also quite a linguist and picked up English and German easily at school and was fluent in both by the time he was twenty. He came to Cambridge labelled a distinguished academic from Europe, and I went to his lectures and to his informal evening dinner gatherings. The subject was Newtonian Mechanics, he was an entertaining lecturer and extremely knowledgeable. He and I happened to get on well, we became friends and remained in touch afterwards. We corresponded from time to time, and I would see him when he came to England which he did periodically, generally once every year. His wife died about twelve years ago; I didn't know her. He lived in southern Russia, and has a daughter who works in Moscow, whom I've met briefly too."

"Did you know much of his work in Russia?"

"No, nothing at all. I thought he was just an academic and university lecturer in Russia. He never indicated anything else, ever. That is, not until he came to see me in London two months ago."

JP paused, and pointing to the coffee and cups on the table said to Sir Alastair, "May I, sir?"

"Yes of course, please help yourself."

JP poured himself some coffee, and offered some to

the others who all declined. He took a sip, and then continued.

"He was quite agitated, and insisted we meet in the open, which we did at St James' Park. It was a fine clear chilly day; we sat on one of the benches on the north side, and that was when he told me of his background for the first time. Frankly I was amazed.

"He said he had been recruited by the KGB in 1977 and worked for the Eighth Chief Directorate in internal and foreign communications, the crypto logic systems used by the KGB to overseas stations, and the overall development of communications technology. He was posted to Germany that same year, 1977, and in fact changed his name from Russian to the German sounding Keppof so that he would fit in with the people where he was living. He was there for almost twelve years. With the fall of East Germany in 1990 he was recalled and sent to work in southern Russia at Stavropol in the Western Caucasus, and also was able to do some university lecturing within Russia. The KGB was closed down, the FSB took over, and the new Russia of course allowed him to travel virtually unrestricted, which he did frequently. His academic credentials made him of interest to Cambridge and hence in 2002 he came to guest lecture at the University, when I met him."

"But why did he come to see you in February, and why tell you all of this?" asked Sir Alastair. "In fact, why did he tell *you* at all?"

"Well, sir, he was very worried. He had discovered an unusual internal instruction and also something about the South Africa connection that together could have major international implications. He of course wanted to put in an internal report but was very concerned that something might happen to him if the wrong person saw it. He was literally in fear of his life. He wanted to tell someone outside Russia just in case. He knew I was military and years earlier I had mentioned just as chat of some of the special forces escapades of my father, so he assumed I would have connections in the security service. So he told me. Rather tenuous, but as usual he was spot on. I was his safety valve. He wasn't betraying secrets, he wasn't a traitor or defecting; just alerting a third party independent of Russia to a possible problem. He came to England as a weekend break. We met, he said he would try to find out more and if he was right would contact me again."

"I see. And so you came to Major Melton?"

"Yes, straight afterwards. I know Keppof to be a brilliant and dedicated individual. What he was saying sounded potentially extremely serious. His work at the KGB may have made one consider him to be an enemy; but from the time that I knew him if there was ever anyone to come out from communism and embrace freedom of the West and the principles of democracy then Keppof is it. Of course there was always the possibility that I was being somehow played and set up by the FSB, but I really didn't think so. In any event, that possibility to decide on was left of course to Major Melton."

"And what about the South Africa connection?"

Melton jumped in with a response. "Well sir, it was that part of JP's story, sorry, Mr Peregrine's story, that within forty-eight hours of our first meeting on the matter had an immediate impact on me. You see, the South Africans had picked up that there had been a sudden foreign interest in their Musina installation, and that had also been confirmed from our CIA friends on the other side of the pond. That was therefore two independent sources confirming the South Africa element of Keppof's story, which meant that what Mr

Peregrine had told me had to be taken extremely seriously. We met again two days later, when JP presented me with his solution for how we could handle the matter."

"Mr Peregrine, it seems that Major Melton is determined to refer to you as JP, and therefore may I do the same," asked Sir Alastair, more as a statement than a question.

"Yes, of course," JP smiled.

"Sorry," said Major Melton, but then continued. "We kicked his plan around, established how it could be put in place, and then I brought it to you for approval, sir. And then things moved very fast when Keppof contacted JP again."

Melton turned to JP.

"Yes," said JP taking up his cue, "that was why I went to Berlin three weeks ago with the intention of meeting with him again. He telephoned me I think from a public telephone box although it might have been from his mobile and said he had heard something else, that he had proof this time and was bringing it to me. He said he had had to make a report internally, but also wanted to tell me. He sounded really scared."

"And what happened when you got to Berlin?" said Sir Alastair.

"Well sir, he checked into the Mondial Hotel on the Kurfürstendamm, I spoke to him on the telephone to arrange a time and he wanted to meet as soon as possible, and so we arranged a time and place for that night, well early morning actually, 2.30am. He arrived slightly early, and I arrived just as he was being killed."

"What do you mean - couldn't you stop it?"

"No, it was too late. I was on the other side of the large road and had taken the precaution of... er... arriving in disguise."

"Disguise? What do you mean? What as?"

"Well...," JP hesitated, and then continued. "Er... well, actually I was dressed as a tramp. I was in shabby clothes, doing my best to appear rather drunk, I smelled, and was looking in waste bins appearing to be foraging for a meal. It seemed to fit Berlin at that time of night."

"Very enterprising, JP."

"Excuse me, Sir Alastair," said Lieutenant Chapman.

"Yes, Lieutenant?"

"Sir, we have this on tape from Mr Peregrine..."

"On tape? You mean you filmed it?"

"Yes, sir," continued JP. "I had a camera sewn into the lapels of the old jacket I had on. Two actually, one infrared. I had a wrist screen with controls to operate them."

"Put it on the screen please, Lieutenant."

"Yes, sir," she replied. The recording was played back on the large screens on the walls, as JP continued.

"You see, I was a good hundred yards away on the other side of the Kurfürstendamm, which is a wide road as you doubtless know - it has three lanes in each direction and a central reservation in between. My first vision - as you can see - is when one man has just stabbed Keppof in the chest and killed him. There was absolutely nothing I could do. A couple of minutes earlier and I would have been there and could have saved him. Given that Keppof was already dead, the best thing for me to do, I thought, was to continue to record the events whilst pretending not to be looking at them, and do my best not to be seen, or discovered, anyway. I could have gone after the two men and brought them down, and found whatever it is that they took from Keppof's pockets; but then we would have lost the two leads linking us with the big players or, worse, have alerted their boss or bosses of our interest in their affairs. At least this way we would come away with something."

"Yes, quite so," agreed Sir Alastair.

There was a slight pause, as all at the table looked at the film showing on the two screens. It was like a gruesome horror movie, only the people on the screen weren't actors and one had just lost his life at the hands of the other two.

"I got some close-ups on them," said JP. "One of them even stared straight across at me. To them I was just a drunken tramp rummaging around in bins."

Major Melton interrupted, "We had nothing on them and so made the usual enquiries from our friends, on who those two unsavoury characters are. It took a few days, but we've got something. Lieutenant?"

"Yes, sir," she replied, opening a folder and handing round head-and-shoulder pictures of the two men from the video. She pressed a couple of buttons on the remote and the same two pictures appeared on the wall screens.

"Aarif Haddad, on the left, and Tarek Raboud. We know that they were involved in the bombing of the American Embassy in Kabul in Afghanistan last September, and these pictures have been facially recognised with the faces on file with our colleagues at the CIA. They are believed to be the cronies for a man called Malekka, about whom nothing is known except that the Americans think he originates from one of the Middle-East countries, is very well connected and extremely wealthy. The name is also known to Mossad in Israel, although they couldn't actually tell us anything more about him either. So far, that's all we have. Other than, of course, that they are terrorists, and considered extremely dangerous."

"Thank you, Lieutenant," said Sir Alastair. "And thank you, Mr Peregrine, for your efforts. I am very sorry about your friend."

"Thank you, sir."

"At least," said Charles Melton, "we have something to work with. Then forty-eight hours ago Stella was taken in St Lucia."

"And what about the poor girl?" asked Sir Alastair.

JP looked down at his hands on the table and intertwined his fingers, thinking for a moment.

"I am booked on the plane tonight to Cape Town to be with her family," he said, "and see what develops. Obviously we should continue to follow through with the plan. I think I should be there; it would appear odd and raise suspicions if I'm not.

"As for Stella herself," he continued, "well we shall just have to hope that she survives. Our intention to holiday together was picked up well in the South African press, and these people clearly saw their opportunity and took the bait. I hate to use the girl in that way, but I couldn't think of any other method."

"This business can be nasty sometimes and often requires great sacrifices," said Sir Alastair. "Or, perhaps I should say in this instance, to be accurate, that it often requires great sacrifices of other people. Which I gather from Major Melton is one of the reasons why you did not wish to join us at MI6."

"Yes sir. But, this is a job that has to be done. Keppof had brought the matter to me and was killed in the process. It's now clear that his suspicions were correct. A great deal depends on getting this right."

"We all certainly agree on that, JP," said Sir Alastair, closing the paper file in front of him and signalling that the meeting was at an end. "You will obviously stay in touch with Charles here."

Sir Alastair stood up. "You must move fast. All of you."

≈

JP left the MI6 meeting using one of the alternate concealed routes. MI6 had three covert meeting rooms in London on the go at any one time, generally underground, taken and used for eight months or a year for the purpose of seeing those who would prefer not to go to the MI6 Headquarters Building on which unfriendly prying eyes could so easily be focused. The rooms were swept electronically each day and were entirely secure.

JP pressed a buzzer on the wall at the end of the long corridor. The door released and he stepped through into the open light of the early afternoon. He ignored the door opposite, which went into another building, turned right and with one hand on the cast iron bannister climbed the concrete steps that a hundred years ago would have been the well-trodden stairway of downstairs servants and goods tradesmen servicing the aristocracy in the house above. His head drew level with the pavement, then the old iron railings. He emerged once more into the heart of London, on the west side of St George Street under which he had just walked. He turned into Brook Street and headed for Claridge's Hotel.

He was in good time for his private meeting, in his suite after lunch.

Afterwards he packed, took a cab to Heathrow Airport and boarded the night flight to Cape Town.

With a bit of luck, nobody would actually notice that his journey from St Lucia to South Africa had taken twenty-four hours longer than it needed to.

5
AWAKING

STELLA HAD COME out of the shower at the beach house. She dried herself and walked naked to the dresser singing quietly and happily to herself, selected her clothes and dressed. She went back into the bathroom to hang the towels and was strolling back out when suddenly from behind an arm went round her waist and a cloth with some foul sweet-smelling scent went over her mouth. She fought hard and tried to scream but the person behind was strong and lifted her off the floor. Her legs splayed all over the place, kicking things over, before a second set of arms grabbed her legs and restrained her, just before she passed out from the chloroform.

The two men threw her onto the bed, bound her hands behind her back and then her feet. One of them threw her over his shoulder and walked to the door. Checking the way was clear, they quickly moved down the steps, hitting the crockery. They rushed to the small boat, the second man kicking the sand behind as they went to cover all footprints. They placed Stella inside.

The electric motor was started and two minutes later the boat was round the point and out of sight. The entire snatch had taken only six minutes. Both Stella and the smaller boat were transferred to a waiting power boat, the big engines were opened up and they almost flew over the waters, heading north-west. Something was injected into Stella's arm. An hour later, when the powerboat reached the luxury yacht *Free Spirit* some fifty miles away out of sight of land and other vessels, it was lifted on board. Stella was immediately carried up to the helipad and strapped inside the helicopter. The two men boarded.

The aircraft routed midway between Martinique and St Lucia at thirty feet above the water and then headed north-east out into the Atlantic Ocean, rendezvousing two hours and two hundred and fifty miles later with the oceangoing super yacht *Excelsior* from which it had departed earlier that morning. The girl was carried from the helicopter, and taken below.

Stella began to regain consciousness. Her head slowly moved side to side, and her heavy eyelids twittered and opened. She blinked repeatedly to get moisture back into her dry eyes, and shook her head more. Finally, she was awake.

Stella realised she was on a bed... and then she remembered what had happened. A feeling of sheer terror came over her. She pushed herself up to the top of the bed and brought her legs up under her chin, pulling the sheets with her and wrapping her arms around her knees. She rocked to and fro, uttering whimpering sounds and little muffled screams. Every inch of her was trembling, her breathing accelerated to the point of hyperventilating. Tears rolled down her face. She opened her mouth and bit hard onto the sheets over her knees, painfully, in an effort to calm herself and vent her anger and fear, and stop herself from reaching the very edge of insanity.

Gradually, very gradually, Stella's breathing slowed. She was alone in the room and, she reasoned, at least not in any immediate danger. She began to calm and her thought processes returned.

Stella glanced around. She was in a rectangular

windowless room. The bed was luxurious, with a deep soft mattress, exquisite silk sheets and fine down feather pillows. She was wearing the same clothes she had dressed in after coming out of the shower - a short skirt, panties, low cut tank top and a bra beneath - and jewellery of rings and bracelets. Her watch said 2 o'clock; but the reading meant little since she could not see outside to establish morning or night, nor how long she had been unconscious nor even what part of the world she was in.

Then with sudden horror she felt the restriction. God, she thought, what is it? She ripped back the sheets. A steel handcuff-like bracelet, only thicker, had been placed around her left ankle. The ankle-cuff, for that is what it was, was fur-lined, presumably to prevent chaffing, and from it ran a long steel chain that ended in a second cuff locked around a metal rail spanning the footboard. It made movement difficult and escape impossible. And even if she somehow managed to shed her shackles she still wouldn't be able to open the keypaded door half way along the left wall. For a while she stared at the ankle-cuff and the footboard, realising she was entirely restrained and at the mercy of her captors, who could do with her what they wanted.

The room was sparsely but luxuriously furnished. A plush sofa, a low wooden coffee stand, an oblong mahogany table with four chairs. A short chandelier dropped from a low ceiling, and two mirrors hung on walls that also carried four small air conditioning vents. The white walls contrasted starkly with the deep red carpet.

Stella now felt curious enough to try to open the doors on either side of the bed. She reached down and slid the ankle-cuff across to the right on the footboard and manoeuvred herself over. She stepped onto the carpet and at once felt the deep pile's plush softness; the chain was easily long enough for her to reach the door and go in.

Inside she found an extensive closet with skirts, dresses, numerous pairs of shoes, a dressing table and chair and drawers that contained an array of other clothes and undergarments. No jeans or trousers, she noticed. Stella exited and this time walked round the base of the bed, pulling the ankle-cuff along the rail to the other end. Beyond the second door was a bathroom, which she used, washing her hands in a marble-topped oval sink with gold-coloured taps that delivered hot and cold water swiftly. There was some pleasant-smelling soap both as a bar in a dish and liquid in a dispenser, and to dry her hands she found a thick pink hand towel on a rail running across the sink base matched by larger towels at the bath and shower. She came out and sat down again on the bed. She was feeling much better now. Her senses were fully restored.

The rooms could be a small but comfortable hotel suite, Stella thought, but there was something missing; what was it? Oh yes. Light switches. There were no light switches anywhere in the rooms. Obviously the lighting was controlled elsewhere. And, as she had already realised, there was no window either. Then for the first time she noticed the constant faint hum and its matching vibration. And every so often the room seemed to move in one direction and then back again; she had noticed that before but thought it was because she was still groggy from the drugs. But no.

I'm on board a ship, she said to herself.

Just then she heard a very quiet series of bleeps, the lock yielded to the keypad sequence and the door opened. Stella jumped up and moved to the top of the bed, her hands down at her sides pressing her back against the wall as though willing it to open and let her pass through.

Three women walked in. Two were dressed in black burkas which covered every part of their bodies except their hands and their eyes, visible through the slits in the material over their heads. The third was dressed in very much western clothing - tight cream trousers, blouse and heeled shoes. She walked with confidence and was clearly in charge, and she smiled at Stella, moving towards her. Somehow Stella's terror began to abate.

"Ah, so you're awake, good," she said, looking Stella up and down. "You must be hungry, you've been asleep for three days."

"Where the hell am I and what do you want," said Stella as forcefully as she could, and thinking that the shakiness in her voice didn't make it sound forceful at all. "And I don't think I've been asleep for three days, I've been drugged and kept unconscious for three days," she added. That sounded better.

"There is some food here, eggs - no bacon I'm afraid - hash browns, mushrooms, toast, and some nice hot coffee," said the woman totally ignoring Stella's remarks, "or yoghurts cheeses and meats if you prefer, and cereals too, so now you will be able to have a good breakfast. I'm sure it's going to make you feel much better."

The woman had a good figure, full and curved, and her face was rounded with a dark complexion, rather small nose and high forehead. The mouth was a slash of deep vermilion. Her black hair hung in a tight ponytail, which seemed to heighten her authority.

"My name is Aisha," said the woman, more firmly now. "You are on board a ship in the middle of the ocean, you are quite totally isolated and, in case you hadn't already realised it, you are under our complete control. There is no escape for you, so do not even begin to think or hope that help is at hand, or that the police will come to rescue you. They will not. There is no help. Nobody knows where you are. You are entirely alone."

She paused to let the words sink in.

"What do you want with me," said Stella. "You have no right to take me or hold me here. What the hell do you want?"

Aisha just continued.

"I will be looking after you until you are required by Mr Malekka. He will talk to you fully about what we want of you and what is to happen to you. I suggest..."

"What do you mean, what you want of me," interrupted Stella in a raised voice this time, "what are you going to do to me? You've kidnapped me, that's a serious crime, you're going to get into..."

Her voice tailed off as Aisha took two steps forwards. Her face had turned to stone and her eyes cold.

"As I was saying, I suggest you try to do all you can to make yourself comfortable and enjoy your surroundings here. *While you can.*" She spoke in a sharper tone that sounded suddenly dangerous, and she had emphasised the last three words. "And whether you continue in pleasant surroundings or unpleasant ones is entirely up to you and will be entirely your choice, as you will see."

Stella stared at Aisha. The woman is clearly ready to kill me at a moment's notice, she thought. She was trembling again now and slowly sat down on the edge of the bed. Her mouth had fallen open and she was breathing quickly.

"Look, what do you want with me," she said again. "Why have you kidnapped me, what is this all about?"

"These two ladies will remain with you now," Aisha went on, indicating the two females in the burkas yet still giving no answer to Stella's question. The other women were quickly bringing in trays from a trolley outside the door and putting them on the table in the corner. They set a place for Stella, crowned by a gold-ringed napkin.

Aisha spoke again, using the softer, gentler tone from before. "After you have eaten, you will I am sure wish to shower or take a bath, and dress. We have a lot of nice clothes for you to wear, as you have already seen..."

What does she mean, thought Stella, 'already seen'. Are there cameras in here?

"... and Mr Malekka would like you to look nice and comfortable for him when he comes in to see you. Oh - by the way, these women do not speak English, so unless you are fluent in Arabic, which our research says you are not, they will not be able to understand you easily let alone answer questions for you. So save your energy. But, they are as I said here to look after you.

"So, eat, drink, bathe, and - today - relax. I'll be back tomorrow. And then I will ask you some questions. Questions about where you work, some diagrams, some codes. And when you are ready to tell us everything, then Mr Malekka will see you."

Christ, the codes. The access codes. It was what she had thought. Oh God.

"I can't tell you anything," she said. "I don't know anything. And even if I did, I couldn't tell you, like everyone else I signed the Official Secrets Act. I can't say anything, even if I knew anything. You're wasting your time. You've obviously got the wrong person."

Aisha had begun to tap the keypad on the door, ready to leave, but turned briefly to look back at Stella. "Don't insult my intelligence," she said harshly. "I really don't like that." And then almost as an afterthought, "And please, no silly behaviour. It would be such a shame to have to restrain you all the time, and so pointless." With that, she was gone from the room. The door closed firmly behind her.

The two women in burkas walked into the bathroom and began to run a bath for Stella. She felt scared and was still shaking a little but the sound of the running water was soothing and she began to calm down, perhaps also because she realised she was not in any immediate physical danger. Aisha was obviously the one to be wary of, and this man Melka, whenever he arrives, but for now perhaps a hot bath would be good for me.

One of the women produced a key and beckoned Stella to come over. Stella shifted to the end of the bed and raised her leg, and the woman undid the ankle-cuff. She ushered Stella to the table, where the food was waiting.

All of a sudden Stella felt hungry. Though she had in fact been fed some nourishment and water via an intravenous drip over the last few days, she could feel real pangs of hunger now. The burka woman looked at her enquiringly. Stella pointed to the hot food, and the other woman, who had spoken only the word Nasrin to indicate her name, put food on a plate and placed it down before Stella. Nasrin poured some coffee too, and the women stood back.

The food tasted good, and at least this was something she could enjoy. As long as it wasn't poisoned or drugged of course; but then, they wanted something from her, they had said, and would need her sensible. She sipped at the coffee.

So it was obvious. She had thought it from the very start, but now she was certain. They are after the codes to the Fincrest Centre. They must be terrorists, or thieves, or both.

Three days, Aisha had said. That was how long she had been held captive and kept unconscious. Stella finished her breakfast, rose and walked to the bathroom. Nasrin and the other woman in the burka who also spoke her own name, Shurafa, were waiting by the entrance.

The water was hot and ready and the bath foam's sweet basil and jasmine scent filled the warm air and made it all the more inviting. Stella tried to close the bathroom door but the other girls shook their heads. So she shrugged off her shyness, stepped out of her clothes and sank into the water.

Once she was in the two girls moved forwards intending to bathe her, but Stella waved with her hands that she did not want that, and they stood just watching her. She began to wonder if they wanted some kind of sexual encounter with her, but, lying back enjoying her soak (such as she could in the circumstances) she decided they were personal servants whose rôle was simply that - to serve. Well - that and, she thought, to make sure that she did nothing stupid to herself like trying to commit suicide, which was why they were keeping such a close eye on her. Clearly she was needed by these people. And that thought brought the reality of her predicament back hard to her again with all the fear and terror. She washed hurriedly to get out of her naked vulnerability.

The burka girls moved forwards intending to dry her but Stella shooed them away once more. She discovered her clothes had vanished, and in fact Nasrin had removed them to be washed. Stella had little choice, therefore, other than to explore the walk-in closet at the other side of the bed. She chose a skirt, a blouse, matching underwear and some heeled shoes that were a little plain but comfortable enough. She was not going to use any of the extensive range of Parisian makeup, lipsticks and perfumes that had been specially provided, but Nasrin and Shurafa made such a fuss that she was obliged to reverse her decision and do so.

Stella was able to get a closer look at the two women. In spite of their burkas she could see their beauty and youthfulness. They were probably both in their early twenties. Their eyes were wide and dark, with liner; their eyebrows were shaped with extended ends to complement the elongated slit. A gentle blue on their eyelids and lower eyes contrasted with the dark tanned skin.

If this was the trouble the girls took over just their eyes, Stella thought, what else had they done to the rest of their bodies? She also caught sight of a shoe on one of the girls, which was a stylish open-toed design with a tie strap around the ankle and about a four-inch heel. That seemed a little contrary to the traditional westerner's idea of what lies beneath a burka, she said to herself.

Then she was startled to see a bulge of what could only be a gun on one of the girls' torsos. Stella had to revise her opinion again of the purpose of these females; to serve and please, undoubtedly, but they were soldiers of a kind, armed and dangerous, and they probably wouldn't hesitate to shoot her dead if so ordered.

Stella picked up a comb to use on her hair but by gesture one of the girls offered to brush it for her. Stella had always enjoyed the feeling and nodded her agreement. She closed her eyes as Shurafa began to brush her hair in soothing full strokes. It was a small pleasure that Stella welcomed, contrasting with the large sine waves of emotion, fear and terror with which she was having to deal.

Another ten minutes and all three girls emerged from the dressing room. Stella was indicated to sit on the couch, which she did, settling down into its soft material and cushions that almost wrapped themselves around her. She was more relaxed, even a little sleepy.

The burka girls cleared the table and tidied, and continued to keep a careful watch over their charge. It was pointless trying to have a conversation with them; Aisha was right about that, only a certain amount could be gained from sign gestures. There was very little for Stella to do other than to reflect on her predicament and worry about what might be about to happen to her, which she surmised, in fact correctly, was probably exactly what her captors intended. The only distractions were DVDs or reading from an array of books made available to her. Every now and then she drifted off into an unsettled slumber. In her enforced, necessarily-circular thinking she tried to formulate a plan of how she should be and what to say when her captors returned.

Stella would spend the rest of the day this way, waiting uneasily. The hours dragged by. But actually she was in no hurry to get to the next morning.

≈

That same afternoon, at the *Bistrot Bizerca* café in Shortmarket Street in the heart of Cape Town, four men sat around a heavy oak corner table eating a late lunch. The air was full of a pleasant mixture of cooked meats and fish, wines, cheeses and the wafting aroma of good coffee. The men were between thirty and thirty-five years of age, fit, outwardly pleasant, dressed in business suits with shirt and tie, and to all intents and purposes were ordinary people enjoying their break from the daily monotony of a work routine.

"He ran twice yesterday, at 2pm and 7pm," said Mateen quietly, "and twice so far today, at 6.30am and then, again, 2pm." Mateen was the youngest of the group. His short gelled hair rose in gathered spikes above a round baby face with quick-shifting dark eyes. "I bet he'll be out again tonight at 7pm. He seems to like to stick to a routine - 6.30am, 2pm and 7pm. And he's obviously some kind of fitness freak, I think."

The others laughed lightly at the comment, but without real humour.

"Just because he likes to stay fit and you don't like running, Mateen," said Samir, "you don't have to berate him. Anyway a little running sometimes would do you no harm come to think of it." Samir liked to run and although his frame was slim it was as tough as whipcord.

Mateen smiled at the banter.

The waiter came over and cleared the plates away, and they ordered some coffee.

"He takes the same route each time," said Walif in a low gruff voice, taking a map out from his pocket and unfolding it onto the table. He took out a pen and used it as a pointer.

"He leaves the Estate at the northern end of the Twelve Apostles, gets down onto the beach road, runs north here along the front, passes Camps Bay in front of the Lion's Head to Sea Point, and cuts through the streets up behind the town; then he heads back south down the Table Mountain road, to the Fincrest Estate. It's about ten miles in all, and he does it in around an hour and a half."

"Good," said Khatib. "Very good. It will make our job all the easier." He looked at the map with a thoughtful stare. Khatib was the leader of the squad. An eagle-like aquiline nose rested on a heavy face of dark mottled skin that had seen much combat and concealed much guilt. "So where would you suggest?"

"We think the best place is here, sir," said Mateen, pointing to a straight stretch of road along the sea front at Sea Point. "There are hotels all the way along there. We have found one that would be ideal. It overlooks exactly that stretch of road and would give us full view."

Khatib wiped his mouth lightly with his napkin and placed the cloth onto the table. He thought a little longer, and then spoke decisively.

"Very well. If he is out at 6.30am again tomorrow morning, we'll do it then. That should make it around 7am at Sea Point. If not, we'll go with the 2pm." He paused, and then continued.

"Now - once again. When we leave here, we split into two pairs. You two," looking at Mateen and Walif, "will go and get the room at the hotel, and set up the equipment. Samir, you check he does indeed leave for the 7pm run tonight and then come back to me at our hotel. I will go back there now and get the item ready. And remember - there is to be absolutely no more contact between the two groups until the rendezvous."

The three men acknowledged their instructions. Khatib pushed away from the table, leaning into the back of his chair. Then he nodded slowly.

"This man seems to be a creature of habit and of routine. And this will be his downfall."

The men paid, and left the café.

At 7pm, JP set out on his third run of the day.

6
BREAKING

THE FOLLOWING MORNING the sun was beginning to rise when JP passed through the black iron security gates of the Fincrest Estate. He nodded to Maltong, the gate-keeper, and then set off at a sharp pace jogging down the incline of the road that would take him to the sea front. He enjoyed running, but he had been in Cape Town less than forty-eight hours and was not running for pleasure. He was running first to ensure he would stay at the peak of physical fitness, which he felt was essential; and, second, to keep his sanity. Since arriving, there had been little for him to do other than wait, and so he had resolved to run three times a day. It kept his mind active and his body tuned. He wore US marine-style shorts, small and tight fitting, a T-shirt; and his favourite running shoes. His frame moved lithely and easily. He made a good pace with no effort.

JP had kept a watchful eye out for anyone paying too much attention to him. The roads had traffic on them of course, though very little early in the morning. A couple of gardeners; a street cleaner; one or two housemaids going to or from work were the only people he had seen up in the hills; and there were always a few joggers, cyclists and pedestrians down at the sea front. He was almost at Victoria Road, and pleased he had been able to find such a good route; although much of it was along the sea front and the road was full of bends with a sharp drop off to the sea, there was pavement all the way and that made for simple running. A car passed him slowly, with the passenger window open and an elbow resting over the edge; another in the opposite direction still had its lights on. Yet again he brought his mind back onto Stella, and wondered where and how she was, and traced through the elements of the plan that he had conceived and that MI6 had adopted, and that was now in full swing.

JP made his way north, running with the traffic flow on the left adjacent to the coastline. The Atlantic Ocean crashed onto the few rocks along the shoreline and the fresh breeze was laden with salt. Another South African autumn day was going to have a clear blue sky. He crossed the wide Peninsula Hotel roundabout, remembering he had seen his first whale from there, basking in the deep waters out to sea.

As JP reached about half way down the straight stretch of Beach Road a car passed him slowly. The passenger window was down, an arm was resting on its edge. He had seen that arm before. The man leant out, his face immediately sinister with its balaclava, and tossed a package out ahead of JP. The car sped off; in an instant JP realised what it was, yelled at the woman walking towards him to get down, knew he couldn't save her, and jumped over the railings at the side of the pavement down to the sandy beach just as the bomb went off. The explosion shattered windows of buildings opposite, knocked him fifteen feet and split his head open on some rocks. JP staggered up and tried to walk, then grimaced, and the darkness of unconsciousness overwhelmed him. He collapsed onto the sand, blood spilling from the wound to his head. But his fast reactions had placed much of his body below the level of the pavement which helped absorb the blast. The woman coming towards him had not been so lucky. She had been killed outright.

In the car Samir accelerated fast from the scene. The two men removed their balaclavas. The car turned into the busy area of the City, slowed and was quickly lost in the early rush hour.

On the balcony of the hotel room Mateen stopped the filming and walked back into the room with Walif. They played back the recording on the camera's screen and then Walif removed the memory card and placed it into the laptop. Without copying the file to the hard drive, he uploaded it via their secure satellite internet connection to the web address they had been given. They checked the file could be viewed; satisfied, Walif erased the temp files, removed the memory card, took it out to the balcony, set fire to it and scattered the ashes over the balcony edge. Mateen popped the second card into the camcorder. The two men left their twin room and went downstairs to breakfast, where the news was all about a bomb blast four hundred metres away.

On board the *Excelsior*, the video file was downloaded a few minutes later. Aisha reviewed it, and smiled.

It could now begin.

≈

Stella awoke from an uncomfortable night. She was ushered by the burka girls, who had watched her on a rotation shift through the night, to bathe and dress. She ate breakfast and then sat on the couch once more. Her stomach felt a wrenching sickening twist as she heard the door keypad bleep gently at 10am, and with fearful eyes she saw it swing open. She swallowed hard.

Aisha entered the room again, this time followed by two large men, Aarif Haddad and Tarek Raboud. Both were wearing T-shirts and jeans that clung to their physique. They looked strong and menacing. Aisha dismissed the burka girls from the room, telling them to wait outside, and turned to face Stella.

"Stand, please," she said to her. Stella looked up defiantly, and did not move. Aisha gestured to Haddad with her head. He walked quickly over towards Stella, and before she realised it had grabbed her by her left arm and pulled her up.

"Ow, let go of me, you're hurting me," shouted Stella indignantly, but Haddad took no notice, and dragged her over to Aisha. He let her go, and Stella swung at him with a clenched fist, catching him squarely on the cheek.

"Keep your hands off me, you ape."

It was a pretty good blow. But it didn't even make Haddad flinch. He just smiled, and grabbed her arm again.

"Tie her hands behind her back," said Aisha.

Raboud pulled out a pair of handcuffs from his hip pocket and the men secured both hands. Stella shouted out, "What the hell do you *want*."

"I'll tell you what we want, and more besides," said Aisha. "Come with me."

She signalled to the men. Each took Stella by an arm and marched her out of the room into the corridor outside, which stretched fifty feet in either direction and was maybe a metre wide, enough for two people to pass sideways on. The red carpet from the room over-spilled into the corridor. Mahogany panels with raised gold edges lined the walls beneath lights sunk into the low curved ceiling.

Stella was taken left thirty feet to the door of a room which obviously backed onto the bathroom and closet of hers. The room had a keypad entrance too, and Aisha entered the number. Haddad closed the door behind them.

Stella looked around in utter horror.

The room was almost identical in size to hers, but otherwise couldn't be more contrasting. The carpet was replaced by cold tiled flooring; the walls were exposed brickwork. Harsh bright light fell from a low ceiling. Two concrete columns eight feet apart stretched from floor to ceiling in the centre of the room, with large steel rings sunk into them at strategic intervals. Off these dangled various chain restraining devices in which ankles or wrists could easily be shackled and held at will, with a similar array embedded into the walls.

The room was reminiscent of a mediaeval dungeon and torture chamber, and it was quickly clear that a torture chamber was exactly what it was. Stella started to feel physically sick, and was on the point of fainting.

Aisha turned to Stella, and spoke clearly and firmly. The quietness of her voice made her all the more menacing.

"I want you to listen to me very carefully. You have a choice. You can either have your life in the room next door; or, you can have it in this room here."

The girl swayed and would have collapsed but for Haddad and Raboud who had hold of her arms. She swallowed hard; her mouth was dry.

"Let me show you around," continued Aisha. "This is where we bring people who either displease us and need some kind of punishment or discipline, or who have some information that we want. Like you do."

"What do you mean," cried Stella, "I don't know anything about anything, I don't even know what you want."

"I think you do. And we'll get to that in a moment." She walked over to a steel table bolted to the floor on which were various leather whips and belts, thick rubber hoses and an array of pliers, pinchers and sharp flat-bladed and hooked knives.

"Such people are stripped and placed into the hooks on the walls or pillars. And then these are used on them," gesturing towards the table.

Aisha picked up a sjambok, a horrific leather whip five feet long tapering from an inch-thick handle to a quarter-inch the other end, and suddenly brought it crashing down onto the top of the table. The sound was terrifying and reverberated around the room. Stella's eyes widened and she jumped visibly.

"You'd be surprised at just how easily and quickly this can bruise and cut through naked flesh."

Aisha walked over to a steel chair that resembled the electric chair previously used for executions in the USA.

"You will probably have seen pictures of this type of chair," she said. "These leather straps restrain the person's arms here, and these straps," she said bending down slightly to hold the lower ones up with her hand, "hold the legs tight against the metal legs of the chair. The helmet hinges down here, and is brought onto the head of the person sitting in it. And then these cables and clips are applied, to nipples, genitals, ears, fingertips... wherever we want. And then over there..."

Stella followed her arm movement to another small table with a box on it, to which the cables were connected.

"...is where we can turn the electric current on and off. It is quite an art, you know, applying the right voltage to cause the maximum pain and burn."

Stella started to cry and struggle but she couldn't move from the grip of the two men. The tour of the room was clearly designed to intimidate and terrify. It was proving very effective.

"And, as is yours, the room is completely

soundproof. Which is why they both have thick walls, a padded door and a slightly lower ceiling than elsewhere in the ship - it's the soundproofing material behind. You see, once we start, the screams can get very loud. Of course if you are like my two colleagues here, they like to hear the screams. In fact they enjoy it. And all the more so when their subject is a pretty young female. Such as you."

"What do you want," whined Stella, "I haven't done anything to hurt you, why are you doing this to me?" She was crying openly now, the tears running down her face and mixing with fluid from her nose. She tried to sniff and clear it.

"Well perhaps we'll stop the tour for now, shall we?" asked Aisha sarcastically and tauntingly of Stella, looking at her without pity. "Put her into the chair," she said harshly.

Stella screamed and struggled violently but she was no match for the men, who had her in the metal chair within seconds. They removed her bracelets and rings; straps immobilised her arms and wrists, one around her neck kept her head up, and her legs were pinned to the legs of the chair, the openness of her thighs heightening her sense of total vulnerability and helplessness. They left her clothes on, which was at least one small mercy.

"For God's sake," she said, "don't, please don't."

"Be quiet," shouted Aisha. Stella was crying and whimpering, begging almost without making any sense. "Be quiet, Stella," said Aisha once more, "and listen to me again. Look up at me."

Stella raised her reddened eyes again. She saw only cruelty in Aisha's face.

"You have some information that we want. When you see Mr Malekka, he will ask you some questions and expect immediate answers from you. It is my job to ensure that you are ready to give that information."

"What information," said Stella, her spasmodic breathing making her speech uneven. "What do you want that I have?"

"We want information about the Fincrest Centre. We will begin with a simple question. An easy one. Say... What is the entrance code to the main door of the administration block?"

Stella's mouth opened in amazement. How did they know about Fincrest and that the front door is on a keypad?

"Look," she said, "it's always open when I go in. I don't know any code. And even if I did, I can't tell it to anyone. It's not permitted. It's..."

"Very well," interrupted Aisha. She moved over to the table where the cables from the chair ended. She pulled out a draw below the top that hinged down forty-five degrees as it extended. Inside, Stella could see a number of blue-labelled phials and some hypodermic needles. Fuck, she thought, what are they going to do to me, I can't do this, I can't do this. She was trembling uncontrollably.

"You know," said Aisha, "there are other methods of extracting information. Mr Malekka would much prefer that your pretty body is not damaged or spoilt, for rather obvious reasons of his own."

"What are you talking about, what reasons?" she asked. Though she had a pretty good idea.

Aisha ignored her again. "And so here we have ten little bottles of some special liquid. Number One packs a nasty punch, and they progress in strength to Number Ten. Number Ten will fry your brain, if I were you I wouldn't let this get that far. When the liquid goes in it will set your nerves on fire, and you will feel pain internally that will start and not end. That is, not end until I put this antidote in," and she held up another small phial, with a red label. She had already selected a third type and was holding it upside down, an inserted syringe drawing some of the liquid out.

"And this one is to stop the screaming. I don't like to be bothered with the screaming."

Stella said nothing. She just listened in horror, her breathing increasing, almost panting now. Aisha approached with the first needle, and Stella tried violently to shake herself but was entirely restrained within the rock-solid chair. The needle went in. Stella let out a scream and a "You fucking bitch" but Aisha was immune.

Almost immediately, Stella found that she was not able to move any more, and her speaking stopped. She tried to shout, but no words came out. She could move her eyes, blink, breathe, but nothing else. She saw Aisha approach again with another needle, felt it go into her arm, heard a loud exaggerated scraping sound in her ears as it was taken out.

Then the pain started. The nerve endings all over her body were attacked simultaneously by a myriad of hideous microscopic nanocells flaying her alive with heat, burning acid, biomaterials and toxicity, as though her entire body were held over an open fire and roasted. Yet there was no flame, nothing touching her skin, no damage done, just the precise work of the chemicals that had been placed inside her, that could continue on with no exertion needed by her torturers. It was unceasing, intense, hideous pain. She breathed fast, her tears rolled, the only sound was her rasping breath. She saw Aisha look down, and say we'll give her forty minutes.

Forty minutes? It wasn't forty minutes. It was one hour, two hours... Or so it seemed to Stella. It was longer than two. It isn't worth it. Nothing's worth this.

Fuck, I don't want it, I don't want it.

Another needle went in, and the pain quickly left her, and her motion returned.

"When Mr Malekka comes to see you, he will ask you for some information. Will you give it to him?"

Stella was panting, not able yet to formulate an answer, let alone give one.

"I will ask you again, Stella. The first, simple question. What is the entrance code to the main door of the administration block?"

Stella didn't want any more pain. She had suffered enough. It wasn't a state secret for God's sake, why should she have to put up with any of this? But she realised something else. Now she hated Aisha. She hated her, loathed her, resented her, more than the pain. I may not last long, you bitch, but I'm not going to make it easy for you. To hell with you.

And Stella looked at Aisha and heard herself say, "Fuck you."

Aisha smiled, and gave a little sigh. "You're a very silly girl, Stella. Why would you put yourself through this? You have no idea of the amount of pain that will come to you, as we move through one bottle to another. And don't think we won't move to some other methods too."

Stella stood her ground, waiting for the next injection, preparing herself for more of the same. But Aisha had another plan.

"Tarek, pick up the curved pliers and cut off the little finger of one of her hands, I don't care which."

Stella wasn't prepared for this. Fuck. To lose a finger? Forever? She screamed, and shook violently in the chair, scrunched up her fists, saw the man walk over with some heavy pliers-like instrument that had two curved sharp blades that could encompass a finger easily and translate the cutting motion into a sever. She screamed again as he forced open her left hand and prepared to put the finger between the blades.

Aisha said, "Oh, wait a moment," and Raboud stopped. "We'll give her one more chance, shall we?" Stella knew she was being teased, played with. Cow. At least there was some relief, her finger was safe for a little longer. She was helpless, they were going to do what they wanted when they wanted. It was up to her to decide when it would stop, how far they were to go. They would carry on until they had what they wanted.

Stella was whimpering and crying uncontrollably.

"So you think you can call me a fucking bitch do you?" said Aisha. She leant forwards a little, and screamed the words again just over Stella's face.

"Another little dose, Stella" said Aisha, looking at the panting, tear-racked face of the girl. Aisha walked over to the phials, and picked up Number Two. Then she put it back down. "No, let's skip the next one. Let's move on a bit, shall we Stella?" She lifted Number Three up from the drawer.

Oh God. What's the point? Bitch. Fucking bitch.

Tears were streaming down Stella's face. One of the men grabbed her hair and pulled her head up. She saw Aisha with the first syringe, the fluid went inside, and once more Stella's movements stopped, she could utter no sound. Then the next syringe with the fluid from the third phial, a little later this time so that the first injection could work more, and she could hear the awful scraping sound again in her ears, a rushing as the liquid was injected into her, and more scraping as the needle came out.

There was no reaction in her straight away this time, and she thought perhaps she had this under control. But then she was hit with a sharp agonising flame again that punched and pummelled every nerve ending in her being, making her throw her head back and her body arch and strain against the leather straps. Her eyes bulged, and face reddened. And then it stopped, as suddenly as it had started. She could breathe again, the pain had gone... Then it was back, hitting her again as if a baseball bat had suddenly begun to beat her everywhere. Her nerves burned, electric shocks were travelling along her skin from her feet to her head. It stopped again, the pain on her nerves went to zero, and then it was back fully again, the range giving her no chance to adjust to the high level and accept and tolerate.

After forty minutes, she was close to passing out. Aisha injected the antidote. She looked at Stella, as her breathing and her skin colour returned to something close to normal. "You don't need to do this, Stella." She could see that her victim was close to the end. Stella was panting and crying, and she had now soiled herself with the terror and pain. There was no logic in resisting, she was not a soldier, she was not at war. Aisha nearly had her.

Aisha said, "Get the video."

Haddad and Raboud wheeled a viewing screen forwards and placed it in front of her.

"Stella, you will answer Mr Malekka's questions." Stella started to nod, unable to speak yet, still shocked by her ordeal that maybe was still far from over. "After you have answered Mr Malekka's questions, you will be placed in his service and you will work at his convenience and pleasure, just as the two girls waiting outside do, just as I do, and just as these two men do. And if there is any problem with you, in addition to the little play room and toys we have here, your father will be killed, your brother will be killed, his wife will be killed and their little baby girl of eleven months, little baby Susan, will die too. As will that fine boyfriend of yours that you left on St Lucia, JP."

Stella looked at her with a mixture of horror and astonishment, and could not find anything to bring to her voice to say. She just cried.

"I am going to show you how easy it would be for us to do this. Watch."

The screen in front of her lit up.

It showed a scene of blue sea, a road, and large pavement, perhaps taken from the fifth floor of an apartment or hotel along the road. The camera panned to a man jogging, and zoomed in. Stella at once recognised JP. And she knew the place, it was Sea Point in South Africa, just west of Cape Town. He was out for a run, in the early morning. She started to cry again. She missed him, she needed him, where was he now? Where was that lovely man, that made her heart race, made her feel warm? The camera panned out. Suddenly a car drove past him and slowed, and a package was thrown out towards the runner twenty yards ahead. The car sped off, the runner slowed, then leapt over the rail to the beach as the package exploded. Stella jumped at the vicious sound, smashed cars, broken glass. JP was hurled backwards and against some rocks. After the dust cleared, amongst the sounds of screaming, JP got up, and staggered forwards, his head bleeding badly, then collapsed. But he was alive, moving. It was different for the woman walking towards him. She had been closer and had taken the full force of the blast. Her lifeless, smashed body lay in three scattered pieces on the concrete pavement.

"You see, Stella? You see how easy it would have been for us to kill him? It could have been him lying dead on the ground. Not that woman. What are you trying to protect? Is it worth his life? Is it worth your pain? And we'll get it out of you eventually anyway. Do you want the next viewing to be of his death?"

Stella stared at the screen. She had somehow become calmer now, the images on the screen had reached inside her and touched the very depths of her soul. She wasn't going to risk his life, or the lives of family. Not for this. Never.

There was no alternative, absolutely none. She had decided. She looked up at Aisha.

Aisha saw her moment. She knew Stella was broken. Stella nodded.

"I'll do anything you want. I'll tell you whatever you want to know."

7
AFTERWARDS

IT WAS FINISHED. The woman was broken and her defences destroyed. There was no more resistance. Only resignation and acceptance.

Aisha had forced Stella over the physical and psychological hurdle and knew she would co-operate fully now, in any and every way. Answers to questions flowed without difficulty. It had taken slightly longer than she had thought, but the result was never really in doubt. She was ready to meet with Mr Malekka.

"Take her back next door," said Aisha curtly.

The men almost had to carry Stella out of the room. Her feet dragged along the floor. Stella was relieved beyond measure to get out of there. She had been severely tortured in a concentrated period, was in shock and seriously scared of what these people could do to her again. She had determined to comply with their wishes in every way. There was no alternative.

The men put Stella on the bed and threw her jewellery down beside her. They went to stand either side of and slightly behind Aisha as the two burka girls cleaned Stella up. Aisha announced she would be back in the morning, and that Mr Malekka would meet with her tomorrow also. Then they left.

Stella's ordeal had lasted five hours. Over the next six, she vomited four times, once on the bed when she wasn't fast enough to crawl to the toilet. She drifted in and out of an uneasy and painful sleep, shivering with cold but then throwing off the bedcovers a few minutes later when she felt the temperature was again high. She was still in the clothes that she had soiled earlier. When her eyes were open the room appeared to be rotating, which only made her retch more.

The burka girls remained. Clearly they knew of the results on Aisha's victims, so they watched Stella closely as she went through the aftermath. Finally, Stella slept for a full uninterrupted half hour. When she awoke she appeared to be more stable and the vomiting had stopped. She tried to relax herself, rocking slightly to and fro and moaning to bring a little comfort.

The burka girls looked at her with sympathetic eyes. They spoke to each other softly in Arabic, and Shurafa went into the bathroom to run a hot bath again for Stella. Nasrin touched her gently on the arm to make her look over and gestured towards the bathroom.

I don't want a bath, you stupid bitches, Stella thought. That's not any good, it's not enough. I want to be disinfected. I want my skin taken off and a new fresh layer grown so that all possible remnants of you people can be removed, made to go away, so that I can get back to life and living.

However, she had to be practical. Perhaps another bath would be good after all. It might help make me feel better, she thought, physically and mentally. She stared at her bracelets and rings beside her on the bed, picked them up and slowly put them back on. That's all I have left now, she thought, and my watch, and a few clothes. They've taken everything else from me. Tears rolled quietly from her eyes and dropped onto the bed. Nasrin put her arm round her shoulders. Stella didn't object or push her away this time.

Stella used the toilet again, then hobbled to the bath and stepped in. The warm water soothed as she sat then lay down. She put her head back and closed her eyes, letting the water come right up to her neck, then suddenly dipped her head under the water. The two burka girls rushed over, thinking she was trying to drown herself, but backed away as they realised Stella was only having a soak. Stella laid her head on the end of the bath, trying to rest and recover.

At least I'm still alive.

And, while she was alive, the rest of the family was safe, and so was JP. She could protect everyone by co-operating with the bastards. Look at what they have done already. They wouldn't hesitate to do more if she didn't co-operate, and maybe the next time they visited JP they would kill him. At least they hadn't hurt her with the violence of a beating or punching, or cutting off fingers, although it had been close. In fact to all intents and purposes, her physical appearance actually had not been affected; except for some inflamed skin and very red puffy eyes, and that would pass quickly enough. If she could ever stop crying that is. And drink a lot of water, she had been told. To flush all of the chemicals out.

She tried to rationalise her situation. The end result had really been inevitable of course. As inevitable as Aisha knew it to be, as those two pigs knew it to be, and as she herself had actually known it to be, right from the start. Submission and co-operation. She had absolutely no other choice.

The most important thing was to stay alive. Just stay alive. As she felt the warmth of the water against her skin, she thought about the two burka-clad girls. Guns under their clothes, dressed beautifully beneath. She had seen their hands as well, they were soft and manicured.

Have they each been treated like I have, she

wondered? Probably, perhaps for disobedience. And probably raped from a very early age too, to train them to serve the male of the species in any way he chooses. Yet those two pigs who accompanied Aisha were under her direction. Who serves them? What was the hierarchy of this place? Aisha seemed to be in charge of everyone Stella had seen since waking up in this hellhole.

And at the top is this man Melka or whatever his name is.

Stella had something he wanted, and she would give him everything, answer all the questions. She knew he would take her body. They had already said as much; get real. She shuddered, forcing the thought out of her mind. However, maybe along the way she can do a little negotiating, to get as much back as possible and make life less hideous. Starting with these females here. If they are to look after me, I'll make them work at it.

Stella lifted one arm out of the water, and snapped her fingers. To her amazement, both girls stood and looked at her, waiting to be told what she wanted. She signalled to the taps at the end of the bath. More hot water. They spoke to each other to check they had understood what Stella meant. Nasrin went to the bath, knelt at the tap end and turned on the hot water. She swilled it around. Shurafa said something to Nasrin who picked up the bottles of scent and foam bath and showed them to Stella enquiringly. Stella nodded, and Nasrin poured some of each into the water again and churned it around. The water got hotter, the bubbles rose and the perfumed smell of jasmine and basil filled the room.

Emboldened, Stella raised her right leg out of the water and placed her heel onto the edge of the bath. She turned to Shurafa and pointed to it, beckoning her. Well this is what you bitches wanted to do to start with isn't it? So if that's your job, you can get on with it.

Shurafa knelt down alongside Nasrin, picked up a soft sponge and soaped it. She pulled her long clothing up to uncover her arms and very gently began to wash Stella's leg. As much as Stella hated these women and everything that had happened to her, the gentle caresses from their hands, the sponges and the warm water, and having these people do this for her, were both satisfying and physically pleasing. They may have forced her into submission, but she was of value to them. She could get back some self-respect, maybe even a little control or influence. That was good for her mind as well as her body.

Nasrin turned the water off, picked up a sponge and started to assist Shurafa. Stella stood and allowed the burka girls to bathe her entire body, except between her legs, which she did herself. She had the girls use the shower head to rinse her, then wash her hair.

When Stella stepped out of the bath the girls encased her in warm soft towels, gently patting her dry. A thick dressing gown was placed around her. Then Stella sat in front of the large glass mirror while Nasrin used the hairdryer and Shurafa went to lay fresh sheets on the bed. The girls brushed and combed her hair.

At the end of it all, Stella found that she was more calm, and extremely tired. She climbed into bed. She held up her leg so that the girls could shackle her, but Nasrin shook her head and wagged a finger. Stella could see from her eyes that she was smiling. Stella gave a little smile back, pleased that she was not to be shackled, and sank into the luxurious covers. Bitch, she thought anyway.

As if by magic, the lights were dimmed - so she is being watched all the time - and within five minutes she was in a very deep exhausted sleep.

8
HOSPITAL

JP WOKE IN a bed in the UCT Hospital. He had drifted in and out of consciousness for six hours. He had numerous cuts and bruises, including one that needed four stitches at his right temple hair line. Thankfully there were no broken bones.

The bomb was a move JP had not foreseen. He knew he would probably be watched, to verify he was a distraught lover, but how had he missed his watchers? Were they that good? Or had he slipped a little in his own professionalism. He had resolved to run three times a day but stupidly the same route and times. He cursed himself for his carelessness. His mind filled briefly of the woman who had been killed. She was thirty-six. What evil monsters these people are, with no respect for life.

The bomb had not been intended to kill him. Not even to shake him, although it had certainly done that. He rationalised it wasn't meant to have any impression on him at all.

"I think it was done for Stella's purpose, Charlie," he said down the scrambled line to his friend in London.

"What do you mean? Are you saying they weren't trying to kill you?"

"That's exactly what I'm saying. They could have got the bomb much closer if they'd wanted to kill me, but they didn't. They threw it ahead of me. I don't think I'm a factor to them at all, I'm just the boyfriend and lover." He paused and took a sip of water from the glass on the table stretched across the bed. "That's good, in fact."

"That they don't see you as anything else you mean?"

"Yes. But I didn't foresee this, Charlie. I should have done, but I didn't."

"Then you're lucky they weren't trying to kill you."

"I'd have survived."

"Maybe. He's a smart, dangerous bugger, Jimmy. With unlimited resources."

"Yes," said JP. "And very professional. I underestimated him. I won't make that mistake again."

"You reckon it was all to make a point?"

"Yes." He paused again. "I think the whole thing was meant for Stella as a threat, to show her that they could get to me easily any time they wanted."

"Are you saying it was staged? Filmed?"

"Yes, I think so. Probably from one of the apartments or hotels there, there are a lot of them. Maybe even a ship."

There was silence between the two men for a second or two. Then Charlie Melton spoke.

"So they're working on her."

"Yes," said JP. "Yes, the bastards are working on her."

After the call JP stared out of the window for an hour or so, his mind rushing with one thought after another. A movie file of the bombing could have been uploaded within minutes for its intended recipient anywhere in the world. For all he knew, there could even have been a live stream as the attack occurred. Although on reflection probably not, in case something had gone wrong and they had killed him, or at the other extreme that there was an error in the construction of the device and the bomb hadn't gone off. No, they would have recorded it. And then the film would be out a few minutes later.

Where is she, he thought again? What on earth had he got Stella into; and what were Malekka and his people doing to her?

JP's thoughts were interrupted by a young nurse who came in to check the wound on his forehead and his vitals once more. She clipped the pulse counter gently onto his right forefinger, briefly held a thermometer in his ear for his temperature and then wrapped the Velcro cloth of the electronic blood pressure monitor around his arm. He welcomed the distraction, and chatted with her while the machine wheezed and sighed taking his signs.

The nurse was pretty, but he missed Stella, not just physically but her company. He put an image of Stella in the front of his mind while the nurse spoke, and then quickly dismissed it. He knew he was a cold calculating man who had no qualms about using people when he had to, and now was not the time for personal feelings. It was probably those that had made him miss the possibility of the attack in the first place.

Finally the nurse gave him a couple more painkillers, and JP watched her leave the room.

JP spat the pills that he had just feigned taking out from under his tongue. He wanted to be sharp and not numbed any more, even if it hurt. He forced himself to focus on the cold reality. He began again to think things through, to explore one avenue of action and its series of consequences; then go back and take another road, considering the outcome; then back again... Just like a game of chess, working out all moves, foresee all of the opponent's options, be aware of the logical and the illogical.

Thirty minutes later, JP decided he was ready. He

dressed and discharged himself. He got into the car waiting to drive him back to his temporary family home. However, he gave the driver some new, additional instructions.

He spent a little time with the worried Fincrests, giving assurances about Stella and that he was fine, then changed his clothes and got into the car once more.

As it sped back to Sea Point, JP still had his chess calculations at the fore of his mind, once more thinking every course permutation through, every avenue of action and reaction, just like a Grand Master. And he knew he couldn't afford to miss a move again.

The Opening had been completed. The Middle Game was about to commence.

And JP was going to make the next move.

9
THE FIFTH RUBRIC

IT WAS JUST after 5pm when the Fincrests' driver dropped JP at the Peninsula Hotel roundabout. The road was still closed to traffic. JP strolled slowly to the police tape strung out across the road in a rectangle cordoning off the crime scene where the bomb had exploded and the woman died.

In a navy baseball cap, sun glasses, a dark sports jacket with the lapels turned up and old camel chinos, JP walked with a slight lean and slow step to make him appear older. Just in case the area was still being watched by the terrorists. He looked carefully around, ignoring the police officers that were still there and the crowd of onlookers.

He could see numerous smashed panes of glass up at the hotels and apartments on the other side of the road that were a direct result of the explosion. Obviously the terrorists would not have filmed from there. He looked in the opposite direction, behind out to sea; the waters had been calm enough and so a ship was a possibility. However the road was slightly raised from the beach - a factor which had lessened his own injuries - and therefore the angle would have been inclined and the viewing perhaps not perfect. He looked back along the road he had just walked; there was no suitable location.

Then JP looked ahead. In four or five hundred metres the road curved slightly seawards and part of a hotel on the other side faced straight down the road. JP gave a grim imperceptible nod. That's where they had been. That's where I would put my camera team if I were going to film the bombing, he said to himself. Yes, it was obvious.

Next JP turned to face the road square on, with his back to the sea. He closed his eyes, and forced himself to think back and remember. He could see the image of the car driving by; he had seen the car before, and the arm resting on the ledge of the open passenger window. He saw the car come down past him not long after he had left the Fincrest Estate... and then he was on Beach Road and it went by again, the left arm and hand down against the door to give the man balance as he leant out... the balaclava, the package lobbed by the man's right hand. The car sped off...

There was something... what was it?

Again, he went through the sequence, and couldn't get it. And then once more. What was it... I know there's something. He had learned in his training years ago that the eyes and brain see and record much more than we focus on. Discipline the mind, train it, find what the eyes have subconsciously seen and that the brain has stored away. Pull out those images. Come on, force them to the front.

And then he remembered. It was the arm - that's it. He had a T-shirt on and the arm was uncovered. What was it... what was it. Yes.. Got it!

It was a tattoo. A red tattoo, a ring around the forearm and something down to the wrist and the back of the hand... No, not quite... a red and *blue* tattoo, with... what was it... a *knife*... hanging down... no, inverted... the hilt of the knife on the back of the hand, and the blade rising up the forearm. That's what he had seen, and couldn't remember. Until now.

So now he had two things to look for. First, find the

room in the hotel. Second, find the man with the tattoo.

"Hello, Jimmy," someone said quietly.

JP smiled without turning to look at the man. "Well Kuhle, it's good to see that the Scorpions can move quickly when there's a chance of making a sting." JP had only called him fifteen minutes ago. The Cape Town head of the Scorpions, the South African police force's most feared anti-terrorist and serious crime squad, had moved remarkably quickly to join him.

"Well, it's not just you, man," said Kuhle. "We don't like it when guests to our lovely country almost get blown to bits by nasties. I kind of take that personally."

JP looked across at him. "I don't like it much myself," he said. "Thanks for putting your men on the hospital watch."

"Well I hope they were discreet enough," said Kuhle. "We didn't want the bomb throwers to have another go at you." He paused, and then added, "I should have put my boys onto you to start with, JP. This might never have happened. You could have been killed."

"No, I don't think so. They weren't trying to kill me...." and JP filled in his reasoning to Kuhle as the two men walked back towards the roundabout and out of view of the hotel. Kuhle Mandingo was a black South African, slightly shorter than JP but the same age, with close cropped hair that was receding heavily at the forehead. A dark moustache trailed around thin lips to meet a small triangle of a beard. He was known for his honesty, integrity and ruthlessness in his pursuit of justice. Black, coloured or white; it made no difference to him.

They got into Kuhle's car, a fast BMW 6 series sports. Kuhle reached down behind his seat, pulled out a canvas bag and handed it to JP.

"A little present from the Firm via the British High

Commissioner. Who says hello, by the way, and hopes that you won't kill too many people here."

"Thanks," said JP. He removed his jacket, slipped on the shoulder holster and quickly checked the chamber and magazines of the Sig Sauer P226. He screwed on the suppressor, pushed a magazine into the gun and pulled the slide to put a round in the chamber. His jacket fitted back comfortably and concealed the Sauer resting reassuringly under his armpit.

"So you want to go to the hotel?"

"Yes," said JP. "It's possible they're still there. Checking out immediately after the bombing would draw attention to themselves, and I gather that you guys closed the area down so tight and quickly that for them to leave today might have been very difficult and very obvious. I'm betting that they're still there, and that tomorrow is the get-out day."

"That's pretty thin," said Kuhle.

"No, not really. Think about it. With the airports and shipping terminals suddenly squeezed almost to a standstill because of the extra searches and checks, anyone leaving would immediately fall under suspicion and have to run that gauntlet. So they're not going to go that way. I reckon they'll leave by car, when the road blocks have gone and they're not in danger of being pursued as a fugitive. Remember, I'd only been here less than forty-eight hours when the bombing happened, and so for them to have put all of this together, and timed it with my jogging, means that they could only recently have checked into that hotel - how otherwise would they have known which one to choose, and how to get at me? No, my bet is they're still here, or at least the film team anyway. Assuming there was one of course. They'll leave calmly and quietly by car when they think they're safe; probably via Durban or into Zimbabwe or

Mozambique. Their job's done, they're in no hurry. That's how I would have played it, anyway. I think we have a chance."

Kuhle pondered JP's words as he took the car along the back road to the hotel. He glanced quickly across at JP. He had heard a great deal about this man, who was ex-SAS, was very smart and tough, and could move very, very quickly. The fact he carried the Fifth Rubric[1] on behalf of Great Britain invoked by MI6 and the British Government meant he had full clearance and was trusted internationally at the highest level. That made him an extremely dangerous operative - for those unfortunate enough to be on the opposing side, that is. Kuhle had been fully briefed about JP and the seriousness of the matter, and he already liked what he had seen in this man. It was Kuhle's job to do so anyway, but he had resolved to help JP as much as he could.

"I know the manager of the hotel well," said Kuhle. "Sheer coincidence; we were actually at college together. But I can use it now to good advantage. He'll want to help us. And, he's black like me, and will enjoy helping out a honkey. So let me go in first, ok, and chat to him."

"Sure," said JP. He smiled at the use of the word honkey.

---

[1] *The Fifth Rubric is an international covenant allowing specified personnel covert operational ability with unrestricted use of firearms at home and in signatory countries abroad, providing maximum security clearance, full co-operation of all internal policing and military forces and immunity from any prosecution for the bearer of the Rubric. It is rarely invoked outside a state of war or extreme national tension. The archaic meaning of rubric is 'red ochre', or 'written in red'. The colour of blood.*

"Just five minutes alone," said Kuhle as he parked up in a side street abutting the hotel, "then follow me in." He took out the keys from the ignition and chucked them over to JP.

Kuhle disappeared for a while and a few minutes later JP duly entered the hotel. He was introduced to the manager, and they spoke discreetly in a side office. "It looks as though you're right, JP," said Kuhle. "Two men checked in yesterday afternoon and asked to be on the top floor with a view overlooking that part of the beach which means overlooking that exact stretch of road. They have a twin-roomed suite. With a nice balcony. And, they're still here."

"Ok, good," said JP. "Let's go."

JP led the way across the foyer to the elevator and as the door closed Kuhle tapped the button for the seventh floor. The two men rode silently for the first couple of seconds, thinking on what they were about to do. Then JP spoke.

"Let's use 'housekeeping'," said JP.

"'Housekeeping'?" Kuhle looked over at him. "You have to be kidding. Nobody's going to answer to 'housekeeping'."

"Why not?" asked JP, indignantly. "I always open the door for housekeeping whenever I'm at a hotel."

"Well I wouldn't," said Kuhle, taking a quick glance at himself in one of the three mirrors that formed the upper halves of the elevator walls.

JP stared at the doors straight ahead, and then turned to his companion.

"Ok then, so what do you want to use?"

"Let's try 'room service'," replied Kuhle.

They stepped out of the elevator and turned left towards 716. The light grey carpet stretched down the corridor with magnolia walls and apartment doors on the right. The windows opposite opened onto the rear car park and brown hills beyond.

"But they won't have ordered any food," said JP.

"Yes, but at least they'd be interested in food, more than housekeeping."

"That's ridiculous," said JP with a laugh. They walked a few more paces in silence. "So, you really want to try 'room service'?"

"Hmm I'm not so sure now," said Kuhle. "Maybe I should get some backup..."

"No, we're here now, we've got to knock on the door."

"So, 'housekeeping'?"

"Yes," said JP. "It's better. 'Housekeeping'. But you do it. You sound South African."

"Yeah, well - that's because I *am* South African."

"Do you always like to get the last word?" quipped JP.

"You're damned right I do. Especially when I'm on my turf."

JP rather liked this man, and smiled dryly as they approached the room with 716 on the door.

JP stood to the side with his back against the wall and his hand inside his jacket under his armpit on the handgun. Kuhle knocked on the door, and called out, "Housekeeping."

"Go away," came a reply. "We're busy."

Kuhle glanced at JP and shrugged his shoulders. He turned and started to walk back along the corridor and raised his hand above his head, beckoning to JP. "Backup," he said.

A startled Kuhle swung round at the sound of a pulverising crash followed by splintering wood and a breaking metal chain as JP's foot kicked the door to the room wide open. Kuhle was already running back as he saw JP with his gun and attached silencer raised at forty-five degrees moving fast into the room. In half a second JP was at the end of the entrance corridor and Mateen almost had reached the gun on the table before JP's Sauer spat out a 'phut'. The round hit Mateen in the leg wringing a scream of agony from the man, reaching Kuhle's ears simultaneously just as he entered. Walif had a fraction of a second more to pick up a machine gun and almost got some rounds off when JP shot him dead between the eyes, bypassing his bullet-proof vest. The man crashed spread-eagled up against the opposite wall and slumped to the ground.

"What the *fuck* are you doing?" screamed Kuhle, now in the room with his own weapon drawn. "For *fuck's* sake, man, what are you *doing*?"

"I'm making the next chess move," said JP.

"*What*?" shouted Kuhle.

JP hit the man on the ground with the butt of his gun to knock him unconscious and stop the screaming. He quickly walked past an astonished Kuhle and closed the door to the room, which still shut to the frame even though one of the hinges was now hanging off loose.

"Look," said JP, standing straight opposite Kuhle and facing him square in the eyes. He spoke calmly, and quietly. "You know what's at stake here, and what's involved. These people put me in hospital and killed a woman this morning, and they have some information that I need. I just don't have time for any niceties, and neither do you."

The two men stared at each other. Kuhle was shocked at the speed and severity of JP's actions; but he knew he was right. He calmed, and very slowly nodded his head. He drew a deep breath, and gave a smile.

"*Shit*. Ok. Ok, JP. But this is still *my* town. You have to tell me what you're going to do. *Before* you do it."

JP smiled back. "Sure, your town. I'm just passing through, bro."

Yeah, and the sooner the better, thought Kuhle. *Fuck.*

JP holstered his gun, went into the bathroom and came out with a large towel. He ripped it lengthways into two pieces, and then got down onto his knees in front of Mateen, binding his leg to stop the bleeding. He looked up at Kuhle.

"I'm going to bring him round, and then I'm going to ask him some questions. It might be better if you go outside and make sure everything is ok there and - just a suggestion - but we maybe could do with a couple more of your guys here. And bring a doctor."

Kuhle could guess exactly what JP meant by 'ask him some questions'. And it was certainly better all round if he wasn't there for it. He stared at JP and said, "Good idea." With that he turned and exited the room.

JP made sure the door was as closed as it could be. He went back into the bathroom and filled the sink with cold water. He picked up the man and tied his hands behind his back with the trouser belt from the dead man, then hauled Mateen into the bathroom and stuck his head into the water. The man spluttered and choked, and then suddenly was fully awake, standing upright on his one good leg, helped by JP. He dragged the man back into the living area of the small suite and threw him onto the couch.

It didn't take JP very long to get the full co-operation of Mateen, who was horrified to find that the person who had burst into their room and shot them both was the man they had been following and filmed that very morning. JP only had to fire two more shots, one into the man's other leg and one into an arm. At the end of ten minutes, JP had everything he needed to know.

Kuhle returned half an hour later with two tough-looking Scorpions and a doctor. They found the wounded man bound hand and foot, gagged to muffle the almost delirious sounds now coming from him and bandages wrapped efficiently round wounds to his legs and arm.

"Gave you some trouble did he?" said Kuhle. He wasn't sarcastic; more, he wanted to cover for JP a little in front of the other men. Though it was pretty clear to everyone what had happened.

"A little," said JP. But I got him under control."

The doctor sat down beside Mateen on the edge of the couch to tend the man's wounds. He was not going to be moved yet, and so the two bullets still in him - the third had passed straight through into the couch - were going to have to be removed there and then. One Scorpion assisted; the other dealt with the body of the dead Walif, zipping it into a plastic body bag.

JP and Kuhle walked over to the balcony. Dusk was approaching, and they pulled the curtains across the closed glass doors to ensure that no-one from outside would be able to see into the room. Kuhle looked at JP and raised his eyebrows enquiringly.

"His name's Mateen. Their instructions are to lie low for today and tomorrow and wait it out," said JP. "Make out they're merely tourists, here for a few days. They're departing tomorrow evening - the rendezvous with the other two, who are doing the same thing and keeping a low profile, is set for 11pm down at the Waterfront. Their plan is to meet up there and drive out together; south down the coast road then east to Somerset West and the N2. They make their way to East London and Durban and fly out, or, if they can't for some reason, they'll drive across the border, he thinks to

Zimbabwe. He doesn't know where to. The head of the squad is a man called Khatib; explosives expert, and the one who actually lobbed the bomb at me. If any of them has any links back up the chain, he's the one. We must get him if we can. And there's a fourth guy, Samir, who did the driving. The car was stolen yesterday and has been dumped. They were at the Cape Grace but checked out yesterday and went to another hotel after stealing and hiding the car close by. Mateen doesn't know where they are, and after the attack there was to be no contact until the rendezvous meet and departure tomorrow evening."

"Ok well I'll send some people over to the Cape Grace anyway; not that it will do any good, but it's possible they could lift a fingerprint or two."

"I doubt it. These people are very thorough; they will have removed all fingerprints and any DNA; and the room has probably been re-occupied anyway. But I agree, it should be checked."

"So what else do you have?"

"I've got a general description of the two from our friend there," JP nodded at the man on the couch, "but it's pretty meaningless and he's not really in any state to co-operate with an artist to get drawings done, so that's out."

"Yes. Perhaps if you'd only shot him twice, he'd be able to help more," quipped Kuhle.

JP smiled, and continued. "But, I have their cell numbers, so you guys can at least try to get a fix on them with that." JP handed over a piece of paper. "If they have them switched on, that is, which I also doubt. Of course there are the cell phones that these two have that you can rip to pieces, and the laptop. But my betting is that you won't find anything of use on them. Like I said the one who has the outside contact if there is any is

Khatib. It seems the other three merely have instructions about me and the bombing, and know nothing else. They are all Arabic and came in from Angola."

Kuhle walked away and spoke to one of his other men, who then left the room to carry out his instructions.

"My guys will visit the Cape Grace," said Kuhle. "And I'm bringing someone over to see what's on the phones, and the laptop."

"Good," said JP. "Can you also get them to check the web address where they uploaded the movie file? It's probably closed down, but it might produce something for us."

"Ok," said Kuhle, "will do. So, our best bet is tomorrow evening."

"Yes, I think so, we should concentrate on getting them then, at the rendezvous."

"It'll be very busy at the Waterfront at that time; it's a smart place to choose to meet up."

"Yes, I know. But, we've a little time to get ready."

"One thing though, JP. What about contact between the two teams, is there a pre-arranged code word or what if Khatib just calls to talk to the others on the phone?"

"No," said JP. "I've checked that. There's to be absolutely no contact at all until the rendezvous. They know phones and a call can be traced or listened in on really easily and so they are not taking any chances. Only after 11pm, if one party doesn't show up. Otherwise, nothing."

"It would be really easy to trick us on that," said Kuhle. "One simple code word that gets the right, or wrong, answer if they call in, and it could tip them off. How do you know he's not lying to you?"

"I don't," said JP. "But, he knows I'm not lying to him."

"Not lying to him?" repeated Kuhle. "What do you

mean? About what?"

"I told him that if the room phone or his or the dead man's cell phone goes off, I'll shoot him dead."

Kuhle looked at JP, and nodded slowly. "Yeah, that would do it, get his honest reply. Sure, that'd work."

JP's eyes were cold and heartless, and Kuhle knew he meant what he said. If it came to that, he would have to stop him. Kuhle just wasn't sure how.

By 10pm the doctor had removed the bullets, and Mateen was sleeping comfortably and out until mid-morning. As the doctor's work was done Kuhle said for him to leave. During the course of the evening, another man arrived with some special electronic equipment and, without turning the phones off, the sims and the phones themselves were dissected. There was nothing of use on them, and the phone company search on the numbers provided nothing. Similarly the laptop, which had been purchased in the centre of Cape Town just five days ago, apparently when they first arrived in South Africa, yielded nothing. The exploration at the Cape Grace Hotel was fruitless, the Scorpions could not get any location signals from the other two phones since they were obviously switched off, and the web address that Mateen had provided had already been closed down. The only avenue left to JP and Kuhle was the rendezvous tomorrow.

One of the other men went out later to get dinner for them all, and the four ate with quiet conversation. Afterwards JP commandeered one of the two bedrooms of the suite. His head had been hurting badly for some time. He had ignored the pain, but now felt he could take a little rest and hand over control to Kuhle for a while. Almost as soon as his head touched the pillow JP drifted off into a deep sleep. His body made good use of the respite and at once began its repair and healing process.

At 2am Kuhle's men discreetly placed Walif's body bag into a laundry basket, took it downstairs via the service elevator and removed it from the hotel. Khule later used the other bedroom and rested, and his two colleagues watched over the room through the night.

Their third man, downstairs at reception in the back office, was also watching.

Just in case.

10
THE PLAN

STELLA WAS WOKEN by one of the burka girls. She saw Aisha at the foot of the bed. "Good morning, Stella," said Aisha with a confident and happy voice. "You have been asleep for eight full hours and I hope you are more comfortable and rested now."

"Is it actually morning?" asked Stella, "or is that just to make me feel better?"

Aisha smiled. "No, it really is morning. It's 7am, and you now have to rise as you will shortly be meeting with Mr Malekka."

"And what will happen to me in the interim," said Stella sarcastically, "are you and your two pet apes going to be returning for another session with me?" Bitch, thought Stella, I hate her.

Aisha laughed. "There is no need for sarcasm. Your two attendants tell me you have been co-operative and are adjusting to your circumstances. But of course we still have to see how Mr Malekka feels about you."

"Is he going to torture me too?"

"Mr Malekka will do with you precisely whatever Mr Malekka wishes," said Aisha. Stella rather wished she hadn't asked the question. "But if you have any sense, you will understand what you have to do and how you have to be to ensure your continued survival. And survival in considerable comfort."

Stella let out a deflated sigh. "Yes, I understand," she said, resigned and unaggressive.

"There was no physical harm done to your body yesterday. Save, perhaps, for some little bruises where you were held or restrained, but those will go quickly. We could have inflicted some, of course, and were close, but it was not necessary. We can move on."

She turned and walked to the door. Just then it opened and Shurafa came in with the breakfast trolley, although it was difficult for Stella to know how long ago she last ate.

"Come, let us talk of other things. The breakfast is here, and I will take coffee with you."

Stella put on her dressing gown. She started to walk over barefooted to the table in the corner, but Nasrin stopped her and indicated that she must put on some shoes. She was given slightly heeled but comfortable slippers.

Shurafa poured the coffee for the two women, and while Stella ate a small amount of food Aisha spoke of the forthcoming meeting.

"Stella, when Mr Malekka arrives, you should address him as 'sir', and always be respectful and courteous. I urge you again, do not be stubborn or disobedient, and when he asks you questions give him direct answers without hesitation. He is not a man to be treated badly, and you would be a fool if you did not take what I am saying to you now very seriously indeed."

She paused as she sipped her coffee.

"So is he Royalty - a prince or something... oil... what?" Stella asked, actually with some interest for the first time.

"I think what you need to know is that he is one of the most wealthy people in the world, is very closely connected with all of the Royal Families in the Middle-east and has particular ties with certain countries, one of which is Iran. He will not hesitate to have you hurt again, or to harm your family or those close to you. On the other hand if you co-operate fully then you won't have to worry about any of that."

"I understand," said Stella again. There didn't seem much point in saying anything else.

"Now, I am going to leave you. You have two hours to prepare for him; he will be with you at 10am. I would add, you would be wise to look as appealing and, er...," she smiled slightly and gazed down at Stella's breasts, "shall we say, as *interesting*, for him as a woman as you can."

"Very well, thank you," said Stella, with resignation. "I'll be ready."

Aisha left, and Stella finished her breakfast. The burka girls busied themselves changing the bed sheets and washing the bathroom, and then even vacuumed the carpet in the room, making it fresh and clean.

So this was going to be the important meeting, was it? Ok. Then she must turn it into a negotiation rather than a one-sided speech. He liked pretty women, like any man; well I'll give him something to look at. And use it to my advantage.

Stella knew she had been gifted with great beauty. She knew what men liked and what they wanted.

It could be a dangerous game. However, she had no other weapon.

Stella went into the bathroom and quickly showered, dismissing the burka girls, although they remained and looked on as was their duty. She had become used to them and her shyness had all but vanished. She had them dry her, and then they went together to the dressing room. She found a deodorant she knew; she chose a beautiful pink chiffon A-line dress, that flowed in slant layers to knee length with enticing décolletage, short sleeves and a bodice that held her slim waist closely; and some dark-pink ankle-strap heels. She put on her makeup and had the girls place her blonde hair in a side-swept updo to expose her neck. She found a simple pearl choker, and with some vengeful delight selected Clive Christian No. 1 Imperial Majesty, the world's most expensive perfume, enjoying the moment of sophisticated fragrance as she stroked her neck, wrists and a slight amount between her breasts. She had the girls carefully paint her nails.

She was ready. She went to sit on the sofa, and waited.

≈

Malekka finished his breakfast. He had been pleased with Aisha's report yesterday and the inevitable result that the girl was broken.

He thought about his enterprise. The boldness of its conception; the use of his spider's web of influence across the globe; the shattering outcome the conclusion would bring. He sipped his coffee, and smiled on what his parents would have thought. They would be proud. Especially his father. Malekka had been born in Iran before the 1979 fall of the last Shah, Mohammad Reza Pahlavi. Malekka's father, Sheikh Khalifa bin Ali Abdin Al-Nahyan, was a close friend of the Shah and enjoyed fabulous oil rich revenues from the country second in size only to Pahlavi himself. However, over the years Sheikh Khalifa found himself increasingly disapproving of much of the westernisation policies of the Shah which were causing internal strife. Though he was smart enough to say nothing.

The Shah began to realise that he might need a quick exit to a new country should the domestic unrest not be stemmed. He thought it prudent to enhance closer ties with his neighbours, the Royal Family of Saudi Arabia, and sent his friend Sheikh Khalifa to do so.

The move proved disastrous for the Shah. Sheikh Khalifa although loyal to his Shah was much more loyal to himself. He quickly became a trusted confidante of the Saudi Royal Family, a decisive factor in their declining the asylum request from the Shah in the 1979 Revolution. The ousted Shah finally ended up in Egypt, where he died in 1980.

For his service to Islam and country, the new regime led by the Ayatollah Khomeini welcomed Sheikh Khalifa bin Ali Abdin Al-Nahyan back with open arms and considerably increased his personal wealth. A grateful Saudi Royal Family also plied the Sheikh with enormous financial and material rewards, including citizenship for him and his family, for having so wisely counselled them away from an uncomfortable alliance with an over-westernised ruler, now deposed.

The Revolution benefitted the Sheikh in other ways, allowing him to ensure his family's profile was first largely lost amidst the upheaval of the Revolution and its years of turmoil, and thereafter remained invisible. The family became almost mystical in the security of its anonymity.

The young Sheikh Barakah Malekka bin Khalifa bin Ali Abdin Al-Nahyan, or more simply Mr Barakah Malekka, therefore enjoyed the most privileged of upbringings amidst fabulous wealth all of which he inherited as the first-born son, together with his father's wisdom over anonymity, upon the untimely death of his beloved parents in a senseless untargeted reprisal bombing in Lebanon where the Sheikh was visiting on official business in 1997.

Malekka, now forty-two, placed the death of his parents firmly at the door of the great Satan America, her infidel ally Great Britain and, most of all, the despised Israel. He swore they would pay for it, again and again. And from their ashes his new order would arise, to bring peace and justice to the world, as though he were the Mahdi. The establishing of the Caliphate and global actions of ISIS were the beginning. The main show was now under way.

The part he had played for Iran in the planning and resource provision of the New York 9/11 attack was unknown except to an elite three individuals. By 2nd May 2011 the last of those, Osama bin Laden, was dead.

Malekka knew his present enterprise would by comparison make 9/11 merely a footnote in the annals of the great Jihad.

At five minutes to ten, Malekka left his suite of rooms and walked down into the depths of his ship to the room that was Stella's prison.

≈

The door opened and Barakah Malekka walked in. Stella liked the jet black hair and his height, not so much the coldness of his dark eyes. She was not sure if she should rise, but decided to follow her instincts and let him have a good look at her. He smiled, and held out his hand.

"Good morning, Miss Stella," he said as she took it. "Do please sit down again and be comfortable."

"Thank you," she replied politely. Yes, I'll shake your hand for now, you bastard; all these pleasantries, yet you had me kidnapped and tortured. She forced herself to put the thoughts out of her mind.

Malekka dismissed the two burka girls, who with lowered eyes scurried away, closing the door carefully behind them. Stella waited.

He pulled one of the chairs over from the table to be directly opposite her. She crossed her legs, knowing he would be able to see higher up her dress that side. He instinctively glanced down. Score one point to me, she thought.

"Stella, I will come right to the point. My business requirements are such that I want some information from you. My colleagues and I considered various options by which we could obtain that information. The result was that you should be brought here."

He paused for a few seconds. His English was perfect; but then so were his other six languages. However, that was merely the result of good schooling and a university education at Oxford. She said nothing, but held his gaze steadily.

"We are not the type of people or organisation who kidnaps and asks for ransom. We will not hide our faces. After we have the information, you will remain within my organisation and be of service to me and to others as I may wish. I believe the various options have been fully explained to you?"

"Yes, sir," she said, remembering how she was to address him. She could see that he liked her response, as he smiled very slightly.

"And I am told by Aisha that you have seen reason and will co-operate. Am I correct?"

"Yes, sir."

He was pleased that this was going well. He wanted this information fast, and could see the girl had been completely broken, exactly as he had planned. She wasn't damaged physically, nor turned into a dithering vegetable either that could only mutter answers to his questions. He would get what he needed without delay, and could move on. It was a shame to have to take her from her family and life; but then, he would give her a good life too. For a while. Not as long as she had been told; but that didn't matter. And, looking at her, he knew he would enjoy the process.

He was about to continue, when she spoke.

"However, sir, there are some things that I do not understand, and, with your permission, I wonder if I may ask you about them, well two things only actually?"

He waited for a moment, surprised, then said, "Yes of course. You may do so."

"Thank you very much. Well, you must know that Aisha and your two men, I believe they are called Haddad and Raboud, were here some hours ago and, well, they 'persuaded' me."

She was sitting back deep in the sofa with her hands down at her sides slightly away from her hips, her spread fingernails a patterned pink distraction. Who wouldn't want to play with her? And this woman has some guts, Malekka thought to himself. She is really quite interesting.

"I am fully aware of what you require of me, although I do not know the specifics of the information you want yet of course. But, my request of you, if I may, is for two small things."

"And what would they be, Miss Stella?"

Stella looked straight at Malekka, and smiled slightly.

"Well, sir, my first request, as I am to be in your service, is this. The only personal mementos and possessions I now have are a few clothes and my jewellery." Stella raised her arms slightly with fingers spread. "Three bracelets, two rings, a watch and the clothes I had on when I arrived here. I feel it will be easier for me to adjust to my new life if I am reminded of my loved ones often, and of what may happen to them if I fail you in any way. These things remind me of my family and boyfriend and so are special. But my clothes have disappeared, and yesterday my jewellery was forcefully taken off me and thrown on the ground, and then tossed back at me later. So, my first and very simple request is, may I have my clothes returned and my few simple possessions treated with respect by people?"

That is a well thought out and logical argument, Malekka said to himself, and so simple and harmless. If the creature wants her things then let her have them, and let's move on.

"That is not unreasonable at all," said Malekka, "and I can understand what you mean and your reasons for asking. I will have it known among all of my people that your possessions must not be disrespected. And the clothes will be returned."

"Thank you, sir." She smiled again.

"You said there were two things?" he replied, smiling back.

"Yes, sir. The other is this. May I speak frankly?"

"You may."

"As I said, I am ready to serve you, for all of the reasons that have been given me, persuasion and the threats over others. I have no other choice, and I can see that it is the only way forwards for me."

"I am glad."

"Yes, sir. But, I would prefer to be of service to the senior male, and that, I understand, is you. My other request, therefore, is that I may be at your disposal only. And, I shall pledge to serve only you without question, without hesitation or resistance, and in any way you choose."

He looked at her as she was speaking. He was very attracted to her. His senses were being flayed by her words. She was a very beautiful, exceptional woman, and although he could have her anyway he knew he would obtain far more pleasure from this female if she was trying to please than if she were forced each time. While this current business is going on, why not?

"Very well. I agree."

She smiled at him, and said, "Thank you, Mr Malekka. You won't regret it."

"I am sure I will not," said Malekka. "But that is for later. Now, I wish to discuss the information I require of you."

"Yes, sir."

He paused for a moment, and then spoke.

"You work at the Fincrest Centre at Musina, South Africa. This is an industrial research and development centre contracted to the South African government. It undertakes a great deal of experimental work in a wide range of areas for your country, including micro technological, computer and automatic systems studies, and it is also a substantial munitions factory providing eighty per cent of large and small bore arms for South Africa's armed police force, the army, navy and air force. Your father owns this company, and you have been playing an increasing rôle in it over the last two years. Your international business studies and business management qualifications from the University of Cape Town and then from Harvard allow you to do this and you have been groomed to take over the business from your father when he retires sometime in the next five years. You presently hold the title of Deputy Director within Fincrest and it is actually you who runs the company on a day to day basis."

Well they have certainly done their research, thought Stella. She said nothing while Malekka was speaking, and waited for him to continue.

"As such you have complete access to all areas of the

complex, and are able to enter any room or safe using the codes with which you have been entrusted. Is this correct?"

Stella took a deep breath. She had lowered her gaze away from him down to her legs once he had started to talk in detail about Fincrest. Now she raised her eyes up again, and looked directly at him.

"Yes, sir, that is quite correct," she replied.

"Good. Fincrest also acts as a storage centre for certain items which are of military importance to South Africa, and they are stored in a room which is essentially a very large safe, in Block B1, Room 151. You know of this room of course?"

"Yes, sir, I do."

"How does one access the room?"

"I have a feeling, sir, that you already know, but the answer to your question is that it has a seven digit security code keypad system and linked fingerprint recognition and retina scanning security system."

"Yes. Within this room, there is an item which I require. It is called a 9M714K-Alpha. Are you aware of this piece of equipment?"

"Yes, sir, I am."

"And, Miss Stella Fincrest, do you know what this item is and what it is for?"

"Yes, sir, I do. It is the launch and control system for a Russian Spider SS-23 five hundred kiloton nuclear ballistic missile. Otherwise known as a Spider Two Three."

11
PREPARING

SO THAT IS what he's after. Stella had suspected as much and was shocked at the lengths to which Malekka was prepared to go to get it. She understood now why she had been kidnapped and brought to this ghastly place. He must be completely mad, or extremely brilliant; she wasn't sure which. How was he planning to get hold of the Alpha, and what was he going to do with it afterwards?

Malekka could see this in her face.

"This is all a little bit of a shock to you, I am sure."

"Well yes, sir, of course. I have many questions racing around in my mind. I'm obviously extremely curious," she said adding the hint of a smile.

Malekka gave a slight smile back. "I will be happy to answer your questions in due course. But first I will continue and tell you what I want of you."

"Very well."

"We are presently anchored some sixty kilometres off Mozambique."

Close to South Africa, close to JP flashed through her mind.

"We arrived here in the middle of the night and at 9pm this evening, the helicopter which is parked on the helipad here on the ship, and incidentally in which you were brought here, will take off and overfly Mozambique at low height. It will have on board something from me that you are going to provide. It will then land in my good friend Robert Mugabe's little country of Zimbabwe just south of Beitbridge and before the New Limpopo Bridge crossing on the border with South Africa.

"There, it will meet up with two more of my men, who entered Zimbabwe over a week ago by land from Zambia in the north. The helicopter will be refuelled, which has been pre-arranged. They will then leave Zimbabwe flying low to the south, cross the border with South Africa and land at the Musina strip which is, as you know very well, about twelve kilometres inside the border."

Stella looked stunned. Her mouth had opened a little. She said nothing, and just let Malekka continue to speak of his plans.

"There will be a Range Rover waiting for them at Musina. They will then drive south-west along the little road to reach the Fincrest complex and the main entrance to the administration block building. They should be there at around midnight. My sources tell me that at night the administration block part of the complex is closed with no security guard at the entrance or within the building and that the munitions factory behind the administration block is the only area where there are guards, both outside and inside. Is that correct?"

"Er, well more or less, sir, there may be some cleaners but, well no not at that time. Could you tell me what day it is please? I have lost track of where we are in the week."

"Ah yes of course," replied Malekka, realising that Stella did not know the day and that the routine probably varied through the week. "Today is Wednesday 15th April."

"Then that is correct, at midnight, in fact overnight, there will be no personnel at the administration block at all."

"Very good. I also understand that the main entrance door is controlled by a security code entry system. Is that correct?" he asked again.

"Yes, sir."

"When they get inside the administration block, my men will proceed along the two corridors and up to the sealed safe room, Room 151. They will open it, and open the casing that surrounds the item that I want. And then, they are going to steal it."

Stella gulped a little at the sheer boldness of Malekka's last sentence. She said simply, "Ok," and then quickly added, "But, even though I give you the codes and the numbers, there is still the issue of the finger prints and the retina scan. Without those you will not be able to access the safe room."

"Precisely," said Malekka.

Stella's heart skipped a beat. Oh my God, she thought, they aren't going to cut my hand off and pull my eye out are they, to use to open the safe room?

"And that is what I want from you. I want all of the entrance codes; and I want your co-operation in getting through those additional security systems.

"You see," he continued, "at first I thought we would take you with us to get us through the security. But you might try to escape, which although extremely foolish for you even to think about could, if you were to attempt it, inconvenience me. So I discarded the idea. And..."

Here it comes, she thought. Her heart was racing now... oh my God.

"...rather than risk that kind of inconvenience, the item could be acquired in a different way."

"Ok, sir," she said, trying to sound a lot braver than she felt.

Realising how her mind was working, Malekka

decided to put her at ease.

"Don't be concerned, Miss Fincrest," he said calmly. "We are not going to deform you and that beautiful body of yours, of which I am expecting so much pleasure later."

Stella heaved a sigh of relief, and then felt sick as his last words hit home.

"I mentioned that the helicopter will carry something from me. That will be the full details of all the entry codes for the Fincrest Centre, which you are going to write down for me later today. And my men will also have an exact replica of your hands, providing the fingerprints for the security system, and a synthetic and very much life-like replica of your eyes, or should I say eyeballs, with which to clear the retina scan system."

"Can you do that?" asked an amazed Stella, "Surely that's impossible? Well, the retina scan anyway, I thought that was unbreakable."

Malekka smiled. He rather liked that she was impressed with his plan and abilities.

"You know, security measures are only good for a limited period of time. However sophisticated they may be, no matter how clever they are, it is only a matter of time before somebody finds a way around them." He laughed and added, "Very often, it's the inventors of the system that make available the method to break it, so that a new security system is needed, and their business continues. Rather like what they say about computer viruses; it's the makers of the anti-virus programmes that introduce the harmful viruses in the first place, so that millions around the world have to buy their anti-virus product to gain protection from that very same new virus." Capitalists, he said to himself. What a bunch of thieving hypocrites.

"Yes, sir, I see," said Stella, relieved that at least they

weren't going to harm her more, thank God.

Malekka continued. "Where is the central storage for the CCTV that operates in the complex?"

"It's just off the entrance hallway to the right as you walk in."

"Obviously I do not want our visit recorded so that it can be played back by anyone. So they will deal with it." He paused, and then asked, "Is that the only recording centre?"

"Yes. Frankly we do not expect this kind of attack. The safe room is impregnable, it would be difficult to breach it even with explosives, which would then bring in the guards from the munitions factory behind and set off the internal alarm, which goes straight to Johannesburg. That would rapidly bring in the army and air force. Twenty or twenty-five years ago I gather the situation was very different. The administration block was very heavily guarded, and the safe room hadn't even been built. Now we are a united country, internal terrorism has ceased and technology has moved on. The room is meant to be impregnable."

He smiled. "Unless, of course, one has all of the access codes, fingerprints and retina with which to move through the system."

"Well, yes, I see what you mean."

"Tell me. What are the opening times of the administration block and factory?" asked Malekka.

She was sure he knew, but she answered anyway. "The arms factory behind the administration block is operational 24 hours a day on two twelve hour shifts 6am-6pm and then 6pm-6am, seven days a week. The factory has security personnel; the administration block has none. There are no chemical or biological weapons stored or in development at the complex, only traditional firearms. The research centre there is open a more normal 9am to 5pm, and those are the standard office hours for staff at the administration block too, all Monday to Friday. "

"Very well, good," said Malekka. "Now, for the fingerprints - do they need your right hand or left, or both?"

"My right hand. The system asks for a different finger, at random, and sometimes for a full palm print."

"Ok, but only of one hand, the right hand?"

"Yes, sir."

"Good. And what about the retina scan. Does the system require your right or left eye or both?"

"Only the right eye. The system is considered to be so strong and unbreakable that only one eye is required."

"Very good. Thank you, Miss Stella. I believe I have all the information I need for now, but I will return again later in the afternoon. In the meantime, you will accompany Aisha and co-operate with her." He paused, and then added, "Your workers at Fincrest are privileged to have such a beautiful and stylish boss." He said the words as a true compliment, with no undertones.

Stella looked at him, surprised at the sudden kindness, and said, "Thank you, Mr Malekka."

Malekka looked up towards the wall opposite the bed, where he knew the cameras and sound surveillance equipment were located, and said, "Aisha, please come in now." He turned to face Stella again, who was already feeling sick at the mention of Aisha's name, but tried to ignore it.

"Actually, sir, may I ask you one thing," she said it as though she had just thought of it, which actually wasn't the case.

"You may." I do like this female, he thought.

"Mr Malekka, this entire thing, my kidnapping, the way I was treated, your questions, where you are sending people tonight... I am frankly scared, but also, I have to admit, I am absolutely fascinated."

That part was true, anyway.

"I have to know, or rather, excuse me, I would really like to know what is actually going on, I mean, what is all of this about? Will you tell me? Or at least, if not now, will you keep me close to you so that eventually I will know why I have been forced into all of this and made to do what you want today and later?" She added, almost as an afterthought, "It will at least make me understand and help with my, er, adjustment."

Malekka thought for a while. He then said, "I can understand what you are asking, and why. And, it is also somewhat pleasing to me that you would like me to share with you what this enterprise is about."

"Yes."

"I cannot tell you now, or over the next three or four days. But what I will promise you, is that I will tell you upon the arrival at our final destination. And so, yes, your curiosity will be satisfied."

"Thank you," said Stella, genuinely pleased that she is going to know the full details. Or, those further details such as Malekka is prepared to let her know. "That makes things easier for me, I think."

Just then the door opened, and Aisha walked in accompanied by the two burka girls. Stella looked at her with immediate fear and a growing sick feeling in her stomach as the suppressed memories of her ordeal came flooding back, and for a moment she thought that the horrors of the previous day were for some reason going to be repeated. But, Aisha merely said, "Good morning, Stella," as though nothing untoward had ever occurred and they were all going on a family outing. Stella didn't quite know what to make of this; whether she should hate her more, if that were possible, or ignore her entirely.

"Yes, sir?" Aisha said expectantly to Malekka, awaiting instructions.

"I have explained my requirements to Miss Stella," said Malekka, "and you are now to take her up to the lab and prepare the items that are needed for this evening."

"Yes, sir."

"Inform me once the preparations have been completed and the items are ready."

"Yes, sir."

"Good." He turned back to Stella. "Now I will take my leave of you. Spend the afternoon assisting and co-operating with Aisha, and later I and Haddad and Raboud will go through the plans of the administration block with you and ask you to write out all of the necessary security codes."

His tone became a little menacing as he said, "Make sure, Miss Stella, that you do not leave out any codes, or locks, or get your directions or any numbers wrong. Life will swiftly become extremely uncomfortable for you if you do."

"No, sir," she said quickly, "I am willing and prepared to co-operate, I promise you."

He nodded. "I will see you again this afternoon for the other information, and then again just before 9pm this evening."

"Yes, ok sir," she said, and stood up as he rose from his chair. He stepped towards her slightly and extended his hand, and she took it. She was expecting a handshake, but instead he gently raised her hand to his lips. She was rather taken aback at such gentlemanly chivalry. He looked deeply into her eyes as he lowered her hand, and said with sincerity, "Thank you, Stella." She was most annoyed with herself to find that she was blushing slightly.

And without waiting for a reply, he turned and left the room.

Aisha, who had noticed Stella's slight reddening of the cheeks, watched Malekka leave the room and then said to her, "He can be very charming when he wants to be, can't he?"

Stella wanted to say that he was a raving lunatic and nothing more than a rich thug, but merely responded with, "Yes."

The door opened again and Stella's two other torturers Haddad and Raboud walked in with a polite "Good Morning." Amazing, thought Stella, we could be colleagues arriving in the morning at the office.

Aisha said, "Right, follow me, please."

She led them out and along the corridor. Stella shuddered as they passed the entrance of the adjoining room. At the end they turned right into an ornate Victorian-esque hallway and right once more up a wide blue-carpeted staircase with golden bannisters, to another corridor at the top. After twenty feet they stopped at some double doors, each with a square glass panel at about head height. Aisha pushed one open.

The room was perhaps forty feet by thirty. Tables lined the walls, and in the centre were two ten-foot benches with a small sink at one end and what looked very much like a Bunsen burner at the other. It reminded Stella of her chemistry lessons at school, but this laboratory wasn't used to demonstrate acid plus base equals salt and water, or how the dividing layer of two liquid monomers can be hooked out in a never-ending nylon polymer strand. The technician running this lab had advanced in skills way beyond simple chemistry, physics and electronics. This was Aisha's world. Her main rôle, in Malekka's empire. Here she prepared the various explosives and detonators that Malekka required from time to time, the odd poison or deadly gas, and the delightful liquids in the phials used on Stella yesterday.

Aisha put on a white coat, buttoned it up at the front and moved over to one of the computer terminals. She beckoned Stella over.

"First of all, please go over to the sink there and wash your hands, dry them in the blower and come back here." Stella did as she was told.

"Sit down here, please," Aisha said pulling another chair over closer to her, "and put your hand down onto this scanner pad. Make sure that you press your fingertips down firmly onto it."

Aisha placed a large thick cloth over the pad and Stella's hand up to around her wrist, and then said, "Keep your hand very still now."

With a low buzz Stella's hand was scanned. An extremely detailed image appeared on the screen. Aisha repeated the exercise with Stella's right thumb.

Aisha then stood, and moved further up the table to what seemed to be a fridge. She opened the door and removed a large tray containing a thick clear liquid two inches deep, that looked like a silicone or gelatinous fluid.

"Sit down again, here, please," she beckoned Stella to another seat. "Put your hand down onto the surface of this gel and press in gently, and then keep still for about ten seconds. I'll tell you when you can remove it."

The gel acted like plaster of Paris, as though she was having a plaster cast made; as she pushed gently into it, the sticky fluid moved aside and then clung to her skin and hugged its contours.

"Good, thank you," said Aisha afterwards, "you can take your hand out now."

Stella removed her hand, and was given a paper

towel to remove any surplus material.

"Wash your hands thoroughly once more please, and then come back."

Stella was then presented with a smaller narrower dish with the same liquid for her right thumb, and the process was repeated.

"You may wash your hands again now," said Aisha, "and that will be the last time, we are done with the messy part."

Stella did so. From the same fridge, Aisha removed a large glass beaker containing some clear fluid, poured it into the casts of Stella's hand and thumb print, and then placed both dishes into an oven situated adjacent to the fridge. She entered a time period into the little digital display at the top, pressed a button, and then walked away. A gentle low humming started and the heating elements began to warm.

"Right, now over here please."

Aisha walked to the other side of the room. Towards the corner extended a five foot by two table with chairs on either side and equipment that one might find in any optician's. Stella was indicated to one of the chairs. Aisha stood opposite busying herself preparing for what was obviously going to be an examination of Stella's eyes. She talked to Stella just as an optician would to a patient in a high street store.

These people are deranged, thought Stella.

"This is a retina scanner. The retina of the eye is the layer of tissue at the back of the eyeball that acts very much like the film of a camera would and, nowadays, like the CCD or charge coupled device does in a digital camera. The light from the image we look at enters the eye and is focused by the lens onto the retina, where its photoreceptor cells, the rods and cones, basically convert the light into electrical pulses that are then sent to the brain which reinterprets them as images."

She paused, and added, "Most educated people more or less know that much."

Stella nodded in agreement.

"But actually," continued Aisha, as she waited for a particular programme to load up in the adjacent computer, "in more detail, the retina is made up of extremely complex capillaries that provide it with blood and oxygen, and that network of blood vessels is immensely diverse and complicated. In fact everyone's retina is unique; even identical twins don't have the same pattern. That's why the concept of using retinal scanning in security is so attractive to companies and the military; in fact, retinography has an error rate so they say of only one in one million. It's actually quite an old concept, and was first proposed in 1935 by two scientists in New York. It's just taken technology a few decades to catch up.

"So. How do you beat a retina scan then?" she asked out loud, as she came to sit down opposite Stella on the other side of the table. "Well, there have been stories of people killing the person whose eye was needed and holding the head up to the scanner quickly before rigor mortis set in; or plucking the eyeball out for the same purpose."

Stella started to feel a little sick. She sat back in the chair and looked down at her feet.

"Oh but you don't have to worry about that, darling" said Aisha quickly. "No, we don't have to do anything so crude. All we have to do is scan your retina here, and then we can play it back in an eye replica machine where the retina part has been replaced by an extremely clever plasma curvature display. This is a little screen curved and shaped exactly to your eyeball and it just plays about thirty seconds of your retina activity... which I am going to film now. And the little model of your eye will even have a working pupil dilator too, light sensitive and iris colour matching of course."

She paused once more, and then said to Stella, "Ok I'm ready now. Stella, just put your chin on the curved piece there, and bring your head forward to touch the upper bar. Then relax. This isn't going to hurt at all."

Stella did so and settled herself, and Aisha lined the equipment up in front. She peered through what resembled a horizontal microscope at Stella's right eye, and made precise adjustments optically and in distance and height.

"Ok, now when I give a little countdown, please stay completely still and keep your right eye steady, and blink as little as possible. Three... two... one... Go."

The machine hummed. A low-energy beam of invisible infrared light crisscrossed a circular path on Stella's retina at the back of her eye. The tissue surrounding the blood-filled capillaries that Aisha had mentioned were absorbing less light than the capillaries themselves, giving a different variation in intensity of the reflection. The machine was measuring this reflection at five hundred and thirty points along every beam path and at the same time recording and grading the reflection between zero and six thousand and thirty. The thirty seconds passed.

"Ok that's it. That didn't hurt, did it?"

That was all that Aisha wanted from Stella. Haddad and Raboud escorted Stella back to her room. They were polite and courteous, opening doors for her and saying that they hoped the examination and work in the laboratory had not upset her or caused her too much discomfort. Stella responded courteously. However, inwardly she was revolted by them. You can say what you like, you bloody bastards, don't you ever think I am going to forget what you did to me.

Aisha busied herself preparing and then finishing the gelatinous model of Stella's right hand, which would by the end of the day have her fingerprints microscopically trimmed and sharpened on it with a laser accurate to one in ten thousand; and in preparing the model eyeball of Stella's right eye that would have the plasma curvature display at the back replicating Stella's retina even to the extent of emulating the temperature degree variation of the blood in the capillaries. She would set the eyeball in a plastic head for ease of moving.

For every new technology, there is sooner or later always a counter-technology, she said to herself.

≈

Stella lay on the bed, staring at the ceiling. She had become involved with a very dangerous group whose leader clearly had his own big violent agenda, and she wanted to think and rationalise what was happening to her.

They kidnap me, bring me onto a huge ocean-going yacht, torture me, threaten to kill family and those I'm close to, to get information out of me. Then they make a model of my hand for fingerprints and my eye for a retina scan. All so they can steal a piece of equipment from the Centre. That's a pretty impressive international operation, well financed, technologically refined, high powered.

Is this man totally mad?

Well I suppose that's a relative point of view, she said to herself. Maybe he's a hero to others. Who knows. However, from where I'm looking he's a dangerous terrorist. The only reason he could possibly want the Alpha unit is to put it into an SS-23 Spider nuclear weapon, either by selling it on to someone who has one or by acquiring one himself. In either case, God help the world.

She wondered how he knew there was an Alpha located at Fincrest, or even within South Africa at all. That was supposed to be one of the country's best kept secrets, and she had had to sign the Official Secrets Act herself before being told about its existence. Although of course one could pick up bits of information from books and the internet - South Africa's past involvement with nuclear weapons wasn't exactly unknown, she reflected.

Stella hadn't been in the apartheid[2] era of South Africa, which coincided with the time of the Cold War. After all it ended over twenty years ago with the release of Nelson Mandela in 1990 and the first free elections in 1994. But she had learned about it. South Africa had become ostracised from the rest of Africa and the western world because of its racist policies against blacks. International sanctions began to be imposed, and for a long time there was apparently a real fear that the country was going to be overrun by either the blacks, or the communists, or that the West's stance would drive the country to economic collapse and civil war.

Angola was in civil war from 1975 which raged for over twenty-five years. The first fifteen were a hidden battle between the United States and the USSR - freedom and capitalism against oppression and communism. A civil war broke out in neighbouring Mozambique around the same time and lasted into the nineties. South Africa's own efforts in South-West

---

[2] *A system of racial segregation promoting white supremacy, where the majority black inhabitants were ruled, and had their rights curtailed, by the minority white inhabitants.*

Africa, as it was known then, which it was governing incurred hostilities from internal warring factions, especially over the apartheid imposed there. South Africa's only ally had been Rhodesia, but she had had her own similar troubles and eventually underwent great change, becoming Zimbabwe in 1980.

She smiled briefly. All those history classes suddenly had a point.

During the Cold War, South Africa positioned herself as a firm ally of the West and was strongly anti-communist; yet the West largely rejected South Africa because of apartheid. On the other hand the communists, who were trying hard then to infiltrate into the entire African sub-continent, especially South Africa because of both her mineral wealth and strategic importance, offered support and help to South Africa in many varied and sometimes conflicting forms, although South Africa very rarely took any of it.

During that time the whole region was a very dangerous place, with a very uncertain future. And, she reflected, the Fincrest Centre played its part.

South Africa had sought to protect herself.

Uranium was discovered in South Africa at the end of the Second World War. By 1977 South Africa's research and development programme at Pelindaba was ready for the first Peaceful Nuclear Explosions tests, or PNEs, but their first device was detected by the Americans. Both the United States and the Soviet Union put pressure on South Africa to drop its nuclear efforts. However South Africa's security had deteriorated so much, with Cuban forces now in Angola and a new military embargo through the United Nations, that the country felt in great danger of being engulfed by overwhelming conventional forces. South Africa wanted to be able to threaten, and if necessary would definitely use, a nuclear arsenal to defend itself, and development work to get one continued.

The surprising and welcome offer from the USSR to South Africa to enhance friendship by the sale of a tactical nuclear weapon was made in 1980. The South African Government agreed, in extreme secrecy, to accept the SS-23 Spider from the USSR in 1981. The weapon was very quietly smuggled across the Mozambique border. Stella's father had played his own part in that.

By 1989 South Africa had developed six of its own nuclear devices. It took great care in protecting its nuclear arsenal, including separating their various parts and storing them across four vaults around the country. Codes were needed to unlock these, including one for the warheads known only by the president himself. One such vault was located at the Fincrest Centre, which held the 9M714K-Alpha, separated from the SS-23 for the same reasons.

And that was how Stella had got to hear of it. Although she still couldn't figure out how anyone else had.

The collapse of the USSR in 1991 saw in a new era. South Africa's government was seeking to end apartheid and rejoin the international community. As part of that effort President FW de Klerk declared South Africa's possession of five nuclear weapons to the world and invited the International Atomic Energy Commission to oversee their removal, which it did. However, whilst winning the desired considerable global praise for its apparent openness and honesty, South Africa quietly retained the Russian SS-23 and the sixth weapon of its own manufacture, neither of which it had declared. The Spider was buried in a vault deep inside a hill close to Johannesburg, where it was properly maintained and could easily be readied as an active weapon. Its essential and intrinsic launch and control Alpha unit was kept covertly at Fincrest three hundred miles to the north-east.

Obviously, then, thought Stella, Malekka or a client has a Spider 2-3 and can't get hold of the Alpha part from within Russia; but somehow had heard of South Africa's weapon and discovered where its 9M714K-Alpha, universal to all variants of the Spider, is located. And so, he has decided to steal the one at Fincrest.

Brilliant. Quite brilliant.

And there is absolutely nothing I can do to stop it, she thought.

≈

Malekka returned later with his two bodyguards, this time with detailed plans of the Fincrest Centre. They asked Stella for the location of coded access points and what those codes were. Some were related to the particular day, as Stella had said earlier, but once you knew the daily digit variations the codes actually were quite straightforward. They even produced a swipe card from her luggage on St Lucia, needed in two places. Finally, she was asked for and immediately revealed the codes to enter the safe room, Room 151, and the one to open the secured metal casement surrounding the Alpha unit. They left her at around 4pm.

Stella ate the late lunch the burka girls brought in for her, and then indicated to Nasrin that she would rest for a while but wanted to be woken at 8pm, as Mr Malekka had asked that she attend when the helicopter departed. She lay down and tossed and turned for a while, but eventually drifted off into an unsettled slumber. She was duly woken at 8 o'clock. She freshened up, dressed simply and thirty minutes later was ready.

The burka girls led Stella along the same route as earlier that day but this time stopped at the top of the stairs at an elevator, which she hadn't noticed before. It took them slowly up to the top deck. They stepped out into a magnificent hallway, but Stella didn't wait to take in its elegance and lovely décor; to the right were a pair of glass double doors to which she walked, almost ran, and passed through.

And then Stella was standing in the open. For the first time in almost five days she was able to see the sky, and smell and breathe fresh air instead of the neutral atmosphere of efficient air conditioners. Her skin was warmed by heat from a southern sun, now set, she could see stars in the black sky above twinkling happily and offering freedom, romance and limitless possibilities, feel the soft breeze on her face blowing gently through her hair, and smell seawater, and fish, and then food that was cooking somewhere below. She was happy to be alive. She put her hands on the railing and closed her eyes for a few moments just enjoying all of the experiences reaching her senses, of which she had been so deprived. She had had a horrible ordeal and had come through it, and now she would just have to take things one day at a time. Just stay alive, she said yet again to herself; just stay alive.

With a quiet courageous sigh, Stella opened her eyes and turned to the end of the deck. A shiny black helicopter with sleek efficient lines and streamlined nose rested on the helipad precisely in the middle of the white landing circle. The pilot, whose name Stella learned from the burka girls was Anwar, who was dressed in typical camouflage battle fatigues of dark brown, black, mid-green and sand, was inspecting the proud outside of the aircraft. A few minutes later Malekka arrived and spoke to him, presumably giving some instructions, for Anwar was nodding. A second man approached and Malekka turned to say some words, and then handed him an aluminium briefcase. Stella couldn't help notice the gun in the shoulder holster around the man's chest, and there was a large long zipper bag resting by the aircraft which she guessed contained firearms and other equipment for their trip.

The man with the shoulder holster opened the rear door and threw the bag in behind the seating. He placed the aluminium briefcase carefully onto the back seat, securing it safely, closed the door and awaited any last instructions from Malekka. Finally everything was ready. Anwar opened his door to the front of the aircraft on the left and boarded, strapping himself in.

Malekka looked over and saw Stella and the burka girls standing just outside the double glass doors, and beckoned them over.

"Ah good, Miss Stella, I am glad you came to join me here."

"It's the first time I have seen the land and the sea and sky for quite a while, Mr Malekka," said Stella back to him, smiling. She was so very pleased to be out in the open world again.

"Yes, of course," said Malekka, in an understanding tone which she thought was genuine. "Do you like my little toy?" he said gesticulating at the ship with his arm.

"Well it's beautiful, of course," said Stella, "and very big." The ship was well lit and had a predominantly light blue colour on board the decks, matching the large swimming pool below.

"It serves its purpose. As do all of my toys," he said. She wondered if he was now referring to her.

"This is Yameen, another of my trusted colleagues. Yameen, meet Miss Stella Fincrest." Yameen extended his hand, and shook Stella's gently. He wore black fatigues, with pockets everywhere. Six foot and about thirty, his eyes were alert and full of authority and pace. He was clearly the leader of the flight team.

"Hello, madam," he said to her in English that had a heavy Arabic accent. She nodded in reply with a smile.

"It is her hand and eye replicas that you are carrying in the case," said Malekka.

"Ah, yes sir, I understand. Thank you, madam," he said to Stella, who just smiled once more.

"Very well, Yameen, it is time."

"Yes, sir."

"You have the other package safely on board?"

"Yes sir. I have checked that too, and it is all exactly as it should be."

"Very well, my friend," said Malekka. "Fi amaan Allah[3]."

"Thank you, sir. Fi amaan Allah."

Yameen walked round to the other side of the helicopter and strapped himself into the seat next to Anwar. He put on his air helmet.

Malekka and the girls walked back to the double glass doors, where Haddad and Raboud had now also appeared, and turned back to watch the helicopter. The lights along the shoreline of southern Africa twinkled off to the right, and beyond the stern of the ship the myriads of stars in the clear, dark sky suddenly vanished as they were cut off at the horizon by the calm ebony waters of the Indian Ocean. The sharp black of the helicopter contrasted ominously with the friendly blues of the ship.

From the cockpit Anwar looked across at them, and Haddad asked for final permission from Malekka, who nodded his consent; Haddad gave a thumbs-up clearance

---

[3] *In God's protection.*

to Anwar, who acknowledged back. Anwar busied himself in the cockpit for a few seconds, and then the twin-engines of the helicopter started to whine as they warmed. The four rotor blades on the Bell 429 slowly started to rotate, gradually getting faster and faster as the powerful engines came up to power. The noise became louder and the helipad deck very windy. Then from the top of their helmets both Anwar and Yameen pulled down what seemed to be a pair of binoculars attached by metal arms to the side of their helmets, to rest in front of their eyes. Stella realised what they were. Of course. Night vision goggles.

The pilot opened the throttle, raised the collective stick by his seat and the helicopter lifted smoothly off the helipad; it hovered, the landing gear retracted smartly into the fuselage and then turning west it slowly left the area of the ship. The people on the helipad deck watched as the helicopter gained a little more height, and then suddenly tilted its nose down steeply as the powerful thrust from the rotor blades was directed towards the rear of the aircraft.

The helicopter moved away rapidly towards the Mozambique shore, its sleek black lines quickly lost in the pitch dark of the moonless night, gaining more and more speed as it flew off on the deadly errand of its master.

12
THE TWELVE APOSTLES

AT 10PM THAT same evening, fourteen hundred miles to the south-west of the *Excelsior*, JP and Kuhle drove away from the hotel. They headed for the rendezvous at the Waterfront.

JP had updated Charlie Melton in London by telephone in the afternoon. There had been no more developments. Kuhle had thanked his friend, the manager at the hotel, and apologised for the state of disrepair in which JP - as Kuhle had put it - had left it, trying to make light of the subject. The manager, who was a proud South African, knew that those who had been staying in his room above were involved somehow with the awful bombing and death of a woman the previous morning, and he was nothing but supportive of their efforts to find the killers, both for the sake of the woman and her family and for the good name of his country. Kuhle left one man in the back reception again for another night, and with an assurance that the cost of putting the room back together would be covered by his government department, Kuhle and JP departed.

JP was glad to be on the move again. He had needed rest and the enforced inactivity had actually been very beneficial to him, and his head didn't hurt any more. If it wasn't for the four stitches, his involvement in the bombing incident the day before wouldn't be obvious at all, and in fact as the stitches were at his hairline his injury was all but invisible.

Kuhle followed Beach Road from Sea Point and then along Helen Suzman Boulevard all the way into Town and the V&A Waterfront. The streets and roads were busy and the sound of live music greeted their ears as Kuhle pulled the car up in one of the disabled parking berths in front of the V&A Hotel. Kuhle walked over to the Doorman overseeing the Parking Reception Area, discreetly took him aside and flashed his badge at him, to ensure there was no issue over the use of the space by the head of the Scorpions.

They walked through the crowds of people out enjoying themselves in one of Cape Town's busiest and most visited areas, set amongst the backdrop of Table Mountain on one side and Robben Island on the other, and immersed within a grand array of fast food shops, fine restaurants, shopping malls, hotels, offices and luxury apartments. They followed the sound of the music to the Amphitheatre and strolled past to sit at one of the numerous open-air tables servicing the coffee shops and bistros at the harbour front marina.

"This is a fine part of town, Kuhle," said JP, who always liked to visit the Waterfront. "You can sure be proud of this."

"Yeah, man, it's good," he replied. "We like to use it just as much as the tourists."

"They've picked a clever place for the rendezvous, it'll be difficult to spot them here. Especially as we don't even have proper descriptions for them. Are your other men in position?"

"Yes," said Kuhle, "and it's not just men. We've got some women scattered around too, some of them paired with the guys to make them not look so obvious. And they're all armed, and good shots."

"Good," said JP. "I'll get a coffee, we'll look a bit odd sitting here with nothing. You want one?"

Kuhle nodded, and JP walked over to join the short queue at the front of a small café. The smell of the pancakes coming from behind the counter was good and he was tempted to get a couple of those too, but decided against it. The staff served quickly, the queue moved forwards and soon there was only one person ahead of him.

The next few seconds went by as though almost in slow motion. The man in front of JP turned round with the cups of coffee and hot chocolate that he'd just bought, one in each hand at chest height, and almost bumped into JP as they moved to get out of each other's way but went in the same direction.

The little laugh on the other man's lips trailed off as he stared into JP's face. JP smiled and started to let out a "Sorr..." but his word muted as he saw the look of astonishment on the man's face and then the tattoo of the hilt of a knife on the back of the man's left hand holding the drink. Mutual recognition was almost equally instantaneous but Khatib knew JP's face and was just fractionally ahead. As the smile fell from JP's lips Khatib threw the hot drinks towards him and went for his gun under his armpit. JP instinctively brought up his hands and looked away to avoid the scalding drinks and began to reach for his Sauer in his shoulder holster. Behind them and slightly to one side, Kuhle saw what was happening and let out a warning yell as he stood up and drew his gun to fire. Five tables off to the left Samir watched the same scene and was faster. His gun fired first, and hit Kuhle in his left side, who went down with a shout. The crack of the shot distracted Khatib who swung to aim his drawn weapon at the sound, realised it was Samir and was about to turn back to fire at JP when he saw JP just had his own gun out and was bringing it round at him. Instead, Khatib took the moment and ran, instantly gaining cover from the onlookers.

There were already screams from the crowd, and then two other people had guns out and Samir and Khatib were firing at them. They didn't need to be as careful as the Scorpions and watch out for the civilians. Three were down within seconds and two of the police had got shots off but had missed. Khatib ran and Samir followed, heading fast towards the street and the cars.

Amidst the screaming carnage JP was quickly over to the fallen Kuhle and knelt down. It was a bad wound. Blood was all over his lower chest and back and was also coming from his mouth. JP yelled out, "Man down, someone get a medic, call an ambulance."

Kuhle looked up and coughed out some red fluid, and saw JP was there. He grabbed at JP's jacket and pulled himself up a little, and spluttered hoarsely, "Go. Go. Just get the fuckers, Jimmy."

JP rested Kuhle's head back onto the cold pavement, and said, "Just take it easy, bro," and then someone was there and helping, calling on the radio for an ambulance and keeping the crowd back. JP grabbed another brief look at Kuhle, then thinking rapidly put his hand in his new friend's jacket pocket, and ran off after the two men.

A couple of more shots rang out, and JP went past a woman on the ground who had been hit and was being tended by a man, also wounded but less seriously. He could still see the two men ahead just going past the Amphitheatre, where all the music had stopped and the crowd had become thick with inquisitive locals and tourists. Khatib and Samir were pushing their way violently through the throng accompanied by shouts and screams. Then they reached the road and were gone.

A few seconds later JP reached the traffic and looked frantically for the men, but they were nowhere to be seen; then the sound of a hard-revved engine and screeching tyres made him turn his head just as a white Mercedes rushed by to the right on the other side of the road. He had no chance to get a shot off, the cars in the other direction were in the way. He ran the hundred yards back to where Kuhle had parked his car, pulling out the keys he had just taken from Kuhle's pocket and pressing the fob to unlock it. There was a car blocking part of the exit, and a man was taking packets from the boot of the taxi.

"Get it out of the way, get out of the way," JP yelled. The driver looked at JP, bemused, and was about to shout something back. But JP was already in the BMW and the engine roared to life. He put it into reverse, slammed the throttle to the floor, the car backed out and smashed into the rear of the blocking car. The smell of burning rubber filled the air as the tyres on the BMW spun on the tarmac with such sustained force that it began to swivel the taxi round out of the way. Two seconds and JP cleared the other car, scraping the full length of the BMW's left side against the crunched rear of the taxi as it came out. Astonished onlookers gazed in amazement and the driver of the other car was screaming obscenities at JP. He took no notice. He was a man possessed, he had one goal in mind, and everything else around him was just scenery for him to move in and between. He pulled the automatic gearstick into forward drive, crossed the fifteen yards to the road and with tyres screeching and a plume of rubber smoke turned right and took off after the Mercedes.

JP flicked the gearstick left into steptronic mode and surged the car forwards. The roads were busy and he steered the car over the dividing centre line, forcing the other cars to move out of the way and ignoring the blaring horns. He could just see the white Mercedes up ahead, taking a left turn to the faster M6 coast road. A few seconds later JP was at the same roundabout and swung left across from the centre line cutting up the two left lanes of traffic as he screeched the car over. The rear of the car came out and JP turned the wheel right to balance the motion, the car slid on four tyres left, straightened up and roared off after the Mercedes, losing little speed in the turn.

The car ahead had slowed and JP thought they might not have realised they were being followed. So he reduced his speed too and began to close the distance gently. The car turned right, then left a couple of hundred yards on into a dual-carriageway. They passed the shining Cape Town Stadium; now there were two cars between him and the Mercedes. All four moved in a staggered convoy across the big roundabout, turning right onto the coast road, the same way Kuhle had driven in. JP decided to wait. He had Khatib and Samir clearly in front of him; if he took them now, the likelihood was that more civilians would be injured, possibly killed. They were obviously heading into open country to make their getaway. When they got there, he would make his move.

They continued to travel the wide dual-carriageway of the M6. The Helen Suzman Boulevard became Beach Road once more, alternating from two, to three, then two lanes again. The dark expanse of the Ocean off to the right was sometimes broken by the eerie outline of a large ship at anchor waiting for a berth at the commercial ports. The two cars ahead became one, then three, and the speed was within the legal limit, so that no police would be attracted. Khatib and Samir were playing it safe. Then they were where the bomb had exploded; the road had been reopened, and it was impossible to guess the macabre events of thirty-six hours ago. Past the Peninsula Hotel, into the Sea Point suburb itself, then an open stretch for half a mile into Camps Bay that had been JP's running route. Suddenly the street lights vanished and the darkness of night was broken only by headlight beams or the calmer lights from a house or eatery. The road began to open out.

The three cars between JP and the Mercedes spaced out. One pulled into the driveway of a house. Two left. More tarmac sped by under the wheels. Another turned into a restaurant. One left. A couple more miles. Then the last pulled into a viewing bay on the other side of the road and its young couple snuggled down. The road ahead became one lane in each direction, winding like a giant snake around the lower curves of the Twelve Apostles mountains carrying the traffic on its back. The road began to climb. There were no other cars, the Mercedes picked up speed and so did JP.

Suddenly the Mercedes took off at a pace and JP knew they had spotted him. There was no need for any more discretion.

JP stepped the gears down with the pads on the steering wheel and the BMW lurched forwards with a roar. This car and its eight steptronic gears was obviously built for speed and was perfect for pursuit; he wondered how many times Kuhle had used it for that purpose. And, whether Kuhle was going to live to do so again. He dismissed the thought.

JP accelerated hard into the bends. A straight stretch, and he pushed the throttle to the floor. The gap began to close, the BMW was within fifty feet of the Mercedes... forty... thirty. He smashed into its rear, the car careered a little from side to side, then revved away; JP matched the engine power and was once again close behind. He put his headlights on full to dazzle the driver when the mirrors caught the beam. The road bent to the left, and then he saw the arm leaning out of the passenger seat, saw the little belch of flame as the gun spat out a round. JP veered right to remove the line of sight.

The road narrowed, the mountains towered above them and the drop to the ocean on the right grew as the cars raced up the incline. The engine roar was deafening, surging the BMW forwards yet the wide tyres hugged the road firmly. The Mercedes pulled right on a straight stretch, the man was hanging out of the window once more. Another belch of white, the round smashed into the windscreen under the rear view mirror and out through the back left. JP braked and pulled back, then his foot was on the accelerator again. He lowered his own window, the added noise through the bullet holes instantly lost in the new decibel onslaught.

JP pulled out the Sauer. He veered left and with his right arm outstretched fired three rounds at the Mercedes. It swerved back over to block his own fire, he came to the right lane, pushed the throttle hard. The Mercedes was again thrown over by its driver, JP now ten feet behind it. The road curved left and both vehicles were matched at a hundred and twenty miles an hour.

Samir, driving the Mercedes, knew his pursuer was blocked from seeing oncoming traffic and the car fast-approaching head on could do nothing to get out of the way except brake. The Mercedes waited until the last possible moment to pull back left and the screaming horn reached JP's ears just when he saw the oncoming vehicle after the Mercedes had swerved over. He veered the BMW left but not in time to prevent its rear wing clipping the oncoming vehicle. The BMW rocked and then began to spin clockwise with a fearful screech of rubber against the tarmac. JP turned left into the spin to counter the motion but overdid it, the car swung the other way and the rear came out right, almost out of control. He spun the wheel right to cancel the pendulum motion, the rear came back round, steadied and the car straightened. Then he had his foot flat to the floor once more, flicked the gears down three steps and the car roared forwards. He grabbed a brief look in his mirror; the car had stopped, the driver ok, getting out. It had been a clever and well-taken move by the Mercedes driver.

JP had the BMW back up close. The gears screamed as he forced the BMW to surge again. He fired two shots. The Mercedes came left to block, JP pulled across right and then its front was three feet ahead of the Mercedes' bumper. He smashed the BMW against the other car.

The tail of the Mercedes hit the landslide brick supports running the left edge of the road. The front of the car swung violently across into the wall, bounced out and began a spin. The driver tried to correct it but lost the effort, the tyres screeched, the car completed a violent half-circle, hit the wall again tail first backwards and flipped up. The inverted car smashed onto the tarmac and bounced, and then a sickening sound of crunching metal and smashing glass accompanied the car's rotation as it rolled savagely four or five times, the revving engine roaring still as the wheels powered but found nothing to grip. The Mercedes landed upright, skimmed across the road, smashed through the barrier of the viewing bay opposite and came to a stop half over the edge of the wall with the two hundred foot drop below. The barrier had just been able to resist the force of the impact and had done its job.

JP pulled up the BMW in the bay, its lights on the gruesome scene. He ran over, assaulted by the sudden sound of night silence, gun drawn. The wrecked Mercedes rested at fifty degrees downwards, all of the glass was smashed and the two left doors were hanging open. JP could make out the figure of the driver slumped over the steering wheel, motionless. Khatib had not been so lucky. He had taken off his seatbelt during the chase to shoot at JP and had been thrown from the car during the roll. His final slide along the tarmac had taken him over the ledge but he had avoided the sheer drop by grabbing the stub of a small tree branch growing out from the rock face a metre or so down from the road surface.

JP holstered his gun, lay down flat on the tarmac and hooked his left arm round the base of a pole of the disintegrated barrier fencing. He pulled himself forwards into the gaping opening so that the top part of his chest was over the ledge, and held out his arm down to Khatib.

"Come on, man, quickly, that's not going to hold for long," he said to him. "If you don't take my hand, you'll die."

Khatib's face was bloodied and bruised, his clothes cut to pieces and his eyes wide with fear. He knew JP was right. The stub had already moved twice, and his desperate efforts to get a hold with his toes on the rock face were fruitless. He nodded up to JP. Avoiding any jerky movements, he reached out for JP's hand and found it. JP's grip was firm and strong. They looked at each other, and JP nodded. Khatib let go of the stub and his body swung away. He dangled above the lethal drop holding JP's hand with both his own, swaying gently in the pendulum of critical mass.

"Now listen to me carefully," said JP, with a little exertion from the effort. "I reckon I can probably hold you for around thirty seconds. So if you don't tell me what I want to know in that time, I will have dropped you."

A horrified Khatib, who thought he was being rescued but now found himself in just as precarious a situation as when he was holding onto the stub, was keen to co-operate.

The man nodded. "I don't want to die," he said, "pull me up, please."

"Some answers first," said JP.

"Yes, ok, yes." Sweat was running from Khatib's face. "Please, pull me up."

"Tell me," said JP harshly, "Where is the girl?"

"I don't know about a girl," panted Khatib, "I swear it, I don't know about any girl."

"Where is the girl," said JP again. "Where did you get your orders, whom do you work for." He was breathing just a little quicker now, and let out a little grimace, as his arm muscles continued to carry Khatib's full weight.

"Alright, alright, I don't know the girl, all I know is you were the boyfriend. We were hired in Angola, by Iranians, that's all I know. I swear it."

"What were your instructions?"

"To follow you, and film a bomb attack on you. We did that. Then upload the image to the internet. And that's it. I swear it. Please," he pleaded, "please bring me up."

"Where is the girl?" said JP again. "Where were you to go next?"

"To Harare - fly from Durban or over the border by car. When they see the film we get the rest of the money."

"How?"

"Cash into a bank. Please," he said, "please pull me up." He scrambled his toes against the rock face, but could still not get any support. JP held his life in his hand.

"Where is the weapon? Where is the girl?"

"What weapon," said Khatib, looking straight up at JP, surprise in his eyes and voice, almost whimpering, "I swear I don't know anything about any weapon, or any girl. Only that you are the boyfriend, and we were to throw the bomb to scare you."

"Where is the girl?" JP persisted.

"Zimbabwe is all I know. Something is happening in Zimbabwe, some people are arriving. The man who paid us the first part said it, some people are arriving in Zimbabwe, like us. He just said it, let it slip. All I know is people are in Zimbabwe."

JP thought he had got what he wanted from this man. He knew nothing of real value, other than that Zimbabwe was where some people were or might be arriving. Khatib had been paid, he was just hired to do this one job. He knew nothing of Stella or the weapon. And, his arm was beginning to hurt.

"Please, I know nothing else. Please… "

JP nodded at Khatib, and braced himself. He closed his bicep to bring the man up, and Khatib closed his arms to bring his body higher and closer to safety, his feet scratching at the sheer rock face again to help the lift and try to find some support. Their faces were almost level, a few inches apart.

"Khatib," said JP coldly, his eyes piercing into the eyes of the other man, "I have a message for you from the family of the woman you killed yesterday."

"What? What do you mean. What message," said Khatib, desperately trying to get himself higher.

"This."

JP suddenly relaxed his right bicep and released his hold on the man's hand.

With horrified terror in his eyes and panic cries of "No… No…" yelled with all the force in his lungs

Khatib tried hopelessly to cling on to JP's hand, scratching and kicking. Khatib slipped away. A gargled scream pierced the air as the doomed man dropped straight down into the darkness, the last sounds from his mouth fading into nothingness.

His body smashed onto the rocks below, blood spouting from the torn flesh and grey lumps oozing from its broken cranium. The pounding waves of the Atlantic Ocean at once began to claim it as their own.

JP pulled himself back up and sat on the tarmac, leaning against the post for a few seconds. He looked over at the car hanging over the ledge. Samir began to stir at the wheel. He wasn't dead.

JP walked back to the BMW. He started the engine, drove forwards a few feet and slipped the car into reverse. He came back hard. The BMW smashed into the Mercedes just as Samir opened his eyes. The last bits of the crash barrier buckled, the car lurched forwards and the cliff edge ripped at the underside as JP sent the car out into the blackness on its final journey.

"And that's for my friend, Kuhle," said JP grimly.

He couldn't hear Samir's long scream. The petrol tank exploded on the rocks below, enveloping what was left of the destroyed vehicle and its driver in a great ball of bright red and orange flames.

JP pulled away slowly, his mind already on how Kuhle was, and the others.

PART THREE

ACQUISITIONS

13
THEFT ONE

ANWAR KEPT THE helicopter low over the ground. The instructions were to fly no higher than one hundred feet above ground level all the way to Beitbridge in Zimbabwe. He had night vision goggles, the latest Garmin GPS glass system and an autopilot doing most of the work. The glass cockpit had long ago replaced the traditional 'six-pack' mechanical instruments of airspeed, attitude indicator, altitude, turn co-ordinator, heading indicator and vertical speed indicator. There were a few back-up mechanical systems, just in case, including the old reliable magnetic compass. The primary flight display screen, incorporating all that had been in the six-pack, was complemented by the multi-function display screen below showing the GPS moving map and engine information.

Their cruising speed of one hundred and fifty knots, about one hundred and seventy-five miles per hour, gave a flight time for the three hundred and fifty mile journey of just over two hours. In planning the route they had taken into account any high rise buildings or pylons; there was none. However, flying in the dark was never that easy, and Anwar's instruments and in particular the autopilot would make this a much more simple trip than otherwise would have been the case, even though he had his night vision scopes. The terrain rose gently from sea level to eight hundred and fifty feet over the first two hundred miles. The two men settled back into a smooth albeit stealthy flight routine.

They ignored the Mozambique air traffic control, such as it was, which frankly wasn't very much. They were below any domestic radar and so invisible to all, and the closest they came to Maputo, which had the busiest airport, was just under three hundred miles. In any event, Mozambique had virtually no air force and so even if they were to be picked up, there was no possibility of their being intercepted.

As they approached the border with Zimbabwe the landscape suddenly began to move up rapidly, and they crossed from Mozambique at seventeen hundred feet. The terrain dropped off again over the next thirty miles; they flew over the Mwenezi River north of Malipati, and then came back up. Zimbabwe, too, had a pretty nominal air force, and anyway was friendly to Malekka; she knew they were coming.

The helicopter crossed the Bubye River. They had sixty miles to go. The terrain came up one last time and the aircraft followed. The weather had not been an issue; there had been virtually no wind that required any compensation in the heading.

Finally the GPS indicated the end of the journey, and they looked for lights; they saw two vehicles. The helicopter touched down. They were one mile south of the little Beitbridge airport and one north of the Zimbabwe-South African border. The journey had taken precisely two and a quarter hours.

The fuel bowser had been borrowed from one of the bigger airports to the north; Beitbridge was a small gravel airstrip and certainly didn't have any Jet-A fuel. Once the rotors had stopped the two fuel personnel drove the bowser close and got to work.

Yameen went over to greet the other two men, also in

black fatigues, who had arrived in the car. They had ensured the fuel's safe arrival. He had hand-picked both Duha and Fadil; like himself, they were tough military men, fit and capable. They swiftly transferred their gear from the car into the back of the aircraft.

Anwar checked the refuelling. He took a sample of the fuel from the bowser before allowing any of it to be placed inside the aircraft; avgas, low-octane car fuel or diesel would have been disastrous. He couldn't actually analyse the fuel on the spot but could make the obvious tests. After all, this is Africa, and things happen. He tested for smell, colour and any water contamination; satisfied, he allowed them to proceed, making sure they used the funnel with the filter that he had brought.

The bowser and car had been provided at the authority of the President, who received a generous deposit into one of his personal offshore bank accounts for his trouble - "a little thank you," as Malekka had said to him a few months before.

Landing some distance from the Beitbridge airstrip had two advantages; it kept their visit away from inquisitive eyes or ears, and the stone gravel from the helicopter engines. Tonight was not the night to take risks of any kind.

Speed was going to be essential now. South Africa's military was nothing like that of Zimbabwe or Mozambique. They had a powerful highly-efficient Air Force, actually the second oldest in the world, with the Swedish Saab Griffin multirole fighter and a number of attack helicopters and a multitude of air-to-air missiles, rockets and guns to back them up. Getting intercepted by the South African Air Force was definitely not a good idea; Anwar knew they would be forced down or blown out of the sky as easily as one might pop a balloon with a pin. So it was essential for very low flying to be clear of any possibility of getting picked up on radar. Even so, there was always the chance that someone would hear the helicopter and raise the alarm, leading to fast escalation. However, that was a risk they could do nothing about. Their incursion into South African airspace had to be fast.

Yameen's team was complete, and they were now ready. Anwar did a final walk-round check of his refuelled aircraft. Yameen dismissed the two bowser crew, and they set off to return both vehicles from where they had come. The men climbed aboard, Yameen this time sitting with Duha and Fadil in the facing club seats behind the pilot. The engines whined, the rotors turned, and the aircraft took off once more heading due south.

Anwar now was flying manually really very low, literally skimming the bushes and tree tops as he followed the GPS carefully, making good use of his NVG. They were across the mighty Limpopo River into South Africa within thirty seconds. They overflew the A1 that led back to the New Limpopo Bridge border crossing and climbed steadily to match the rising terrain, but still hugged the ground. Within five minutes they reached the little Musina tarmac airstrip just over three miles from the centre of the town. Anwar landed the aircraft deftly on the holding bay at the south-east side of the strip, by the waiting lights of a car.

Before the rotor blades had stopped the three soldiers, with rucksacks, NVG, balaclavas and wielding automatic rifles with suppressors, were out of the helicopter and running hard over to the car, a Range Rover. They exchanged silent greetings and places with Mulayl, who had brought the car to the airstrip, bundled in, started the engine and headed off. Mulayl ran for the helicopter, took a rifle and ammunition from Anwar and crouched down beside the aircraft outside as guard.

Anwar had turned the engine off. All was quickly quiet again at the airstrip. The noise from the Range Rover died away as it raced off into the stillness of the night.

Duha took the car on several small dirt tracks to the tarmac road running around the outskirts of Musina, then turned left to head away from the town. They drove south-west, taking care not to exceed the one hundred kilometres per hour limit. An interruption for speeding was attention they did not want, however unlikely.

At seven miles exactly was a turning right. The road ran straight west for one and a half miles, and Duha slowed to reduce the engine noise. At the end was a small one hundred-foot hill surrounded by trees and the road bent sharply left around it, to the Fincrest Centre located discreetly on the other side. Instead of continuing they drove off-road and stopped the car. They got out, crouched down and listened. Apart from a few clicks from the cooling engine and the night sounds of semi-wild bush South Africa, mainly crickets, there was no sound.

Twenty seconds later Yameen gave a nod. They ran the remaining five hundred yards of the curved road in complete silence. Five minutes later they were at the approach road to the administration block, out of sight of the factory and guards behind it. They stopped and crouched down again, waiting, listening. Nothing. Good, thought Yameen.

Another few yards crossed in silence and they were at the entrance door to the block. Yameen looked at his watch. The journey from the aircraft had taken them exactly fourteen minutes.

Yameen took out the swipe card and small sheet of paper with the security codes. The green beam of Fadil's torch cut through the darkness for three seconds as Yameen swiped the card through the slot by the door and punched the access code into the keypad. The entrance door clicked open. The men passed inside, ensuring the door locked back in place behind them. They turned left, to the alarm control box on the wall, and with the help of the green torchlight again entered the code and turned the alarm off. They moved to the door opposite, entered the pass code and Duha went inside. Twenty seconds later he had turned off the CCTV system and emerged with the current disk recording safely in his rucksack.

They went past the central reception desk and moved swiftly down the long corridor, which divided into two at the end. They turned right to enter B Block, and were faced with double doors; Yameen used the swipe card again and entered the code. Eighty feet further they reached a second corridor division; B1 to the right. Then some solid metal double doors. No requirement for a swipe card; they were getting close.

The torch came out for a fifth time. They passed into the B1 block. Room 151, the fifteenth room on the ground floor, was at the end. They stopped outside and looked at the security system.

Duha removed the aluminium briefcase from his rucksack and popped it open on the floor. Encased in soft protective sponge, like lenses in a photographer's carry case, were the replicas of Stella's right hand and the fabricated head with the model of her right eyeball. Yameen looked once more at the code list and punched the long access number.

The display screen above the keypad suddenly sprang to life:

Code accepted.
Verify print with the second finger
of your right hand.

Yameen picked up the gel hand, bent the other fingers slightly out of the way and placed the middle finger up against the scanner on the wall. The screen was large enough to take the full hand; although that clearly was not what the machine wanted tonight. The scan bar flicked on and ran quickly top to bottom, then turned off and went back up.

A few seconds later the LCD screen displayed some more text:

Scan print accepted.

Good, first stage done ok, thought Yameen.
It then displayed:

Retina scan required.
Please approach Retina Scanner
and place your eye up to the scanning lens for
Retina Scan Certification.
Press Red Button below to activate.

Yameen lifted out the head. He pressed the small button on its top to run the plasma curvature display, put the chin on the bar below the retina scanner and pressed the Red Button. There was a gentle hum.
The LCD lit up:

Scanning declined, access refused.

What?? Scanning declined, access refused. Shit, what the hell is happening now, thought Yameen. What the fuck do we do? The three men looked at each other. Fear crept into their stomachs. What's gone wrong? What do they do now? A little bead of perspiration trickled down from Yameen's brow.

The LCD screen display changed suddenly, and said:

*Please repeat exercise and attempt
Retina Scan again.*

*Please approach Retina Scanner
and place your eye up to the scanning lens for
Retina Scan Certification.
Press Red Button below to activate.*

Yameen's mouth had suddenly gone very dry. He swallowed hard. He looked at his companions again; they weren't in any better shape. He lifted the head up again and this time gave it a little kiss. Once more he pressed the button at the top of the head and placed it onto the chin rest. He made sure the forehead was up firmly against the top bar... perhaps he hadn't had the angle right...

He pressed the Red Button under the scanning lens. The low hum came again quietly from the machine. They waited for what seemed eons. Finally the LCD lit up once more.

*Retina Scan accepted.
Access approved.*

The three men collectively heaved a sigh of relief.

And then a motor whined, the bolts in the thick steel door slid back into the wall and the door opened. Bright lights snapped on and the men removed their NVG quickly. There were no windows in the room or corridor; the light was contained.

The men had their composure again. They moved swiftly inside and immediately saw what they wanted. The 9M714K-Alpha was mounted in a tilted metal box on a waist-high steel pedestal. Yameen entered the code at the keypad to the right. There was a click and the lid popped up.

They have it!

Yameen looked at his two colleagues, who also were grinning triumphantly. He nodded, and the team moved silently on.

The Alpha was grey and metallic, thirty centimetres by twenty and maybe ten deep. On the top was a series of switches, a small keypad and an LCD screen. Fadil produced a second briefcase from his rucksack on the floor; Yameen knelt down and positioned the Alpha into the case. It fitted perfectly. The foam sponge that enveloped it would provide secure protection from vibration and movement.

It was going to need it.

He handed the closed case to Fadil, who carefully placed it back into his rucksack. Yameen took out four chrome tubes the diameter of a man's fist and maybe twenty centimetres long, and handed two to each of the others. They set the timers to forty minutes. Fadil threw one of the incendiary bombs down and it rolled over to the Alpha pedestal. They went back into the corridor, Yameen looked at the code list for the last time and entered the number onto the keypad to close the safe door. It thudded solidly shut. The men put their NVG back on.

They retrieved the head and hand and made their way back to the exit, using the release buttons now available on the doors. Duha dropped a tube bomb in the B1 corridor, and the other two were placed in the main corridor and reception area. They quietly exited the front door, heard it click shut and crouched down again, listening. Thirty seconds. Nothing.

The three men ran quietly from the centre, back onto

the road and covered the five hundred yards to the car. Without a sound to each other, they opened the doors, got in and Duha started the engine. The Range Rover sprang to life and they rejoined the road, and drove off the way they had come.

Eight minutes later they were approaching the Musina airstrip. As soon as Anwar saw the car lights he powered up the helicopter, and the rotor blades were beginning to turn as the car drew alongside. The men exited the vehicle. Yameen pulled out the last tube bomb from his rucksack and handed it to Duha.

"Ten minutes." Duha nodded, and rolled the bomb under the car.

Thirty seconds later they were all safely on board the helicopter with all of their equipment, and the 9M714K-Alpha. As they sped over the border into Zimbabwe once more, Yameen glanced at his watch. The operation had taken exactly forty-six minutes.

And the only thing they had left behind in South Africa were five bombs.

≈

Thirty-thousand feet above them the American drone UAV that on a shift watch with its twin had silently been circling the Fincrest Centre for the last seventy-two hours centred its crosshairs onto the helicopter, and went into automated track mode as it too crossed stealthily into Zimbabwe airspace.

14

OUT-FOXED

NONE OF THE men said anything. They were all elated at their incursion into what they perceived for that night as enemy territory. It had gone perfectly, save for the little glitch at the retina scan, which had been terrifying. However that was all it was, just a little glitch. The mission had been a total success.

Yameen sat back in his seat and stared out of the window. He knew Mr Malekka would be proud of him and his team, and that meant a great deal to him. So too did the large second payment they would be receiving.

Behind Anwar the four men looked at each other. They began to grin, then let out loud shouts of jubilation, and both Mulayl and Duha turned to shake Anwar on the shoulders too. It had been Mulayl who had arrived in Pretoria a week previously from Zurich. For three days he had acted like a tourist and taken in the Union Buildings, the Zoo and the National Botanical Garden; on the fourth day he quietly purchased the car and left his hotel. It had been an easy drive north to Musina, and he had arrived in perfect time for the rendezvous that night.

The bomb under the car was the first to go off. A huge explosion launched the vehicle a hundred feet off the ground and tore it to pieces. A large orange flame mushroomed up three hundred feet, quickly replaced by thick black smoke rising higher still. The shock wave shattered the glass windows of a few deserted buildings close to the airstrip and rocked the frames of those in the town three miles away. What was left of the car smashed back onto the tarmac inverted, in a rainstorm of molten shrapnel and burning debris. People in the town awoke from the noise and saw the airstrip's reddened sky.

At the Fincrest Centre the bomb in the safe room was first to go, with a violence amplified by the room's confined thick metal shell. The explosion instantly destroyed everything inside and then physically twisted the room out of shape, into a deformed cuboid. By the time the rumble of the explosion reached the munitions factory behind, the steel bolts of the safe room door had already become twisted and no longer able to open. Exactly as Malekka had planned. It would be some time before anyone could get inside to find out exactly what had happened.

The explosion in the B1 corridor demolished the two metal doors at one end and travelled up the corridor in the other direction to destroy the safe room keypad and the retina and fingerprint scanners; the bombs in the main corridor and reception area blew the front of the building apart and took the roof off. The shock waves knocked the guards off their feet as they ran to the administration block. The blast lit up the sky for miles around. The Centre was on fire and burning furiously.

≈

JP sat down on one of the benches outside the Groote Schuur Hospital at the top of its long approach road, put his elbows onto his legs and with a deep sigh looked down blankly at the ground between them. He had just come out from visiting Kuhle. The head of the Scorpions had caught a very nasty wound, but was still alive, if only just. The bullet had entered his chest between the fifth and sixth ribs, clipped his left lung and then exited his back, mercifully damaging no other vital organs. The traumatic pneumothorax it had caused and the severe internal bleeding made his life teeter on the brink for a while. However, the paramedics had brought him to the trauma unit very quickly and the doctors had moved fast. He was still in intensive care and under sedation, but was out of danger, and expected to make a full recovery.

He's going to need a new car, though, said JP to himself, looking across at the vehicle with a dry smile on his lips. The lovely BMW now had dents and scrapes down the length of the left side, the front was crumpled, the rear bashed, the windscreen had a bullet hole in it as did the rear left window, and the engine was in dire need of a service and tune up.

His cell phone rang. It was Charlie Melton on a scrambled secure line.

"It's blown up, Jimmy," he said. "They've got it and blown the place to pieces."

"Bloody hell," said JP sitting upright at the news, "is anyone hurt?"

"We don't think so, but don't know for sure yet. They didn't touch the factory part, but the admin building at the Centre is blown to bits and on fire."

"How did they do it?"

"A helicopter and a team from across the border in Zimbabwe. As bold as brass, flew in, did the raid, and then went out. They were really fast, really professional."

"Are they tracking it?"

"So far, yes. They're back over the border again now but the Yanks have sent the drone in across the border anyway. I hope to Christ they don't get spotted, it'll be an international incident and all hell will break lose if they do."

"Far worse than that could happen if they lose track of it," said JP, and then continued, "Charlie, a few things have happened this end." He gave a quick summary of the essential details of the recent events in Cape Town. Melton listened in silence.

"...so it seems that Zimbabwe is the link, or the next one so far anyway," said JP, "and your assumption that they came into South Africa from there is doubtless right. That's where the focus should be now. We have to pick up the lead from there."

"I'll pass all that on," said the voice on the other end of the phone. "The Yanks have got the ball for now; get yourself back here, JP. There's nothing else for you to do there. We've told them at Ysterplaat, and the South Africans are laying on a flight in one of their nice Gripens for you. You can give us a full report when you're here. We've scrambled the refuellers."

"Ok," he said. "Thanks Charlie. I'll see you in London."

He hung up the phone.

Well then, there could be no more doubt about it at all. For sure, they are getting, or have already got, an SS-23 nuclear weapon, and they now have a fully working Alpha with which to launch it. Of course, they could always set the bomb off anyway, wherever it's located, but then why go to the trouble of stealing an Alpha unit? Their plan is obviously to launch it from some place to somewhere else.

Where in the world is the bomb? It could be anywhere, he said to himself grimly as he drove back to the Fincrest residence. And that was a terrifying thought.

JP joined the Fincrest family in the large lounge. He

had known from the start that there was never going to be any serious ransom demand. Now it was perfectly clear. The two communications to the Fincrests - *'Do nothing, change nothing, tell nobody. Or she dies'* straight after Stella first vanished and *'USD $20m, small notes, forty-eight hours'* (now just expired) - were merely a brilliant diversionary ruse.

Stella hadn't been taken from St Lucia for money. And now there was no need for JP to stay any longer. Malekka's people had what they wanted. The search was on.

He showered and packed quickly. He took out his second mobile phone that he had bought in London and sent a quick text. It read, *'Arriving L early hours today, suggest meet tonight if poss.'* The reply came back, *'Ok, will confirm details.'*

Good, he thought. Good.

He reassured Stella's parents once again as best he could, thanked them and said goodbye, keeping it all as brief as possible. First because he had to, and second because the events were so distressing for them. And, for that matter, for him too.

Particularly as it had all been his idea.

The Fincrests' driver took him out to AFB Ysterplaat, the South African Air Force Base just north of Cape Town. He was taken quickly through to the kit room where he suited up for the Saab Gripen, and within the hour he was in the air seated behind the pilot, heading north in excess of Mach 2. He hoped to God the CIA would be able to track the helicopter to wherever it landed, and then trace the Alpha to where the bomb was located.

Though that could still be fraught with problems.

≈

Eight thousand miles away in Langley, Virginia, in a room deep underground at the CIA headquarters, a small team of personnel watched the progress of the Reaper UAV in Zimbabwe airspace. The aircraft was doing a good job keeping up with the helicopter, which was at twelve thousand feet and once again moving at one hundred and fifty knots, or one hundred and seventy-five miles an hour. The Reaper could match that comfortably.

It had taken over the surveillance at Fincrest from its partner UAV some twenty hours before and so could stay airborne for another six or eight. The Americans had already launched a replacement from the Makhado Air Force Base at Louis Trichardt, fifty miles south-west of Musina, which they were discreetly visiting courtesy of the South African Government. The second UAV was racing towards its brother at its top speed of two hundred and sixty knots to take over.

It was potentially a dangerous operation. A top-secret UAV in unauthorised airspace running out of fuel or crashing would cause an international furore. More worryingly for the Americans, if the aircraft came down in Zimbabwe it could end up in the hands of the Russians or possibly the Chinese. Both would love to be able to dismantle a Reaper or even parts of it. Twenty-five years of more cordial relations since the Cold War could be quickly erased, as events in Ukraine were showing.

The team tracked the helicopter usually in close-up and with a combination of highly-sensitive infra-red, image-intensifying and thermal imaging cameras. The ground passed by at high speed below, but the Reaper's crosshairs remained relentlessly steady on the centre of the helicopter through course changes, air turbulence and height variations. While the night imagery wasn't nearly as detailed as that from daylight it was certainly refined enough to detect any large change in airflow, or an infra-red source such as a man jumping, or a door opening. The CIA had already placed their operatives in Zimbabwe on high alert.

The helicopter was taking basically a northerly direction, making course adjustments with sharp turns over various landmarks, such as roads; so far it had flown north-west, turned north-east and then north again. Each time, the UAV mirrored the changes.

The helicopter could either track north across the border into Zambia, east into Mozambique or of course simply land in Zimbabwe. It had just turned eastwards again at the Sebakwe Dam and so Mozambique looked a viable destination; but then it turned north at the A4, the main road to Harare.

Suddenly the helicopter's speed slowed, and so the Reaper's reduced with it. Finally the helicopter landed at Harare International Airport. The Reaper went into its standard tight figure of eight above at forty thousand feet, keeping the crosshairs of the cameras still neatly on the centre of the helicopter.

The UAV had already switched over to optical light cameras for the brightness of Zimbabwe's main airport. It saw a bowser approach the aircraft and refuel it; it saw five helmeted men come out of the helicopter to stretch their legs; and it saw the same five men get back into the aircraft and the rotors begin to rotate. Then, just before the helicopter took off again, two of the men came out once more with rucksacks and a kitbag and ran quickly into a covered van alongside the aircraft. The helicopter took off again and the van drove off towards the main terminal building.

All hell broke loose in the centre. There was an

immediate barked order to get the operatives in Harare over to the Airport and try to find out about the men, who they were, where they went, who helped them, who drove the van, could they get fast access to it, get prints, talk to the men that had helped refuel the aircraft. Had one of them got the Alpha? If so, which one? Half the people in the room left in the space of thirty seconds. The two controllers of the UAV suddenly had their adrenalin flowing and were sitting bolt upright in their seats, minds focused fully on their piloting and guiding movements and instructions.

The helicopter and three of the men were now flying to another unknown destination. Should the UAV stay with the aircraft or follow the van? The Reaper had already terminated its figure of eight flight path. The decision was made to continue shadowing the helicopter. It started off north, but then suddenly changed course north-west more or less following the direction of the A1 road, picking up speed quickly and climbing to twelve thousand feet once more. A little over an hour later the helicopter crossed the border with Zambia, and again the UAV crossed into airspace for which it was not authorised. Thirty minutes later and the helicopter landed at Lusaka, the capital of Zambia.

This time there was no refuelling; the remaining three men carrying rucksacks and their kitbags got out of the aircraft into a waiting adjacent van, just as their colleagues had done at Harare, and the van sped off to the terminal. As soon as the helicopter had started on its north-west track, the CIA issued instructions to their men in Lusaka, who then started to make their way out to the airport.

Unfortunately, there were suddenly inexplicable road works along the route and all traffic throughways to the airport were blocked off and closed for the next few hours. Malekka's web of power had infiltrated into Zambia with ease and a great deal of internal disruption and influence could be bought for a ridiculously small amount of money, despite the governmental cordial relations between the USA and Zambia. However, cordial relations in the hands of government ministers were no substitute for US dollars in the hands of the common worker.

Just as their friends had done in Harare, the three men that had landed at Lusaka left the terminal by different means, in different vehicles, to different locations that only they knew.

Two countries, five men, five rucksacks, five kitbags. Five different movements.

It was hopeless.

The CIA terminated the overhead surveillance at Lusaka, and the second drone that they had sent earlier to take over from its twin turned round and headed back to base, as its brother had already done.

Despite all of the CIA's expectations and great efforts, the five men and their bags simply vanished.

≈

A little earlier that evening, a few minutes after Anwar had flown the helicopter across the South African border and into Zimbabwe, Yameen had looked at his watch and noted that the bombs should be going off just about then. He smiled at the devastation they would cause and the brutal damage that would be wreaked on the door of the safe room.

He said to Fadil, "Check the Alpha again please."

"Yes, sir," replied Fadil. He carefully took the smaller aluminium briefcase from his rucksack on the seat next to him and removed the Alpha from its comfortable foam cushioning. Duha opened his kit bag and took out the scanner. It could detect any kind of radio emission in the vicinity on any frequency. He switched it on, and as Fadil held the Alpha out with both hands Duha ran the box around the unit for the second time since they had left Musina. Just to make sure they had not been outsmarted and there was some kind of tracking beacon installed and operational in the Alpha.

There was none.

"It's still clean, sir," said Fadil.

"Good," said Yameen. "Put it back, and then let's put it in the container."

Fadil placed the Alpha back inside the aluminium case. From the end of the seat row Mulayl unstrapped a black object shaped like an oversized rugby ball with angled sides stretched into a three-dimensional hexagon. He handed it to Yameen.

Yameen levered out a flap located on its centre rim, inserted a small black double-sided key and turned it. The container popped open two thirds from the top as though cut across with a knife. Inside was thick sponge and sprung cushioning that supported a central rubber frame. It matched the outline of the aluminium case containing the Alpha perfectly. Fadil placed the case into the rubber frame, brought the two halves together and snapped them shut, locking them. Mulayl strapped it down beside him once more.

The men settled back into their seats. Mulayl took out a flask of coffee and poured for everyone. They sipped at the hot drink in silence as the aircraft continued to speed along in the night.

Anwar had taken the aircraft up to twelve thousand feet, since there was no need for them to hug the ground as they were in friendly territory. It made for a smoother flight and an easier one for him too, since he could relax more and let the autopilot do its work without so much overseeing from him. At one hundred feet there was not much time to spare if something went wrong; twelve thousand feet gave a much bigger safety buffer.

He was routing slightly west of north, and they had a journey time of one hour and fifty minutes to their next landing point at Harare. He had programmed the autopilot to dip the aircraft suddenly and then raise it again to emulate the effects of air turbulence. He could see when the bumps were about to occur on his screen and called out a warning to his passengers. When they crossed the A9 road at Pambuka the aircraft turned hard to the north-east, followed the road for seventy miles to Mashava, then turned sharply north. Anwar now had the helicopter on a course of 355° True. The minutes passed. The only noise was the whine of the turbines as they powered the aircraft forwards.

Anwar broke the silence.

"Fifteen minutes."

Mulayl lifted the black hexagonal container off the seat and handed it to Yameen opposite him.

"Check everything is secured down," said Yameen.

They looked about them, and placed anything that was loose back into rucksacks or kit bags, and tightened their seatbelts around them.

"Ten minutes," said Anwar, "and dip coming."

The aircraft jolted down and then up, disturbing the airflow behind it yet again.

Duha leant forwards and felt beneath his seat for the small button. The men moved their feet away from the centre of the floor and Duha pressed the button. An area two feet square dropped down at one end in front of him and then started to slide away beneath the aircraft. Instantly there was a loud rushing as the air poured in. Duha released the button; they wanted the temperatures and air pressures and flow around them to be altered only very gradually, just in case anyone was watching them. As indeed they were.

Duha pressed the button again and then waited; he repeated the process several times, and the hole in the floor in front of them grew bigger.

"Five minutes," came Anwar's voice through their headsets.

Duha looked at Yameen, who nodded. He pressed the button and opened the floor the final couple of centimetres.

"Four minutes."

Yameen had the black container on his lap, and was waiting patiently.

"Three."

Another minute passed.

"Two minutes."

"One."

Anwar gave a countdown from fifteen seconds.

"... Four. Three. Two. One and dip."

The aircraft lurched.

"Zero and drop."

Yameen dropped the black container through the hole in the floor. The helicopter had reached exactly the map coordinates of Latitude 19° 08' 00.02" South and Longitude 30° 20' 25.47" East.

As it plummeted downwards the helicopter banked hard to the right and flew off at a ninety degree angle east, apparently coinciding with the Sebakwe Dam. The container had been immediately swept behind by the oncoming air; the dip had disturbed the airflow to obscure the ejection and now the helicopter was flying away fast at right angles to the parabolic line that the container was dropping along.

Eight thousand miles away in Langley, Virginia, the

UAV Pilot and the surveillance team saw the helicopter make yet another turn, this time to the east. They watched as the UAV automatically mirrored the turn and continued on at one hundred and fifty knots. The dielectric composites and negative index metamaterials of the container's construction, its dark matte paint on its surface, its unusually angled shape, and its sheer small dimensions all combined together to make the container undetectable at night in all ranges of the electromagnetic spectrum. It could not be seen visibly, nor in the infrared, nor by thermal imaging, nor picked up by radar, and by the time it had reached terminal velocity of one hundred and twenty miles an hour twelve seconds later, the helicopter was already over half a mile away to the east. The container continued to freefall, unnoticed, undetected and unexpected.

Except by the men below on the ground who were waiting patiently for it.

The helicopter and the UAV above were two and a half miles away when the container reached twelve hundred feet. Its parachute opened and the black silk material and cords expanded quickly to slow its descent virtually to zero. The hexagonal object with the Alpha finally floated gently down to the ground. As it touched the earth the strings of the parachute relaxed and were ejected from the object. An internal timer began a fifteen-minute countdown.

The men on the ground heard the sound of the helicopter disappear in the distance. They switched on their sonar listening devices and infra-red scanners, and trawled the sky directly above searching to see if there was a UAV looking down at them after the drop. There was nothing.

And then the operator smiled as he picked up the UAV thirty thousand feet above the helicopter, both now low on the horizon and heading in unison east towards the A4 road, when it would make its final turn north to take it up towards Harare.

They had suspected the South Africans might be able to respond very quickly to the attack on the Fincrest Centre. Especially as the border guards at the New Limpopo Bridge crossing would be able to report they had heard a helicopter travelling south across the border and, just before the explosions, one crossing north. The South African military obviously had been sharp, able to catch up with the helicopter and track it.

Or so the men on the ground thought anyway.

The helicopter was gone below the horizon, there was nothing above them. There would be no need for him and his two companions to follow the backup plan to split up and each to travel off in different separate directions by land and then air, with one of them taking the Alpha to the alternative rendezvous point.

The CIA didn't know it, but their effort over the next three hours in following the helicopter first to Harare and then to Lusaka, and then later of their operatives over the next few days in trying to locate the five men, was utterly pointless from the start.

They had been out-manoeuvred, and out-foxed.

15
DELIVERY ONE

WHEN THE TIMER inside the hexagonal container reached zero, it began to emit a low-power radio signal. It had a range of eight hundred yards or so.

Certain there was no UAV above them after the passage of the helicopter, Zaim, the three-man ground team's leader, pulled his night vision goggles down again and from his pocket took out the directional indicator, no bigger than a cigarette packet. He turned it on, the small LCD screen lit up and a series of dashes began to cross the screen from the centre bottom to the top slightly over to the right. It cleared, then the moving dashes started again. The small digits at the bottom right showed the distance: two hundred and fifty-four metres.

Zaim turned to Qudamah. "Do you have the co-ordinates?"

"Yes, sir," he replied, "they've just come in." He passed a small sheet of paper to Ghazi who copied the GPS data into his flight book for later, then handed the sheet back. Qudamah pocketed it.

"Ok then," said Zaim. "We'll pack up the equipment and then go and get the drop. I'll guard; you two get the gear."

The three men got out of the Range Rover that they had been using as an operations base and Zaim stood with his machine gun and suppressor levelled, watching for any animals that might want them for dinner. The area was meant to be farmland, but they knew there had been trouble with lions and hyenas recently and they weren't taking any chances.

They had parked under a tree for concealment but had also placed a green and brown camouflage netting over the car earlier in the evening. They took the netting down, then disconnected their camouflaged electronic equipment. They retrieved the two parabolic receiving dishes ten metres away that had been tilting back and forth scanning the sky for sound or an infra-red signature, and their netting.

"That's it, sir," said Ghazi. "We're all secure and ready."

"Right, get in. This place gives me the creeps, I keep feeling we're being watched. Let's collect the drop package and get the fuck out of here."

Qudamah drove slowly using the powerful headlights as Zaim guided with the directional indicator. It didn't take them long. They found the hexagonal container on the ground close to a bush about six feet high, which its black parachute had all but enveloped. Zaim covered once more as Ghazi got out and picked it up, pulled in the small chute and got back in.

They were pleased to have the metal cocoon safety of the car around them again. Qudamah drove slowly back to the small barn they had thought at first they could use to conceal the car but had then decided against once they had looked inside - it was full of old farm equipment, rusty machinery and foodstuffs for animals. They headed north, and then were soon on the dirt track heading west. They travelled almost two miles in the heartland of the wild Zimbabwe farm terrain, and then the track turned sharply right. At the top was the Mahamara airstrip.

They stopped close to the only building on the site,

an open brick hanger where the airstrip's two or three visitors a year would park their aircraft, mainly to be out of the blazing sun during the day, and which otherwise was empty. However, tonight it was not empty. Tonight it housed another sleek efficient, Bell 429 helicopter, that had been fully refuelled after its arrival in the early evening by a second bowser, that had then departed back to Harare one hundred miles north-east.

Ghazi had flown the helicopter in with Zaim; Qudamah had rendezvoused with them in the four-wheel drive Range Rover. He had entered Zimbabwe on a commercial flight from Paris three days before, obtained the vehicle in Harare, then driven down to meet his colleagues. Once the bowser had departed they had pushed the helicopter on its wheels into the hanger. The hangar was large enough to cover it completely.

Now they reversed the process, and the helicopter came back out to rest a few feet from the hangar under the starlit sky.

Ghazi got on board, prepared for flight and then came out again to give the aircraft one final walk round. Qudamah and Zaim busied themselves transferring to the helicopter, first making sure that the hexagonal container holding the Alpha was securely strapped in, and then loading everything else.

This time there was to be no blowing up of the car. That would only attract unnecessary attention. Instead it had been arranged to leave the keys in the vehicle as a thank you to the farmer who worked the land with the airstrip on it. The car was another form of US dollars, this time being put in the hands of a lowly worker instead of a high government official. The farmer's sudden acquisition of a nice new vehicle would undoubtedly attract attention in the local area, but not nearly as much nor as quickly as an explosion.

The team had been careful not to leave fingerprints by wearing gloves, although Qudamah had been in it for three days prior. So the car was driven into the hangar and then he and Zaim sanitized the vehicle first with an efficient wipe-over and then with a bleach spray to destroy any DNA. Not that they thought DNA could ever really become an issue in the centre of wild Zimbabwe. However, they were professionals, and did their job thoroughly and according to instructions. They removed the logbook, petrol receipts and any other paperwork. Excess papers from the helicopter were also removed, including Ghazi's flight book sheet, and the two blank sheets beneath, on which he had written the GPS coordinates, now entered. Just in case the aircraft was forced down over the coming journey. The GPS autopilot would erase the co-ordinates next time the engine was closed down, but papers might remain. There was to be nothing left to lead anyone to their rendezvous point. The small bundle was put on the ground in the back corner of the hanger and set fire to. The number plates and Vehicle Identification Number in the engine were not important; they would lead nowhere in Harare, thanks to the assistance from the Presidential Office.

When they were all on board and helmeted, Ghazi started up the engines, the rotors started to sweep round, but then Qudamah remembered the folded paper in his pocket. He jumped out while Ghazi reduced power, opened out the last item he had nearly missed and put it onto the embers of the fire to let it burn with the rest. He ran back to the helicopter and the blades picked up speed even as he climbed in. Ghazi took the helicopter off the ground and raised the gear. The familiar whine was a pleasing sound for the men to hear. The route was to be a straight line, fast speed and at a height of one hundred feet again above the ground, just as Anwar had done. The aircraft was identical to Anwar's. Ghazi watched over the systems closely for the entire journey.

They had a fairly level flight for the first thirty minutes, but as they left Zimbabwe and crossed into Mozambique the terrain rose up to over six thousand feet. There was a steep drop-off of four thousand feet in under five miles. The helicopter hugged the terrain faithfully and reliably at a steady hundred feet. Then they were clear of the mountains and the last ninety miles tailed off in a gentle slope down to the sea.

They crossed the coastline just to the south of Nova Sofala. The *Excelsior* had been cruising slowly north for eighty miles over the last five hours, and was exactly in position. As Ghazi flew the aircraft out across the water the men were pleased to see the shore lights get smaller, replaced by the friendly blue-white of the ship forty-five miles out to sea.

Ghazi pulled back the power, reducing the speed to a mere hover. He lowered the landing gear and skilfully manoeuvred the helicopter inch by inch directly over the helipad circle on the ship.

It touched down perfectly in the centre.

The entire operation had taken seven and a half hours, and had been accomplished with perfect results.

Deep in the hold of the ship, oblivious to the helicopter's arrival, Stella slept uneasily, but unchained, in her soundproofed room. She tossed and turned every now and again, while one of the Burka girls sat on the couch in the low light, reading, ever watchful over their charge.

It was 4.30am, on Thursday 16th April.

16

SOCHI

MALEKKA'S PLAN HAD been playing out well. In South Africa the events of Wednesday through into the early hours of Thursday morning had worked brilliantly for him, although he did not yet know of the destruction of Khatib's group. That wouldn't matter though; they had accomplished their mission for him.

However, the days' events were not yet concluded.

In Russia six thousand miles away they would host the key element planned with General Evgeny Kutuzov Vashinsky.

At about the same time that Malekka began talking to Stella on the *Excelsior* of his intent to steal the Alpha, General Vashinsky was arriving at his office in Moscow.

Today, Vashinsky said proudly to himself, years of planning would come together. The asset would to be moved. His friend Colonel Anatoly Linchuk would be relying on certain crucial actions.

Vashinsky was ready.

In fact, he had been ready for a very long time.

Vashinsky knew he belonged to a different era. He was the product of a union between a hardworking poor Muscovite of good character and a fine-looking merchant seaman who had served at Murmansk in the Second World War. The marriage started well, but the husband turned to drink which over several years increased considerably in volume. In addition to hitting his young wife when it pleased him, in one furious drunken stupor he also laid into the young Evgeny, then aged four. That proved to be a mistake. His wife had fought in the Army at Stalingrad and forgotten little of her training. Two days later she lay in wait for her drunken husband on his way home. He was eventually found in a roadside ditch, with his throat slit from ear to ear.

Evgeny enlisted in the army, excelled and rose in the ranks swiftly, making his mother proud. His qualities of calmness under pressure, great attention to detail and action devoid of emotion came to the notice of the KGB, which he was invited to join and within which he thrived. His one regret was not being able to pass on some of the later benefits of high position to his devoted mother, who sadly died of pneumonia not long after he joined the KGB. He was alone in the world with no relatives.

At thirty there was a short marriage, to a young girl from Leningrad, and for a while Evgeny was happy and enjoying life. But she died in childbirth, a personal blow from which he never really recovered. His career benefitted all the more from his undivided attention and energies. It became full of outstanding intelligence work from a fine mind and exemplary actions in the military, often with his friend Anatoly in the Spetsnaz. As he rose in the ranks of the KGB he executed, tortured and assassinated enough people to warrant both being rewarded accordingly and handled carefully. As Deputy Director of the FSB he became one of the ten most powerful men in Russia and the legitimate successor to his own boss, the Director himself, General Bortnikov.

However, time passed, and disillusionment festered. And so Vashinsky used his power, influence and skills in developing his project with Malekka, to create the wealth he should have had years ago.

Yes, he had been ready a long time.

Vashinsky planned to work late. Now, as he drank his morning coffee in his office, waiting calmly for events to unfold through the day into the evening, he reflected on what was needed later. It was all in place. And on how he had solved, somewhat brilliantly he thought, its most fundamental problem.

The solution had come quite innocently when Russia won its bid in 2006 to host the 2014 Winter Olympic Games at Sochi on the Black Sea, although at the time he hadn't even met Malekka. Vashinsky had smiled when he learned later of the number of new buildings that would be needed for the Winter Olympics. One hundred and ninety three. Plus the supporting infrastructure that embraced virtually every conceivable area of construction and development. It was perfect. He thought how the holiday town of Sochi that he knew and loved, which even before work began was the second largest and most popular holiday resort in Russia, had changed.

The overall Olympics development concept had been straightforward enough. Two clusters of buildings each containing an Olympic Village, one on the coast and the other in the mountains. The coastal cluster at Sochi itself would contain the new Olympic Park in the Adler district, closest to the airport, and comprise six new venues including a skating arena and the main Village.

The mountain cluster would be at Krasnaya Polyana, thirty-five kilometres north-east up in the Western Caucasus Mountains. It was an ideal setting for the snow events. Its summit was over two thousand three hundred metres and the ski runs would drop fifteen hundred metres, providing fast challenging courses. Krasnaya Polyana needed five ski complexes and a bobsleigh track, and its own Village.

The power grid for the region had to be upgraded two hundred and fifty percent, with a thermal power station at Sochi, five substations and the Krasnopolyanskaya hydroelectric station. New or upgraded telecommunications facilities would include broadcast infrastructure for radio and TV and the laying of eight hundred kilometres of fibre optic cables.

Transportation facilities would get new highways, roads and the enlarging of existing ones, especially the M27 coast motorway, railway modernisation and a new high-speed Moscow link. Sochi airport would have an extended runway and new terminal. Sochi's sea port and Tuapse's, eighty kilometres north-west on the coast, would be enlarged. There would have to be a considerable upgrading of the sewage and waste management facilities. A multitude of hotels and guest houses would go up, and, importantly, the housing development would stretch on five years after the end of the Games.

His thoughts were interrupted by a knock on the door to his office.

"Come in," said Vashinsky in answer.

Praporshchik[4] Tchepikova entered. Ah, this is the good looking one, thought Vashinsky. The messenger from Director Bortnikov walked over. He never knew which of the Director's staff was going to be sent down the corridor with the day's personal communiqués.

"Good morning, General," said the Praporshchik. "I have today's traffic from the Director for you."

"Good morning, Praporshchik. Thank you," he added as he held out his hand for the data stick.

This was a simple method by which to transfer

---

[4] *Similar to Warrant Officer.*

private messages and various 'Eyes Only' files to his immediate subordinate, and vice versa. The Director had decided that sometimes not everything should be recorded on the internal computer files and emails. A private code was still needed to access the data on the stick, of course, but it was useful to have this close and entirely private exchange between two of the most powerful men in Russia.

He plugged the stick into the usual USB port on his personal laptop, which immediately sent a coded email response to the Director to confirm receipt of the stick and of today's traffic. This was required within fifteen minutes of issue or the data would self-shred, so the stick was always plugged in promptly by the other party.

"Anything to go back, sir?" asked the Praporshchik.

"Just a little," replied the General, and handed over his own coded data stick.

"Thank you, sir. Will there be anything else, sir?"

"No, Praporshchik, thank you, that will be all."

"Yes, sir," and the young woman turned and headed towards the door. Vashinsky's eyes followed her legs as she walked off. Such a nice pair of legs, he thought.

He returned to his thoughts on the Olympics.

The vast construction work, he had first read in the Government papers, would require both massive land movement and use of large prefabricated parts. The world's largest diggers, cranes and plant were needed to maximise efficiency, and large lorries to transport them. A suitable corporation to handle this had to be found.

This had suited Vashinsky's own needs perfectly. As had the investment requirement. The cost of the Winter Olympics was enormous. Three hundred and twenty-seven billion Rubles. That's almost eleven billion US dollars, Vashinsky had said to himself. Plus the housing.

Russia was very proud to have won the bid for the

2014 Olympics; but that had been in 2006. In 2008, the global economies collapsed, and the worldwide financial crisis hit Russia badly too. Expenditure budgeted in the good times of 2005-6 but ending eight years in the future quickly became a liability. Suddenly foreign investment in Russia was much sought-after.

The asset would require a very large truck to move it. The Olympics development project needed oversized trucks. And money.

Vashinsky had a brilliant solution.

In 2008, he along with others from his Government attended the signing in Geneva by El Salvador of the Geneva Protocol[5], not because he attached any particular importance to El Salvador but because it offered him the opportunity to travel to Geneva and see his terrorist partner - for that's what Malekka is, Vashinsky said to himself, a terrorist; or does that make him someone else's freedom fighter, as they say? - but then, what do I care, he thought.

He had stayed in a magnificent suite in the Hotel des Bergues, the oldest hotel in the city and still one of its finest, overlooking Lake Geneva and the famous Water Jet inseparably linked with the city.

The two men met up quietly one afternoon. Vashinsky outlined to Malekka the importance of the 2014 Winter Olympic Games.

"... and so after the Games, when the media has left and the spotlight gone, the large transportation that our enterprise requires is available and already in place."

---

[5] *The Protocol for the Prohibition of the Use in War of Asphyxiating, Poisonous or other Gases, and of Bacteriological Methods of Warfare, referred to as the Geneva Protocol, is a treaty prohibiting the first use of chemical and biological weapons. 137 nations have ratified the Treaty. El Salvador signed on 26 Feb 2008.*

"Yes. I see. Yes, very good indeed, my friend," said Malekka. "What size do we need the trucks to be?"

"Internal dimensions of fifteen metres long, four and a half wide, four metres tall. And they must be able to carry a weight of thirty-eight thousand kilograms. This will meet the Olympics development specification easily, and, more importantly, handle the asset."

"Can you guarantee the contracts?"

"Oh yes," said Vashinsky, with conviction. "My colleagues in the Ministries will always listen to the FSB. And all the more so if you and your Iranian brothers bring long-term financial investment along with the construction companies."

Shortly afterwards, the Russian Government had been delighted to award three construction contracts to foreign corporations that also took a sizeable chunk of the Russian Olympics and housing investment portfolio. It was particularly pleasing that these should come from one of Russia's most important allies, Iran. It was particularly pleasing to Vashinsky that the corporations should be owned or controlled by Barakah Malekka.

The road haulage corporation also operated essential dedicated shipping. In a simple 'roll on, roll off' ferry fashion, the huge lorries were loaded with their oversized cargo, then put to sea, driven off at the receiving port and taken directly to Sochi or up to Krasnaya Polyana. The process was reversed as required. Tuapse proved to be the ideal port; its facilities could accommodate the weight and length of these monster trucks, the M27 virtually ran alongside the dock and the trucks could easily join the road and roll straight down to Sochi.

The personnel at the port soon became accustomed to seeing these huge trucks roll off and on their mother ships, as did the people travelling the M27 highway and the site personnel at Sochi and Krasnaya Polyana. Their movement became just another ordinary part of the great proud 2014 Russian Winter Olympics project, and the extensive housing development of the area that continued after the Games had finished.

The meeting in 2008 had ended with one last little negotiation with Malekka.

"Now of course," Vashinsky had said, "when you are awarded these government construction projects, you will obviously make millions of dollars from them."

"I sincerely hope so," smiled back Malekka. I can see what's coming now, he thought. This old Communist is more of a Capitalist at heart than many we already do business with in the West. "What do you have in mind?"

"Cuba."

"Cuba?" asked Malekka. "What, all of it?"

They both laughed.

"That would be a little hard even for me to achieve."

Vashinsky smiled. "No, not all of it. Just a little piece of it. I thought, perhaps a thirty acre estate along a nice sandy shoreline and perhaps a five thousand square metre villa on it."

Malekka thought for a moment, and then said, "Agreed." And then added, "But there is one thing you haven't told me."

"What is that, my friend?"

"Why Sochi? I mean, I understand about the trucks and the dimensions. It's perfect. Brilliant. But, what is the importance of the Sochi area to us?"

"Oh, didn't I mention it?" smiled Vashinsky. "Deep in the mountains, directly off the road connecting Sochi and Krasnaya Polyana, is our West Caucasus Defence Base. And, within it, the West Caucasus nuclear arsenal."

17

THEFT TWO

THE FOUR MEN drove along in silence from Sochi towards Krasnaya Polyana. The highway was hewn impressively out of the West Caucasus mountains left of the Mzymta River, which began as a trickle in their heart and drained fifty miles later into the Black Sea at Sochi. As the mountains soared above the Akhtsu Gorge the thick greenery of spruce and fir gave way to grey rock and then snow-capped summits at nine thousand feet. The scene carried the essence of nature's pure beauty.

Colonel Anatoly Linchuk had enjoyed many holidays at Sochi's good beaches and hotels, and had often skied at Krasnaya Polyana. Sadly, the local area had changed drastically because of the Olympics. Too much concrete, too many big hotels and houses. It was almost unrecognisable to him now.

They were nearly at the Akhtsu Tunnel which snaked through the mountains for almost two miles. The largely secret West Caucasus Defence Base was located behind. Fifty years before, several million tons of rock had been blasted out from the heart of the towering mountains to create an enormous cavern not too dissimilar from the American NORAD centre in Colorado. The WCDB had extensive communications facilities and command and control personnel in direct contact with Stavropol to the north-east and Moscow itself. Its most ominous and bleak rôle was to house the West Caucasus nuclear arsenal.

The most fearful weapon was the RT-2UTTH Topol-M, which NATO had given the name SS-27, or Sickle B. It carried an eight hundred kiloton warhead, fifty times more powerful than the Hiroshima bomb, had a range of six thousand five hundred miles and was a true Inter-Continental Ballistic Missile. Launched from a mobile platform it would be virtually impossible to detect or counter in a wartime situation.

The older OTR-23 Oka, named formally by NATO as the SS-23 Spider and known more colloquially as the Spider 2-3, was a weapon Anatoly knew well. Three decades had passed since it had first appeared, although technically the weapon had only actually been in service for four or five years.

It too was very much a mobile weapon. Enclosed within a transporter, the missile had a nuclear payload of five hundred kilotons, around thirty-five times the power of the Hiroshima bomb. Its range was five hundred kilometres and therefore the Spider wasn't an ICBM but a tactical theatre weapon, intended as support for conventional Russian forces on the battlefield, particularly in Europe. Its shorter range had taken the Spider into considerable controversy that made it perfect for Vashinsky's plan, which Anatoly and his hand-picked crew from the Spetsnaz were about to execute.

When the Spider 2-3 first appeared in 1980 the USSR had claimed its range was two hundred and fifty kilometres. The Americans knew the range was in excess of four hundred. The USSR conceded, and the missile was included within the Intermediate-range Nuclear Forces Treaty then under discussion between the USA and the USSR. In 1987 Mikhail Gorbachev and Ronald Reagan ratified the INF treaty, by which a number of tactical theatre nuclear weapons would be dismantled and destroyed. This included the USSR's SS-23 Spider, traded with the American Pershing Ib and II missiles.

A considerable number of the Spiders were destroyed. Unfortunately the exact number of SS-23s that the Votkinsk machine building plant in the heart of central Russia had actually manufactured had, either through an innocent error or a deliberate one, been mis-declared. In order to comply those omitted from the Treaty merely had their 9M714K-Alpha launch and control units quietly removed and returned to Votkinsk. This allowed genuine deniability by the USSR of their present existence as an in-service weapon, yet retained an eventual re-deployment ability of the remaining part of the system if ever required.

The situation was more confused since at least one hundred and thirty had also been deployed to Warsaw Pact countries, including East Germany, Bulgaria and Czechoslovakia, in part to avoid declaring them in the INF Treaty. However, although these were recalled, when the USSR itself collapsed in 1991 a number of the countries of which it had been comprised not only suddenly found themselves to be independent states once more but discovered SS-23s still sitting within their territory.

Frankly, thought Anatoly, when the Berlin Wall fell and the Soviet Union finally went these dangerous weapons had ended up scattered all over the place. There had been similar stories about submarines and their missiles, both nuclear and conventional, located at various ports of countries that one day had been part of the Soviet Union and the Warsaw Pact and then the next had not.

Thankfully order was eventually restored, the weapons were brought back and the new Russia had control!.

Every now and again one of the present total of twenty-four Spiders at the WCDB arsenal was quietly moved back up to Votkinsk and destroyed along with its Alpha. This was done discreetly. An *en masse* movement of the weapons would certainly alarm foreign intelligence located in Russia and be spotted by American satellites.

Actually the fact that Russia still had the SS-23s and that their destruction was quietly ongoing was known to American intelligence. The Russians generally made the transport of an SS-23 coincide with an American satellite pass. If missed, another would see the transport train come down from Votkinsk to Tuapse and go back up. Images would also be captured of the Spider being removed from the train to the factory two miles from Votkinsk station.

This kept the West calm and satisfied, and no great fuss was made. After all, although the weapons had been fully maintained they were old, their Alpha units had been removed and, in spite of the Ukraine, relations with the Russians were still better than they had been for decades. There was no point in seeking to embarrass the Russians over this issue. Particularly as doing so might then also focus Russia's, and global, attention onto the actual number of the USA's own Pershing missiles due to be destroyed by now but that in fact still existed.

Apparently the Americans, too, had also incurred a considerable delay in keeping to the timeline of the INF Treaty. This could prove to be extremely embarrassing for the Americans and the current Presidency. So there was a kind of mutual understanding, to leave the matter alone and let the destruction of the weapons on both sides, although late, proceed along quietly, watched by their respective eyes a hundred miles or so above.

General Vashinsky and the FSB knew the overhead timings of the satellite that, amongst its other duties, watched the West Caucasus Defence Base. In fact, the FSB knew the orbital movements of all American and other foreign satellites. Tonight, it was critical that Anatoly's actions were definitely *outside* that viewing window and so not picked up by the Americans.

They were exactly on time. At the Akhtsu Tunnel the central reserve and safety barriers of the two-lane highway disappeared. Immediately before the tunnel was an unsignposted off-road similar to a works entrance or unfinished lay-by. It appeared too late for traffic travelling south exiting the tunnel to use, and traffic heading north had to slow well in advance before turning across the carriageways. It was intentionally designed for use only by those who knew of its existence.

The driver slowed and crossed the carriageways proficiently. Thick hedges and tall trees ran off left; the dirt road bent right and paralleled the tunnel for fifty yards. The truck was quickly lost to traffic. The road curved left, widened and suddenly acquired a tarmac surface.

The truck halted at a gated checkpoint. Steel fencing extended ten feet either side and turned at right angles to run along the road a hundred yards to the mountainside. Bland lampposts switched themselves on in the failing sunlight. At the rock face a large gaping hole pushed into the very heart of the mountain.

Two armed soldiers came out of a hut and Colonel Linchuk presented his credentials. He and his three companions wore the uniform of the 54th Guards Kutuzov Rocket Division of the 27th Guards Missile Army, with the flashes of the Strategic Rocket Forces of which they are a part. Quartered north-east of Moscow at Vladimir, the closest Rocket Forces base to the manufacturing plant at Votkinsk albeit 1,000 miles distant, its members were fairly frequent visitors. Linchuk had had himself and his Spetsnaz companions stationed covertly within the Division. His credentials did not say Colonel Anatoly Linchuk. For two months now he had been Major Sergei Rozhkov, and his colleagues similarly carried covert IDs.

The men had travelled down two days before, in accordance with their orders received from Moscow. They took a military flight from Vladimir to Stavropol, drove down to Sochi and up the A148 to the WCDB.

The gates were opened. They drove through in silence and on to the tunnel. Four metres high and six wide, it stretched ominously into the interior. No other people or vehicles were anywhere to be seen. In fact the tunnel ran for over a mile westwards before opening into a similar area with another manned command post. It then led very discreetly onto a small public road running north further into the mountains and, in the other direction, back down to the coast.

The tunnel was designed to channel the majority of a nuclear strike blast out to the other end, bypassing the WCDB itself. Two massive thirty ton blast doors were set into the north wall. The first gleaming steel door slowly began to open thirty yards away, extending like the tongue of a giant Iguana to snatch all it found into its dark belly. The lorry turned right through the hole in the rock face.

None of the men was prepared for what they saw; someone let out a "God Almighty".

They were facing Armageddon. The awesome power of nuclear technology encased within cold titanium, steel and complex composites, ready to wreak instant horrific destruction upon the flesh and blood of millennia of humanity. A vast rectangular hall two hundred feet high and four hundred wide stretched a third of a mile straight ahead. Harsh cold lighting thrown down from a grey roof illuminated the voluminous cavern, glinting on row after row of Russia's nuclear and conventional missile arsenal laid out before them. Fifty of the very latest Topol Ms (SS-27s), eighty-two Topols (SS-25 Sickles), the twenty-four R-400 Okas (SS-23 Spiders), and a myriad of non-nuclear missiles, other launch and support vehicles, mobile radar guidance systems, tanks, and transporters of all shapes and sizes down to the most basic truck and five-seat four-wheel drive, all stood to attention in hideous rows of pending lethality. Numerous technicians, maintenance crews, office personnel and armed soldiers milled around in their designated tasks, oblivious of the enormity of their routine. The five two-story buildings that were the complex's nerve centre were off to the right.

Nevertheless, as a soldier and a good Russian Rozhkov felt pride and excitement, too, at the sight before him. He was also pleased to be on the brink of generating a considerable amount of money for himself as a result of the madness of this super-power one-up-man-ship.

Sergei got out of the truck at the guard post. One of the two soldiers manning the entrance approached. "Good evening, Major, we've been expecting you."

"Good evening, sergeant," replied Rozhkov, returning his salute.

"I hope you had a good journey down."

"Yes, yes, it was fine," said the Major, "but somewhat tiring. Vladimir is a long way away from here. Which is the item?"

He knew perfectly well which was the item, but this

sounded better.

"Well, sir, they all look alike don't they," said the sergeant, but then seeing that his attempt at humour was neither appreciated nor shared by the senior officer in front of him, quickly looked at his own paper notes and added, "It's the next one in the row of them, sir, serial number 3974389df2. A five hundred kiloton one."

"Thank you, sergeant," said Sergei. "Where do I find Lieutenant-General Ramazanov for verification?"

"The first building, sir," said the sergeant, indicating the closest of the five brick structures over on the right. "If you go through the main front doors and through the pair of doors directly facing you as you enter, you get to the Central Control. His office is straight across the other side to the rear."

"Right," replied Major Rozhkov. He turned and shouted out, "Stanislav," and beckoned to one of his men to get out of the truck. The man who had been sitting next to him got down and walked over.

"Stanislav, you need to come with me."

"Yes, sir."

"Sergeant, where do they park the truck?"

"Oh yes, sir, I'll go and tell them."

"Good, please go ahead."

The sergeant walked to the driver and gave instructions of where to park up, and said for them to bring the keys to him. Major Rozhkov and Stanislav walked smartly over to the building indicated and opened the door. A wide corridor went off right and left and directly opposite was the sign 'Central Control' by a pair of doors. They passed through.

A maze of long tables and computer screens filled the room, staffed by close to fifty men and women of various ages and rank entering data, instructions, monitoring streams of figures, talking quietly into headsets or viewing glowing radial arms methodically sweeping a circle. The WCDB not only had a nuclear arsenal but was the military's control centre of its forces for the southern part of the Russian Federation, responsible for border monitoring of neighbouring Georgia, Azerbaijan, the Ukraine and Kazakhstan, the airspace above and any overfly infringements, the control of all ground troop and Air Force movements in the area and all surface and submarine movements of the Navy in the Black Sea to the west and the Caspian Sea to the east.

Major Rozhkov and Stanislav followed the passageways at the walls round to Lieutenant-General Ramazanov's office opposite. Sergei knocked and they went inside. The General and another Major were both leaning over a table looking at a screen in the outer office and straightened as they caught sight of their visitors.

After salutes and the preliminaries the General said to Rozhkov, "Major, may I see your orders."

"Yes, sir." He handed them over, and then took them back once General Ramazanov had flicked through them.

"Please now open your Code Envelope, Major."

"Yes, sir." Rozhkov brought out a sealed envelope from his inside breast pocket, broke the red seal and removed the card inside. A series of numbers and letters in large bold typeface was printed on it.

The General turned to his accompanying officer and said, "Major Tutov?"

Tutov brought out a similar envelope and handed it to the General, who then also broke its seal and removed the card inside. He said to his visitors, "Verification procedure."

"Yes, sir," replied Sergei.

Sergei held out his card to show the printed characters. Tutov read them and checked them against those on their own card, and said, "Character match confirmed, sir."

General Ramazanov said, "I confirm character match."

He then said to Sergei, "Your Code is confirmed, Major Rozhkov."

"Thank you, sir."

Tutov then took the card from General Ramazanov and held it out before the two visiting officers. They both looked at the series of numbers and letters, and compared them with those on their card.

Stanislav said to Major Rozhkov, "Character match confirmed, sir."

Rozhkov acknowledged with, "I confirm character match."

He then said to Ramazanov, "Your Code is confirmed, General Ramazanov."

"Thank you, gentlemen," said General Ramazanov. "Now step this way please."

He walked them over a few yards to a man sitting in front of one of the control consoles. The man looked up.

"Final verification please, Captain."

"Yes, sir." The Captain sent the authorisation request to the Central Control in Moscow. A series of large numbers and letters appeared across the middle of the screen in response. Both pairs of officers confirmed that the on-screen characters matched those on their cards.

Vashinsky had organised this well, thought Linchuk.

"Very good, gentlemen," said General Ramazanov. "Now we just need the hand prints, please."

"Yes, sir," said Major Rozhkov, and placed his right hand on the scanner where the Captain indicated. His hand print was quickly scanned, sent to Moscow, compared and the confirming verification came back.

Sergei said, "Your turn, Stanislav."

"Yes, sir," and Stanislav did the same. The WCDB promptly obtained the positive verification result back from Moscow.

The General said formally, "Very well Major Rozhkov, you are authorised to proceed."

"Thank you, sir."

"Have a good journey back."

The men saluted, and Sergei and Stanislav were escorted out of the building by Major Tutov, who was tasked with confirming to the guards personnel that the verification and authorisation procedures had been completed, and that they may now permit the vehicle to be accessed and removed from the arsenal, to begin its journey to Votkinsk. Tutov said his goodbyes, and returned to the operations building.

Sergei looked over at the Spider 2-3. It was as impressive as he had always remembered. It might have been a little older than some of the others in the Arsenal, but it was still a terrifyingly lethal and effective weapon. The missile was entirely enclosed within a Transport Erector Launcher, based on the remarkable amphibious BAZ-6944, and was slightly over three metres wide, three high and just under twelve in length. Eight drive wheels with wide-section pressure-changing tyres rolled the vehicle along, with two fixed double-axle pairs in the rear and two steerable in front.

The TEL's four hundred horsepower diesel engine could not only achieve a road speed of sixty-five kilometres per hour but also, as it was amphibious with excellent buoyancy should it have to plunge into a river or lake, could make water speed of ten kilometres an hour. It was impossible to guess the deadly contents lying within; it appeared just as any other military vehicle, as innocuous as a troop carrier, in a standard dark green and brown camouflage paint. Except, it was much larger.

Sergei walked over patted the side of the vehicle, feeling the cold metal underneath ready to spring to life at a moment's notice.

The sergeant had briefly returned to the command box to get some papers needed for the sign-off. He was back quickly, and held the clipboard out to the Major.

"Would you please sign here, sir," asked the sergeant.

"I will once we have done the usual inspection," replied the Major. He indicated to Stanislav and the other men, waiting by the Spider, to run through the usual pre-motion checklist that applies to all SS-23s.

"She's fully fuelled I take it?" said Sergei to the sergeant.

"Oh yes, sir."

"I know we're only going up to Tuapse to get the transport train north, on that ghastly journey to Votkinsk," he said, smiling for once to the sergeant and with a hint of a moan, "but I like always to have a full tank to start off with."

"Yes, sir," replied the sergeant, who was glad to see that the Major seemed more relaxed now.

Sergei's men finished the inspection. Stanislav came over.

"Sir, the check list has been completed, and all is satisfactory. We are ready to depart at your order."

"Very well, Stanislav, thank you."

Major Rozhkov scribbled a signature on the papers that the sergeant held out once more, and called out, "Ok boys, fire her up." His men opened the doors to the front cabin on both sides and got on board. He took his file copies and put them in his pocket.

"Ok sergeant, we're ready."

"Very well, sir, I hope all has proved satisfactory."

"Yes most satisfactory, and I shall mention so in my report." He asked for the sergeant's name and made a note of it, which pleased the young soldier considerably. Praise of any kind from a senior officer in the army was good but one from a Major in the Strategic Rocket Forces was particularly worthwhile.

"Goodbye, sergeant."

"Yes, sir, thank you, sir. Goodbye."

They saluted.

Major Rozhkov climbed aboard, took the end of the comfortable four-berth bench seat and pulled the armrest to his left down to get settled. With guidance from two movement marshals who had come over once they heard the massive engine roar into life, Stanislav first put the motor into reverse and watched in his mirrors as he was signalled back. He put the gears into forward, and on clearance from the front marshal nudged the vehicle ahead and to the right.

He passed slowly through the command check post, and paused as the enormous blast door was opened up again for them. The vehicle moved out into the tunnel and followed the road back to the first command post; the two soldiers there opened the gates, saluting the Major as they passed by. Major Sergei Rozhkov returned their salute and then smiled quietly to himself as they pulled away.

The night was pitch black. They reached the A148 at the Akhtsu Tunnel, turned right and headed south, the powerful head beams of the TEL lighting the way. The roads were completely deserted. They joined the M27 at the outskirts of Sochi and headed up the coast. Construction crews on the other side of the M27 at Sochi were working under night lights but nobody paid any attention to the TEL. In fact they probably hadn't been able to see or hear them, the din from the site was so intense.

The TEL moved swiftly along the road. When the vehicle and its deadly missile passed the outskirts of Khosta five miles along the M27 the transporter slowed and pulled into one of the new lay-bys, a large parking area created behind a row of trees left standing as a natural windbreak. There was still no-one else on the road, no-one else in the lay-by.

Except, that is, one of the now-familiar very large haulage trucks, brought in specially for the Olympic work sites from 2009 by Malekka's corporations. Its specific purpose was to move oversized items of plant machinery and other very large objects.

Including this Spider 2-3 nuclear missile.

The truck had been waiting only six minutes. The driver saw them. Leaving the engine running and in the parked position, he jumped down from the cabin, walked quickly to the end of his truck and unlocked a recess box housing a series of hydraulic levers.

He pulled one, and two large stabilising legs at each corner of the rear of the truck lowered down to the ground. The man worked another lever and the rear door slowly began to lower. Three supporting legs midway along the tailgate extended and sat solidly on the ground as the end of the tail door came to a rest on the tarmac. The tailgate now formed a gentle-sloping and extremely strong ramp into the truck.

The TEL containing the five hundred kiloton Spider 2-3 slowed to a crawl. Without stopping it moved smoothly onto the tailgate ramp. As soon as the vehicle was inside the man at the hydraulic levers reversed the procedure and the tail door of the truck closed.

The entire loading process had taken ninety seconds.

The driver got back on board, put the truck into gear

and began to pull out onto the M27. As he did so, there was a cheer from inside the cabin of the mobile launcher of the SS-23, as the four men congratulated themselves. They just had enough room to get out of the machine and walk around a little. Major Sergei Rozhkov had gone now; Colonel Anatoly Linchuk was back. He got out his cell phone and sent a coded text comprised of six numbers. The recipient, his friend General Vashinsky, sent a numbered response.

Two minutes later, the commander of the unit at the special heavy transport train waiting at Tuapse was brought a message by the communications officer received from Moscow. The message read: *'Operation cancelled. Return to base immediately.'*

With a deep sigh and quietly cursing under his breath, wondering what was the point of such a huge waste of time, the commander told the waiting communications officer to acknowledge the order, and to instruct the train operators to pull out and begin the journey back to Votkinsk. The man disappeared to carry out his instructions.

It seemed an awfully long way to have gone only to have the exercise cancelled at the last minute; but then, he thought, this was Russia, and these things sometime happen. And if his superiors wanted to send him this long distance over three days, only to have him return empty handed another three days later, then that was their concern and nothing to do with him. Why should he worry? He just followed orders.

The train was under way in fifteen minutes. It jolted forwards as it started to pull out of Tuapse. The commander sat down in his carriage once more, put his feet up on the seats in front of him and picked up his book, returning to the page he had just left.

At the same time, the Central Records Bureau at the

Kremlin, the computer database at the headquarters of the Spetsnaz and all associated electronic records facilities were simultaneously wiped clean of any traces of a Major Sergei Rozhkov and the three members of his unit, including records of their orders, fingerprints and the movement allocation numbers and letters for an SS-23 contained in the Code Envelopes. Any indication of the movement of a Spider, or of any link between Colonel Anatoly Linchuk, the other three and the operation that they had just successfully undertaken, instantly vanished.

The truck left the M27 at the Tuapse South Port Heavy Junction and rolled slowly to the Quayside embarkation point. The driver handed some paperwork down to the young Customs Officer who had left the crew room and the final twenty minutes of the football on TV. The man quickly looked at the papers, said it's a heavy load you've got tonight, the driver laughed and said yes it always was. The young Customs Officer didn't bother with an inspection; that had stopped long ago, when the Port Authorities had relaxed such protocols because of sheer quantity and the need not to slow the construction schedule. And who wanted to inspect yet another piece of large plant machinery anyway.

It was lucky for the young Customs Officer that he had chosen not to inspect the truck. Tonight his wife would not become a widow, and the four very capable Special Forces soldiers of the Spetsnaz inside the truck, crouched low with their suppressed nine millimetre AS Val assault rifles ready, would not have to kill him, nor would they now have to raid the service office and kill the other Customs officials on the night shift, before embarking quickly on board the ship and putting to sea.

Instead, the driver and the young Customs Officer

both signed off their respective forms, and one headed back to his TV, and life, and the other put the very large truck into gear and slowly drove it onto the waiting ship. Thirty minutes later, the ship was at sea.

The silent men in the hold of the truck saw the red warning light go off and before long could feel the gentle swaying motion of the ship. They stood at the front of the hold, congratulating themselves again, waiting for the connecting door to open so that they could go out onto the deck of the ship.

It was then that Colonel Anatoly Linchuk again released the safety catch on his AS Val rifle and with a quick burst of virtually silent automatic fire shot his three companions dead.

He knocked four times on the front wall. A door opened and he got out of the truck. Some of the ship's crew entered and removed the three lifeless bodies. The journey to Istanbul would be around five hundred and fifty miles.

As soon as the ship was over deep water and the bodies had been weighted with chains and concrete slabs, and just as Ghazi was landing the helicopter with the Alpha on board the *Excelsior*, the bodies were dropped quietly over the side.

Colonel Linchuk lay on the bed in his small cabin, enjoying the large vodka and his new circumstances. His friend Vashinsky would be pleased with his success. Linchuk knew that the train wouldn't be arriving back at Votkinsk for another three days or maybe four, depending on the interaction schedules of the public and freight commercial trains. His superiors wouldn't even connect up the two ends of the puzzle for a week or two at least. If they ever did, that is. He thought about the money he was to be paid. He thought again, too, about the Spider.

One of the great advantages, he knew, of the Spider was that the entire weapon was self-contained. The crew has no need to step outside the TEL to prepare the missile and needs no extraneous instructions or command centre relays to input calculations, target details or flight trajectory for launch. The newer ICBMs need a support vehicle. But not the Spider. The Spider 2-3 was neat and tidy and lethal - a true stand-alone nuclear weapon. And it could be prepared for firing in less than ten minutes.

That is, once it has had its launch and control 9M714K-Alpha unit put back inside it.

Thirty-five hours later the ship passed through the Bosphorus into the Sea of Marmara, then routed through the Dardanelles, out into the Aegean and on towards the open Mediterranean Sea.

The Spider 2-3 rested in the truck below deck in the hold, rolling and swaying with the ship in a waltz of calmness and gentleness that belied the assimilation of lethal ferocity encased within its shell.

18

TRACKING

DESPITE THE DEADLY seriousness of the circumstances, JP still managed to enjoy the flight in the Gripen back to the UK in the early hours of Thursday morning. The engine belted out an impressive eighteen thousand pounds of thrust at takeoff with afterburner, and then a steady twelve thousand dry for the majority of the journey. The flight was supersonic, except when the pilot refuelled three times en route. JP declined the pilot's offer to handle the controls for a while. Any other time; but for now he wanted to stay focused.

The fact that Malekka had taken the Alpha unit from the Fincrest Centre was actually good news, in a number of ways. It meant that Malekka already had, or was getting, an SS-23 Spider and was planning to launch it, not just park it in some city and blow it up. So, follow the Alpha, and we can get to the bomb. He was sure of that more than ever now. Second, it also meant that Stella had given them the information they needed about the Centre, and so they will have stopped working on her.

JP just hoped and prayed that she hadn't put up too much resistance. He was well aware of the cruelty people can release on each other to obtain information. His father had experienced it in Vietnam as a prisoner whilst in the SAS attached to Australian forces. And his grandfather had been the guest of the Gestapo in France in World War II when captured on a mission for the SOE. After telling them nothing for over a month he made a spectacular escape, returned to England and resumed his work against them. Following four months in hospital, that is.

JP had had his own experiences in the SAS and undergone much torture resistance training. He would not wish any of it on Stella, and hoped she had not been physically or psychologically maimed. Assuming that she had survived. They might have just killed her as soon as they had the information, he thought soberly. Though his calculation was that they would keep her alive and put her to other uses. He didn't much like where that thinking took him either.

The flight was six hours. The Gripen touched down at 8am at RAF Northolt on the outskirts of West London, a full twenty-four hours ahead of the earliest commercial flight. Saving a day in critical times could be very useful.

A car was waiting, and he went straight to Claridge's Hotel. On the way JP called Melton on a secure line who asked that they meet as soon as possible after he had checked in.

JP also sent a quick text message on his other phone. It read, *'In town. Stand by.'* The reply came back almost immediately. *'Ok.'*

He showered and by 11.30am was walking into the same safe meeting venue at Hanover Square.

"Ah, JP, good," said Charles, getting up from the boardroom table and strolling over, again, to shake his friend's hand.

"Hello, Charlie," said JP, and added, "Good morning, Lieutenant," to Jane Chapman who was in the same chair as before.

"Hello, Mr Peregrine," said the Lieutenant, "I hope

the flight we laid on for you was a smooth one?"

"JP, or Jim, please," said JP, and the Lieutenant smiled in response. "Yes, it was smooth, and very fast, thank you." He sat down. "So, what's the latest?" The head was now taken by Melton.

"Well they certainly made a real mess of the Fincrest Centre," said Charles. "There was a team of five of them in all, they came in from Zimbabwe like I told you and were very slick and very professional. They were in and out of the building within just a few minutes, and had a helicopter waiting for them at Musina, which then flew them across the border. At least, we assume they came in from Zimbabwe, because that's where they flew out to, although we don't actually know that for sure as we only picked them up three miles from the Fincrest building in the car on their way in. But it seems logical enough, and fits with what you discovered from the terrorist cell in Cape Town that threw the bomb." JP gave a silent nod. Melton continued, "They flew across Zimbabwe, landed at Harare, some of them left the aircraft which then took off again and crossed over into Zambia. The helicopter landed at Lusaka, where the remaining three left the aircraft and split up. They all basically vanished."

"What about the helicopter," asked JP, "What did they find out from that?"

"Well that seems to have been a bit of a botched-up job. The drone hung around for another hour or so; actually there were two, they sent a replacement in as the first was getting very low on fuel and came back after the switch. But the drone couldn't follow the men at Lusaka, as they had all but vanished. There was nothing for it to see or do any more, or so they thought, and…" Melton paused.

"Oh, no, surely not," said JP with exasperation in his

voice.

"Yes... as they weren't supposed to be there anyway, Langley recalled the UAV back to Makhado."

JP put his elbows on the table, and his head in his hands.

"I don't think that was so smart," he said.

"Well, no. The Americans sent their agents out to the airport straight away. As soon as the helicopter landed they immediately asked the Zambian government to impound it, and the understanding was that it would be. So the drone was recalled. It was the middle of the night there and by the time things got moving in Zambia diplomatically and their instructions implemented at grass roots it was all too late."

"So - don't tell me - when the Yanks arrived the helicopter had vanished?"

"Yes. While they were trying to get out to the airport, mysteriously there were sudden road works that sprang up from nowhere, and they couldn't get in for two or three hours. Apparently another pilot took the aircraft two hours later and flew it off somewhere. No flight plan was filed."

"Damn," said JP quietly. "Damn. This man Malekka's a nightmare. He's got it all planned beautifully."

"Like I said Jimmy, he's a smart one, for sure."

JP paused and then asked, "Anything in Harare?"

"No, nothing. That's considerably more difficult even than Zambia. As you know the Americans' relationship with Zimbabwe isn't much better than ours."

"So are there any leads from this at all?" asked JP.

"Frankly, no," said a dejected Melton. "Malekka - if he actually *is* the one running this thing, we still don't even know that for sure - has outsmarted us all the way.

And what hasn't helped us one little bit is the fact that they seem to have had the full collaboration or co-operation anyway of that madman Mugabe in Zimbabwe. They were given right of overfly in the country, and they refuelled at Harare. It seems quite logical to assume the operation started from somewhere in Zimbabwe too, as I said."

"We have all the film, JP," said Lieutenant Chapman. She turned to Melton. "Shall I run it, sir?"

"Yes, Lieutenant, go ahead, please," said Melton. He spoke again to JP. "The UAV tracked them throughout. You can watch the whole bloody thing on television, just like a 9pm family movie."

The Lieutenant worked one of the remote controls on the table. The video of the Fincrest Centre taken from forty thousand feet appeared on the screens, and the three people in the room watched silently. They saw the figures of the men move up to the administration building, go inside, exit a few minutes later and then drive off. They saw them take off in the helicopter from Musina and route through to Harare, watched some of the men leave at the last minute and the aircraft take off again. And they saw the helicopter cross into Zambia and land at Lusaka. They watched as the last of the men exited the aircraft, split up and were driven off.

The screens went blank and then flickered back on again. The last images from the UAVs were of the bombed car burning at the Musina airstrip and the destruction at the Fincrest Centre.

"Ok, thank you, Jane," said Melton. The Lieutenant switched the screens off.

There was silence for a while. JP poured coffee for them all.

"Charlie, this man Khatib that had thrown the bomb in Cape Town... I was holding him over a two hundred foot drop and trying to pull him up onto the ledge, and he was keen to answer my questions. I don't think he lied. He was a mercenary, not a Muslim extremist; he wanted to live, not die. He was adamant that Zimbabwe was important, although he just didn't know in what way. Now it might just be that it was because the helicopter was overflying and landing at Harare and dropping people off to escape. Which means that the Alpha was flown on to Zambia. But, it's also possible that there was more to it than that. Maybe the Alpha was left in Harare and one of the three men has it. Or... maybe they got the Alpha out of the helicopter in some other way."

"What are you saying, JP, that they dropped it? Parachuted it?"

"Sir, that might explain something that I've been wondering," said Lieutenant Chapman.

"What, Jane?"

"Well, sir, it zig-zagged. The helicopter zig-zagged in Zimbabwe, but then when it left Harare it flew to Zambia in a dead straight line."

Melton and JP stared at each other, and then turned and stared at her.

"Did it?" they asked at the same time. Neither of them had spotted that.

The Lieutenant smiled, and said, "Yes, gentlemen, it did. Not often, but it definitely zig-zagged."

Melton pointed to the remote close to her, and they looked at the screens again as the Lieutenant played the video images once more. It was unmistakable. Three or four pronounced course variations in Zimbabwe; none on the route to Zambia.

When the screens went off again, Melton spoke first.

"You're quite right, Jane. So that leads to the next question - why. Why did they do that? Temporary instrument failure so they had to follow land markings, roads? Zimbabwe air traffic control required it? Or, the most obvious - they were covering something."

"I think they knew the South Africans have a very sharp and well equipped air force," said JP. "The Fincrest is a military centre, and they were concerned the Saffers might respond quickly and get some tracking over them in Zimbabwe, possibly even Zambia. Of course, the South Africans wouldn't know if or what has been stolen at that time, since the Centre's been destroyed and is still on fire."

"If they thought the Saffers could respond that quickly, then they were definitely covering something," said Melton.

"They thought they might be followed," said Jane. "Which mattered to them in Zimbabwe, but not in Zambia."

"Yes. We know they've gone for the Alpha. And I think they dropped it," said JP. "It wouldn't have been left in the helicopter in Zambia as it could have been impounded. Either it's a massive double play, to make the South Africans think they dropped whatever they stole when they didn't; and that would mean the men on the ground that left from the helicopter have the Alpha. But I think that would be more difficult and more risky. If I had been planning this, I would have dropped it and then made everyone think it was going out overland."

"That's really clever," said the Lieutenant. "But, if that's what they did, then how did they drop it, and where?"

"I bet there was another crew on the ground," said JP.

"With another aircraft?" said Jane.

"Yes," said Melton, "that would work. A separate ground crew, drop it down to them, and fly it out when it's safe an hour or so later. But fly it to where?"

"Your guess is as good as mine," said JP. "And I don't know how they got it out of the helicopter and dropped it unseen. Maybe there was a trapdoor. Maybe that's why they didn't abandon the aircraft finally in Lusaka, because a trap door would be discovered quickly and give the game away." He paused. "Charlie, we need the Americans to look at the imagery again. And, I think they should get some more birds in the air."

"The Yanks are already reviewing all of the recordings as we speak. I'll go and pass all of this on. Now that we have an idea of what may have happened they can focus onto trying to find something, anything, that could have been dropped from the helicopter in Zimbabwe. And I think we mean around the turns?"

"Yes," said JP, "I think so."

"Ok. And, I'll tell them we need every inch of the route looked at again from the air, in daylight, and ask they get the drones airborne straight away. Maybe they'll come up with something yet."

"It's possible, said JP. "It's slim; but, they're the best in the world at this. If anyone can find something now, it's the Yanks." He smiled slightly at Jane Chapman, and then at his friend. "There's still a chance, Charlie," he said.

≈

On board the *Excelsior* that same morning, an excited Shurafa woke Stella just before 7am to let her know that the helicopter was back and that there would be an early buffet lunch at 11am. She would be required to attend.

Stella had thought it was the same aircraft returning, but learned from Shurafa that it was actually a different one. She didn't understand why it was different, or what had happened to the other helicopter, and Shurafa didn't offer any explanation. It seemed there was much jubilation and excitement on the *Excelsior* and it would be a busy morning.

Stella decided to stay in bed for a while longer but couldn't sleep. Her mind was racing with thoughts of what had happened and where the Alpha unit now was; she presumed that Malekka's people had been successful in stealing it. She wondered what had happened at the Centre and whether anyone had been hurt or maybe even killed, although Malekka had said that it was their intention to get in and out quickly without being seen and avoid any kind of confrontation.

However there was another far more cogent reason why Stella couldn't get back to sleep. The same one that had made sleep almost impossible for her through the previous night.

Stella had given all of the information to Malekka that he wanted. She was now haunted by one simple question. Why would they keep her alive any longer? She was of absolutely no further value to these people, and she knew them to be ruthless enough simply to kill her. Or those two men, her other torturers, could just be given her to play with. Or Aisha might torture her to death as an experiment. Or someone might just simply put a bullet in her head and throw her overboard.

So to stay alive she knew she needed to give them, give Malekka, a reason to keep her alive. Her thinking brought her to one simple, inevitable, loathsome conclusion.

Malekka wanted her physically, and she would have to do it and accept it. And she would have to be the best fuck he had ever had so that he would want her again and again.

If she didn't, she knew she would die.

She was revolted, disgusted at the prospect; but far

more terrified of the alternative.

The engine sound from the *Excelsior* had increased. It was not loud, but it was noisier, and of a higher pitch; she thought the ship must be steaming at its top speed, which actually was the case as the *Excelsior* was travelling at her top cruising speed of thirty-five knots. The ship's top speed was actually an impressive forty knots, but that could strain the engines if sustained for long periods, and so the Captain liked to maintain a steady thirty-five when his master wished him to proceed with all speed. And anyway, it was always useful to hold something in reserve, just in case.

At 8.30am Stella had a nice long hot bath, and put on a tight-fitting dress that was low-cut and allowed a good proportion of her generous breasts to be seen; it was cleavage that any man would be interested in, and she knew Malekka would like it. If she was going to have to adapt to this lifestyle and accept it, then she was going to be the woman of the top man and not be given to anyone else. She would use every effort to make Malekka keep her near him. And she needed to prepare herself mentally for the inevitable physical onslaught.

The dress was just slightly above the knee, and she chose a pair of high-heeled shoes to complete the outfit. Her hair was swept back, but she brought it around her neck and down over her left shoulder. Just stay alive, she kept saying to herself; just stay alive. By the time she was ready to leave the room with her two servant girls (for that was how she had now come to view them) it was 10.45am and she was hungry.

The girls took her to the lift and then up to the penultimate deck, which she learned was Malekka's personal suite deck. She was shown into a large lounge; a variety of sumptuous sofas and chairs were scattered around. Tables boasted varied and delicious-looking spreads of food. As she entered she could see Malekka talking to two men, but he noticed her at once and excused himself to walk over.

"Ah Miss Stella," he called out in a loud voice so that others could hear. All eyes in the room were on her as they walked towards each other. She noticed Haddad and Raboud looking at her too and took great delight in totally ignoring them both. "I am so pleased that you have joined us."

"Good morning, Mr Malekka," she replied and held out her hand to take his. She was once again caught out by his chivalry when he raised her hand to his lips accompanied by a little bow. And she was again annoyed with herself when her cheeks reddened slightly. She must stop that from happening, she said to herself.

"We have had a very successful night," said Malekka, "and it is in no small way due to you and your good co-operation."

"I am glad for you," replied Stella. "May I know the details? What's happened?"

"Yes," he replied. "But first, meet the three men of my second helicopter," and he beckoned over Zaim, Qudamah and Ghazi. They were presented to Stella with great formality and aplomb. Each of them bowed slightly as they shook her hand, and the conversation flowed in English. Stella heard how the first team had got in successfully and stolen the Alpha, how it had been parachuted down unnoticed by the UAV aircraft above, how the three men had recovered it and flown it out of Zimbabwe through Mozambique in the second helicopter, to bring the unit here onto the ship. And whilst they spoke she could tell that Malekka was looking at her, at her body - not leering, just a subtle glance of both admiration and desire - and sometimes she would look at him and they would exchange a smile.

"Then you must each have great skills and bravery to accomplish such a mission, gentlemen," said Stella at the end of the tale, rather flatteringly to them all.

"We are all well trained in our profession as soldiers, Miss Stella," said Zaim.

"Yes, that is true," said Ghazi, and added, "but then some are exceptional men as they are not only soldiers but are also skilled pilots too."

The other two laughed, and Malekka also.

"Ah, I see," said Stella. "And I wonder which of you is the pilot. Now let me guess... ummm... would it by any chance be you, Ghazi?!"

There was more laughter.

"Well, Miss Stella, as it happens, you are correct."

She smiled. These are actually nice people, she thought to herself. If they weren't all murdering lunatics.

"Come, Miss Stella," said Malekka. "I want to show you something now, which this part of our endeavour has been all about."

"Yes, sir." He led her through a door into a small anteroom. There, on a table, and still in its open carry-case, was the Alpha unit.

She gasped a little when she saw it. "You really did it," she said. "You really did it." In a strange way she was really quite impressed.

"Yes, Stella, we did it," replied Malekka.

"May I ask a question?"

"Yes, of course."

"Well, I am wondering if anyone was hurt, at the Centre I mean, any of the people there. I know most of them, and I have to hope of course that there was no loss of life or even injury to anyone there. Or your own men," she added as a quick afterthought.

"No, nobody was hurt," replied Malekka. "The team

went in quickly, the retina and fingerprint scanners recognised your copies without difficulty," (he ignored the little glitch), "the codes worked perfectly and the men took the unit out from the safe room."

She looked up at him and waited for more.

"Of course, the Centre itself has been blown up."

Stella's mouth opened slightly, but still she did not speak again yet.

"Do not be concerned, Stella," said Malekka. "Nobody was hurt. And as for the damage, your father will doubtless be able to recoup that from insurers in due course. In fact, what is most likely to happen is that your father will both get paid out for loss of earnings and be compensated too for the destruction of the building. He will end up with a newer better facility as a result."

Well that was a blessing anyway. Nobody killed or hurt.

"Yes, I see, thank you."

And, actually, he was probably right about the insurance and the net result too, both financial and in terms of the new structure of the building. Not that that mattered in the slightest right now.

"And so, sir," she continued, "what is happening now, where are we going? Of course, the Alpha unit is not good for much on its own."

She held his stare; he was obviously considering whether he should tell her now or not. Malekka put his arm around her slim waist and walked her back into the lounge.

"Well, Stella," he said, "we are now cruising at close to our top speed back to what is the base for my little project. Where, and you are quite right, there will be another larger cargo delivery in due course, to which the Alpha unit was designed to be attached. In fact the other cargo is already on its way."

"You mean, you have it already?" asked Stella, with a genuine hint of astonishment in her voice. Malekka noticed her tone, and liked it.

He smiled. "Yes. On the other side of the world, some more of my colleagues have also been busy. They have the Spider, and it is now on its way to my base."

"A Spider 2-3? You have it?" Stella said again. She was taken aback. "That's, well, that's quite impressive, Mr Malekka," she said.

"Thank you, Miss Fincrest."

"And so where is it that we are going, how long will it take to get there?"

"Well, you will forgive me if I don't tell you where we are going," he said, "as that must remain confidential to me for the moment. But I can tell you that it will take perhaps five or six days to get there. And, we will arrive just after the other cargo."

"Yes sir, I see."

"And what you must do, my dear, is try to rest and enjoy yourself a little. You are on a luxury cruise liner in open waters. You can relax, take massages, swim, sunbathe, eat anything you wish, read. Unfortunately I cannot permit you to listen to television or radio, for obvious reasons, or be on the internet, but there is a very well stocked DVD library here and a very large screen on which to view in the private cinema. And any movie that you would like to watch that we do not have we can download easily enough, so just tell Nasrin or Shurafa, and it will be done. In the evenings we will dine in our own restaurant and enjoy live music here on board."

This is all too surreal, she thought.

"I understand. And, Mr Malekka, when we get there, will I be able to see the Spider itself? I've never actually seen one, ever. Even though I have known about the Alpha unit, the missile itself is just a term to me, just words."

"Yes, you will. I promised you that I would show it to you when we get there, to your new temporary home, and I will do so."

Actually, you will see more of it than you anticipate, he smiled to himself.

"Thank you." And then she asked another question. "Temporary home, sir?"

"Well, yes, of course," said Malekka. "We can hardly stay after we've launched a five hundred kiloton nuclear ballistic missile from there to its target, now can we?"

19
REFLECTIONS

JP LEFT THE meeting close to 4pm and went back to his hotel. He was very dejected at the lack of progress from the Americans. He needed to rest and wanted to think everything through again, but first ordered an early dinner. He ate in silence, relaxing. When he was finished he had room service take the trolley away, put out the Do Not Disturb sign, locked the door, lay down on the bed, put his hands behind his head and stared up at the ceiling.

JP thought back to when Dr Keppof came to see him in London in February. It was always good to see his old tutor. Actually JP felt rather privileged that the professor liked to stay in touch. They met on a cold day, and a clear blue sky belied the crispness of the air. They sat on a bench in St James's Park, throwing bread to the ducks and swans. The scene was a bleak contrast to the dark story that Keppof unfolded. They spoke quietly, their breath white as it condensed.

"...so you see," said Keppof, "my position in the KGB gave me a lot of exposure to the movements of the nuclear weapons inside Russia, or the Soviet Union rather as it was then, and I know a great deal about them."

He put away the bread and lit a cigarette, breathing in on it deeply.

"I do not believe it would be possible for anyone to obtain an Alpha unit from within Russia. They are held too securely, the location is too central within Russia and the monitoring of these and other such sensitive items is just too tight and prohibitive. However, the Spiders themselves were, and are, scattered all over the place, in several arsenals on the fringes of Russian territory. And here's point number one. In 1981, the Soviet Union sold one SS-23 to South Africa."

JP looked across at Keppof. "Really? To South Africa?"

"Yes."

"Well that's a pretty closely guarded secret," said JP.

"Yes. And despite what South Africa says about not being a nuclear power, we know that they still have it. It has been maintained, but it has been separated and the parts are in different areas of the country. Of course, it can still easily be put back together."

"But, how do you know this?"

Keppof looked over at JP, and smiled.

"I believe that current terminology in your country might classify that question as being 'a blonde moment'."

JP laughed. "You're right. Stupid question. For just a moment there I was forgetting that you're FSB."

Keppof smiled again. It disappeared quickly. "As I was saying, the South Africans still have an SS-23 Spider although separated. Its Alpha unit was placed in a high security centre in the north of the country at Musina close to the border with Zimbabwe, called the Fincrest Centre."

"Ok. So, what's the problem?"

"Well, here's point number two. The problem is, my friend, that I have intercepted two separate internal coded messages."

"What did they say?" asked JP simply.

"The first was seeking confirmation of the

whereabouts of the South African Alpha unit." He paused, to let the words and their meaning have more effect, and then continued. "Now, why would anybody be interested in knowing about that?"

"Hmmm, yes, I see what you mean," said JP. "That's a good question. If an Alpha is linked only to a Spider, then it can only be in relation to an SS-23."

"Exactly."

"And the other? You said you intercepted two messages?"

"Yes. The other message indicates the movement within Russia of an SS-23. That in itself isn't unusual; like I said, that happens from time to time. However, the problem with this message is that it referred to a movement to be made specifically *outside* the time of the American satellite pass."

JP turned slowly to look at Keppof again. Keppof looked back at him deep in the eyes, and just then JP could see the hint of fear in his old tutor's face.

"Yes, that's right, JP. I think someone is trying to move a nuclear weapon so that it isn't seen by the Americans." He paused again. "Now, why would anyone want to do *that*?"

"That's a second good question," said JP.

"I could be overreacting. I could be getting a little senile and imagining things where there is nothing. But, let me tell you something, JP." Keppof leaned forwards and put his elbows on his knees, and JP followed suit. Keppof lowered his voice further. "I've been in this game a long time. I knew the KGB. I know the FSB. Frankly, despite the new name, the difference isn't all that great. And I trust my experience, and I trust my instincts. I know when something feels right, and when something does not feel right. And this, my friend, does not feel right."

"So what do you think it adds up to? What exactly is happening?"

The questions were redundant; just then JP understood what he meant. Keppof turned to look ahead at the ducks in the water. He nodded slowly.

"Yes. You have it. I think someone is trying to sell a nuclear weapon to someone that they shouldn't. Or - which is worse but probably more likely - someone is trying to steal one." He took another drag on his cigarette and added, "And I think they are planning to steal the South African Alpha with which to launch it."

Keppof had been spot on, thought JP. He remembered how Keppof had said that he wanted to tell someone outside Russia that he could trust, and chose him also because he knew that he had been in the SAS and had 'friends'. "Just in case anything should happen to me," Keppof had said.

"Why not report your worries, what you have found, to your boss?"

"I've thought of that, of course," replied Keppof. "But, maybe it's my boss who is trying to organise these things."

"Yes, I see. What about going higher up?"

"Well, the same thing applies. How high could this be coming from? Perhaps it's the Director of the FSB, or the head of the Special Forces or of the Army, or somebody in the Federal Assembly, even Putin himself. How do I know? And of course if I do report it now and go above my immediate superior, and it proves to be nothing at all, then I am in trouble for going over him. Well, her, actually. That sort of thing does not sit well in the FSB specifically or in Russia generally. I could get moved out very quickly, and I'd prefer that that did not happen. I have no particular wish to end my days in a Gulag Archipelago in Siberia or a modern-day counterpart."

"Can you not tell who sent the message, is there a signature, a department, a location?"

"No, nothing. They came in on the general internal communications crypto logic batch, of which there are hundreds every day, and it would just require a simple reply through the same coded system. There is usually an identifying numeral known to the sender or receiver, or both. It is purely by chance that I spotted it. It just happens to be the case that I know about the SS-23s from my time in Germany. And I know about the timing of the release of the SS-23s to be linked with the American satellite passes. Having found the one about the Alpha and South Africa, I watched more closely over the next few weeks and spotted the second, about the Spider itself."

He paused for a few seconds. "Actually," said Keppof, "when you look at it like that it sounds really thin. But then, this kind of work is often like that. And I don't think I'm wrong. Something is not right here, Jimmy, I just know it."

Keppof had gone on to say that he would try to find out more and then contact JP again. Which he had done. What had he found out that had cost him his life? Why did he want to meet with JP again so very urgently, in Berlin this time? JP knew that it was very easy for Keppof to get to Berlin, and holding a current German passport would raise no queries.

He must have learned which Spider was going to be sold or stolen, or its location. Perhaps when or why, or who. Or maybe it was about the theft of the Alpha. Whatever it was, thought JP, he was going to tell me and hand me the evidence that night in Berlin; only the murderers got to him first. They silenced him forever and then took the evidence just after they killed him. As well as his wallet, to make the murder look like a robbery.

Keppof's killing would only have happened if someone had found out that *he* had found out about what was going on, and they wanted him silenced. So maybe Keppof had chosen to report it higher up the chain after all, once he was sure of his facts. Did it really come from that high up?

Yet Keppof's murderers were Iranian, not Russian. I know that for sure, thought JP - I saw them, filmed them, and MI6 has confirmed they were. Yet the Russians are perfectly capable of killing people when they want to. So why were Keppof's murderer's not Russians?

Suddenly JP sat up on the bed, and said out loud to himself, "Of course."

To stop anybody looking into Keppof later. That's why they weren't Russians. *It could lead back to the man in Russia.*

As things are, Keppof died just as a result of a mindless murder in Berlin over theft when he was holidaying for a weekend break. Very tragic of course; but nothing for the man in Russia to have to worry about any more.

JP lay back down slowly, his hands back up behind his head.

That means that the man in Russia is so close to the people from Iran that he passed them Keppof's execution. No link back to the man in Russia. Very clever. And much more dangerous too. A powerful man in Russia, well connected within the bureaucracy of the new Russia, is closely linked with a rich and powerful Mr Malekka from Iran.

Christ. It's not just a sale, or a theft. It's a collaboration.

But this plan hasn't been thrown together in a couple

of months, thought JP. This has been getting planned for years. Time was needed, and had to be taken, for contacts to be made, seeds to be sown, discretion, covert action, a gentle step here, a gentle step there. I mean, we're not talking about stealing a firecracker here, are we, it's a bloody nuclear missile for Christ's sake. This has taken some time to put together. It's a class act, run by some pretty powerful smart people.

And then comes along dear old bright, brilliant, loyal Dr Keppof, and spoils it all with his intelligence and sharpness and intuition. What else could they do, except get rid of him?

Bastards, he thought.

JP thought briefly of happier times with Keppof. At Cambridge, studying; in the wine bars in the evenings, with Keppof holding court; of when he met his daughter with him in London last year, a lovely girl just turned twenty-three.

Just give me the chance, and I'll get them for what they have done.

What of this man in Russia? A traitor; someone to whom killing means nothing. And what does he expect for himself after the bomb has been detonated? Or it might be a woman of course. And what is Malekka actually after, what's his goal? Where is the SS-23, when is it to be united with the Alpha and become launchable? And when? Tomorrow? Next week? Next month?

It was a tragedy that the Americans got nothing from the UAV surveillance and their agents. Charlie said that our own people in Zimbabwe had found nothing either. So are we just going to wake up one morning and find some city has been blown up in a nuclear explosion? New York again? Los Angeles this time? London? Are the news channels going to show a mushroom cloud rising up where one of the world's great cities used to be, after a few million people have just been vaporised in a microsecond?

JP's plan had worked and got them so far. Get a very public introduction to the beautiful Fincrest daughter who actually runs the Centre, sweep her off her feet, let the media publicise the romance, take her to an open holiday location, make her the bait, wait for her to be taken. She is the solution to the terrorist's problem of how to break in and take the Alpha. And then, once they have it, the Americans can track it. Then, we can find the missile itself and the bomb. It was solid enough.

Except, we've been outsmarted.

Well at least we know Keppof was right for sure.

And what of the girl? JP sat upright on the bed and crunched his eyes shut, trying to make those thoughts go away. They kept coming back. What had those people done to her, to make her give up the codes? Yes, that had been the plan, that they take her for that purpose, it's true.

I'm not such a nice person, thought JP; I can't be, if I can come up with that sort of plan, using people in that way. All for my purposes, for my country's purposes. So I'm trying to save a few million lives. That makes it all ok then does it?

He sat up, swivelled round to the edge of the bed and ran his hands through his hair, staring at the floor. He took a deep breath. Enough, he said to himself. No more negatives. I'm not going to self-destruct.

He took a long shower, dressed and a little before 10pm was ready to head downstairs to the bar.

What we need is a breakthrough, he said to himself as he closed the door to his room. Soon.

Charlie Melton arrived a few minutes later and joined JP at his discreet corner table. They ordered their drinks and spoke quietly together, their words covered by the general chatter and gentle background music. Nevertheless, the two men were careful in their choice of words.

"I've passed on our thinking to our friends," said Melton, "and they should have had the first flights this afternoon. And they're going through what they already have with a very fine toothcomb, as we discussed."

"Good," said JP. "You know, I'm sure they must have had a trapdoor. I would have. I can't find any other reasonable explanation for the zig-zagging. If the item had just been dropped and the helicopter carried on in the same line, then they would both have been in the same grid and for longer. It would have been more easy to detect. Veering off at a right angle takes the immediate attention away. Very clever."

"Yes, I agree," said Melton, "The more one thinks about it, the more obvious it all becomes. It's a good distraction and disguise. Now our friends know what to look for, and when, they have a good chance of finding something."

"It's such a cockup that the helicopter wasn't grabbed, then we'd know for sure about the trapdoor."

"I think it's a genuine slip of the system, JP. Our friends did all they could on it. It should have been enough to secure the aircraft, and if it hadn't been night time they would have got it. Apparently the President of Zambia is furious and very embarrassed. They like us, and our friends."

"Well I hope to God they find something, and find it quickly."

"Yes." Melton paused for a few seconds, and then said, "I want to ask you something, Jimmy. Just between us." He moved forwards and placed his elbows on the table, and JP did the same, so they could speak more quietly.

"And this is off the record."

"Ok, go," said JP. He knew what was coming.

"In South Africa. Khatib. I happen to know you've got a grip like a vice, Jimmy. He didn't just slip from your hands did he, like you said in your report. That just doesn't gel."

JP eyed the elegant glass he was holding up in both hands.

"No," replied JP very quietly. "He didn't. Charlie, they're after a bomb to kill millions, they have Stella and were working on her, he'd thrown a bomb at me, and had killed a totally innocent civilian. The woman had two kids, a six year old boy and a three year old girl. You're right. I got the information. And then I dropped him."

"And I don't suppose the car went over the edge totally on its own, did it?"

"No. It was hanging over, held by the remains of the barrier, almost gone. When I was done with Khatib, I reversed the car and helped it over the edge. The driver was still alive as it went, just."

There was a little silence. And then JP spoke again.

"What would you have done, Charlie?"

Melton smiled. "The same, boyo."

"I'm glad the desk job hasn't mellowed you too much then," said JP. "These are vile, evil people. They go around maiming and killing others. In my book they don't deserve to live."

"I agree," replied Melton. "But remember, JP. We've invoked the Fifth Rubric over you. I know of no-one else that I would entrust it with. And the whole operation is your plan, which I and my boss and our friends over the pond and everyone else back you in one hundred per cent. We all know that you may have to do things in, er, let's say an unusual way; that's why you now carry the Rubric. Sometimes the only way to fight fire really is with fire. To deal with these people you have to fight in their world and on their terms. They use democracy and the law against us all the time. They twist it at every opportunity, to hamper our self-defence and the ability of our own forces to protect our homes and our loved ones and our way of life. So, we all know you have to be free to operate outside of those very laws and restrictions that we as members of a civilised democracy cherish the most."

Melton paused and took a sip of his whiskey and soda. JP said nothing. He had great respect for his friend and former commanding officer. When he spoke in this way, which was rare, JP listened. There were few whose words he felt had meaning and depth, but Charles Melton was one of them.

"What I want to say is, Jimmy, don't go too far over the line. Just be careful. Don't lose yourself in this."

JP looked across at Melton and smiled. He knew Melton was looking out for him, and he appreciated it.

"I hear you, Charlie," was JP's natural response.

There was a short silence, and they finished their drinks.

"You know Charlie, I did only shoot one of them in the leg first, and there was only a little persuasion, and he's still alive."

Melton and JP laughed at the sentence that suddenly brought some light banter to the table. "Let's have another drink," Melton said.

Not long after, the Major left. JP signed the tab and went upstairs to his room. He was suddenly very tired. It had been a very hectic twenty-four hours. Just the previous night he had been racing round the base of the Twelve Apostle Mountains in South Africa.

He stripped off his clothes and slipped naked under the sheets, and within two minutes was in a very deep sleep.

≈

On board the *Excelsior*, as the ship proceeded at its top cruising speed to its destination, Stella dined with Malekka in his private quarters.

She knew the inevitability that the night must bring.

20
THE TRAIL

THE INTELLIGENCE COMMUNITIES of the Americans and the British had gone into overdrive in both Harare and Lusaka. They carried out their work quietly, efficiently and thoroughly, moving discreetly from one person to another to root out any possible leads that could take them forwards.

At the CIA headquarters in Langley the Americans were undertaking a complete in-depth re-analysis of all imagery from the UAVs. After the phone call from Charles Melton the Americans promptly flashed instructions to their Reaper team at Makhado Air Force Base at Louis Trichardt south-west of Musina, and the drones were in the air within thirty minutes, heading into Zimbabwe at forty thousand feet to retrace the flight of the helicopter. They stayed in the air that afternoon, through the night and into the next day, searching.

Similarly the analysis team that was pouring over the earlier images worked late that day and planned to go through the night. Although the close focus camera had stuck rigidly on the helicopter, the two wide-angle cameras still had several minutes' worth of imagery of the land passing beneath and behind the Reaper as it sped along, and it was that in particular that they were now examining, especially following the turns made by the aircraft.

At around 11.26pm in the dimmed light of the

analysis room, Corporal Susan Coker pointed excitedly again at her large screen. "There, sir, there it is again, do you see it?"

Colonel George Bravington saw it. "Yar, ah sure do, Cokee," he said in a southern accent that was civilised and laid back, but which covered a sharp aggressive temperament about to be awakened. "It's just a shimmer; but there's sure something there."

"Yes, sir," said Corporal Coker. "We're not getting the image of an object itself, it doesn't seem to have any infra-red emissions or reflected light in the darkness."

"No, ma'am; ah see what you mean, it's something that's passing over the *other* images and disturbing the patterns."

"Yes, sir, that's it. I've seen something like it before once or twice with a bird at night time, but of course there's always an infra-red source of some kind with a bird even though it's not very large. Here, there's nothing, just the shimmer."

"Yar, I think you've got something. I'm going to get the Chief down."

He picked up the red telephone at the side of the adjacent desk. "Get me Mr Wilkins." Bravington waited, and then there was a click.

"Yes, George."

"Sir, ah think we have something here. And ah think you should come down and see it."

"Ok, George, I'm on my way."

Simon 'Slim' Wilkins, the Deputy Director of the CIA, had spent half of his professional career in the Marines and the other half at the CIA, and he was liked and respected by the military and the politicians. In the elevator he punched one of several buttons below zero to go down to the operations centre. He took his six foot three inch light frame through the large double doors opposite the elevator, over to Bravington and where a now rather nervous Corporal Susan Coker was sitting. It wasn't every day the Deputy Director of the CIA dropped in to look over her shoulder, thought Cokee... Thank God.

Wilkins raised his eyebrows as he approached and said to Bravington, "So what have you got?"

Slim Wilkins watched the large screen as he was shown the strange shimmering effect that, under high magnification of the images taken by the wide angle camera of the area behind the helicopter, could just be made out.

"It has no visual or infra-red signature at all," said Corporal Coker, "and so what you're seeing, sir, what I think is happening, is the interference by *something* of the other established signatures coming from the ground, as a slight shimmer."

Wilkins watched from two minutes before the turn of the aircraft at the Sebakwe Dam, saw the slight drifting of the shimmering effect continuing along the previous line of the helicopter's direction of travel before the turn. And he saw the forward motion of the shimmer eventually stop, just as that of a falling object would be finally halted by horizontal air resistance, and then only marginal drift against the land beneath as, it would seem, some object continued its fall downwards to the ground.

"And then finally, sir," said Susan Coker, "look at this outline here, we think it's a bush... see how there is a small shimmer again, its signature is altered slightly... and then the motion stops."

"Hmmm, ok," said Wilkins, then added, "let's see it again." There was another play back, and then one more.

He thought for a while, then looked at Bravington

and Coker.

"That's pretty thin," said Wilkins.

"Yes, sir," said Coker, "but I'm sure it's movement, it's not a natural…

"Relax, Corporal," said the Deputy Director. "It's good enough for me."

"I think we should get the drones over the area, sir," said Bravington, "and let them see what else they can find there in the daylight."

"Yes. Give the order," said Wilkins. He was just turning to go and then said to Coker, "Well done, Corporal. Good work."

"Thank you, sir," said Coker who quickly reddened slightly at the praise from someone who was almost at the same level in her mind as the Almighty Himself. Susan Coker didn't see the knowing wink that Wilkins gave Bravington as he turned and walked away. The two older soldiers each knew, remembered, what a deserved pat on the back meant.

The order from Colonel Bravington to Makhado AFB went out one minute later at 12.30am, when the sun was already rising in the sky of a new day in Zimbabwe, at 7.30am local. The Reaper reached the quadrant at 9.00am. For six hours it looked down onto the area surrounding the bush where the CIA analysis had concluded something had landed by parachute; and then wider afield around the Sebakwe Dam to the north, the little airstrip and the farm. Langley received hour after hour from three visual cameras of imagery of cattle, fields, poor farmers toiling in the heat, lions and hyenas in the wilder open areas surrounding the plot; in fact the UAV was searching an area of about a hundred square miles virtually inch by inch.

There was nothing. Everything appeared completely normal. The drones viewed two farms, maybe five people that worked on each, some skinny oxen pulling ploughs on dry parched terrain, much of it with pits, ditches and furrows to catch as much rain water as possible, to try to increase an ever-dwindling crop yield. The two or three cows were milked, goats fed, a beaten up old truck started up and rolled out to the edge of a farm border to repair broken railings. Every now and again as the temperature rose through the day the low wind would blow up a mini tornado, tracking across the arid land fifty or sixty feet in the air, finally petering out a half mile or so further on. At the basic housing the women hung out washing, beat a carpet or two, took out trash bins to secure containers away from scavenging wild animals, brought drink to their men and gave them lunch. Life there must undoubtedly be very hard; but there was nothing untoward anywhere that the piercing eyes of the Reaper could see.

But then the true brilliance of the American intelligence services came back into play.

A UAV finally found something. They found something unusual. Just after 4pm the farmer three miles to the north of the Mahamara airstrip wandered into his ramshackle old barn and drove out, heading off towards Gweru in the south presumably to buy some goods. There was nothing so unusual in that, in itself. What made it unusual was that he drove out of the barn in a brand new shiny black four wheel drive top of the line Range Rover.

Now how did a poor farmer in Zimbabwe get hold of that?

Forty-five minutes later, Slim Wilkins was on a scrambled video call with Charlie Melton in London, passing on the details of their findings.

"So it would seem, Charles, that there is obviously some kind of link between the shimmering caused by something that we reckon's been dropped, and the shiny new car the farmer has," said the Deputy Director of the CIA to his opposite number at MI6. "The area is just south of something called the Sebakwe Dam, and is a very isolated piece of terrain. It's wild farmland, very parched, almost desolate. And guess what - it's got a tiny airstrip there. Called the Mahamara airstrip. Nothing more than a flat strip of land, although there is a small old open hangar at one end. It's a perfect drop point."

"Very clever," said Melton. "And if there's a hangar it's a perfect place to hide a plane or a helicopter overnight too. I guess the airstrip is something left over from the profitable times of Rhodesia. Can you see any signs of recent use of the strip?"

"No, there's nothing we can see. We've been through it all really thoroughly. I think what's needed is to get someone down there."

"Ok, Slim, do you want to send one of your guys in? Do you have someone from Harare that could go down?"

"Frankly, no," said Wilkins. "We've looked at that, and the two men we have in Harare are still working on trying to get any leads from when the helicopter landed and the two men left. Anyway, it's your operation. It needs a very quick look. Twenty-four hours. We think you should send Peregrine. Now."

"Yes," said Melton thoughtfully.

"Well - he's briefed, he knows what to look for, he's qualified; hell, it's all his plan."

"Ok. We'll drop him in. He can have a nose round, and see if he can pick up the trail. Actually - hold on a minute, Slim."

Melton turned to the other side of his desk, picked up a file, leafed through some sheets of paper and then turned back to the camera and screen.

"We've got a Hercules in Eastleigh. Kenya to Johannesburg is a pretty straight line. They'd have to overfly Zimbabwe. We'll stick him on that. It'll have to be a night drop, and it's too late for tonight. We'll get him out tomorrow daytime, and he can go in tomorrow night.

"Ok. Look Charles, it's really lion country there you know, you don't want to leave him there for too long. He'll be on his own, there's no help."

"Indeed." Melton paused, thinking quickly. "Slim, just a thought - where's the *Ronald Reagan*, isn't she somewhere around there heading up to your 5th Fleet?"

"Yes, the Group's steaming north, just off Madagascar. Why?"

"Isn't there a 'T' on there?"

"Yes, I reckon so. Oh, I see where you're going. Sure, let me know what you want. We can send Jimmy a bit of warm US hospitality."

"Thanks. I'll get back to you. And - great work, your boys and girls have done a fine job."

"I'll pass it along. We're sending you all the imagery in the next few minutes." Melton nodded and smiled. "Nice chatting, Charles."

The screen went off.

Melton glanced to the right of his desktop at Lieutenant Chapman. "Jane, get hold of JP, and get him in at the House. In two hours. 6pm tonight. And stop that Saab pilot going back tonight. Tell him we're going to need him again."

"Yes, sir," and she left the room to make the calls.

≈

JP had slept well and woke late, refreshed and relaxed.

He went for a long run, showered again and then was ready for lunch with the person to whom he had sent the text message leaving RAF Northolt yesterday morning. He had one more private meeting in his rooms at Claridge's in mid-afternoon.

JP got the call from Jane Chapman around 4.15pm. He took another extended route to the House and was there with Charlie Melton and the Lieutenant at 6pm sharp. Melton gave a quick summary of his conversation with Slim Wilkins and of the CIA's findings. They settled down to review the imagery.

They switched the screens off after the third viewing.

"That's really good work by the Yanks," said JP. "Very hard to spot the shimmering, whoever noticed that must have eyes like a hawk - even if they were helped by motion detecting software."

"We think it's worth going after, Jimmy," replied Melton. "So do the Americans. It needs a fast look on the ground, as soon as possible, to see if we can discover what did actually happen and if we can pick up the trail of the Alpha again."

"Obviously we have to assume that the bomb can't be in Zimbabwe," said JP. "After all, what would be the point? If Malekka was to blow it up in Zimbabwe, that's not exactly a major terrorist target or strike against the West, and anyway it's clear Mugabe has been helping them. If the range of the Spider is five hundred kilometres from the drop point, that hardly gets it out of Zimbabwe. So I think we can assume that the weapon itself isn't there and isn't going to be."

"I agree," said Melton. "The focus has to be to pick up the trail of the Alpha. The Americans have two people in Harare, we have one, but they're committed. This job needs to be tackled separately.

"Are you saying you want me to go in?" said JP.

"Yes. That was the suggestion from our American friends, and they just beat me to saying the same thing. It's our game really anyway. Neither the Americans nor we have a clue where the Alpha has gone. We're now assuming that it was pushed out of the helicopter and dropped down to this location, and then moved on from there. What we need is confirmation. Proof. You have to find out how and where. We need the trail."

"Fine," said JP. "I'll do it, of course. What's the plan?"

"We have a Hercules in Nairobi that is flying on to South Africa. Pure coincidence. They're carrying aid goods donated by the Government to the South Africans for refugees from Zimbabwe. The influx has been set off again by the violence over the coming elections there – if you can call them that of course; they'll just be a rigged showcase. The Hercules had a twenty-four hour stopover in Kenya and is due to fly on tonight, but in about..." Melton looked at his watch... "forty minutes they're going to develop engine trouble and tonight's onward flight will be delayed. The pilot that brought you here yesterday from Cape Town is also getting an extra stopover in London tonight, which apparently he's delighted about – and his South African superiors are pleased to help out. He's going to fly you to Eastleigh in the Saab tomorrow at 2pm departure from Northolt. You'll join the Hercules and depart Moi Air Base with them at 11pm local tomorrow evening on the rescheduled flight plan. They'll overfly Zimbabwe and the drop zone on their direct route to Pretoria. The flight's just under four hours, so you'll jump at 2.55am."

"Fine, that's clear enough. I hope they're accurate, a night drop will have to be absolutely on the money, I really don't fancy hiking in the African bush."

"They'll have the new instructions later this evening

and so twenty-four hours to prepare. They'll be fine. The Hercules will be at twenty-eight thousand feet for the duration and will depressurise the hold slowly thirty minutes before. You'll have a suit, oxygen and the latest night vision HMD with the exact GPS coordinates to guide you in. The moon will have set just after 5pm Harare time, sunrise is at 6.06am, so you'll be in total darkness."

"One thing occurs to me," said JP, "have they pulled the UAVs off? If they haven't, I think they should. There may be a team on the ground with detection equipment, placed to check that the drop hasn't been discovered or to see if there is any follow up from the South Africans. We don't want to alert Malekka; it's best he continues to think he's got clean away with it. So let's call the drones off."

"That's good, JP, I agree. Now that we've found the drop site they're not needed any more and their continued presence could endanger this mission, and actually the entire operation."

"Not to mention endangering Stella's life as well," added JP soberly. "If Malekka thinks we're on to him, he could easily decide to kill her. If he hasn't already, that is, of course." JP's heart skipped a beat as he said the last few words.

"Sir, may I suggest, then, that the withdrawal's done gradually," said Chapman. "If they have detection equipment, let them use it also to detect that the drones have no interest in them by looking at the adjoining areas too, and gradually pulling away and flying off elsewhere."

"Yes," said Melton, nodding thoughtfully. "We'll ask the Americans to do just that."

"What's my drop target?" said JP.

Melton turned again to Jane.

"There's a shed or barn just under three hundred metres to the west of where we saw the final bit of the shimmer on the screen, which is presumably a bush or tree where the parachute came to rest," said Lieutenant Chapman. "The barn is your drop co-ordinate. It will provide cover and safety from animals through the rest of the night. In the morning, the first target is the bush, to see if anything can confirm that a drop was made. Then, we'd like you to visit the old open hangar on the airstrip two miles to the west. To check out for any evidence of an aircraft. Third, the farm house, three miles to the north of the hangar, where the Range Rover is located. Check the vehicle, get what you can out of the farmer. Extraction is that same night."

"Ok," said JP.

"You referred to the African bush," continued the Lieutenant. "I thought I should check. You're going to have to be really careful, JP. We all know that Zimbabwe is extremely poor, there are sanctions against her by the international community because of the on-going human rights abuses against the people by the State forces, and of course the President continues to drain the coffers for his personal benefit. People are starving. The water situation in the country is pretty critical too. Lions and hyenas should be in the conservation areas and national parks but borders aren't maintained and they stray all over the country; there are current reports that lions have eaten people and livestock on farms in that area, and over one hundred donkeys have been taken by hyenas in the last months. Where you're going is one of the poorest areas of the entire country, and what's more there are several tributaries that serve the Sebakwe Dam, although most of them are dry presently. However, where there are watering holes, animals will appear. You're only there for less than twenty-four hours and so you may see none at all; but be ready for them just in case."

The briefing and planning discussion went on for three more hours. JP was back at the hotel at 11pm, and before settling down he went through everything in his mind once more over a last drink of hot chocolate. He didn't like to take alcohol before going live; he preferred the calming influence of a warm beverage and a clear head. There was only one thing that was playing on his nerves. It wasn't the thought of a long fast journey to Kenya; it wasn't the thought of a parachute drop on oxygen at night from five miles high; nor was it the thought of a possible tangle with forces he might find on the ground at the farm. It was the thought of an encounter with flesh-eating bone crunching four-legged animals and the possibility of being eaten alive. He had seen enough of that on TV nature programmes, when a pride of lions had their kill and tucked into dinner while the meal was still breathing. *Be ready for them just in case*, Jane had said. He had never liked cats. Especially when they were bigger and more powerful than he was.

JP did his best to sleep comfortably through the night. He ran in the morning again, and was ready in good time for the car that collected him at 12.30pm and took him out to RAF Northolt. He was reunited with the Saab pilot, and whisked to Nairobi at speed by the powerful Gripen, arriving on schedule four hours later at 9pm local.

He joined the three-man crew of the Hercules C-130. They left Moi Air Base at exactly 11pm. Three hours and forty-five minutes later they were at twenty-eight thousand feet in the heart of Zimbabwe airspace midway between Kenya and South Africa, and, at 2.45am, JP was standing in the rear of the aircraft.

The hold had been in almost total darkness for the

last hour to help JP's eyes adjust and preserve their sensitivity, and had also now been depressurised. JP was dressed completely in black, parachute on and wearing the specialised HMD helmet that also provided oxygen. A crew member, also masked, stood by the rear ramp controls. After a thumbs up to JP he lowered it. The raw noise of four propellers and gushing air tore into the aircraft as it was pulled through the atmosphere at two hundred and ninety knots. An ominous black gaping hole at the tail stretched out and down for five miles. The man nodded to JP, and JP nodded back. They both looked at the two lights at the exit, waiting.

Suddenly the red light was on, and JP was at standby. He moved closer and placed a black gloved hand on the side of the open walkway, waiting calmly. The seconds ticked by. He exchanged a final nod with the crewman.

Then the red light went out. The green was on.

JP took a deep breath and leapt forwards, hurling himself out of the aircraft into the rushing darkness of the cold unknown beyond.

The crewman closed the ramp.

In the cockpit of the Hercules, the pilot and co-pilot both saw the red indicator light go out to confirm ramp closure and the exit of their special forces cargo.

They looked at each other momentarily, then turned back and stared ahead out of the cockpit window.

Neither spoke. They didn't need to.

PART FOUR

USE OF ASSETS

21
INTO ZIMBABWE

IN SIX SECONDS JP was stable in the standard free fall position, his body spread-eagled, slightly head-up, shins almost vertical. Another six and he reached terminal velocity of a hundred and twenty miles an hour. He was already studying the information on his visor. The exact GPS co-ordinates for both his present position and the drop target showed as green digits on the black background. He could see height, vertical and horizontal speed and a small graphic marker that indicated where he was and where he needed to be. He had a total of maybe two minutes of drop time.

JP was off by one point six miles. He put his right hand out and down to turn, then back again to stop. Then he placed both hands at his hips, put his legs together, tilted down and shot across the ground tracking horizontally. The new shape was more like a wing and gave slightly less negative lift, and his vertical speed dropped to ninety miles an hour as he sped over the terrain, still three miles high. The sound of the rushing air lessened and in his visor the diagram of the target and position began to merge together. The GPS figures scrolled and a minute later the only discrepancy was the vertical displacement. JP knew he was exactly overhead and changed his body shape back to continue the vertical free fall. He pulled his cord at two thousand feet. With a flapping noise and heavy jerk to his shoulders his chute opened, and he drifted down in a gentle descent.

JP unpinned one side of the oxygen mask and breathed the warm Zimbabwe air. The rest of his body was quickly warming inside his drop suit. The night vision cameras either side of the helmet provided good imaging to the display visor. He could see the barn that was his drop target; the surrounding terrain was made up of grassland and intermittent low bushes and small trees. JP could also make out some moving four legged creatures three or four hundred yards to the east from the target barn. They looked very much like hyenas; they weren't big enough to be lions, he said to himself, but he knew that where there was one there was most probably the other not far away. The hyenas were gathered around a small mound of something, he presumed a dead animal that was their kill, and the eight or nine he could count were tearing into its flesh. Or perhaps the kill belonged to the lions and the hyenas had stolen it by sheer weight of numbers. They were feasting.

JP was not intending to spend the rest of the night in the open Zimbabwe bush and wanted to get inside the shed as quickly as possible. He was a fearless soldier with courage in battle, but it was another thing entirely to deal with hungry wild animals that would like to eat him alive or dead if they got half a chance. And they would have excellent night vision, were stronger and heavier than he and could move faster too. An encounter with one, or more likely several, was something that he did not relish.

JP was on the ground in another thirty seconds. He took off his helmet, listening intently as he shook himself out of the one-piece flight suit. He knelt, opened his rucksack and put on his night vision goggles. He took out his C8[6] and attached the suppressor; now he

---

[6] *Diemaco C8 CQB: Close Quarter Battle carbine assault rifle.*

could defend himself if something came out of the blackness. He quickly pulled in his parachute and stuffed it into its de-harnessed carrier, and threw the rucksack onto his back once more. He was just about to raise himself up from his one knee crouch, but froze. He was sure he could hear a rustling of something through the grass or against a bush.

JP stayed still, straining to pick up all sounds. A rich plethora of noisy pulsating insect chorus, buzzing, ticking, humming, stridulating, filled his ears as the night symphony backdrop; the hideous whooping giggle of the hyenas; croaks from reed frogs; bats fluttering; every now and again a deep rumbling from a distant elephant. And then a lone roar of a lion a few miles away. Was its pride close by, had their kill been stolen? Were they now looking for something else? For him? The primeval fear of man versus predator was raised in JP's being, it touched a raw nerve. The hairs on the back of JP's neck stood up and a small bead of sweat appeared at the top of his brow. Through the silence of the noise, he knew, he just knew, that he was already being watched, could feel several pairs of eyes looking across at him through the emptiness. The night was jet black, the air crystal clear and the stars glanced gaily down at him but cast no shadows. He had to fight to resist the instinct to run.

Thankfully his night vision goggles were efficient and provided a clear image of his surroundings; he could make out the low grass, thorny bushes and small trees off fifty or sixty yards to his right. He was in a very exposed position.

There it was again, another rustling sound.

The light breeze had already taken his strange and interesting scent to the animals downwind of him, they were curious, interested, hungry. He needed to get out of there. He cautiously walked the thirty yards to the shed. JP felt better with something solid at his back, even if it was just a ramshackle wooden siding. He was crouching low, staring, keeping perfectly still. He was just about to head for the doors to force them open when he caught sight of the first, slightly forward of the bushes fifty yards away. It had raised its head from its stalking crawl to look directly at him. A pair of white eyeballs stared eerily; and then they were suddenly joined by another pair, and then another. *You're only there for less than twenty-four hours and you may see none at all...* Well it hadn't quite worked out that way. The lionesses were there, and he was on the menu.

JP decided he wasn't going to, couldn't, wait any longer. He wanted to maintain absolute silence, but wasn't certain that he could get inside quickly enough before the lions made their move. And he wasn't about to take any chances. So he levelled his carbine and pulled the trigger. Two short bursts of fire made virtually silent by the rifle's suppressor cut the lead lioness almost in half. With sudden roars and snarling the others quickly bolted, before turning round staring again, shocked and confused.

At the Mahamara Airstrip two miles away the man sitting quietly just inside the entrance of the open hangar suddenly sat bolt upright. He heard the noises from the lions. He was used to that every now and again in the night, their main time for hunting. The man also saw the two sets of three flashes of light. He was not used to seeing that. Except in a gun fight. He had been in enough of those to recognise muzzle flashes when he saw them.

JP took his moment and went to the front of the barn, taking care not to run lest it incited an inherent instinctive charge from the big cats. With his knife he levered open one side of the double doors and stepped inside, pulling it closed firmly behind him. He breathed a sigh of relief, and wiped his forehead with the back of his hand.

JP sat down cross-legged at the corner by the doors, his carbine resting upright on the ground, his head back against the wood. For the next two hours he heard the hyenas scavenge on the dead lioness's body, cackling and giggling. And then the lion pride was back, with the males this time, and their more equal numbers together with the sheer raw muscle power of the males made the fight simple and quick. The hyenas were gone. The lions devoured what was left. It was no longer one of their own; it was now merely meat they had smelt on the wind and been attracted to by their noisy millennia-old enemy.

As the sun began to rise beneath a blue sky, the night symphony quickly vanished. At 7am JP stood and ventured outside. The lions were gone, the hyenas were gone, there was little sound. He brought out his binoculars. The land was predominantly flat and barren to the horizon, save for low brown grass and some bushes. There were no mountains; not even any hills to speak of. Just mile upon mile of open savannah. The monotony of the desolation was broken by a few simple trees. Nothing moved, except the odd bird in the sky and the vultures grouped in circular glide some distance away, who were waiting for their own moment to land and feast, perhaps on the last parts of the meal provided by JP.

JP went back into the barn and closed the doors. He took out two rectangular electronic units from his rucksack, each about twelve centimetres by seven, one twice the thickness of the other. He wrapped the thicker one in a plastic bag, and then looked around the barn. It was full of old rusty tools and farm machinery that hadn't been worked for decades. Broken implements were strewn all over the place. The only thing he could see of any potential use were a couple of old buckets and a pitchfork. The barn wasn't very high, perhaps fifteen feet, but as he looked upwards he found what he wanted. He walked to the middle of the right wall and stood on a pile of broken bricks and metal and wood offcuts, and reached a large old jug perched on a ledge. He wedged the plastic bag behind the jug so that it was entirely obscured from view, then backed away kicking the dirt floor as he went to remove his footprints. He left his parachute and harness in the corner, put his rucksack on again and slung his rifle over his shoulder. A few more seconds and he was out of the barn and had closed the door securely behind him.

He noticed the tyre tracks pretty much immediately. They ran off north and south from the barn and it was clear that someone had driven past and then back up again. They also ran off east.

JP turned on the GPS locator. It had been programmed with the exact co-ordinates of where the last shimmer had been detected by the Americans. In a few seconds the screen was bright with a string of figures and a simple direction indicator. JP set off east at a slow pace, and realised he was mirroring light tyre tracks but of the reverse direction. He was holding the locator in his left hand out in front, the rifle resting on his left forearm. He moved alert and poised ready to respond to anything coming at him from the terrain. But this time there was nothing; he was able to move freely and uninterrupted.

There was little in the way of flora or fauna. JP passed low bushes and a few trees that rustled in the breeze, watching for snakes. A whistling sounded as air flowed into the holes of the bulbous swellings that grew at the base of the acacias' thorns. The spikes along every branch and twig were two or three inches; the elephants loved the taste of the acacia trees and the thorns were of no consequence to them, but the ants burying after the nectar could get inside the elephants' trunks and sting the sensitive areas. That kept the huge mammals away. Once the ants had left, though, the trees were defenceless. Twenty minutes later JP was at the destination bush, an aptly-named Whistling Thorn six foot high and just as wide. JP put the locator back into his pocket and studied the bush and the surrounding area.

It didn't take him long to spot what he had hoped would be there. However, it took some fifteen minutes and cost him several nasty scratches and a little blood to get it. At the top of the bush he pulled away the small piece of material caught by one of the thorns, torn from the parachute when it had been pulled down by whoever had collected it. He looked at the little piece of material, maybe two inches square, and turned it round in his fingers. Black silk. Typical parachute material.

JP looked at the ground again. The tyre tracks had been difficult to make out in the taller grass, but he could tell by the direction of bent stalks and radials in the dirt that they had left on the track he had just followed in, and could make out the other along which they had arrived, slightly south of west. He checked the bush again, to see if there was anything else caught in it, and found one more smaller strip of material on the other side. He placed both into a small plastic bag, closed the pop-in zip and put the bag into his rucksack.

So this was what had happened; the Alpha had been dropped. Or something had anyway, but JP was convinced it was the Alpha, not a ruse. And, it had been collected by a ground crew, in the car.

Then what had happened to it?

He wanted to follow the tyre tracks by the ramshackle barn so he retraced his steps back. He brought out his GPS locator and changed its mode to camera. He took three or four pictures from different angles of the tyre markings, placing his C8 carbine down beside them to give a dimension measure. The make, size, model and car specification for the tyre could easily be deduced from the pictures. As he took them each image was instantly whisked away to the American satellite above.

JP followed the tyre marks south although it was difficult once again when the clearing around the barn began to give way to the brown grass of the savannah. But then it seemed to stop anyway at a slight clearing around a tree. JP stared at the ground.

There was a considerable amount of broken and flattened blades of grass. Something had rested there. He could now make out their route off to the drop area, which he walked out and back, but found nothing along the way. He was just turning to go back north to the barn when something glinted up at him from the ground. He walked over to it, knelt down and pushed the other blades of grass out of the way. He pulled out the hooked skewer. The sort used to secure a tent tie cord firmly to the ground. A tent? No. A camouflage net. He checked the area with renewed care, and although he couldn't find anything else, the one in his hand was enough. They're easy to miss when taking them out in pitch blackness, he said to himself. This was where the ground team had been based, probably in the car for safety, and had awaited the delivery from the sky.

JP moved back to the barn. He lifted the binoculars from his chest and surveyed the area again. There was no movement, nothing to concern him. He set off again following the tyre marks, this time to the north. The tyre marks moved onto a small dirt track that led away west from the barn, towards where he knew the Mahamara airstrip was located a couple of miles away. He could soon see the old open brick hangar and within half an hour was standing close to it, looking down the length of the tiny runway to the south-east. He couldn't see any marks of interest at the top of the runway and walked over to the hangar. He could see tyre marks from the car, but then almost immediately spotted another type of tyre track. This one was thinner, a little deeper, and fresh, he could tell, because of the sharpness of the impression, and it definitely wasn't a radial tyre. JP smiled. A helicopter tyre. This was how the Alpha had been taken out; by helicopter.

But, to where?

He placed his carbine on the ground next to the mark and sent a series of pictures skywards once more.

The excessive heat of the late morning or the diversion of having just found helicopter tracks perhaps made JP lose a little concentration, for he missed the almost silent approach of the man behind him until the last moment. Too late, he began to spin round. All that did was make the swing of the man's rifle butt hit his head more towards the temple than the back. JP collapsed in an instant, unconscious.

When he awoke two hours later, he first felt the pain coming from his wrists and hands. He groggily raised his head and looked above. His eyes slowly focused on the biting handcuffs. Their joining chain was slung over a hook that dropped down from a lintel beam spanning the width of the hangar six feet in from the open front. The hook was at the end of an aircraft tie-down chain, curled around the beam and secured off at one of the side walls. JP had been stripped naked, apart from underpants, socks and boots. His feet were tied together with rope and he was dangling a foot off the ground like a carcass of meat. He then noticed the pain in his head from the blow. He blinked his eyes again and shook his head a couple of times to help restore his senses. He cursed at his stupidity.

The three men sitting on the ground at the hangar entrance looked up as he started to move. To their left was his emptied rucksack, its contents strewn onto the ground. The men were black and JP presumed they were Zimbabwe army, or more likely ex-army. It was another confirmation that JP had found the right area for the Alpha search. Why else would a rear-guard be here? Although it was a confirmation that, just then, he would happily have done without.

One of the men spoke.

"So, you are awake at last, my friend." His smile revealed brilliant white teeth, but no humour. "We have been waiting for you. You have been asleep a long time."

The other two men laughed a little.

"I'm afraid Mandeeb here must have hit you a little too hard," he continued. "And I think you are going to have a bit of a headache for a while also."

The men laughed again.

He stood up, and the others followed. He was six feet tall easily, about forty-five, strong and looked unpleasantly dangerous. With his hands nonchalantly behind his back the man strolled over to JP and walked slowly around him, stopping to face him squarely in front. His dark eyes were cold and penetrating, a smile played on thick lips and he seemed eager to begin on JP.

"You will I am sure want to talk to me in a little while. We want to know who you are and what you are doing here."

JP said nothing, and merely looked away from the man, staring out into the Zimbabwe bush. The smile on the man suddenly went, partly through annoyance and partly through surprise. He hadn't expected to be ignored. He stared at JP a little longer, and then said, "Loosen him up, boys."

The two men took off their shirts, and, ceremoniously for JP to see, put on tight-fitting leather gloves. They were younger than the other man, very muscular and clearly used to physical encounters; the one called Mandeeb locked his fingers and stretched his hands out in front to crack them. The men moved in.

Over the next two hours Mandeeb and the other, Eltong, used JP as they would a heavy bag in a boxing gym. They moved lightly around him, punching with a jab, a straight, a hook, an uppercut, reigning the blows generally onto the upper torso, the chest, back, sides; however it was that JP happened to swing in their direction. Sometimes they would punch his thighs and buttocks. They ignored his testicles lest they kill him, except for an occasional uppercut every thirty minutes. JP's face was constantly contorted, his head up and back, sometimes down on his chest; his breathing was faster, he twisted one way then another, his biceps flexed to help relieve the pain. He let out a moan, a pant, a short cry, a shout, he passed out twice. The sweat poured off him. But he spoke not one word.

The faces and chests of the two torturers glistened in the sunlight as they worked on their victim with great vigour, stopping only when JP passed out and then wading in again when he had regained consciousness. And all the time Akunda, the leader of the trio, sat on the ground at the entrance with his head up against the wall and his legs outstretched looking across to the other side, bored, glancing right every now and again at the spectacle of his men punching the rotating body swinging side to side.

After two hours, Akunda stood up holding the second large cigar that he had lit up since they had started work on JP. He walked over, and studied the fast breathing, the pained twisted facial expressions. Akunda puffed the cigar and blew the smoke over JP's face.

"You're very strong, my friend," he said, going around behind JP. "Very strong, and very fit." He completed the circle. "How does a man get to be that fit?" he said to JP's face. "Come now, a simple question; tell me your name." JP ignored the man, and just stared out ahead looking at the Zimbabwe savannah.

"Just your name," said Akunda as he started round again. When he was behind JP he suddenly pushed the cigar's red tip onto JP's skin at the area of his right kidney. JP let out a low scream and tried to move away, twisting sharply round.

"Hold him for me," said Akunda. The other two wrapped their arms around JP's torso and held him steady.

"Tell me your name, my friend."

Akunda spent the next half hour burning JP's skin, around the kidneys, under the armpits, and the upper thighs. Once when he was being held facing towards the rear JP noticed a little pile of ashes and paper in the far corner. Then he was twisted round to the front again as the cigar came onto him once more. Each time JP let out a forced shout through clenched teeth.

And then his head dropped onto his chest and his whole body went limp.

"He's out again," said Mandeeb.

"He's taken a lot, and has said nothing, not one word," said Eltong. "Who do you think he is?"

"He's a very unusual man," said Akunda thoughtfully, "that's who he is," and stuck the cigar into JP's side again to check. There was no reaction, the body stayed limp. Akunda walked away to the entrance, puffing on what was left of the cigar. "South African for sure," he continued. "Somehow they traced the helicopter drop to here."

"You think they got onto us that fast from the attack?" said Mandeeb. They didn't know the details of the attack, only the time, and that it was across the border.

"I'm afraid so," said Akunda. "They are very good, the South Africans. Much better than our poor little Zimbabwe, my comrades. Whatever our employers took from there must be very important."

"It looks like the drones were interested in us here after all then."

"Yes," said Akunda. "I thought they had gone away, but no. They've probably sent a few guys in to different areas for all we know. Including us. And we got this one. We were lucky he had to shoot at the lions."

"And I was very sharp in seeing it, sir" said Mandeeb. Akunda smiled and nodded back at him.

"What do you want to do then, sir?" asked Eltong.

"Oh, we'll carry on and get something out of him. It's only a matter of time. We'll radio in our capture of this man tonight if we have some information on him and if not then tomorrow evening at the communication time. But like I said, for the South Africans to go to these lengths… it must mean that whatever they stole is worth a lot. A lot of money."

"What are you thinking?" said Mandeeb.

"Well, we are guarding this hangar on this deserted strip. And the pathetic farmhouse. Now *we* have something ourselves that is valuable. Perhaps *very* valuable to our employers."

The other two men began to smile.

"Well that should be worth a little bonus then?" said Eltong greedily.

"Exactly," said Akunda. "Perhaps we can do a little trade, do a little more business." He thought some more, and took one final puff on the cigar before killing it with his shoe on the ground. "We will continue the work and find out what we can from our guest. And then pass on the information we get from him and his picture, tonight or tomorrow night, or as long as it takes to break him. But, only for the right price. Only after the money is in my account."

"How much extra can we get do you think?" asked Mandeeb.

"I'm not sure. I will think on it." He turned back to look at the other two. "But now, I am hungry. I am going to go up to the farmhouse and have some food and a little drink. And to fuck the daughter again. And then I'll come back. Mandeeb, you can come up to the farmhouse now, eat. Then you can have the wife."

"And I suppose all I get is the guard duty then," said Eltong disgustedly.

"Well this isn't a democracy," said Akunda, "but let's face it my young friend, it is your turn."

"Bring me back some food then, please, I'm hungry too."

"We will. And I'm going to bring more than that," said Akunda. "I'm going to bring back some sharp knives and begin slicing skin off this man. And some other tools to crunch his balls up."

"Fuck, that's nasty," laughed Mandeeb.

"And if he still isn't talking to me by tomorrow I'm going to cut his balls off and stuff them down his throat one by one."

Akunda and Mandeeb sauntered off in the direction of the farmhouse, and Eltong took Akunda's place on the ground, his back propped up against the side wall, staring out across the entrance. He closed his eyes and rested.

The pain had been severe. JP's mind had shut down twice into unconsciousness. However, the torture had done something else. It had raised his pain threshold, brutalised his anger and awakened utter ruthlessness. All of which JP directed inwards mentally upon his body, to be devoid of further pain.

Acting was not one of JP's major talents. However, he had learned how to feign fainting during torture and had become good at it. It had been a difficult part of his training, especially if the infliction of pain continued afterwards to check unconsciousness. Faking collapse was a useful way of getting a break from the pain, or some information from the torturers unbeknown to them. Even in turning the tide of the struggle. As JP now planned to do.

For the third passing out was not genuine.

JP waited a few minutes until he judged the other two had had enough time to reach the farmhouse three miles away. Then, he moaned and pretended to regain consciousness. He raised his head, shook it slowly and began to pant as he faked the pain hitting him once more. Well, that part was real. The pain had never left him.

Eltong looked over. He smiled and gave JP a little wave.

"Please," said JP, hoarsely.

Eltong stopped his smiling. The man had said something. The first words, and he had heard them. Not his superior officer or his colleague. *He* had heard them!

"Please," said JP again, a little louder this time.

"Please, some water."

Eltong stood. He walked over to JP and stood with his hands on his hips right up close to the man, as he had seen Akunda do.

"So, now you speak something at last."

"Please, some water."

"I will give you some water. But first, you must give me something."

"Yes," said JP hoarsely again, "yes. No more."

Eltong was very pleased. He was going to get some information from the man, when Akunda and Mandeeb couldn't. He was going to be the first.

"What is your name, my friend?"

"Dezi," said JP. "Dezi de Klerk." It was the first South African name that came into his head, the surname of an earlier Prime Minister. "Please, some water."

Eltong smiled. "Ok," he said. "A little water."

He turned to get a water bottle. It was what JP had been waiting for. As Eltong turned away, JP brought his legs up silently, opened them at the knees and in one swift movement brought them down onto Eltong's shoulders, wrapping them around his neck. Before Eltong realised what was happening JP pulled the man backwards and lifted himself up using the support from Eltong's shoulders, took the handcuffs up off the hook and twisted left, pulling the man down with him as he fell. JP clenched his legs tighter and twisted violently as they hit the ground. There was a hard snap as his legs broke Eltong's neck.

JP sat up for a minute stretching, clenching and massaging his hands to get some movement back into them. Then he crawled over to the dead man and foraged in his pockets. To his relief, he found some keys and quickly was out of the handcuffs; he wouldn't have to pick them. He slowly peered out of the hangar, north towards the farmhouse; there was nobody to be seen. He went to his rucksack. His GPS locator had been smashed and his rucksack cut up as they searched for anything in the lining. The small plastic bag with the material lay on the ground, ignored. His C8 and ammunition were intact. He imagined the rifle was going to be a proud trophy for one of the men, probably Akunda, as well as the Sauer with its silencer and holster. His trousers and shirt were there, torn but wearable. He checked that the carbine and Sauer were in firing condition and had not been spiked, put his clothes on and the bag with the material in his pocket. He attached the silencer, strapped on the shoulder holster and pushed the handgun into it. It felt good to be dressed properly again. His knife was still there in its sheath on the back of his trousers. Fortunately his torturers had not got around earlier to the idea of peeling him.

Then he went over to have a look at the ashes on the ground in the corner of the hangar. Somebody had obviously been having a fire, to destroy some papers. And then he saw one complete piece of badly scorched paper about three inches square some four feet away from the rest, that had obviously been on the verge of igniting but hadn't actually done so. Perhaps because it had been taken off the fire by a sudden gust of wind. JP couldn't possibly know, of course, how Qudamah had remembered the final piece of paper and exited the helicopter with the rotors turning to burn it with the rest, nor could Qudamah know that the quick re-acceleration of the rotor blades moments later pushed a downdraft too early into the hangar and lifted the browning paper clear of the fire just before it could ignite. It was one of those silly oversights, an amazing fluke of luck or twist of fate that so often down through history turns the tide of battle and on which wars can be won or lost.

And, there was some writing on it that was still legible.

JP didn't try to pick it up, in case it disintegrated; instead he got down closer to the paper and moved his head around to catch the sunlight at the best angle. He smiled to himself. This was it.

He memorised the GPS co-ordinates, found another of the plastic zip bags, thrown away by his captors, and as carefully as he could picked up the half-burnt paper.

JP was ready. He ached all over, he was very badly bruised, he probably had some cracked ribs, his burns were extreme in places and viciously sore, and he knew he was obviously not in such good physical condition just then.

But, he said to himself as he moved stealthily out of the hangar to make his way up to the farmhouse, you should see how the other fellas are going to look in just a little while.

22
KAWALA

THE FARMHOUSE WAS a large rectangle on one level, with the entrance door in the centre of one of the longer walls and three windows either side. JP could also see one of the side walls, which had no windows. He was three miles away. His plan was to run around the flank of the house to be out of sight, and then approach the farmhouse square on to the shorter wall. He would have to risk an initial dash across open land in full view of the farmhouse to one of the deeper irrigation ditches, but once there he would be obscured. There was, he felt, only a small chance that he would be seen over open ground, but if spotted he would fight it out in a straight gun battle. He had already reduced the odds considerably to two-to-one with the death of Eltong, and if it came to that he had a good chance of killing the other two.

Not that he was actually planning on killing them.

He had one more look through the binoculars, and started. He covered the three hundred yards at full pelt, and jumped into the irrigation ditch. He peered over the top of the small bank; it was clear. He ran low the entire length of the ditch, stopping once to check his position; and then finally was square on to the windowless side of the house. He left the ditch, and ran the remaining two miles silently. He paused at an old cart twenty yards from the wall, listening intently. There were sounds, but they were garbled. He moved to the wall, then the left corner. Now he could hear through the open windows.

The sounds were strange and unpleasant. There was a regular knocking and a young girl's panting cry in rhythm, intermingled every now and again with a scream and then a shout asking for someone to stop. She was obviously being raped. There was a man's voice, calling out just then for more food, and a second woman who said yes, yes. He thought he could hear a third man, in a quiet sob or whimper.

JP moved silently to the front, his back flat against the wall, and very slowly peered round the first window. It was a bathroom, and was empty. He moved to the next window. A man of about forty was sitting on the ground with his right wrist handcuffed to the D-handle of the bathroom door, with his other arm round a young boy of about ten, clasping him close to his chest. Across the open sitting area a man was at a table facing the kitchen beyond, where a woman was heating a pan on a simple stove. To the left, three doors led presumably to the bedrooms that made up the other half of the house, one of which was the source of the girl's screams.

JP dropped down low and went past the other two windows to the open door. He stood again and had another quick look in; there was no change. He levelled his C8 so that he was ready to fire, and silently walked through the doorway. The man and the boy looked up in astonishment. JP quickly put his finger to his closed lips urging them to remain silent. The man's eyes were wide in a mixture of amazement and fear but he nodded and also put his hand over the boy's mouth. JP moved forwards and in a few silent strides was behind his target. Mandeeb had just wiped his plate with some bread when the rifle butt made contact his head. Mandeeb's face rested in the remaining food. The woman heard and turned round with a gasp but also responded to JP's finger urging silence.

The sound in the bedroom continued unabated. JP looked at the handcuffed man and pointed to the first door, closest to the kitchen. The man shook his head. JP pointed to the second, and the man shook his head again. JP smiled slightly, raised his eyebrows and pointed to the third. The man nodded.

JP rested his carbine and drew his gun. He walked over silently and quietly opened the door. Inside the sparsely furnished room the young girl on the double bed had her hands tied to the headboard railings and her skirt up to her waist. A simple blouse had been ripped open to expose her bare breasts. Akunda was on top of her, naked apart from his boots, riding her with heated vigour, oblivious to his surroundings and her cries for him to stop. JP stepped forward and pointed the Sauer at his back. He slowly and deliberately cocked the gun.

Akunda froze in mid-motion. It was a sound he immediately recognised. The girl continued to pant and cry, and then stopped too when she wondered with relief what had made the man stop. Then she saw JP at the foot of the bed and answered her own question. Akunda turned his head round, and saw his torture victim standing with a gun pointed at him. His eyes bulged with petrified astonishment.

"Let me make myself perfectly clear," snarled JP with a viciousness that surprised even himself. "If you don't do exactly what I tell you to do, I will shoot you dead. Do you understand?"

Akunda looked away and nodded.

"Get up." Akunda obliged. It was instantly clear there was no possibility of his further carnal activity. Akunda used both hands to cover himself.

"Put on your underpants." Akunda did so. JP moved to the right of the bed, his gun held straight out pointing at Akunda's heart. He gestured with the gun for Akunda to kneel and then move through the doorway. JP followed.

"Stop," he said. Akunda froze.

JP de-cocked the gun and then brought it crashing down onto Akunda's head. JP looked down at the unconscious man with contempt.

The man with the boy spoke first. " Who are you?"

JP looked at him and the boy. The father still had fear in his eyes, wondering if they were now to be attacked by this new visitor and merely have one misery replaced by another.

"A friend," he said.

The father's fear abated a little, but then he added, "There's one more."

JP shook his head. "No, there isn't," he said with a slight smile. "Not any more."

The man stared at JP, and a little smile broke out on his face too as he began to realise that his family and he were safe. He hugged his son close to him, and nodded at JP.

JP turned and spoke to the woman. "Ma'am, your daughter needs you in there." Silently the woman nodded, and smiled with gratitude. She walked and then ran into the other room. There was immediately more crying and screaming, but of a different kind, the sort that means relief, comfort and security.

JP looked for the handcuff keys on Mandeeb. He hadn't thought to keep the others he had used at the hangar, although they might not have fitted anyway. He found them, walked over to the man by the door, released him and knelt down looking at the boy.

JP smiled and said, "Hello, young man. My name's Jim. What's yours?"

The boy's eyes were red from crying and he was

frowning constantly. He held a brave but pitiful look of innocence and confusion that showed he didn't understand anything of what had happened in his home. Except, that the other men had hurt his mummy and sister and daddy and that this new man had stopped that. Suddenly the boy flung himself forward and put his arms around JP's neck. JP hugged him back. Just as quickly, but with a smile on his lips, the boy withdrew back into the comforting arms of his father.

"Just a minute," said JP to the father, who had opened his mouth about to speak again. He walked over to Akunda, pulled his hands behind his back and bound them with the handcuffs. Then he knocked on the open door of the bedroom. The mother had untied the girl's hands from the headboard and was holding her in a strong embrace. She had closed the torn blouse and brought the skirt down to provide at least a little comforting modesty. The woman turned to look at him and nodded as she rocked her baby. JP went to the headboard and took the rope with which the girl had been restrained. The boy and the father came in; the family all sat on the bed and hugged, crying together. JP wasn't needed. He quietly walked back out, closing the door behind him.

JP dragged Mandeeb over to lie adjacent to Akunda and tied his hands behind his back with the rope. Then he sat on one of the simple cushioned wooden chairs in the lounge and waited. Half an hour later, the father came out.

"I do not know how to thank you," he said with a smile. "Who are you? Can we do anything to help you?"

"Yes," he said, "but first I would like to finish making these two secure. Do you have some more rope or any wire that I can use?"

The man went off for a while and returned with some of both, and helped carry the two outside. They were still out cold. JP placed them on their fronts and bent their legs back up behind them. He looped rope from their feet round their necks and down to their wrists, pulling tighter before tying the rope off. His torturers were firmly hogtied.

"Now, please, come and sit at our table," said the father, "we must speak. And, let us offer you some food and drink."

The man sent his son into the middle bedroom as the mother and girl came out of the first, a large blanket wrapped around the girl's shoulders as she walked to join her brother in her room. She got to the doorway, and then turned and walked over to JP. The girl was only about sixteen, thought JP. She was very beautiful, and her brown skin glowed in the lessening sunlight and belied the brutality that had been inflicted upon her. She stood two feet away from where JP sat, and looked down at him.

"Thank you," was all she said. He smiled and nodded; her eyes filled with tears again. She turned and walked back to her bedroom, where her brother was now lying on the bed. The girl went to the bathroom to bathe thoroughly; to freshen and try to begin to heal from what she had endured. The boy would wait. Even though he was only ten, he knew enough that he should try to comfort her.

The woman brought some water and the three adults sat at the table, the man at the top opposite where Mandeeb's head had crashed into the plate. They both looked at JP expectantly.

"My name is Jim Peregrine. My friends call me JP. I'm British, but I've been working in South Africa. I'm here trying to trace something that was stolen from some friends of mine south of the border at Messina, and find the people who took it. I would very much welcome any help you can give me in bringing the thieves to justice." That sounded simple and uncomplicated enough, he said to himself. "I would like to ask, and to know, what has been happening round your home recently, over the last week or so."

The man and his wife nodded.

"My name is Oshimba," said the man. "Oshimba Kawala. My friends call me Simba." The three of them smiled. "This is my wife, Eshe. My daughter is Chaneen, and my son is named Tongol. About two weeks ago a man came here to see us. We didn't know him; he just arrived in a car from nowhere. He said that he would like to have use of the airstrip on the farm. The airstrip is hardly ever used, it is from another earlier time, before our country was called Zimbabwe. I was offered one hundred US dollars in cash and I was told I would be given a new car afterwards, if I gave no objections, asked no questions and kept quiet. Well I didn't ask any questions. We needed the money, the car would be wonderful and so of course I said yes. We were to stay away from the airstrip for two weeks. So, we did."

JP said nothing, and continued looking at the man. Simba's son, Tongol, was a replica of his father; only Simba's frowns were more numerous and set in deeper furrows on the forehead, and the black frizzy hair had twinges of grey and was receding.

"On the 16th, we were allowed to go back. There was a car in the hangar; well it wasn't just a car, it was beautiful. It was a brand new Range Rover, a four wheel drive! An amazing help for me, and a great gift. It is worth a large deal of money. I was very grateful.

"But then, these other three men - animals - came.

Three nights ago, the evening of the very day we went back to the airstrip. They said they had come to be here for a week, to guard the area for us, they said. In case any other men came and harmed us, they said. I was grateful to start with; they were pleasant enough, they asked if they could put some equipment up in a tent outside at the back of the big barn that's close to the house. We didn't see them at all. The next day I drove into Gweru to get a few supplies. That night they turned up and said they wanted dinner. We fed them. And then after dinner they wanted more."

The man paused and looked over to his wife.

"They started on Eshe first. When I tried to stop them, they knocked me out... they had guns and there were three of them... and they tied me up. And then they took Chaneen. Our lovely little girl." His eyes were full of tears again.

JP reached over with his hand and put it onto his shoulder. "Let me tell you something, Simba. These men are now my prisoners. These men will pay for what they have done to you and to your family. They will pay heavily for it. And I promise you: they will never, ever, hurt any of you again."

Simba smiled at JP, and nodded. "You are a good man, JP. A good man."

And Eshe smiled too. Then she put her hand onto Simba's on the table. "And you are a good man too, my husband."

Simba returned the loving gaze. He looked back at JP.

"They knew we had the Range Rover. They took the keys, and the keys to the other old truck we have. They told us to tell our workers to go for a few days, and come back in a week. We were on our own. And then they did their 'guard duty' by coming here and abusing all of us whenever they wanted. Two nights. This is the second day. And then, you came."

"I am glad I came when I did then," said JP. "Tell me; before these three came, did you hear any sounds from the airport?"

"Yes," said Simba. "We didn't go there, as we were told not to; but, we heard sounds. A helicopter."

"What exactly did you hear, and when? Can you remember?"

"Yes, it was on the last evening, before we returned to the airstrip and found the car. We heard a helicopter arrive in the early evening just after sunset. And then it took off again, late, perhaps two in the morning."

"I am wondering, and this is very important; do you happen to know in which direction it headed?"

"Oh no, JP. We were in the house here, in bed. The noise woke us; we are both very light sleepers, and in fact I think I was actually awake anyway, dozing. We heard it but I couldn't tell you the direction it took."

"Did the noise get any louder, I mean did it come and fly over the house?"

The man and wife looked at each other and thought.

"No," said Eshe. "No, it didn't get any louder. It just faded away."

"Excuse me, father." Tongol was standing at the open door to his sister's bedroom.

"Yes, Tongol, what is it?" All three adults were looking over at him, and paused their conversation. The boy started to walk over to the table.

"Tongol you should be in bed and staying with your sister for now," said Eshe.

"Yes, mother, but I can help."

"Help?" said Simba. "What do you mean, son? How can you help, and help us with what."

"Excuse me, Mr Jim," said the boy now also to JP,

who smiled back at him. "Father, the door was open, I could hear."

Simba looked at his wife and smiled. They should have closed the door. Tongol continued while he had the chance.

"Mr Jim, I can help. I heard the helicopter. And I saw it."

There was a stunned pause.

"You saw it?" said Simba.

"Yes, father, I saw it."

"Where did you see it, Tongol," said JP. "How did you manage that?"

"Were you up on top of the house again, Tongol?" said Eshe, "And at night time?"

Tongol looked down at the ground. "Yes, mother," he said sheepishly.

"What were you doing up there? I've told you not to go up there especially at night."

"I'm sorry, mother, I couldn't sleep. It was hot, and I just went."

"Well this is one time when you will be excused," said his father. "But only if you can help Mr JP here. Isn't that right, mother?"

Eshe smiled. "Yes," she said. "Yes, Tongol, if you can help Mr JP then you will not get into trouble."

JP took his cue. "Well, Tongol, what did you hear and what did you see?"

"I heard the helicopter take off. And I saw it fly away."

"You saw it fly away?" said JP. "How could you do that, if it was night time. Wasn't it very dark?"

"Yes, sir," said the boy. "It was dark. Very dark. But it was clear, there were thousands of stars looking down at us. I saw it fly off with the stars behind."

JP looked over at his astonished parents, and then

back at the boy. "Tongol, could you take me to where you were watching the helicopter from? And show me the direction it went off in?"

The boy nodded, held out his hand and tugged JP. With the parents following, Tongol led JP into his bedroom, opened the window and climbed out. Hidden round the corner at the back of the house lay a broken tree branch ten feet long, which Tongol lifted and placed up against the house rear wall. He climbed up the branch and stood on top of the roof, beckoning to JP with his hand. "Come," he said.

JP knew that the branch would snap as soon as he put his weight onto it, and looked around for something else. Simba saw what he was doing. "Here, JP." He bent over, offering his back.

"Are you sure?" he said.

"Sure, man. This is a farmer's back. It's strong, you know."

JP smiled. He climbed up onto it, stood and then was up onto the tiled roof too. The boy took his hand again and walked him up to the apex that spanned the longer length of the house. They turned round and then both sat on the ridge tiles at the top. They stared out over the rear of the house and across the savannah.

"Ok, Tongol," said JP. "What did you see?"

"The airstrip is there," he said, pointing behind them and off to the right, towards the hangar three miles away. "I was sitting here like this, looking ahead and up at the stars. And I heard the helicopter start up. I turned round to look. The noise slowed down for a while, and then it started up again, and it took off. I could make it out clearly."

"You're a clever lad," said JP. "So which way did it go?"

"It stayed low. And it flew across and off in that

direction," and the boy pointed with his arm outstretched.

"Did it change course at all?"

"No. I could see it for a few minutes. And it went straight."

Tongol was facing across the rear of the house, still pointing. Forty-five degrees off to his right.

Straight towards Mozambique and the Indian Ocean.

The time was approaching 5pm. Over the next two hours, JP had a good and simple meal with the Kawala family. Eshe warmed the meat, Tongol got the water and put the jugs on the table, Simba carved more bread. And when they were sitting and just about to start, Chaneen came out from her room, and joined them, sitting quietly, and ate too. She didn't speak often, but she listened, and laughed once or twice too with the others; it did her good to be with her family, and with the stranger who had rescued them all and saved them. When the meal was finished, the first sounds started to come from the two men who had been dragged outside in front of the door.

"Do you happen to have any duct tape, Simba?" said JP, who wanted to prevent any abuse coming from the two men. He for one had had quite enough of them, and he was certain the family had too.

"Are you kidding?" said Simba. "A farm like this one is held together by that stuff."

JP wrapped some tape firmly over the mouths and round the back of the head of the two torturers. Then he went back inside and sat in the sitting area. The children had been sent to their rooms, and this time the doors were firmly closed.

JP put his head down into his hands; he was suddenly feeling a little giddy. He had been ignoring the pain from his torture, but it was attacking him badly now and in particular he needed to do something about his burned skin. He asked if Eshe had any Vaseline or similar cream, and she asked why; then it was quickly clear to Eshe and Simba what had happened earlier. JP filled in some of the details that they hadn't been able to guess.

Both Eshe and Simba demanded that JP remove his shirt. They were appalled at what they saw. JP's chest, in fact his entire upper torso, was covered in blue and black bruises. The burned skin was red and some very unpleasant-looking large blisters were already appearing; in fact it was the blisters that were the most painful. They had to be pierced. Eshe got to work. With a sewing needle that she repeatedly heated in a candle flame and then let cool she pierced the base of the burn blisters on his lower back and under his armpits. She pushed the fluid out from beneath with a thin cotton cloth and soaked it up. She carefully dabbed the wounds clean with fresh water, and then applied some burn cream and added a layer of Vaseline; she then bandaged the wounds.

In view of what had happened to Eshe and Chaneen JP refused to remove his trousers for treatment to his upper thighs. Instead, JP doctored himself in the family bathroom. At the end of the second hour he was feeling much better and was once again comfortable enough to be mobile. He looked at the clock on the wall again, and said, "I have to go."

"Go?" said Simba, surprised at the statement. "Go where? It's almost night! Where can you go at this time?"

"Aren't you staying with us overnight, JP?" said Eshe. "You need to rest, you should stay until morning."

"No, thank you both," replied JP, "but I have to leave you now and go and meet someone. I am being collected."

"Oh, well, ok," said Simba, "of course."

"But there is something you could do for me, please, if you can."

"Anything, JP. What do you need?"

JP put on his shoulder holster, and gathered his carbine and other things together. There wasn't much, for he had entered the farmhouse with little other than fighting gear. He then said goodbye to the Kawala family. Eshe hugged him and gave a kiss on the cheek, Simba shook hands and then hugged too. Chaneen came over, and smiled, and then she too put her arms around his neck and reached up on her tiptoes to kiss him on the cheek. JP smiled back, and then knelt down to see Tongol. They shook hands solemnly - traditional, then thumbs up with fingers round the ball of the thumb, then traditional again. Tongol smiled and flung his arms around JP once more, hugging tightly.

JP hugged back. "Be good for your parents and look after your sister, young man. And thank you for your help."

JP felt a lump in his throat and had to swallow hard. He wished good for this family; he knew he would probably never see any of them again, and he was grateful for their brief help and friendship.

Simba and JP went outside, and closed the door. Eshe kept the children away from the windows. The sounds of the African savannah night were already loud again.

Simba went off and returned with his Range Rover. They put the back seats down, and put the two men, who were complaining bitterly through the tape around their mouths, onto the back. JP stowed his gear and added the few extra items he had asked of Simba. They got in. Just before Simba started the engine again, JP spoke.

"Simba, are you sure you want to do this?" he said.

"You don't have to, you know. This is my world, not yours."

Simba put his hands on the top of the steering wheel and lowered his head onto them. He took a deep sigh and then turned to JP.

"JP, I'm not a fighting man, not like you, with guns and your hands; I'm a farmer, I fight with my hands in another way, every day, trying to drag a living and a life out of this land for Eshe and the children. But if I were able to fight like you, I would do what you are doing. And this is my chance, for me to put things right a little bit, for my family, for what these people did to my woman, and my little girl, and to me, and to my boy who had to see it all too. So, yes, JP, I want to do this. If you'll let me."

JP looked at Simba. "Right. That's clear enough. And, by the way, if I were in your shoes, I would want to do exactly the same. Come on then, let's go." Bravery and courage come in all sorts of different shapes and sizes, he said to himself.

Simba drove first to the hangar. He got out with JP and helped him pick up the dead body of Eltong, and put it in the back with the other two. They moaned loudly when they saw the lifeless corpse, and realised they were all going for a drive. Then JP took the chain by which he had been suspended earlier that day down from the lintel beam, and got back into the car.

Simba knew the dirt tracks very well and the night blackness didn't confuse him at all. They headed east guided by the car's powerful headlights, past the barn area and on into wilder territory. The tracks virtually disappeared in another two miles and the car bounced along at a slower speed, navigating the bushes and the odd tree carefully. They stopped at the next clearing they came across. They lifted the dead man out first and put him on the ground in front of the headlights.

JP fetched the paper and blackened piece of wood that Simba had provided. He took Eltong's right hand, rubbed the man's fingers onto the burnt wood and pushed the charcoaled fingers carefully onto a sheet of paper. Then he took the fingerprints of the left hand. He folded the sheets up neatly and put them into his pocket with the others of the two men he had done earlier.

They dragged the two hogtied men from the car. Simba fetched the sledge hammer and the fence-wire pegs; JP brought the chain. Simba placed the point of a peg through a middle link and hammered it into the ground. The thicker upper part wedged the chain tight and entirely secure.

JP put one end of the chain through the loop of rope around Akunda's neck, took it down around his arms still secured behind him and then back up. They pulled the squealing, wriggling man away from the peg to take the slack out of the chain. Then Simba hammered a peg through the end link and one just above Akunda's head, fixing him to that spot. With some delight Simba held the man's legs while JP took out his knife, cut the rope from the man's neck to his feet and tied the top part off at his arms. He pulled the bottom part to straighten Akunda's legs. Simba hammered in another peg and they secured the rope to it. The man was pinned to the ground on his back wearing only his underpants and boots, his hands tied behind him, his legs outstretched.

JP and Simba then took Mandeeb onto the opposite side and secured him similarly. JP used his knife to slice the man's trousers open on both legs, up to above the knee. In five minutes the two torturers and rapists were fifteen feet from the central peg and Eltong's body, and thirty feet apart at opposite ends of the chain.

The strong lights of the Range Rover cast heavy

shadows over the two men on the ground in the ominous, eerie scene. JP walked to Akunda and pulled the tape off from around his mouth and head. He was oblivious to the whines and the mixture of pleading and abuse.

"I want you to listen to me, Akunda."

He certainly had Akunda's attention.

"If you think you can do what you did to me, and to Mr Kawala here and his family, and get away with it, you are very much mistaken. What you did was very wrong. Now I want you to apologise to Mr Kawala."

"Yes, yes, I am sorry, I am really sorry. And I apologise to your wife and your daughter and your boy. Please. Please don't do this to me, please."

"What did you think of that, Mr Kawala?"

"It helped a bit," said Simba. "A tiny bit."

"Good. That helps a tiny bit, Mr Kawala says. Now, you can tell me something..." JP took out his handgun from his holster, suppressor still attached, and pulled back the hammer to cock it. He bent down a little and placed the end of the silencer two inches from Akunda's right kneecap. The man screamed in terror, the whites of his bulging eyes contrasting strongly with the darkness of his black skin.

"No, please, please don't."

"Tell me, Akunda. Tell me. If you do not..." JP's voice trailed off and he shook his head. "Well I think it will be better for you if you answer my questions. Who are you, where are you from, what were your instructions."

The man was very keen to talk. In five minutes, JP had everything out of him that he could possibly want. Then JP and Simba walked over to Mandeeb who also apologised profusely to Mr Kawala and his family. And was also very keen to talk.

They walked back to the car. It was time for them to leave.

"Can I say a... 'goodbye'" ...Simba spat the word out contemptuously... "to them?"

"Absolutely," said JP. "Be my guest."

JP stayed by the car. He saw Simba go over to Akunda first, kneel down, put his head down close the man's, and say some words. Then Simba went over to Mandeeb and did the same.

When he came back, JP didn't ask what he had said, and Simba didn't tell him.

"Right, let's go," said JP. The two men on the ground heard, and screamed at them to come back. JP wandered back over, and stood at Akunda's feet, looking down at him.

"I've told you everything," said Akunda. "You said you would release us if we answered your questions."

"Did I?" said JP, with a confused tone. "I don't think so, actually. What I said was, that it will be better for you if you talk. And it was, wasn't it?"

He stared down at a horrified and confused, begging and perspiring Akunda. He shook his head.

"I mean," said JP, "you confessed. And you know what they say: confession is good for the soul. Oh, by the way. I thought the cigar trick was especially unpleasant. So, this is just a little professional courtesy. Something from me to you."

And with that, JP calmly took out his Sauer, cocked it again, aimed slowly at Akunda's right kneecap and this time pulled the trigger. The gun gave a quiet 'phut' sound. The night was filled with a hideous piercing scream from Akunda as the bullet shattered the skin and bone, and blood and fragments scattered out around the man's leg. Akunda was almost fainting from the shock and the pain, and he knew that he would never walk properly again. If he ever got the chance. JP then aimed at the other knee, and fired again. There was another gurgling scream.

He walked over to Mandeeb, who knew what was coming. He was screaming for mercy. He screamed much louder, and differently, after JP had fired twice more.

JP and Simba climbed back into the car. Simba started the engine. He put the car into first gear, and slowly drove away. The men who had tortured JP and raped Simba's family saw the car lights vanish, heard the purr of the engine fade away. All that remained were the sounds of the African night bush, and the noises that each of the two men made.

Their screaming stopped, replaced by painful moaning and panting; and then that quietened, as their eyes and ears became adjusted to the night that now enveloped them. Their struggling lessened too. Because they knew any sounds would only draw attention. From the creatures, the predators, that hunted at night. Even if they were able to escape, they would not be able to walk, let alone run; only crawl. The man had made sure of that. And the smells - of sweat, of blood, of fear - were already in the air, fanning out into the bush, searching for sensitive nostrils, to be appreciated, welcomed, evoking instinct and stealth. A hunt. A slow death.

The two men in the car didn't speak for a while. They thought of the two men they had placed right in the heart of lion country. Once the car was gone and darkness returned the lions or hyenas would soon hear the whimpers, soon smell the blood from the smashed knees, soon pay them a visit. They knew the men would be eaten alive. It would be a fitting end to some particularly nasty people.

Simba found the dirt tracks again easily. He drove down to the small out barn that had been JP's drop target. Simba unlocked the doors - JP said he hoped he hadn't broken the lock and in fact he had not. JP went inside, quickly retrieved his spent parachute and helmet and collected the other box that he had wisely separated and hidden earlier. Then they were back in the car and driving to the hangar.

JP removed his kit from the car and placed it just inside the hangar entrance. Then the two men stood before the Range Rover. It was time for the final parting.

"Remember, Simba," said JP. "I don't think you'll see or hear from anyone in connection with those three, or the other first visitors, again. But if you do, you just tell them the truth. Say that a man came, and took them away."

"Ok, JP, I've got it."

"The stuff behind the barn that you showed me - keep it hidden safely for a few weeks, and then take it up to Harare and sell it. Get what you can for it, and enjoy the money."

"And what happens now? Where are you going, what's going to happen to you?"

"Me? Like I said, I'm going to be met in a little while."

"Will you be OK, JP? And what was stolen - you never did say?"

"I'll be fine, Simba, don't you worry about me. I can't tell you what was stolen. All I can say is that it was important, and it's my job to find it."

"You're special forces, aren't you? It's pretty obvious," said Simba, feeling safe in his remark now that he was away from his family. "Or a spy, or something."

JP smiled again at Simba. "I'm just a man with a job to do."

"Ok, I'll stop asking," said Simba, who could see JP wasn't going to say more. "Thank you, again. For everything. You saved us all. And take care of yourself."

"You too, Simba. And that lovely family of yours."

They shook hands one more time, hugged and gave each other a slap on the back. And then Simba was in the car driving back off to his home, his family and their life together. JP watched him go.

JP strapped his night vision goggles back on and removed the electronic box from its plastic bag. He turned the unit on, walked a little distance away from the hangar and pressed the one button on its front. A red light went on for two seconds, and then blinked steadily. He walked back over to the hangar, sat down and waited. His C8 carbine was on his lap. Just in case.

In just over an hour, he heard the distant harsh roar of lions mixed with a man's screams. It was repeated a few times over the next twenty minutes. Then the usual noisy bush sounds returned. The men were gone.

In another hour, JP heard what he had been waiting for.

He picked up the electronic homing device once more and when the flashing red light had turned to green he entered a safety sequence.

A minute later, the night symphony of the African bush was shattered by the scream of the single Rolls-Royce turbofan engine of the Harrier AV-8B II jump jet as it came in for its vertical landing. It was a 'T' version, the two-seater trainer type that Charlie Melton had suggested to Slim Wilkins that he might like to send from the *USS Ronald Reagan*.

JP stood just outside the hangar with his hands on his

hips, and the pilot landed the aircraft fifty feet away. The engine went off.

JP walked over carrying his gear. The curved glass cockpit bubble opened as he approached and the pilot stood up. He said in the darkness to JP, in a lovable New York drawl, "Cab for Captain Peregrine?"

"Good evening," said JP in response, "How I do like door-to-door service."

The pilot, Major Art Murtha, climbed down, and then up again to the rear seat. He took the flight suit out and handed it to JP who quickly put it on.

JP climbed up and buckled in with the help from the Major. JP was rather squashed, as he had to sit with his carbine, redundant skydive helmet and the rest of his kit on his lap, but he would manage.

The pilot got down, and then back up into the front seat. The glass cockpit bubbles closed on their hinges, and sealed tight.

"You ready, JP?" came Art's voice over the headset.

"Ready," he replied.

"Right. Here we go."

The pilot started the engine again, its massive thrust went down towards the ground. The pilot pushed the throttle forwards more, the thrust increased and then suddenly the Harrier rose majestically into the air, and kept on going, straight up, rising higher and higher in its graceful vertical rise from the ground. The aircraft tilted to forty-five degrees in its climb skywards and gradually increased in forward speed, the wings giving lift as the passing airflow grew and the pilot directed more and more of its twenty-three thousand five hundred pounds of thrust towards the rear.

It wasn't entirely an unseen departure. Several bush animals turned to look at the noise and saw a strange bird rise into the air and fly away.

And one pair of human eyes was watching too. They belonged to a small ten year old boy.

Over at the farmhouse, Tongol was supposed to be asleep, but he wasn't. He was sitting on top of the roof again and had seen the aircraft land at the hangar. He knew it had come to collect his friend. And now he saw the aircraft take off and soar up into the sky.

He would never forget his new friend, and nor would he ever forget that his friend took the bad men away and saved his family.

"Thank you, Mr JP," he said in a small grateful voice. And, with a quivering lower lip and tear-filled eyes still fixed on the fast-disappearing aircraft, added, "Goodbye..."

The Harrier was quickly high in the sky and tearing through the air at over six hundred miles an hour, heading north towards London.

≈

In another part of the world, the ship carrying the deadly Spider 2-3 inched backwards into a canal dock at the quayside set in an enormous metal hangar, and was quickly tied up. The stern divided into two curved halves, and the large ramp of reinforced steel within lowered on hydraulic arms either side to touch the solid concrete ground of the quay.

The large truck came off the ship. The door at the rear right corner of the hangar rolled off against the wall giving way to a tunnel and closed again smoothly as the truck passed through. The tunnel was short, and a second door at its end rolled away to open into another hangar, smaller and more compact. The second door closed, creating a soundproof seal for the smaller hangar. The truck's rear ramp panel was once again lowered and Colonel Linchuk reversed the SS-23 out. Ground marshals helped him manoeuvre the Spider onto the crosshairs painted on the floor in the centre of the building.

The truck went out the way it had come in, and back into the hold of the ship. The main lights of the docking hangar were dimmed, the rope lines of the ship were cast off. The huge hangar door rolled back. Slowly the engines moved the ship forwards very gently, the bow thrusters working to inch the ship away from the quay. As she moved out into the harbour the hangar door began to close shut, and the lights went out. The ship had been in dock for just under one hour. The only lights of the harbour that could now be seen were the two on either end of the breakwaters two hundred yards forward. The ship slowly moved towards them.

Abisali, the truck driver, left the confines of the ship's hold and came up onto the deck. He went to the stern, to look back at the harbour. The captain steered the ship through the centre of the gap between the breakwaters, and then ordered the revolutions of the propellers increased. The ship began to pick up speed and the lights on the harbour breakwaters became smaller and dimmer as the ship moved further away.

Abisali thought of the man he had left in the harbour, of the deadly cargo that they had just delivered, and wondered if he would ever see him again. He had come to like Colonel Anatoly Linchuk during the days of their sea voyage together. He looked from the rear of the ship until the harbour lights went below the horizon, as the ship moved off out into the open sea.

Inside the hangar, encapsulated in its mausoleum of painted white steel and aluminium, the Spider 2-3 rested quietly alone, a cold and lethal combination of man's most ingenious scientific endeavours perverted by evil and fear, now awaiting its afterlife by a rejoining with a 9M714K-Alpha.

She wouldn't have to wait long. The Alpha was already on its way.

23
BACK HOME

THE FIRST THING JP did when in the car whisking him away from RAF Northolt at 6.30am was to call Charlie Melton, who wanted JP to go straight to MI6's private and exclusive top-security ward at the Cromwell Road hospital. JP was hurting again badly and needed medical attention. However they agreed the discussion would take priority so that JP could first report the intelligence gathered from his mission into Zimbabwe.

The second thing he did was to stop at his hotel, collect his cell phone and send two text messages on the new one. After a little toing and froing over timings he had a late lunch and a late dinner organised for the day. He quickly washed his hands and face - there was no time for a shower and he was in too much pain anyway to change his clothes. So he went in as he was.

This time Sir Alistair Crewe took the meeting at the House. JP gave his report, and passed on the various items he had brought back. Finally, he outlined the information he had obtained from Akunda and Mandeeb, that they knew nothing of the bomb or the purpose of the Alpha, which had been confirmed when JP had heard their conversation while he had feigned unconsciousness under torture, although they knew the name Fincrest and that something valuable had been stolen from there.

"They were merely to guard the place and report any

unusual relevant activity by radioing in to a specified frequency at a certain time in the evening. They were more interested in seeing if they could get an additional payment for me, before handing over the information they believed they could extract from me. They said they were former members of the Zimbabwe army and left because of the bad pay and conditions, and found the attraction of the work for which they had been hired of much more interest. They'd been brought in by a local middle man in Harare known for recruiting mercenaries." JP handed over a small piece of paper with the man's name written on it. "Though I very much doubt it will go anywhere."

"Probably not," said Sir Alistair. "That's the trouble with these cells, they're all separate from each other and connecting them up is nigh on impossible. Still we'll try." He handed the paper to Melton. "What happened to the two men?"

JP was silent for a while, and then said. "We had a fight. They lost."

"No loose ends I take it?" said Sir Alistair.

"No, sir. None."

Sir Alistair nodded. He had nothing further to ask on the subject. His man had been beaten and tortured by these people, and their demise was of no interest to him. They had got what they deserved. Although, JP hadn't exactly given the details.

"We have some information on the tyre data from the pictures you sent us," said Melton, looking over at Jane.

"Yes," she said. "The larger tyres were just standard issue for a Range Rover exactly like the one the farmer has. And incidentally, the number plates that the drone got of the vehicle went nowhere; it was purchased legitimately in Harare for cash using a name and false French passport, our man there says. However, the other tyre marks that you took were definitely of an aircraft, used on a variety of makes, including a Bell 429 helicopter, exactly the same as the one that was followed by the UAVs from the Fincrest Centre."

"Well, all things considered I believe it's pretty obvious that we now have the trail of the Alpha," said Melton. "I think we can discount the possibility that any of the men who left the helicopter in Harare or Lusaka took it with them. Thanks to JP, we have the evidence and proof that shows the Alpha was indeed dropped. It was parachuted down very cleverly; flown out to sea, and is, or was, on a ship somewhere."

"Yes quite," said Sir Alistair. "Do you have the position of those GPS figures, Lieutenant?" asked Sir Alistair.

"Just working it out, sir," said Jane looking at her laptop. "Yes, sir, I do, I have it now. Not the exact full location, as the figures JP found were partially scorched and came up a couple short. But it would appear that they are approximately fifty miles out to sea to the south-east of the Mozambique coastal town of Nova Sofala."

"Then that has to be our next target," said JP. "Fincrest was blown up at around midnight; the helicopter drop was an hour or so later, then a two hour flight to a sea rendezvous. The Kawalas said the helicopter took off at around 2am. You can work out the figures more accurately, but I would say that we're looking for a ship that was at those GPS co-ordinates between 4am and 6am the morning after the Alpha was stolen.

"Yes," said Melton. "But tracing a ship that was in that position four or five days ago is going to be an enormous task. Finding a satellite that was over there that day and time, sifting through the data... well it's not going to be easy."

"And of course," said the Lieutenant, "it could easily have been helicoptered off to another city or airport and then flown out in a private jet. So they will have to check all of those too."

"It's a very big job," said Melton. "It's going to take a week or two at least."

"Yes. Well, pass all this new information on to the Americans and let them get on with it," said Sir Alistair. "The sooner the better."

"Yes, sir," said the Lieutenant, "right away."

"JP," said Sir Alistair, "you've done a fine job, at some considerable discomfort to yourself. Thank you."

"Thank you," said JP. "However I feel I must apologise for the awful aroma coming from me, I came straight here after splashing some water on, I didn't bother to shower or change, as you can doubtless tell."

The others smiled, and they all rose. "Come on, JP, let's get you to the medics," said Melton.

Melton was disgusted at the torture his friend had had inflicted upon him, and appalled to see the bruising and burns. Fucking bastards, he muttered under his breath, several times, as with the help of nurses JP stripped to show the damage to the doctors. "I'll be outside, JP. They'll look after you." The medics got to work. He was x-rayed pretty much over his entire torso to check for broken or fractured bones, and then they also checked for internal bleeding. Mercifully, there was none, only the nasty bruising. It would appear that his torturers were skilled and knew how to inflict pain without breakages. The burns were the worst. Mainly very painful second-degree ones, but one or two verged on penetrating through both the epidermis and dermis skin layers and becoming more serious third-degree category. He was treated with cold water splashes, cold compresses and special creams, particularly narcotic pain relievers that helped almost immediately to ease JP's agony. Finally, the medics covered the burns with soft dressing gauze pads and he was bandaged again. They would visit him twice daily, to redress the wounds and ensure speedy recovery.

Charlie Melton drove JP back to Claridge's. Neither said much, each lost in his own thoughts. Then JP spoke.

"How do you think she's doing, Charlie? Do you think she's still alive?"

Melton pondered for a while. "If you want my cold assessment, which I know you do," he said quietly, "then I would say that I think, yes, she is still alive. I'll tell you why. She gave them all of the information - that's obvious as the raid on the Fincrest Centre went smoothly for them. They forced it out of her, of course. If I were in their shoes, in Malekka's shoes, I would keep her alive, and for three reasons. First, I would enjoy showing off the results of my efforts to her, showing we'd taken the Alpha, that we have the weapon too, maybe even keep her for the time of the launch itself. Second, she's a very beautiful girl. I would enjoy having that, and also relish in the knowledge, the statement, that having her would make - to me, to her, to everyone - another victory by Malekka over the enemy, the infidel. And third, if all else fails, if something happens and the plan for the bomb isn't achieved, then I would use her as a final weapon, publicly humiliate her and the family. I'd pretend to trade her. Maybe even get some money. But then, instead, I'd kill her." He paused for a few moments. "So yes, JP, I think she's still alive. And, thanks to you, we have the trail again now. I have no doubts about that."

"Me neither," said JP. "But you know what the

trouble is." It was a statement, not a question.

"Yes, I do, only too well, my friend," he said as he pulled the car up outside the hotel. He turned to look at JP. "If they have the Alpha, we have to assume they have the bomb. And no-one's going to steal a nuclear weapon and sit on it for a couple of weeks. There's too much danger of getting discovered and caught."

"Exactly," nodded JP grimly. "Once it's been taken, it's going to be used, and used sooner rather than later. We're running out of time."

And everybody knew it.

"Get some rest, Jimmy," said Melton, "if you can."

≈

It was 11.30am, but JP really didn't have time for rest. He took off the casuals that the hospital had lent him, and with a bit of effort managed to change - some clean underpants and socks, light trousers and fresh open-necked shirt, slip-on leather shoes. He even managed a red cravat. When he was downstairs at 12.15pm, the concierge had the rental car waiting for him in Brook Street. JP set off for lunch, the first of two private meetings that he had set up that day, unknown to Melton and MI6.

JP had first met Steve Montague seven years previously at a party, and the two had become good friends. On Thursday, the day he arrived back from Cape Town, JP had called Steve and they met up at Claridge's the next afternoon. Now he was heading for the follow-up.

He drove to Abinger Hammer, just outside Dorking in Surrey. He had known the village since boyhood. It was a special place for him. He pulled into the car park of the Abinger Arms, got out and waited, as he always did. He gazed briefly at the cricket ground and thought of the trout in the Tillingbourne that flows by. What a beautiful quiet village, full of decency and civilisation; what a contrast to the madness of the violent world in which he was presently immersed.

JP looked up at the village clock. Ceremoniously, Jack the Blacksmith raised his hammer and hit the ornate cast iron bell twice to signal 2pm. JP smiled. Then he read the inscription on the clock. *'By me you know how fast to go'*. He stared at it grimly for a few seconds. He may soon have to go faster than he had ever gone before.

JP drove down the road a little more to reach the Michelin-starred Drakes on the Pond Restaurant, parked up and went inside.

"You look like shit," said Montague, who had spotted the slight stiffness JP had in his movements. "What's happened to you in three days?"

"Don't ask," said JP. And Steve knew better than to do so.

As soon as they had ordered and the waiter had gone off, JP looked across the table at Steve and said quietly, "Is it done?"

"Yes, it's done."

"Good. So let's have it, Steve. Hand it over."

Montague grimaced a little, sighed and put his left hand into his jacket pocket. He pulled out a small slim box, three inches long by one deep, and under an inch high. He put it on the table, slid it over to JP and said in a low voice, "You know that that is totally illegal, don't you. That's a highly advanced little gizmo and it is totally bloody illegal."

JP picked it up.

"And if there were any MI5 or Police around in here and they knew what it was, we'd both get arrested and thrown in the clink. And then they'd chuck away the key."

JP smiled at his electronics genius friend as he put it calmly into his own pocket.

"Then we'd better not tell them, had we," he said.

Just for a second, JP's eyes had a mischievous but deadly twinkle in them.

≈

As JP drove back to London two hours later he wondered for the thousandth time how Stella was. He hoped that Melton's assessment was right. He pondered again on his trip to Zimbabwe. And on the little item that Steve had given him.

He knew they needed to crack this conspiracy and they needed to do it very soon. He just hoped and prayed they would be in time, before the phone rang with news of a nuclear explosion somewhere. Or maybe he would see it first on CNN. Or be in it, if London was the target. Any second, it could all end.

JP was back at Claridge's in good time for his final meeting at 8pm, with the same person who had come to see him twice before. First, after he had arrived in London from St Lucia before going on to Cape Town, and again as a result of his text sent as soon as the Gripen had delivered him safely from Ysterplaat four days ago.

After their dinner in his rooms and his guest had left, JP had a visit from the Doctors at 11pm who changed the dressings on his wounds. They would be back tomorrow at 10am. It seemed they were pleased and that he was healing well.

JP put on a T-shirt for the night and climbed into bed wearing nothing else, although a large part of him was covered in bandages.

He laid his head exhausted on the pillows. His last thought, before he fell into a deep sleep, was that while the world has much evil in it and people like the Malekkas abound, it also has truly good people in it. Some with great courage, and great bravery.

Like the person who had dined with him that evening...

≈

JP slept late into the morning, and wasn't even up when the Doctors arrived at 10am to change his dressings. He did nothing all day except sleep, eat and rest. He had a late breakfast, and slept; and a late lunch, and slept. He knew that his body was recharging, re-energising, and by the end of the day he felt able to have a bath unaided. He removed his bandages and had a good soak in comforting warm water. When the Doctors came again at 6pm he felt refreshed and much better. Into the evening, he was invigorated, restored and full of strength and energy once more.

It was just as well that fate had permitted him a day of rest and recovery.

Because, although he didn't yet know it, in just over twenty-four hours Jim Peregrine was going to need all his strength, ability and determination in ways that he could not possibly imagine. And he would be tested to the extreme on his Regiment's motto of *Qui Audet Adipiscitur*.

Who Dares, Wins.

24
HERMES

THE JOURNEY HAD taken just under six days. On board the *Excelsior*, most of the time Stella was kept indoors in her cabin, or in Malekka's state rooms. He had taken her that same night, when they celebrated the arrival of the Alpha unit five days ago; he had asked her to join him for dinner on his deck, and she had of course been obliged to do so. They had been served a wonderful meal, as fine as the best restaurant on land could have managed, and then he had required her to stay the night with him.

She had no choice. He was not a brutal lover; it was not a violent assault rape, as it could be. The only reason she consented at all, if consented was the right word, was because of what else would happen to her and to people she cared about if she did not. She knew that Malekka could kill as easily as he could make love, and she had become resigned to the fact that she must surrender to him physically; totally, completely and unreservedly. When she was with him, she comforted herself by thinking of JP, and of imagining that she was with him and only him; and when Malekka told her to do things to him for his pleasure, she imagined that she was doing them to JP, for his pleasure. In the cold world in which she was now forced to live, her imagination warmed her heart and her soul, and helped to keep her sane. And alive. Malekka was pleased with her, and wanted her time and time again. She knew she now lived as a whore, selling her body in exchange for life itself.

Sometimes she was allowed onto the pool deck to swim and sit in the sun, but never under the open sky; always, there was a cover that extended from the deck above and screened her. When land or another ship appeared on the horizon or radar she was immediately taken back inside by the burka girls. She assumed, correctly, that the additional controls were precautions in case she was seen by others, a ship, a passing satellite, powerful binoculars from land, unknown UAVs making a general sweep of the area. Malekka was taking no chances. He ran a tight operation, in every way.

Malekka would often tell her how he wished her to dress for the next evening or afternoon - she was rarely required by him before 3pm. But then after the first couple of nights she had been with him, he told her that she would be obliged to wear a burka, as the other women on board the ship did; all with the exception of Aisha that is, who never wore one. The reason why Aisha was excused from this was never explained to her; perhaps, thought Stella, it was because of the senior authority she held in the organisation, unlike her burka servants and the other women whose position in the hierarchy was low.

Stella hated the burka. She hated the material and what it stood for and, strangely, she also hated being perceived to be on the same level as her burka girls. She did enjoy one element of it, and that was the great care and attention the women paid to their eyes, the only body part generally visible. So Stella metamorphosed from one creature into another; first sometimes in a skimpy bikini on her personal time by the pool; then into a burka on a par with most of the other women; then into a sexy female of pleasure for Malekka when he wished it to be so, in more traditional western afternoon or evening attire. She wore her jewellery through the days and nights; how she had come to love and cherish it more than she ever thought possible, a reminder to her not only of her life outside from which she had been wrenched, but also of how her co-operation kept the people she loved and cared for safe and alive.

She had no idea where the ship was going. She was not allowed out at night and could not see the stars, and anyway she was busy entertaining Malekka. She was not allowed sight of land, and they clearly didn't want her to know or discover her location or destination. However as the days passed she did notice that her watch stayed more or less in time with the rising and setting of the sun, and so she assumed the movement of the ship was more along a line of longitude and so south to north. Travel east or west would cause her watch to slide out of step, and that did not seem to be happening.

Unless, of course, someone was secretly altering the time on her watch when she was asleep, which although difficult was entirely possible. She didn't think that was happening, but couldn't know for sure. Indeed she couldn't be sure about anything, which was why she was co-operating so fully with Malekka, she reminded herself again. Just stay alive.

Stella thought often of her family, and of JP, the man who had come into her life and with whom she thought she had fallen in love. She wondered how he would be if he knew what she was doing every evening, and doing willingly, with full compliance, no resistance. He would understand, wouldn't he? Yes of course. Would he still want her afterwards, if there was an afterwards? Understand, yet reject her? Could life really be that cruel? She had always had JP in her mind when she was with Malekka, that's how she got through it; but now there was, suddenly, a bigger problem. She had actually had orgasms on the last two nights with Malekka, and Stella was finding that sickeningly confusing. That was bad, it just wasn't right. How could it ever happen, she thought? Why didn't she stop herself, when she felt the climax approaching? Was this just another part of Malekka's sick plan, to break her even though she was broken, to reach inside her heart and soul and tear out the most personal and private part of her existence and take that from her too? What is going on in my head, she thought?

After four days, the ship dropped its speed down to five or six knots for a full twenty-four hours and she was confined to her cabin. It reminded her of when she first awoke on board the ship; she shuddered at the memory. One good thing was that she was left alone by Malekka for that night, and she was grateful for the respite.

Then at around 4pm the sound of the engines suddenly increased and the ship moved at speed again. She was allowed back up onto the pool deck and enjoyed the late afternoon sun for a couple of hours until night began to draw in. She wondered why Malekka hadn't sent for her before now, but then Shurafa came and told her that the ship would be docking just after midnight. She was to stay in her cabin for the evening and prepare to disembark.

Stella was elated. She was going to be on dry land again. She was sure she would still be restricted in everything but somehow the thought of her feet actually being on firm ground, wherever it was in the world, made her feel much more free and like her old self. On land she could survive; on board a ship she was more confined, surrounded by water, reliant on others. And on land, there was always the possibility of escape.

Stella enjoyed a quiet meal on her own, without

Malekka, although as usual one of the burka girls was with her. She rested a little, and then later thought she could feel the ship change direction to the right, which in fact it had by almost ninety degrees. Then finally after another hour or so the engines slowed again and she knew the docking was close. She was keen to go onto the deck to watch, which she was told she could do. She had very little luggage of her own, of course, since most of it had been left on St Lucia; but what little there was she packed carefully into the small suitcase provided by Nasrin.

The burka girls indicated to her that she need not worry about any of the other clothes or anything else in her cabin, as her new accommodation had copious similar items for her to use and enjoy. Stella left the suitcase by the foot of the bed, and then accompanied Nasrin and Shurafa up onto the deck.

The air was still warm from the heat of the day, the sea was calm and untroubled and the stars already twinkled down from a clear dark sky above. In the distance, Stella could see lights of a harbour and, once her eyes had adjusted, that the ship was slowly paralleling a breakwater maybe a hundred yards off the starboard beam.

Stella couldn't quite make out the shape of the harbour, but it seemed there was a land peninsula from which the first breakwater extended at right angles, and then itself curved round another ninety degrees. She was right, for, slowly, the ship turned starboard to follow the breakwater line a couple of hundred metres; then there was a gap, and another began. The ship slowly turned right again, moving between the breakwater end walls with the single light on each into the harbour entrance and the quiet protected waters beyond.

The *Excelsior* slowed almost to a full stop, and used

its powerful bow and stern thrusters to rotate clockwise on its central axis, then push sideways towards the dimly-lit quay twenty yards wide running along the land's edge. Then the ship started to move backwards.

Suddenly the lights of the harbour blazed out as bright as day. Five men were walking along the quayside paralleling the ship as it reversed. The quay continued in a right angle, but at the corner the waters opened into a large canal-like berth within steel and aluminium panels and girders of a huge hangar some sixty yards by twenty. With infinite care the ship was reversed in by her captain and gently manoeuvred into place.

The massive door that had rolled open onto the landward side was already beginning to close. It sealed off the night with a loud metallic clang that reverberated around the cavernous building. The ship was entirely enclosed. Ten minutes later, the *Excelsior* was moored securely.

Stella disembarked from the ship down a gangway behind Malekka and his two bodyguards, followed by Aisha and two other burka-clad women that she had not seen before. Nasrin and Shurafa were behind. As she went, Stella noticed the large exit door at the far corner of the hangar off to her left, and wondered where that led to and what it was for.

Stella rejoiced quietly to herself as soon as her feet were once again on firm ground, even if it was just the quayside. The group moved straight ahead towards the hangar wall, where wide double doors opened automatically giving access to a short corridor and a pair of much more solid doors at the end. One side opened, held ajar by a man who appeared to be a valet, and the party walked into a luxurious reception hall.

Malekka turned round to Stella and said proudly,

"Welcome to Cuttle Cove, my little temporary home. So named, by the way, because of all the local cuttlefish."

"That's a charming name," replied Stella.

"Thank you, Miss Fincrest," said Malekka, ever the gentleman, on the surface at least. Then in Arabic he spoke to Nasrin and Shurafa, who quickly moved off to a door right and beckoned Stella to go with them.

"Your suite is that way," said Malekka, "and I will join you later, perhaps in half an hour."

Stella followed the burka girls. She was very dejected at that moment; she was hoping she might be left alone for another night but apparently it was not to be.

Her rooms were down another short corridor, and the valet accompanying them unlocked the door and led the way into the most opulent suite Stella had ever seen. The lounge was easily three times the size of the room on board the ship and lavishly furnished. The bedroom was off through double doors in the middle of the left wall and on either side were further rooms one of which was the large bathroom, finished in Italian marble with solid gold taps and gold-rimmed sinks and faucets. The dressing room contained an enormous walk-in closet with an extensive variety of designer clothing that all seemed to be exactly her style, and taste too, she admitted to herself.

Even Stella was impressed by the sheer lavishness of her new surroundings. She made use of the amenities of the bathroom and freshened herself a little; there was no time for another shower, if Malekka was arriving that soon. When she came out into the lounge again Nasrin had disappeared, presumably to go to her own rooms, and Stella was just about to go to explore more of her suite when there was a knock at the door.

Shurafa quickly opened it and Malekka walked in.

"Miss Stella, I was going to wait until tomorrow morning," he said, "but frankly I don't want to. I am going to see the other piece of cargo this evening before retiring to bed, and I thought you might care to accompany me."

"Oh yes, sir, I would," she replied, and then added as she walked slowly over to him, "After all, this is why I was taken from St Lucia, isn't it."

"Yes, that is correct."

"So, yes, I would like to see what you needed the Alpha for, very much."

"Of course. Well, come with me." He held out his arm. She took it and walked out with him. Together with Nasrin, who had reappeared, he led her across the main reception hall to doors that opened into the warm evening air, and Stella could at once smell the gentle aromatic waves of oranges and olives and hear the crickets that hid in the grass. They followed a covered path round to the back of a facing smaller hangar. Malekka opened a door, and they walked through.

Stella gasped. "My God," she said.

In the middle beneath the bright clinical light was the Spider 2-3 in its transporter, a monstrous machine forty feet long and ten wide in dark camouflage green. The top was split open along its back, from the cabin on the right down to the rear. Raised and sticking out at thirty degrees was the missile, over twenty feet long and a metre in diameter at its base, an intimidating epitome of cold lethal terror and ominous terminal dread offering the end of existence itself.

The engine of the transport vehicle was running. Its exhaust fumes were being taken away in a thick plastic pipe into an exposed floor panel, presumably exiting somewhere in the open. There were four thick heavy tyres on both sides, and at each corner of the rectangular machine the extended hydraulic legs gave absolute rigidity to the launch vehicle and its deadly missile. Alongside the Spider were a small range of desks, computers and a plethora of electronic equipment set on various tables. Several people in long white coats stood close by.

There was steam coming from the area at the base of the rocket. Stella looked along its length to the tapered pointed front that she knew encased the nuclear bomb itself. She thought of the ghastly effect it would have wherever it goes, wherever it lands, and thought of New York, of 9/11, and a brief image flashed through her mind of the decimation that would follow if this weapon were to detonate in the City's midst.

Stella looked over at Malekka. He was staring at the rocket in awe, with absolute delight on his face, pride too. He looked down at her, and said, "Well Miss Fincrest, what do you think of my SS-23 Spider? Beautiful, is she not?!"

Stella had to force her reply out. "I am staggered, sir. Terrified. Yes, terrified, more than anything."

They walked over closer to the weapon. Aisha was obviously the head of the science team, and she turned as they approached.

"Mr Malekka, we're just about to shut it down for the evening, if that's all right with you, sir," she said. "I just wanted to come in quickly and see it, and bring the Alpha unit in ready for work on it tomorrow."

"Yes, yes, of course. You should rest, and then start fresh on it tomorrow." Malekka turned to the man. "And you are Colonel Linchuk, are you not?"

"Good evening, Mr Malekka," said Linchuk, "it is a great pleasure to meet you at last." He extended his hand. Each gripped the other's firmly.

"The pleasure is mine, Colonel," said Malekka.

"And first, I should say, I think, thank you, and congratulations, on a job very well done."

"Thank you, sir," he replied, standing smartly and almost to full attention.

"How is she, is she behaving herself?"

"Oh yes, sir, the equipment is in perfect working order," replied Linchuk. He looked over briefly at Stella, and then back to Malekka. Malekka noticed his brief distraction.

"I'm sorry, Stella may I present Colonel Anatoly Linchuk of the Spetsnaz, the special forces of the Russian Federation. Colonel Linchuk, this is Miss Stella Fincrest, from South Africa. Her father owns the Fincrest Centre, which Miss Fincrest runs and from where our Alpha unit has just been commandeered."

"How do you do, Miss Fincrest," said Linchuk, taking her outstretched hand in his and giving it a firm but gentle shake.

"Good evening, Colonel," replied Stella.

Linchuk continued directly to Malekka. "Sir, we are just about to close down as Miss Aisha says, and with your permission I will continue?"

"Yes, please, both of you, finish up."

The Colonel walked back over to the Spider, and climbed up inside the rear of the front cabin where the launch controls were located. In a few seconds there was a whining of hydraulics and the rocket began to lower, gradually sinking back down into the heart of the launcher. The sides closed up above it, making it both air-proof and water-proof. One would never know or even be able to hazard a guess what was inside.

Linchuk switched off the engines, and the reverberating sound of the motor vanished. A contrasting calm settled in the building. Aisha turned off the last of the terminals and screens, and the place fell silent, save for the gentle sound of air conditioning.

"Stella, come closer," said Malekka, "see what my men have procured for me, all the way from the heart of Russia."

She walked up to the launcher. Its dimensions were intimidating and its stark threatening coldness more evident.

"It's incredible," said Stella. "And the Alpha, may I see it again?"

"Yes you may, Stella."

The Alpha unit was on the centre table adjacent to the Spider 2-3. Just a simple cold box of electronics, coded uniquely with a launch sequence linking the missile and its bomb, making all three parts work as one. The Spider stolen somehow from within Russia. Inoperative without the little box brought from South Africa. Quite an operation, she thought. One couldn't help being impressed by the resources and abilities of this man.

"I am astonished, sir," she said. And she really was. They had been talking about the weapon for almost two weeks now, and here it was, and here was the Alpha alongside it.

"I can see that you are a little shocked, Stella. And you are probably tired too."

She looked back at Malekka and smiled. "It's true, sir, this is a shock, it's incredible. And, well, more scary. Very scary. Actually," she added with a sigh, "perhaps I am just really tired too. May I be excused and go and prepare for bed?"

"You may, Stella. But I will not be with you tonight. I want to talk with the Colonel here."

"As you wish, sir." Her heart leapt for joy. "In that case, I will make my way back to my room, with your permission?"

"Yes, that is fine, Stella, go ahead," and with that he

turned to talk to Linchuk and Aisha, who was herself looking to lock down the hangar and leave for her own quarters, for she too was tired after the sea voyage.

Stella turned followed by Nasrin, and started to walk back to the door. Almost as a habit she put her right hand onto her left wrist to rearrange her bracelets. Only, this time, it wasn't to do that.

The second bracelet was of embroidered gold made in two halves, hinged on one side and secured by a push-in clasp on the other. A short chain on either end of the halves kept them linked when opened.

Stella's heart raced. When she was almost at the door, and unseen by anyone, she pushed the two halves of the closed bracelet in and applied a little more pressure. The ends of the bracelet moved together by another two millimetres as the little pointed clasp inside reached the waterproof protective seal, and first split it, then touched and activated the tiny circuit beyond.

Seven weeks before, one of the many transistors that made up the older-era electronic circuitry of the Alpha unit had been removed, opened and a tiny micro-circuit placed inside. It had then been closed and put back in the Alpha. The procedure had been carried out so well that even a microscope wouldn't show where the cutting and resealing had been done, and the Alpha unit itself was unaltered and remained fully functional.

The small electrical pulse emitted by Stella's bracelet was picked up instantly by the additional circuit in the Alpha, and the radio signal that it in turn sent skywards lasted only three seconds but was extremely powerful, and it was enough.

In under a tenth of a second the signal reached five GPS satellites orbiting twelve thousand six hundred miles above the surface of the Earth. Each relayed a signal with slightly different positional data down to the ground both to the CIA in Langley Virginia and MI6 via GCHQ in England, allowing an exact calculating and pinpointing of the signal source. As the signal went skywards, Stella felt a quiet vibration in her left first molar tooth, where the crown contained a tiny receiver, confirming the Alpha had transmitted.

Stella knew that the people receiving the signal would now be certain of three things. First, that she was alive. Second, that the Alpha unit and the Spider 2-3 were side by side. And third, they would now know the exact position of the Alpha to within one metre, and so the location of the Spider.

Stella suddenly felt exhausted. A huge wave of emotion came over her, as she knew she had achieved what she had set out to do, and she had to make an effort to steady herself as she walked. As she passed through the door and headed back towards her suite, and with tears suddenly welling up in her eyes as the emotional release of what had finally just occurred began to hit her, she kept repeating one phrase to herself.

Come on, JP. Come on, JP.

25

TARGET

JP GOT THE call from Charles Melton at 10.25pm. "We've heard. Come on in, JP, fast. Come straight to the SIS."

"Right. I'm on my way."

The phone went dead. JP's heart was pounding. He had heard the tension in his friend's voice. JP left the hotel room within two minutes and grabbed a cab, wondering for the twentieth time so far since Melton's phone call what, exactly, MI6 had heard. A message from Stella? Was she still alive? Had the Americans found the ship? Was that it? The cab went round Hyde Park Corner and down Grosvenor Place alongside the walls of Buckingham Palace gardens, onto Vauxhall Bridge Road. His mind was racing. Things were coming to a climax, he could feel it.

JP drew comfort from the feel of the Sauer under his armpit. He looked down at his hands. Probably, within the next forty-eight hours, he would have to fight and kill people again. He began to push his mind back into its military frame, his combat training and abilities. He ignored the residual pain from his torture.

The taxi turned off the Albert Embankment at the entrance corner of the MI6 Building. JP put on a cap from his jacket pocket and turned his lapels up full. He stepped out of the cab and walked briskly to the entrance door five feet away, held open for him by one of the security officers. The door closed, JP presented his ID to the officer and then was allowed through the heavy internal metal security door. As he passed through he saw Jane Chapman walking towards him.

"Hello, Lieutenant."

"Hello, JP. Follow me please."

In silence he was escorted along a short corridor to an elevator. Jane pressed the fourth button below the one marked 'G'. She led him along another corridor, still each lost in their own tense thoughts, and into one of the rooms off on the right.

The inside was almost an exact replica of the conference room at Hanover Square. Sir Alastair was at the top of a larger table with Melton, and this time there were three or four others. As JP walked over, everyone stood and started to clap. Charles Melton said in a raised voice above the clapping, "It's Stella, JP. We've had the signal!"

They shook hands, and as much as he tried to conceal it a visible sigh of relief escaped JP's mouth. He gave a smile in acknowledgement at the praise coming from around the table.

Sir Alastair began to speak and the clapping subsided. "JP, first I must say, congratulations on the success of your plan. You have done this country an enormous service with your ingenuity and brilliance. As a result of your efforts we have located a rogue nuclear missile, that otherwise would have gone undetected. So, thank you."

"Thank you, sir, and all of you," replied a rather embarrassed JP as he sat. "It may have been my plan; but it's Stella who is there in the front line against Malekka. That is one very brave girl." There were murmurs of consent around the table.

She's alive, he thought. She's alive. This was the best news he could have hoped for. She's alive.

"Yes, we owe her an enormous debt of gratitude too," said Sir Alastair. "But, that is for later. Now, we have to do something with the new knowledge that we have acquired."

"Yes, sir," said JP. "So - where is it?"

"Cyprus," replied Charles Melton."

"*Cyprus*," said JP. "What the devil is it doing there? *Cyprus!*"

"That is what we are now going to try to ascertain," said Sir Alastair. "I am meeting with the Chief of the Defence Staff and the Secretary of State for Defence at 2am. By that time, we must have a proposal in place on which to proceed. We don't know how much time we have, and the one thing we need to do is to move very fast, as I said once before at an earlier gathering of ours. This weapon could be launched at any moment, and we obviously need an attack to take these people out. The SAS have been placed on standby and told to be ready to move within a couple of hours."

"How on earth did they get a nuclear missile to Cyprus in the Mediterranean," said JP. "The American Sixth Fleet is at Naples, the Royal Navy is active in the area, we have the two Sovereign Bases on the island at Akrotiri and Dhekelia, the RAF at Akrotiri and a few thousand troops. Turkey has thousands of troops there too, and so does Greece. What are they up to?"

"Let's reason this through," said Sir Alastair. He turned to Jane Chapman. "Lieutenant, your briefing please?"

"Yes, sir." She pressed a button on the remote control to activate the three screens on the walls around the room. A large map of the Mediterranean Sea area with neighbouring countries and Cyprus at the centre of the display, and a large circle drawn in red around it, appeared on the screens for everyone to look at.

"The signal we have picked up pinpoints the location at the northernmost point of Morphou Bay on Cyprus, at a place called Cape Kormakitis. The closest town is Livera, some three kilometres to the south-east. Ever since July 1974, when Turkey invaded Cyprus in response to an attempted coup d'état by Greek Cypriot nationalists and the Military Junta that ruled Greece at the time, the island has been split in two. The southern and west part - about sixty percent of the island - is the Republic of Cyprus, which has around eight hundred and fifty thousand Greek Cypriots and close ties to Greece. The northern and east part - the other forty percent - is the Turkish Republic of Northern Cyprus, population three hundred thousand Turkish Cypriots. The Military Junta in Greece fell in 1974 and Greece has of course been a democracy ever since."

The Lieutenant paused for a sip of water from her glass on the table, and then continued.

"Northern Cyprus, as it is known, is a democratic republic, and claims Morphou Bay as its own territorial waters. Only Turkey recognises Northern Cyprus. The rest of the world, including the United Kingdom, recognises the sovereignty of the Republic of Cyprus over the entire island, including the portion currently under the control of Northern Cyprus, and the thirty thousand troops that Turkey maintains on the island are seen as an illegal army of occupation. Northern Cyprus is heavily dependent on Turkey for economic, political and military support, and it is said that nothing is done in Northern Cyprus without first checking with Ankara. Northern Cyprus is mainly Muslim; the Republic of Cyprus, Christian.

"Turkey and Iran have very close ties, which would make this an ideal and easy base for a man such as Malekka; Iranian, rich, influential, very powerful, and

Muslim. We believe he has probably been established on the island under the radar for some time. We are finding out more about this as I speak.

"We know the range of the missile is no more than five hundred kilometres," continued Lieutenant Chapman. "The circle on the map shows a radial distance of five hundred kilometres emanating from Cape Kormakitis. As you can see, this brings in the seaboards of Turkey, Syria, Lebanon, Israel and Egypt.

"There is detailed background on the weaponry in the folders in front of you, ladies and gentlemen. In summation, though, the Spider 2-3 has a range of three hundred and ten miles, or five hundred kilometres, and a flight speed of six thousand eight hundred miles an hour, or Mach 9. Although an older weapon, it is terrifyingly efficient and deadly, is mobile, can be launched easily and quickly from its launch vehicle, and there is some considerable doubt that the Patriot Missile or the Arrow[7] system could actually stop it with absolute certainty. The Patriot does not have a one hundred per cent success rate; and neither does the Arrow which is a relatively new system. They might stop the SS-23; but they might not. In any event, it is entirely possible that Malekka has some kind of radar jamming system. Or, the Spider may be modified to detonate if it detects an incoming missile, and even if it does not, and if a SAM Missile succeeds in killing it, the resulting explosion would release radioactive material into the atmosphere that could easily kill thousands through radiation poisoning,

---

[7] *The MIM-104 Patriot and Arrow are Surface-to-Air Missile (SAM) systems, designed to destroy incoming theatre and intercontinental ballistic missiles. They are the primary weapons of its kind used by the United States and several nations, including Egypt, Saudi Arabia and Israel, which, with the US, was largely responsible for the Arrow development.*

depending upon the wind strength and direction that prevail at the time.

"It is our conclusion, therefore, that - perhaps rather obviously - this weapon should not be allowed to become airborne, nor should it be blown up on the ground with conventional explosives since that will spread radioactive material around Cyprus and still kill hundreds possibly thousands of Cypriots and tourists. Therefore the weapon must be *disabled* on the ground."

Jane Chapman turned to look at her boss. "That's it, sir."

"Thank you, Lieutenant."

There was silence for a few seconds, while the people sitting around the table considered the details in the Lieutenant's briefing. JP was the first to say something.

"Well, I can see some immediate problems," he said grimly. "If I were Malekka, the first thing I would do is to rig the Spider to be easily detonated, with a backup of being blown up with explosives, where it sits on the ground now, just in case I get discovered and attacked. I might lose my overall intentions, but I'd make sure that the bomb blows up everyone and everything for miles around me come what may."

"Yes, I agree," said Melton. "A sudden attack could result in the destruction of half of Cyprus. Even if we use a cruise missile or an aerial laser guided bomb in a surprise attack, the weapon would be destroyed but there would still be some pretty unpleasant radioactive material in the atmosphere with deadly effects as a result, as the Lieutenant has just said, and thousands could still die.

"Looking at the circle on the screens, the target obviously has to be Israel," continued Melton. "But then, having said that, the target could just as easily be

Port Said and the Suez Canal, which would make a nice terrorist target," he added. "Blow up the canal to damage the economies of the world because of the closure of the waterway. The nuclear fallout would prevent its repair for decades, let alone use."

"Well of course we don't even know that Cyprus is the final intended location of the weapon," said JP, "and so it might not be the launching place of the missile."

"That's right, sir," agreed David Pearce, a senior data analyst sitting to JP's left a little further down the table. "It could merely be that Cyprus is just the first place where the SS-23 and the Alpha have come together, and so the first time that the signal could be sent to us as Mr Peregrine planned."

"Yes," agreed Melton. "It is entirely possible that they plan to launch the missile from a ship after moving it somewhere else around the world. It could be that there is a ship leaving to take the weapon out into the Atlantic towards the USA; the target could be New York, or Washington. Or they could launch from the ship and attack the Saudi oilfields; imagine what global chaos that would cause. The price of oil would go through the roof, it would elevate Iran up in the front line of prime suppliers and so offer them much more power and influence around the world. Just what we don't want."

"And Malekka is Iranian," added someone else further down the table.

A general discussion broke out, with several people talking at the same time amongst themselves, which Sir Alastair allowed for a few minutes. He himself spoke in earnest to Melton on his right, and Jane Chapman. The one who was silent was JP. He was listening, and thinking. Then, suddenly, he spoke.

"I know what they're intending to do."

The voices suddenly fell silent around the table.

"What do you mean, JP?" said Melton. "What are you thinking?"

"I know what they're intending to do," said JP again, grimly. "What's the date today?" he asked openly.

"Er, 21st of April," said Jane. "Actually, as it's just passed midnight, it's now the 22nd.

"Yes, 22nd April. Malekka isn't just a man who's a terrorist. He's an Arab terrorist. He's going to launch his SS-23 missile tomorrow, on 23rd April. His target *is* Israel, and he's going to launch it tomorrow. Because 23rd April is Israel's Independence Day."

There was a short silence.

JP added, "So we've now got just under twenty-four hours to stop him."

"Bloody hell," said Melton softly.

His sentiments were echoed around the table.

26
COUNTERING

SIR ALASTAIR SPOKE decisively. "I think it's time that I went to have a chat with Mossad and the CIA." He pushed his chair away from the table. "Obviously Israel must be told, and then convinced to do nothing. I do not believe Turkey should be told, not yet, since Malekka and the weapon are on Turkish soil and there may be someone high up in the government in Ankara who is helpful to Malekka, and might tip him off. For the same reason we're not going to speak to Moscow yet. The last thing we want is for Malekka to find out that we are on to him."

"Yes," said JP. "He may decide to blow up Cyprus just for the hell of it, as I said before. And if I may suggest, I don't think there should be any involvement of UAVs at the moment. Malekka is a very resourceful man, and he'll doubtless have equipment to detect them even at high altitude. His team in Zimbabwe did after all."

"What are you saying, JP?" said Melton. "We need immediate surveillance and intel."

"Yes of course, but not by a UAV. We need to go higher, to be sure of non-detection."

"Well there is one possibility that we could undertake, and that is a conventional overflight," said Melton. "It's busy airspace at Cyprus, and what's one more aircraft at thirty thousand feet flying in the usual commercial airway?"

"Yes, that would work," said JP. "But we still need something above in situ, giving the latest on a regular constant live feed."

"You mean re-task a satellite?"

"Yes. We can't be too careful; don't give Malekka any possibility of detection. Overhead UAVs are out. A satellite would be safer."

"JP, that will take longer," said Sir Alastair, "and, not that it matters, also cost much more. To re-task an orbiting satellite into a different orbit or orbital position involves quite an effort."

"Yes, sir, I know," replied JP, "but look at what is at stake here. If we get it wrong, literally a few hundred thousand people could die, if Malekka detonates the weapon on the ground in Cyprus. We need total, complete surprise."

Sir Alastair thought for a moment, and looked over at Melton. Melton nodded in agreement.

"JP's right sir," he said. "No chances. These are high stakes, and we shouldn't risk it."

"Yes, I must say I agree too." Sir Alastair looked briefly around the table. "Does anyone else have any comments on this point?"

There was silence.

"Very well. We will leave you for a while, and I will make some phone calls, and we will get a sortie flown out of Akrotiri, and the higher surveillance organised."

He turned to Melton and JP.

"And for God's sake, find a solution."

The head of MI6 stood up to leave the room, and as he did so four others from around the table stood also.

"Oh, JP, I am sorry," said Sir Alastair. "This is Caroline Tewkson, my Personal Assistant. Melton, introduce the others." And with that, he and the woman swiftly left the room.

Melton quickly ran through the names of the others at the table, and JP shook hands with them briefly as they moved to leave the room. David Pearce was head of Data Cartography Analysis, Europe; Mary Shipton, Strategic Communications; George Daytron, Control, Eastern Europe Section. They followed Sir Alastair out, to go to their respective work locations and continue with as much detailed intelligence gathering about Cape Kormakitis and Malekka as they could, and quickly. Within five minutes the head of MI6 was on the telephone, placing a call first to the CIA and then to his opposite number at the Mossad.

JP, Charles Melton and Jane Chapman remained in the room at the table.

"Right," said Melton. "Let's get a timeline on this. It's now 12.30am. That means that in Cyprus it's now..." - he paused to look at Chapman - "1.30am?"

"Two hours forward, sir," said the Lieutenant.

"Thank you; make that 2.30am in Cyprus." He thought for a moment, and then added, "and in Israel?"

"Also two hours, sir."

"...and 2.30am in Israel. Flight time to Cyprus is, maybe, five hours?"

"More or less, sir" said the Lieutenant. "Five is safe."

"Ok. Two hours ahead of the clock. Flight time is five hours. Allow, say, six hours if we're lucky to re-task a satellite, and another hour to get pictures back and a live feed established, if we can get one; say seven in all. That's fourteen. One hour to get you, JP, to the SAS at Hereford, and then thirty minutes to transfer the group to Brize Norton for the flight over to Cyprus. Half an hour to get from RAF Akrotiri in the south to Morphou Bay and the target area at Cape Kormakitis in the north. Sixteen hours in all. That takes the clock to 6.30pm this evening, Cyprus time. And you haven't seen one intel picture yet or had any time to formulate a plan."

"If we go in at 11pm, that will give us four and a half hours between now and then to make that plan," said JP. "That's not a long time. And, that would be four and a half hours if I left now."

There were a few seconds of silence once more.

"I don't think I should go to Hereford," said JP.

"No," agreed Melton. "You want to go straight out there?"

"Yes. I am assuming that I still have the sanction to go in first, to get the girl out?"

"Well that was what was agreed at the outset," said Melton. "But looking at the time frame and the location, and the lives involved. I don't think we can hold up anything at all, JP, not even for her. We can't risk millions of lives, or tens of thousands minimum, against saving the life of one person."

"I know what you mean of course," said JP. "But we have to try. I have to try," he added. "I promised."

"Yes, I know. And I think that if I said to you, no, you'd go in anyway."

"Well, Charlie, remember, technically I don't work for you," said JP with a slight smile.

"Don't worry, JP," said Melton, "I want you to go in and get her just as much as you do. She can't just be left and ignored. Especially not after what she's done."

JP looked his friend in the eyes. They both knew exactly what had to be done. Stella couldn't be left alone at the mercy of Malekka and his people, to die in the coming onslaught, or to be vaporised by a nuclear bomb exploding in northern Cyprus. She had done too much and sacrificed too much.

"You go get her, JP" said Melton. JP smiled slightly, and gave a gentle nod.

"I'll get her, Charlie," he said.

Lieutenant Chapman interrupted. "Sir, I have some things that need consideration, along with all the other parts of the jigsaw."

"Yes, Jane." said Melton.

"Cape Kormakitis is in northern Cyprus. RAF Akrotiri is in the south. There is an international border to cross, to pass from the Greek side to the Turkish side, and a UN buffer zone is still there separating the two territories. Not very active, I believe, but it's still there. We are planning an assault on the foreign soil of a fellow NATO state, as they see it anyway, against their knowledge or agreement. I presume the Greeks won't be told either. Even though the Prime Minister invoked the Fifth Rubric over JP, we're actually supposed to advise the participating country in advance of the bearer's arrival on their soil, as we did South Africa, and of course that's only JP; the SAS aren't covered by any such agreements. We are apparently warning the likely target country, Israel, who will undoubtedly go nuts and want to make an assault against Cyprus immediately, to ensure the weapon can't be launched at them and so protect themselves, but with little or no consideration of the effects that destroying a nuclear weapon on the ground on Cyprus would have to the local population."

"They will have to be persuaded against that course of action," said Melton, "and if I know Sir Alastair he's probably on the telephone to the Foreign Secretary about that right now."

"Yes, sir."

The Lieutenant continued.

"There has recently been much friction between Turkey and Israel over the prospective drilling for oil and gas in the eastern Mediterranean, and if Israel were to try to bring war planes close or into Northern Cyprus airspace the Turkish Air Force would not take kindly to it and quite possibly shoot them out of the sky.

"And in addition to the matter about crossing the border, should we not tell the Cyprus Government too, if we are telling the Israelis? This whole thing could blow up into a war even if the weapon doesn't get launched, because of the violations and infringements of international boundaries and territories."

"Lieutenant, you are completely correct in what you say," said Melton. "And, there is absolutely nothing we three can do about that. That is the diplomatic side of this game, and, as they say, that is not my problem. Right now I will confess to being pleased that I am merely the Deputy Head of MI6. Those kinds of niceties will fall onto Sir Alastair's shoulders to deal with. But I do agree, there are going to be enormous international implications over this whatever happens."

"Yes, you're right, there will be," said JP. "But today I don't care about the international borders or the politics either. Today I only care about saving life, and our focus has to be on our job and on that, on getting it done. Leave the politics to the politicians. What we have to do is get in and disarm that Spider and get Stella out at the same time." Then he looked straight at the Lieutenant. "Just as I would if you were in her position instead."

The Lieutenant smiled at the two men in front of her. She knew they were strong good people, willing to fight and even die for what they believed in to help others, when their duty or loyalties required it. She was proud to be working alongside them. She dispensed with other possible ramifications from the course of action they were beginning to plan. But she still had a practical question arising and so pushed it again.

"There still remains the problem of how you get

across the border from the Republic of Cyprus through the UN buffer zone to Northern Cyprus."

"Yes I've been thinking about that one," said JP. "They allow tourists across quite freely and without any difficulties, don't they? I have been to Cyprus before, to Akrotiri; and I've had a vacation on Cyprus too. They just let you drive across with no difficulties. If I can have a decent car in Akrotiri when I arrive, with things nicely concealed, I'll drive myself up and across the border."

"Yes, that sounds good enough, JP," said Melton. "We can make sure that as well as the normal kit you have some additional communication items and other useful bits and pieces."

"Ok. So, I'll go through as a tourist, drive myself up to the Cape as close as I can - what was the name of the closest town you said?" said JP, turning to Jane.

"Livera. Three kilometres to the south-east."

"Thanks. I'll go to Livera, hang around a little, act like a tourist, and then slip away and drive north a bit more. I'll park up, and then do the final bit on foot. I can spend the last couple of hours sending the latest pictures back to you for the SAS. Who's going to do this one, Charlie, is it Mike, with 2-2 Alpha?"

"Yes."

"Good." JP was pleased to hear that. He knew Major Mike Durford well, and he and the sixty men that made up his squadron couldn't be bettered. They'll tear the bloody place to pieces, he said to himself. The trick is not being around when they do it.

"JP, whatever time the SAS decide to go in, you'll just have to be ready to move in before them. That way we can honestly say we started the operation as soon as was humanly possible, and didn't delay for any reason at all, not even to help save the person on the inside. You see what I mean."

"Yes, I understand," said JP.

"How long do you think you'll need?"

"Well if I go in too soon, I might have the girl and the missile, but not be able to hold them. If I go in too late, I might not have enough time to get the job done before Mike and the team hit the place."

JP paused for a while, and then continued, "I think half an hour. The very latest they can go in will be 11.45pm, probably earlier, 11.30pm. They will want as long as possible to study the intel of course and formulate their actions, and as there is so little time to do that they will want to use as much available time today and this evening right up to the last minute before committing to action. So, I'll be aiming for 11.15pm tonight local time, and bring it ahead as necessary to be thirty minutes before whatever time the lads set to move in if it's before then. We have to assume the missile will fire from 12 midnight; or maybe three minutes beforehand. So they'll work on that timeframe."

"I take it the three minutes is the flight time of the Spider?" said Melton.

"Yes, a rough estimate but I think that's what it will prove to be, so if they want to hit Tel Aviv at midnight on Independence Day they'll launch at 11.57pm."

"Why would it be Tel Aviv, and not Jerusalem, or one of the other cities?" asked Lieutenant Chapman.

"It certainly won't be Jerusalem," said Melton. "That city means far too much to Muslims for them to make that the target, just as it does Christians and the Jews."

"Yes that's right," said JP. "The target won't be Jerusalem. And there's a specific reason why it *will* be Tel Aviv."

They both looked at him enquiringly.

"Because the Declaration of Independence of Israel was signed in 1948 at a place now called Independence Hall, but known at the time as the Tel Aviv Museum. The target is downtown Tel Aviv."

≈

JP left the briefing at 5am. A car with darkened windows took him out from the SIS straight to his hotel. He ordered a large breakfast from room service. Then he took his suitcase from one of the large wardrobes, threw it onto the bed and took out the new mobile phone he had bought on Monday on his way to see Steve Montague.

He tapped in one message and sent the text. It said, *'The sun is shining brightly today'*.

The breakfast arrived a few minutes later and was wheeled in on a trolley. Just as JP sat down to eat, the phone bleeped its incoming message notice. The text read, *'And the grass is green'*.

JP looked down at the phone. Good luck, my friend, he said thoughtfully to himself. He wondered what the day would bring, and what the results would be of the actions he had just instigated with his text a few moments ago.

He turned the phone off and removed the sim card. He bent it in half, and put it in his pocket with the phone. He would bin them both outside. He sat down again and tackled his full English breakfast heartily.

The car would be outside at 7am sharp, ready to take him back to RAF Northolt.

≈

As JP began his breakfast shortly after 6am, in Cyprus

two thousand miles away to the south east, at 8.10am local time, Barakah Malekka was authorising a transfer of funds. His instructions were received in Tehran, one thousand miles east, at 9.42am local. At 10am another half billion US dollars left the Central Bank of Iran in five equal separate wire transfers, following the same routing as before.

In the afternoon another half billion US dollars would be in Vashinsky's numbered Swiss account.

≈

Not long after the same car with the darkened windows whisked JP away from Brook Street at 7am sharp, fifteen hundred miles to the east in Moscow, at 10.05am Moscow Standard Time, General Vashinsky heard the usual knock on the door to his office. It generally came between 10.00am and 10.15am each day.

"Come in," said Vashinsky in answer.

He looked up as the door opened. He was pleased to see that the delivery of his personal communiqués from the Director was being brought to him by Praporshchik Tchepikova. She smiled at him as she glided across the floor, and his eyes couldn't stop themselves from lowering briefly to look at the girl's legs. Was that hemline a little shorter today, he asked himself?

"Good morning, General," said the Praporshchik. "How are you this morning, sir?"

"Good morning, Praporshchik, I am well thank you. I have a feeling that today is going to be a lovely day."

"Yes, sir," replied the Warrant Officer. "I believe you may be right. I think the warm weather is on its way."

"Let's hope so."

"I have today's traffic from the Director for you, sir." As she reached his desk she sat down rather cheekily on its corner, which was a familiarity that he would never usually have allowed but he had begun to relax his own rules a little over the last week or so. At least with Praporshchik Tchepikova. And as she sat, the skirt moved up a little higher. He didn't mind. It was a nice distraction.

He plugged the stick that he had just taken from her into the usual USB port on his laptop, which immediately sent the coded email receipt in response back to the Director.

"Anything to go back, sir?" asked the Praporshchik.

"Yes, here it is," replied the General.

She took his coded data stick. "Thank you, sir. Is that all, sir?"

"Yes, Praporshchik, thank you. Have a good day, my regards to the Director."

"Yes, sir," and the Warrant Officer stood and turned to walk back towards the door. She could tell that Vashinsky's eyes were on her legs again. A girl can always tell that. Normally, she didn't like it. Today, however, she did.

Vashinsky was expecting another very large delivery today. An hour later he went into the secure banking system at his Swiss account to see if there was anything new. Nothing yet; only the half billion US dollars from before.

He would check later. Yes, he said to himself as he leaned back in his leather chair, today was indeed going to be a lovely day.

For him, anyway.

27
ARRIVAL

AT RAF NORTHOLT, a Typhoon T3 twin-seater Eurofighter had flown in ahead from RAF Coningsby, refuelled and was waiting for JP on the tarmac. He suited up and joined the pilot, who took the plane airborne at 8.30am, and first routed south-west towards the Celtic Sea and the Atlantic Ocean. The aircraft passed one hundred miles abeam the French coast at Brest at fifty thousand feet, and then turned due south, accelerating through the sound barrier to Mach 2, just over fifteen hundred miles an hour. By the time the sonic crash reached the water its intensity had lessened considerably. The carpet boom fifty miles wide followed the aircraft as it tore along.

It had been decided the best route would not be a straight line to Cyprus. A direct flight path would involve passing through the airspace of nine, possibly ten, countries including Croatia, Bosnia-Herzegovina, Serbia, Bulgaria and Turkey. That would require far more overflight permissions and the speed of the Typhoon would have to be subsonic; populated areas and sonic booms do not sit well together. Indeed the flight might raise awkward questions from some of those countries, including Turkey. Although Turkey was a full member of NATO, it was possible someone in Ankara might be well aware, or even be a part, of what was going on at Cape Kormakitis and inform Malekka. Therefore a longer but supersonic route largely across water had been selected. "The scenic route," as JP had quipped.

Spain had granted its NATO ally permission for the RAF aircraft to fly supersonic at fifty thousand feet over a narrow lightly-populated corridor of its territory. The plane flashed across the northern coast of Spain east of Bilbao, followed the general south-east line of the Pyrenees and crossed the Mediterranean coast well to the north of Barcelona. It stayed over the Sea for the rest of the flight. Midway between Sardinia and the coast of Tunisia it was refuelled by the VC-10 tanker sent from RAF Akrotiri, and then sped on once more, past Malta and Crete, landing at Akrotiri two and a half hours later, at 1pm local.

JP quickly got out of his flying kit and was led off towards an office complex at the north end of the airport. Satellite pictures of Cyprus were easily available commercially - even Google Earth could show useful images, although their pictures were a year or two old. However, the images that JP had viewed with Melton and the others in London were two months old. They showed the general layout of the topography of Cape Kormakitis and in particular of the various buildings within the private complex at the very tip. The actual building which fitted the location co-ordinates of the Alpha unit and the Spider sent to them by Stella had been identified, so JP knew exactly where the weapon was, or at least where it was twelve or fourteen hours ago. The complex was quite extensive; there was an excellent man-made deep-water harbour with breakwaters, and a construction that appeared to be a large hangar over the quayside that was obviously used to house a big ship. There were considerable residential buildings, much of them reaching down to the water on the north-east side of the Cape. On the west side, running almost the entire length of the property in a north-south direction, was a private tarmac air strip, at the southern end of which was a substantial hangar, presumably enclosing at least one if not two large aircraft and possibly a number of smaller ones. There was a wall that stretched the entire width of the complex from west to east that JP would have to breach. It was unknown what kind of protection the wall carried; whether it was electrified, or whether it was patrolled by guards, as he suspected it would be.

While it had been agreed at the SIS that they should not use UAVs to spy on the Cape both Melton and Sir Alastair had made the point that Cyprus had a particularly busy airspace. It was a Mediterranean holiday destination all year round and even in April there was a constant stream of planes and holidaymakers arriving and departing. Also, because of its geographical location, there were standard air routes above or abeam along which passing aircraft were constantly flying at altitude. What's one more aircraft amongst all of those, Melton had said? So it had been deemed safe to send an aircraft up from Akrotiri, have it climb to thirty-thousand feet south-west, turn to fly abeam Cyprus and take extremely detailed pictures with a live feed to obtain current intel on Cape Kormakitis, then, when sufficiently past the island, descend, come about and return to the RAF base.

MI6 had briefed the Commander British Forces Cyprus and requested the flight. The Commander had immediately arranged the sortie and the resulting very detailed imagery was relayed to London. That same imagery was now also available to JP two hours later in the privacy of the digital data analysis room at the airfield.

The Group Captain who had collected JP knocked on

a door and entered.

"Mr Peregrine, sir."

"Oh thank you, Tom," said Air Vice-Marshall Sir Donald Gaunchon, Commander British Forces Cyprus, as he stood and walked round his desk to greet JP.

"Welcome to Cyprus, Mr Peregrine," said Gaunchon, taking JP's hand in a vicelike grip. "It's a pleasure to meet you, although I of course wish it could be under better circumstances."

JP could feel the calloused skin covering hardened muscle and toughened bone of a hand that had held ropes and scaled rock faces all over the world as a distinguished mountaineer, as well as worked the controls of a myriad of aircraft. "How do you do, Sir Donald," said JP, "I couldn't agree more."

"Group Captain Williams here flew the flight, and we have some interesting things to show you. I know you're a little short of time, so we'll move straight on." He turned to a fourth man in the room, and said, "Right, Jenkins, let's see it."

The four men sat down on plain wood chairs set around a simple rectangular table, used more for flight debriefings than espionage surveillance presentations, their eyes on a large screen on the wall a few feet in front of them.

"You'll see, Mr Peregrine," said Tom Williams, "that the imaging comes from about thirty thousand - well, thirty-two thousand actually - feet up, and as instructed by London we didn't directly overfly the island, and so the views are slightly at an angle, which in any event often helps with identification and orientation anyway, as you know of course. But the detail of the resolution is quite ample to get a pretty good idea of what's going on on the ground."

The recording ran through the first sixty seconds or

so. The image was sharp, in black and white, and the resolution was clear enough almost to be able to tell the time on the watches worn by people on the ground, had they wished to do so. There were maybe ten people visible in the complex in open plain view.

"There are quite a few people milling around at the perimeter of the complex," continued the Group Captain, "and these two - just pause it, Jenkins, please." The image froze. "These two are clearly carrying some kind of assault rifle strapped around their necks."

"Yes, so they are," said JP. "Malekka obviously has his own kind of private army, perhaps mercenaries. That's only to be expected, he's going to keep the place guarded very securely." I wonder how many, he thought.

Williams indicated to Flight Lieutenant Jenkins to continue the playback.

"Also there are some women wearing burkas," he said. "Surely strong evidence backing up what MI6 has said, that this is a Muslim complex with an Arab, this man Malekka, at the top. Of course the religion of the Turkish Republic of Northern Cyprus is Muslim anyway. So the establishing of this centre within Northern Cyprus was a natural blending of ideals and beliefs in terms of culture, social customs and behaviour, and in that way at least it obviously fits right in. Very clever."

"That's interesting too," said JP. "See how that one is walking up to the wall on the right, on the south-east side in the corner? And then right over to the building by the sea."

"Yes?" said Sir Donald. "And?"

"Well it's a bit of good news," said JP. "I was concerned that the open area just on the other side of the wall might be mined, but it seems that it isn't. That makes things a little easier."

"Oh I see what you mean, no I think you're ok there," said Sir Donald. "The personnel are moving quite freely generally, in all areas."

"One thing did occur to me, Sir Donald," said Flight Lieutenant Jenkins.

"Yes, Jenkins?"

"Well, sir... Doesn't it seem to be a rather active place? It's quite busy. And every now and again a box or something is being carried into the hangar at the end of the air strip, presumably an aircraft hangar."

"Yes. Actually, you're right. In fact," said JP, "a fair amount of activity". He thought for a while, and then added, "They're packing up and getting ready to leave. They're going to launch the weapon tonight, but they need to be able to get off the island too, as soon as the missile has been successfully fired. That's what all that activity is."

"Yes, of course," said Gaunchon. "Nobody's going to want to hang around the launch site of a nuclear ballistic missile that's gone off to kill millions of people."

"There has to be an exit strategy," said JP, shrugging his shoulders. "And that's it. They'll be in the air immediately after the weapon has been launched, probably heading straight to Iran or some other Arab safe haven."

"So they're packing up and loading the plane in the hangar," said Jenkins, "ready to leave as soon as they have launched the thing? Why don't some of them leave first? Wouldn't that be easier, perhaps?"

"That's a good point, one which we debated in London," said JP. "The question was, would the weapon be left on automatic launch to be fired on its own, or would most of the personnel depart in advance first leaving a handful of people to launch the weapon, or would everyone stay until the launch, and then they all leave together. We think it depends entirely on the whim of Malekka, who has absolute power over all of these people. The key point therefore is this: would he really want to leave the island before his work of presumably several years has actually taken place? Would he want to miss the final big grand event?"

"No," said Group Captain Williams thoughtfully. "No, if I were he I think I would want to stay and see it launch, especially if I've put years into this plan. And presumably a great deal of money."

"That was precisely the conclusion we came to as well," said JP. "And if Malekka stays, everyone else will too, because if he sends anyone else away that would just weaken his own security and protection, so why do that? Or his thinking might not even go that far or encompass that; simply, that if he chooses to stay, those who serve him will of course stay too. It could also be the case that it is only a small number of his people that even know what the real plan is or that there is a nuclear weapon at the site, and so most of them won't be concerned at all about the need to leave the site shortly."

"In any event," added Sir Donald, "MI6 as you know has already made arrangements with us and the Navy, as well as the US military, that any flights or ships leaving the complex would be tracked, and we have an AWAC in the air now. Anything that leaves, we'll know where it goes."

"Good," said JP. He paused as he looked at the screen. The angle was getting greater now, as the aircraft was nearing the end of its view window.

"Do we know anything more about Malekka yet, or about his home at Cape Kormakitis?" he asked.

"Well," replied Jenkins, "Cape Kormakitis is one of the most deserted and sparsely populated parts of Northern Cyprus, in fact of Cyprus generally. The tip of the Cape was purchased five years ago, and for the first four years of that new ownership, there were extensive building works carried on there. The public records merely show that the place, which is called Cuttle Cove - a rather nice name actually - is a private estate owned by a wealthy businessman.

"We haven't wanted to pry too deeply or quickly on the island at this stage, in case it attracts too much of the wrong kind of attention," said Sir Donald.

"No, of course," agreed JP.

"Other than that," said Jenkins, "we have found out nothing more."

"However there is one other interesting thing on the feed," said Group Captain Williams. "Just before we were out of range. Look at the square building at the south-east, where the weapon is located. We're almost at that part now. Hang on... Just a few more seconds... coming up... There!"

All of a sudden, the roof of the building where the Spider 2-3 was situated suddenly split open in the middle and started to open. Then the motion suddenly stopped; a few seconds later the direction of the two halves reversed and the roof closed up again.

"There, did you see it?"

"I certainly did," said JP. "The roof opens up, and that's so that the weapon can be launched from inside. They're testing the roof and making sure it works properly. How interesting," he added thoughtfully. That knowledge, he said to himself, could be very helpful later. Perhaps.

"Interesting? That's a bit of an understatement, Mr Peregrine," said the Air Vice-Marshall. "I would have said how bloody terrifying."

JP and Sir Donald looked at each other. JP smiled grimly, and nodded.

"Yes, sir, you're right."

"These devils, on Cyprus of all places. Right under our bloody noses." He shook his head almost in bewilderment. Then he looked up, and spoke again.

"Mr Peregrine, I have one question that I am a little confused by."

"Yes, sir?"

"Well, the SS-23 is an older weapon. Still very deadly, but its technology comes from an earlier era. The Israelis have one of the most advanced missile defence systems in the world, the Arrow, developed with the Americans. It's supposed to be even better than the latest most advanced American Patriot missiles - and incidentally there are a couple of US Navy destroyers with some Patriot batteries on board steaming towards Israel."

JP nodded in acknowledgement, although he knew this already. The image on the screen they had been watching had come to an end, and the screen went blank.

"It's actually a three-tier missile defence system," continued Sir Donald, "covered first by the Green Pine, now the Super Green Pine, radar system, which is extremely sophisticated. I have been present when they did a test fire and interception, and the Arrow blew the target missile out of the sky with ease. I'm not at all sure an SS-23 would get through all that."

"No, I agree," said JP. "There is not a one hundred percent chance of success for the missile, although I still wouldn't want to take a chance on those odds even so. It might get through."

"Yes, quite, but given that the odds are not totally secure in favour of the missile - then how's he going to do it, with certainty?"

"Frankly, we don't know," said JP. "Obviously Malekka will have had the same thoughts. He seems to be an extremely resourceful man, and we have to believe that he has come up with some kind of solution. He may have acquired, or developed, an extremely effective radar jamming system. Or, he may have had the missile system itself amended to detonate anyway on detecting an incoming SAM aimed at it, so that nuclear fallout kills people in Israel. We don't have the answer to that one. Other than, given that he has been able to operate and develop this international plot this far, he obviously has no intention of launching the missile only for it to be obliterated."

JP paused a moment.

"The Arrow system, and because the SAS are going in, are frankly the only reasons that the Israelis haven't launched a pre-emptive strike against Cape Kormakitis and taken the weapon out already. A pre-emptive strike will spread a great deal of dirty radioactive material around Cyprus and kill thousands of people on the island, but from their perspective it saves millions of lives and quite possibly Israel herself."

There was silence for a while, as they all waited for JP to continue.

"No, he has a solution somehow," said JP. "We have to assume that. We just don't know for sure what it is."

A few minutes later, JP was ready to leave. He thanked the Commander for his help, and the other two men. There was nothing more he could do to assist, Sir Donald said, other than to provide JP with the car MI6 had asked for. On the other hand, there was much preparation needed in his support of the SAS team arriving later in the day, but Akrotiri would be ready.

"I trust the car will be satisfactory," said Sir Donald,

"it has everything in it that was asked for, placed where it was asked to be placed."

"Thank you," said JP.

They all walked out of the room and through the exit to the outside. The air was warm and the sun shining brightly; the Mediterranean Sea off to the south across the runway was blue and calm, and some simple sailing boats were having fun crossing the water. It was a welcome contrast to the gravity of the discussion they had just had.

The Air Vice-Marshall turned to JP and held out his hand.

"Good luck, Mr Peregrine. And don't worry about things this end. I'll make sure the lads get there exactly on time."

"Thank you again, sir."

JP changed his clothes for the drive north, and then Tom Williams took him to the car that Charles Melton had requested. The car had indeed been fully, and discreetly, kitted out. He drove through the exit gates of the Base at 2.30pm.

JP was keen to get to a reconnoitre point at Cape Kormakitis as soon as possible. Another thing on his mind was the time of sunset, 7.27pm that evening, which meant total darkness from 8pm. He was still a good two hours from the border cross point, which had been set in London as Astromeritis, virtually due north from Akrotiri. However, driving north would take JP through the mountainous region of Cyprus along a myriad of small winding roads; today was not a day to risk a wrong turn.

So JP would stick to the main roads, even if it took slightly longer. He headed out east along the A1 motorway, passing the outskirts of Limassol and then along the coast. The road turned north-east, inland.

Traffic was fairly light once he was out of the built-up coastal area. At Nicosia JP headed west and just before Kokkinotrimithia turned off the main A9 road towards Astromeritis. He was at the border crossing on schedule, at 4pm.

There was one car behind him and two ahead. All JP had to do was follow their example for the customs and border control officers. With his camera round his neck and binoculars on the passenger seat, and in shorts, short sleeved shirt and sunglasses raised up from his eyes resting on his head, and helped by his British passport, he was waived straight through with smiles and good wishes, both as he left the Republic of Cyprus and entered the Demilitarised Zone, and then again on the other side crossing into the Turkish Republic of Northern Cyprus.

He drove on.

JP passed through the little town of Morfou, which had given its name to the Bay and twelve miles of coastline to the west, and then on to Kapouti. The road was small, the afternoon temperature a warm twenty-four degrees Celsius. He drove by multitudes of different trees, of oranges, olives, lemons, grapefruits and pomegranates interspersed with fig trees, which also seemed to be in every house garden he passed. It was a luscious peaceful setting, in stark contrast to the deadly landscape to which he was heading.

Shortly after Kalkanli the road started to wind and climb, and JP was soon almost at a thousand feet. He turned off just before Myrtou, heading away north-west to Kormakitis. Two miles more, after a particularly dense area of olive trees, JP suddenly caught a glimpse of the sea off both right and left, and knew he was getting close to the narrowing peninsula of Cape Kormakitis. Livera proved to be nothing more than a grouping of small farm houses and a couple of basic shops, and JP decided against stopping. The road became narrower and its tarmac surface was replaced by gravel, stones and potholes. He was almost there.

Just over a mile after Livera JP pulled the car off the road onto a dirt track. The only house or residence past that point was Cuttle Cove. Any traffic in the opposite direction would be coming from there, he would then be seen and suspicions aroused. The tiny dirt track went into the ever-present olive trees and the car was quickly lost to view.

JP got out and opened the rear door. He reached for the centre of the bench seat towards the back and pulled hard on the leather loop to raise it, revealing the storage beneath. He took out his rucksack and kit bag and transferred everything to the former which soon bulged fully laden. He had checked the contents of both before leaving the base. He locked the car securely, strapped the rucksack onto his shoulders and with binoculars and camera dangling around his neck walked off to the north-west. He was a holidaymaker taking pictures and bird watching, doing some camping and just having a quiet evening to himself.

JP walked nonchalantly through the olive groves. The land started to rise steeply as he approached the western side of the Cape, and after seven or eight hundred yards he was almost at the summit of a hill which fell off sharply down to the sea to the left as a shallow cliff-face. He moved slowly forwards until he could just see over the hill, to the very tip of Cape Kormakitis. His target, Cuttle Cove, lay four hundred yards before him. He stepped back a few paces, removed his rucksack and crawled forward on his stomach to have a clear view of the complex, remaining well hidden amongst the olive trees and other bushes.

He began to scan Cuttle Cove with his binoculars.

In there was a hideous nuclear weapon that a madman was getting ready to launch, to wipe out a nation and kill the best part of three million people.

And somewhere in there, too, was a girl that JP very much wanted to find.

28
SURVEILLANCE

IT WAS JUST after 5pm. JP surveyed Cuttle Cove for another ten minutes, before moving back on his stomach down to his rucksack. He began to empty the contents.

He took the two small cameras on their solid short tripods, moved back up to the crest of the hill and positioned them so that they were well concealed but in clear line of sight of the complex. He placed the third camera, rather like a sniper sight with a powerful infrared laser below, alongside the other two. Then he fanned out and added the small parabolic dish of the audio surveillance system. He moved back down again to the rest of his equipment. He booted the laptop, raised the small antenna dish on the top of the communications box and hooked them up. The box would receive, filter, heighten and then send the signals to his own screen and earpiece and up to one of the orbiting satellites for GCHQ and MI6. The feed would then be relayed to Durford and his SAS team, who were already well advanced in their attack plans, to the CIA at Langley and to a small operations room at RAF Akrotiri sixty miles south.

JP took out the camouflage and erected a half-dome of cover, giving some protection from the bright evening sun and from possible peering eyes above, not that he expected any. Finally, he popped in the earpiece, flicked one of the tiny switches on the communications box and spoke quietly.

"Broadsword calling Danny Boy. Broadsword calling Danny Boy."

The words came from one of JP's favourite films, Where Eagles Dare. Two thousand miles away in London, as JP's voice came in on the secure link, Lieutenant Chapman wondered how these men, doing dangerous deadly work, could always make light of their situation. Don't men ever grow up?

JP spoke again. "Broadsword calling Danny Boy. Broadsword calling Danny Boy. Are you getting this, Charlie?"

There was a slight crackle, and then JP could hear his friend's voice as clearly as though he were sitting five feet away.

"Danny Boy calling Broadsword, Danny Boy calling Broadsword. Yes, JP, I can hear you. We're getting the live feed now."

"Copy that." He paused a little, and then said, "Are you ready for control."

"Standby, Broadsword," came Melton's reply. A few seconds later, he spoke again. "Affirm, go ahead."

JP flicked another of the tiny switches, and then said, "You have control."

"Copied, Broadsword, we have control."

The operation of the daylight vision and the highly-sensitive night vision cameras as well as the audio ears were now under the direct control of MI6 in London. Every now and again JP could hear a very quiet short whine as one of the small motors was activated to move a camera up or down, left or right, or zoom tiny lenses for more detailed or wider images, or small adjustments to the dish. The sound from the laser equipment, control of which JP retained, was equally quiet but more regular, as it automatically scanned Cuttle Cove in great detail.

JP moved back up to the crest of the hill again and settled down for a prolonged viewing of the Cuttle Cove complex.

He was looking first for any external perimeter guards. He thought that, as the operation was coming to fruition, Malekka might add some guards on the outside of the wall. They weren't too difficult to spot. Three of them. One sitting at the centre at the main gate; the other two wandering out to either end of the wall at the sea, east and west, where they turned and walked slowly back. They wore local clothes but, he could tell, were fit professional soldiers from some country or other. Each was carrying an automatic weapon strapped around his shoulder. Perhaps these were the same men he had seen in Akrotiri with Sir Donald, now moved to outside. He would have to deal with these three first before affecting his entry.

The wall itself was about twelve feet high. A little bit of a challenge, but he could manage that. JP presumed there would be some kind of alarm system on top; he could see metal frames jutting out at forty-five degrees towards the complex at maybe three metre intervals along the wall, with some wire between. He looked left. For a while he studied the aircraft hangar just to the east of the south end of the runway; it was certainly large, and he guessed that in there was perhaps a Boeing 737 or Airbus 318 to carry everyone out, maybe a Learjet too. That would need sorting by the SAS lads too.

His glasses followed down the length of the runway to the end, and then over to the right to take in the residential buildings. There were a couple of swimming pools with sun beds placed around them, although they were all unoccupied. Further across to the east, he could see a large quayside hangar, easily big enough to cover a large yacht or several smaller craft. JP surmised that inside was the ocean-going yacht that had been waiting at the GPS co-ordinates. The helicopter had flown with the Alpha and docked; then the ship had taken the Alpha and Stella half way round the world, first north in the Indian Ocean, then into the Red Sea, through the Suez Canal and into the Mediterranean. To dock here at Cuttle Cove at Cape Kormakitis. It was unusual, he thought, to have a quayside hangar that encloses large ships. The reason was obviously concealment. On top of the roof was a rectangular construction maybe forty feet deep and thirty high set slightly off square, facing south-east. JP had no idea what that could be.

His target would first be the residential buildings. It was from there that most of the women, all in burkas, and some men were moving items into the aircraft hangar. There had been no time for any local intelligence gathering, to try to ascertain where Stella was within the complex. An all-out gun battle would probably ensue once the SAS raid started, as Malekka seemed to have a small army at the place. The girl would have no chance; she would either be killed outright by her captors, or quite probably in the crossfire.

However, one man, on his own, might have a chance. JP had thirty minutes to locate her and get her to safety. He didn't know how yet.

JP kept up the surveillance at Cuttle Cove over the next hour, dropping back frequently to check on his electronic equipment. He had already activated the CCTV detection and acquisition software to see what camera surveillance the complex had and whether he could hack into it. Doing so, if possible, would provide great assistance to the SAS and give him much better knowledge of the buildings; he might even locate Stella.

What a shame, thought JP. The system at Cuttle

Cove had no such vulnerability. It was obviously hardwired and entirely internal. Still it had been worth a try. Never mind. We'll just go with plan B.

He could see three CCTV cameras himself through his binoculars, one located at each end of the perimeter wall by the sea and the other by the entrance gate. The software had picked up five other cameras inside. Each had been identified, its coordinates fed into the firing system and the laser was ready to take them out, at the simple flick of a switch. The infrared laser beams would not be visible and would melt the lens of the camera or burn a hole through the casing to damage the inside, blinding it completely. All eight CCTV cameras that the system had detected would be immobilised within one minute. It would mean that eight views would be lost from the CCTV control station, wherever that was, more or less immediately; that would appear to be a system outage or fault, since the playback of the last recorded scenes would show nothing untoward. There would first be an effort to reboot the system and get the cameras up and running again, and then if that failed, which of course it would, a more serious physical look at the cameras, one by one. That would take time. It would be a while before the laser attack would be discovered. All he needed was thirty minutes and then the SAS would be there anyway. It would confuse the control station long enough before an alarm sounded out somewhere.

So he hoped, anyway.

Darkness began to fall. JP once again returned to his electronics station, and reached for his rucksack. He replaced his colourful shirt and shorts with a jet black T-shirt and trousers, and swapped his trainers for black boots with a flexible rubber sole, important for the wall climb. He strapped on his shoulder holster, attached the suppressor to the Sauer and holstered the handgun. He strapped on a bullet-proof vest, and his black jacket over that. He attached the suppressor to his C8 assault rifle. He pulled the balaclava over his head.

In the spate of thirty minutes he had been transformed from a casual holidaying tourist into a subversive attack and killing machine. Darkness finally settled around him.

The screen on his laptop had automatically dimmed. JP took the level down even further as his own eyes adjusted to the darkness. He took out the night vision goggles from the rucksack and strapped them on his head, raising them up. He replaced the binoculars with powerful night vision ones. He sat down and crossed his legs, placed the C8 on the ground in front of him and his hands on his knees, almost in a classic yoga position. He waited quietly, listening intently around him, adjusting to the cooler air and night sounds of the crickets. A memory of the night sounds of the African bush flashed into his mind; but here the background was much less noisy, and neither was there the roar of lions or the laugh of hyenas carried on the breeze. There were no man-eating predators. The only predator loose in the area that evening was Jim Peregrine. And in this environment, his environment, he was far more dangerous to the men in the buildings below than any big cats could ever be.

After thirty minutes JP once again crawled on his stomach to the crest of the hill and looked over. The place was almost in total darkness. The people ferrying boxes out to the aircraft hangar had stopped, presumably having completed their work. There was now little movement. There was dim lighting at the entrance gate and the external side of the perimeter wall where the three guards were situated. Again JP saw the two men walk to the outside edges of the wall, turn and then come together to meet with the third in the centre at the gate. It was better for them too of course that there was only low artificial light at the wall; their own eyes would be able to see better. Once the three were together they lit up cigarettes again and chatted quietly.

His earpiece suddenly came to life, with the 9pm check-in call.

"Danny Boy calling Broadsword."

"Broadsword," whispered JP back.

"The holiday folk are on their way, e.t.a. two two four five."

"Copy that," said JP very quietly again.

"And we have some live pictures from across the pond for you," said Melton. "Prepare to receive."

Fantastic, thought JP, God bless America, the Yanks have done it. They have re-tasked a satellite and from a hundred miles above him there is a live feed of Cuttle Cove.

"Copy, please standby."

JP moved back down and readied his communications box. He needed to see this; there may have been changes since the RAF images earlier that day. In fact, he could no longer be certain even of what was immediately on the other side of the wall that he was soon to breach, or round on the other sides of the other buildings, or what current movement there might be on the blind side of the quayside hangar.

"Ready" he said simply.

In a few seconds, the image of Cuttle Cove from directly above started to come through onto his laptop screen. This was what he needed. The images were crisp and clear, and he was able to scroll around and zoom in or out to view the current status in great detail.

"Nice and clear," said JP. "Say thanks for me."

"Wilco, JP. Confirm status."

"Status green," he said.

"Out." The radio went silent again.

Good. JP spent the next fifteen minutes studying the live feed on his laptop screen. A couple of people come out of the buildings around the pool and he zoomed in to see what they were doing: an evening smoke. He watched as the two went back inside a few minutes later. He looked at the external stairs at the south-west side of the building that contained the Spider just as a man went up them and into the door at the top; he came out again two minutes later, went down the stairs and back to the large rectangular building that was the start of the residential part of the complex. He was able to view the inside base of the entire wall, and could see clearly that there were no obstacles or personnel there, only clear ground. Good, he thought again.

The SAS would be at Akrotiri at 10.45pm, Melton had said, right on time. He knew that Sir Donald would have the five Bell 412 helicopters of 84 Squadron, based permanently at Cyprus, fuelled and waiting for them, to bring the lads north low over the mountains and up to Cape Kormakitis, dropping them in the open countryside a mile south of Cuttle Cove to maintain stealth. They would then run in and be in place ready for the assault at 11.30pm. JP would move in at 11pm. He didn't know what method of entry the SAS had decided to use. He didn't need to, although he thought it would probably be around the ends of the walls on the east and west parts of the Cape. What he did know was that, whatever the route, they would execute it fast and with terrifying efficiency. The speed and brilliance of their operations were legendary. JP had no doubts at all that they could complete the action in minutes, and secure and neutralise the Spider before Malekka's people knew what hit them.

Other units would take out the aircraft in the hangar and disable any ships on the quayside. They were ready and expecting a full battle with Malekka's people once they realised they were being hit, but by that time, if all goes well, the bomb will be nothing more than an impotent lump of metal and chemicals resting harmlessly in its launch vehicle in the safe hands of the SAS. JP was to get Stella out into the water to the northeast of the Cape in whatever craft he could find before the assault began. The regular British armed forces at Cyprus, now on standby, would then move in to take over.

The Premiers of the two Cyprus Governments would be telephoned by the British Government and appraised of the SAS operation as it began, so that both the Republic of Cyprus and the Turkish Republic of Northern Cyprus would in the eyes of the world be seen to be participating in a joint international venture to defeat terrorism. They might not like being informed at the last minute, but informing them in advance might compromise the operation to the media or, worse, to Malekka. So silence would be maintained until the SAS were approaching Cuttle Cove.

JP moved back up to his observation post at the crest of the hill, and was peering down once more through his night binoculars. The minutes ticked by slowly. He hoped that he would soon see Stella and that he could make her safe again. All of this desperate craziness would then be over. It seemed months ago that they had been on the beach in St Lucia enjoying the sand, sea and each other. It had been the plan to draw out the terrorists, but in the process, in the time leading up to her kidnap, the two of them had found something special in each other and become close, far closer than JP would like to admit to himself. Now, he had to find her. He just had to. If she was still alive. He had hoped that the sound surveillance might pick up something to help him locate her. However London had quickly ascertained that Cuttle Cove was very heavily soundproofed, as they had thought. What chatter was picked up was of no value. It had been worth a try; but Malekka had covered this aspect just as thoroughly as he had everything else.

Just before 10pm JP moved back down from the hill again, and checked the complex on the satellite feed, paying special attention to the internal perimeter of the wall. It was clear. In fact, there was nobody to be seen anywhere. The images were firm and steady. Amazing, really, what can be done, he said to himself. And thank Heaven for it.

At 10pm his earpiece came to life again.

"Danny Boy calling Broadsword."

"Broadsword."

"Confirm status."

"Status green."

The radio went silent once more. There was nothing further to report on either side. The operation was on schedule, he was ready, he had one hour, the SAS had forty-five minutes before they landed at Akrotiri. He moved back up and looked out again around the Cape, taking in the view on either side of Cuttle Cove. The sky was beautifully clear and the stars twinkled from a cloudless sky. Malekka had planned this so very well, he thought. On 18th April there had been a New Moon and today, four days later, the tiny crescent moon, which gave off no light of consequence, was already setting and would be below the horizon at 11.13pm. To all intents and purposes, the night was jet black. The air was still warm from the heat of the day, there was a gentle breeze blowing from the north towards him that every now and again rustled the leaves and branches around him, and he could hear the distant, soft sound of the sea lapping calmly onto the beaches around the Cape. He could see a few specks of light out on the water belonging to a couple of ships or yachts settling down for the night, where people were probably having a drink or a late meal, or couples were making love and enjoying the calm Mediterranean on this quiet peaceful evening. As he lay on his stomach and looked at the complex through his night binoculars, he wondered for the hundredth time where Stella was. He hoped that all his training, all his abilities and skills would come together in the right way that evening, and work to free her, and bring her life again.

Not long now, and he would know. Or, he would be dead. One or the other.

Just then a quiet but unmistakable hum could be heard coming from the complex. He scanned the place again with his binoculars; he could see nothing new. Was he mistaken? No. No, he could definitely hear something new, that wasn't there before. Perhaps it was just a new generator starting up. He continued to watch for a couple of minutes. The sound settled and maintained a steady low, very quiet whine.

At 10.23pm, his earpiece came to life again. This time the voice was agitated and much louder than before.

"Danny Boy calling Broadsword. Urgent."

"Broadsword."

It was Melton's voice once more.

"JP, Israel's under attack."

"*What?*" said JP in a louder whisper incredulously, moving quickly back down from the crest of the hill.

"It's Israel. She's under attack. In the last twenty minutes, there has been a massive, sustained cyber attack, which has already started to cripple her computer networks and communications systems. They think it's coming from Iran. Public and private facilities, overnight finance operations, transportation, hospitals, government departments, they're all being hacked and disrupted. Viruses are going in, screens are freezing up, things are being switched off that should be on, even the traffic stop lights have all been made green and there are car crashes everywhere. It's chaos."

"Bloody hell," said JP quietly.

"They've got into the military systems too, and are causing total disruption," continued Melton. "They're crippling the country. They've even got into the electrical grids there and are taking them over and turning off power all over the place. And a few minutes ago, some extremely powerful and effective radar jamming has started that seems to be coming from at least three locations, aimed directly at Israel and the surrounding area including the western seaboard. Directly at the Super Green Pine Radar system. It's gone blank, nothing at all. The GPS there is down too. The Arrow system is useless. And the Americans say the same about their Patriot System. All totally inoperative."

"This is it, Charlie," whispered JP as loudly as he dared. "This is how he's going to get it there. He's not going to send it *through* the Arrow defensive shield. He's turning the whole bloody shield *off*."

"That's not all of it," said Melton. "Listen to me, Jimmy. The Israelis say that at this rate they are going to be completely exposed and helpless by midnight. They are terrified, they see they will have no defence network at all. They're trying to battle it, but it's so strong and so sudden they are losing. So instead they're launching an air strike, JP. Now. They're going pre-emptive and will kill the weapon on the ground in

Cyprus with a laser-guided bomb. The dirty radioactive fall-out will kill people on Cyprus, but they're going to do it anyway. They have to. The aircraft are almost in the air. They're going to hit it at 10.55pm. You have to get out."

There was silence.

"Jimmy, for Christ's sake, can you hear me?" Melton was almost shouting. "I said they're going to hit it at 10.55. You have to get out. You haven't a chance. For God's sake save yourself."

There was still silence.

"JP?" he yelled.

There was no reply.

On the viewing screens in London, the night camera could make out the vision of a man running fast down the hill towards the complex. The only sound they could hear was from the discarded earpiece on the ground close to the cameras, of the whining and quiet pop of the laser gun, as one by one it took out the eight CCTV cameras at Cuttle Cove.

29
THE LAST DAY

AS SOON AS JP learned what the Israeli's were going to do and when, he flicked the switch to start the work of the laser, grabbed his C8 and started his run, throwing his earpiece onto the ground as he went over the hill past the cameras with Melton's words still coming through. There was no point in waiting; he knew what Melton was going to say, and every second was going to count now. In that instant he committed totally to his course of action. If he was going to die it was going to be on his terms, and he certainly wasn't leaving without trying to rescue the girl or disarm the Spider. If in trying to do that he died, then that was his choice. The SAS weren't even on the island yet. To hell with everything else.

Now he had to go fast.

At full pelt JP ran silently down the hill like a black panther leaping towards its prey, all residual pain from the torture dismissed, winding his way past olive trees and leaping over bushes and rocks. His NVG were working well and providing vision that was almost as good as if he was in broad daylight. His body operated as a well-oiled machine, lithe capable and fast; there was no perspiration, no panting; just smooth, efficient motion, combined now with grim determination.

As he went he was calmly formulating a plan of action. The weapon, now, had to come first. He had to get to it and disable it; and then somehow find Stella.

He had already decided what to do about the three men on the outside of the wall. They were following a more or less consistent routine. The wall was around five hundred and fifty yards across and was curved slightly from the west seaboard to the east side of the Cape. When the men walking reached the water's edge either end, none of the three was in sight of the others.

He was running down a line equidistant to the west end of the wall and the gate at the middle. He slowed when he was about a hundred and fifty yards from the wall, and then dropped silently to the ground onto his stomach, lifting up his NVG to the top of his head. He put his elbows on the ground, placed his rifle on single round fire and aimed through the night sight. The man walking to the western edge was first.

One minute gone, twenty-nine left.

When the man reached the end of the wall and began to turn, JP fired. The silencer on the C8 reduced the sound of the fire to a quiet pop, which was lost quickly in the gentle northern breeze and the few rustling bushes around and behind. The bullet hit the man in the head and he dropped to the ground dead. JP turned the rifle towards the man at the centre of the wall at the gate, took aim and fired. That was two down.

He stood, lowered his goggles again and ran off fast to the right due east. The third man had got to the end at the sea and was starting to turn to walk back. A few seconds more, and JP dropped to the ground again. He took aim, and fired. The top of the man's head came off as the bullet ripped into its target, and the third guard dropped silently to the ground.

Twenty-eight minutes.

JP was on his feet again now, and running quietly towards the east part of the wall. The land was flat and had become permeated with sand, and the olive trees and bushes had given way to little more than clumps of moss and lichen. JP would go over the wall at the curve.

He got to within thirty feet, paused and crouched on the ground again. He strapped his machine gun over his head and shoulder on his back, so that his hands were free. He no longer needed the NVG as there was sufficient low light for him to be able to see well enough, and he slipped them into a jacket pocket. JP stood, took a deep breath and ran fast straight at the wall.

At about a metre away he raised his left leg high to the wall and bent his knee in hard, pushing off his right leg and leaning back slightly. The momentum gripped his left foot against the wall and he pushed up with his toes, his other leg moved fast under his chest as he ran up the wall and found grip a metre higher, and he pushed up again, raising both arms in a great leap skywards, stretching his body to its full length, his hands reaching for the top of the wall.

They found it. Without losing momentum his biceps took over and pulled his body up. He leant forwards slightly and then first his right foot was on the top, then the other, his body contracted like a coiled spring. He pushed hard with his legs, propelling himself up and forwards in a leap straight over the three rows of angled wires that ran along the top of the wall. He stretched his legs as he dropped the fourteen feet on the other side, ready for the impact. As his feet touched the ground he rolled, absorbing the energy of the drop.

He was in.

JP moved forwards quickly to a row of storage buildings, crouched low and looked around, listening intently for any sounds that might herald his arrival. There was nothing. Nor could he see anyone. He looked back towards the wall, and then further round to the gate. All was still and quiet.

JP followed the building along to the right. He silently went round one corner and at the next had his first close-up view of the missile hangar twenty yards away. There was a door on the side facing him, but he wanted to check the perimeter first before going in. He ran over and moved along to the right corner. He peered round and saw the corridor leading off to the bigger quayside hangar. He could see the water of the Mediterranean beyond.

JP turned to head back when he heard voices from behind and quickly dropped down as a door opened and closed. He went back to the end of the wall but could see nothing. He thought he should check out the corridor joining the hangars and make sure it was clear. He moved over quietly to the door that had opened and closed just a moment ago. There was no lock or keypad. He quietly turned the handle and opened it, and saw the back of a man standing against the far wall.

JP didn't hear or see anything. He just felt a massive blow on the back of the head as he was about to go inside. He fell forwards into the corridor with stars in his eyes and slumped to the floor, fighting away the darkness of unconsciousness with all his might. He shook his head and looked up. Dazed, he found himself on his feet; his C8 had somehow already been removed from him and so too had his handgun, and knife, and they lay in a pile on the floor by the door. There were two men. One of them was holding his arms in a vicelike grip behind, and the other was standing there in front of him, glaring at him with cold vicious eyes. The man pulled his right arm back and smashed his fist into JP's jaw, and JP's head came back hard to the right. He felt the blood starting to drip from a split lip and his head reeled some more with dizziness. The man behind him released his grip and threw him against the wall. The two men now stood in front of him. JP recognised them immediately. Aarif Haddad and Tarek Raboud, the two killers of Dr Keppof. They ripped off his balaclava so that they could see his face.

"So, are you English or American?" said Raboud. "What are you doing here? How did you get here? What are you after? Come come, you need to talk, and quickly."

Haddad laughed. "Yes, you need to talk my friend," he said, and he smashed another fist into JP's face, on the other side. "And we can help you talk to us." JP was almost down on his knees.

They liked that. They had somebody new to play with. They would enjoy getting some information out of him. Who was this man, that had appeared from nowhere? They would get a little information out of him and then take him to Mr Malekka.

"So, my friend," said Haddad, "what are you doing here?"

JP thought quickly. He had recovered fast, but he started to feign his near collapse onto the ground. Haddad took another step towards him, ready to hit him again, but JP raised his arm.

"No, ok, no more," he said.

"Ah, English, ok my friend, good, you are very sensible," said Haddad. "So now, what are you doing here?"

"Tell us, you pig," said Raboud, who decided to hit JP again just for the hell of it and smashed his fist into JP's right cheekbone. JP felt as though his head was close to falling off.

"No, no more, please," he said, spitting out some more blood onto the floor.

"So tell us what you are here for," said Haddad. "Or we can continue like this for the rest of the night if you prefer."

"Ok. Ok," said JP, making out that he was gasping for breath. "I'm here to find a girl. She was kidnapped from an island in the Caribbean, and I've come to find her."

Haddad and Raboud looked at each other, and smiled, and then started to laugh.

"You mean Stella?" said Haddad. "The girl with the nice tits, that we played with and fucked this afternoon? Given to us today as a little present from our boss?"

"The bitch with the nice long blonde hair that cried all the time and whimpered as we screwed her cunt and her arse?" said Raboud leeringly. "What's she to you?"

"I didn't know that," said JP, ignoring the question. Never mind about fighting them; he had to fight himself, to control and conceal his own anger at what he had just heard. Now he wanted to kill these two more than ever. They had moved further away from the weapons on the floor, which now couldn't be of any immediate help to him, or them. He needed to remain calm.

"But that's not the only reason I'm here," he said.

"Then tell us, you fucker," said Haddad. "Why else are you here? Or shall we beat it out of you a little more?"

"No, no, there's no need to do that," said JP. "I'll tell you."

"Ok, so tell us then, we're waiting, and then we'll decide what to do with you," said Haddad. "Why else are you here? Who are you? What is the girl to you?"

"You don't recognise me, or remember me, do you," said JP, bringing himself upright a little more. "We've almost met, you know."

The smile started to go from the faces of Haddad and Raboud. They glanced at each other quizzically, and then back to JP. And then the realisation came to them simultaneously, as they recalled the images played to Stella whilst she was being tortured. Of course. The man running along the promenade, the bomb, the explosion as he jumped over the railings. They peered at him, matching the man with the images.

"You're the boyfriend," said Haddad nodding his head slowly, his eyes slightly widened, his voice carrying shocked surprise. Raboud stayed silent, but JP noticed the throat movement as he swallowed. Good. Confusion and a few of seconds of distraction. It would help.

"Yes," said JP. "I'm the boyfriend."

"You're here for her?"

"And we almost met, too," JP carried on regardless. "In Berlin. A couple of months ago. It was in the Kurfürstendamm. In fact, you looked straight at me." JP paused. "Just after you killed my friend, Dr Keppof."

The faces of both Raboud and Haddad had drained a little of blood and become whiter. All was not as it had at first seemed with this intruder.

"And the other reason I'm here," said JP as he stood up to his full height of six foot three and looking at the other men, "is to kill the two of you."

Haddad and Raboud didn't like this any more. Haddad's face snarled, and he drew his fist back and aimed another blow at JP, but this time JP had had enough. He stepped to the right of the blow, caught Haddad's arm and pulled him forwards, stepping across his legs and forcing Haddad off balance and over in front of JP. As Haddad went down on his back, JP quickly punched the man's throat, almost killing him outright. While he was bent over Raboud came forwards to attack him from behind and JP gave a harsh kick up with his left leg, finding Raboud's face with a vicious blow that sent the man reeling backwards. JP was up and bouncing now in a classic karate pose, with his left hand out to the front and his right arm drawn back alongside his chest. The weapons were behind him. They would have to fight through him to get to them.

Haddad staggered up from the ground. He ignored the discomfort at his neck and forced himself to breathe deeper to clear his head. Raboud was back up now, too, trying hard to overcome the damage the kick had done.

But JP was ready for them both.

Haddad moved in with a series of fast punches. JP just leant back and dodged them all helped by light footwork. Haddad gave another right swing; JP raised his left arm and blocked it, stepped in and right elbowed Haddad hard in his stomach. The man bent from the blow, JP's hand slipped under his armpit and pulled him forwards off balance, then JP stepped around and behind, brought his left arm up around Haddad's neck and pulled back. In one fast blurred motion Haddad was held from behind. JP dropped back and down, Haddad hit the ground hard and JP smashed first at the neck, then the groin, then the neck again. The man was curled up in agony on the ground.

Raboud swallowed hard at the lightning speed with which this intruder had brought down his very experienced battle companion, and snarled, going in at him again. But JP was up and facing him. Raboud rotated to bring his right leg up in a three sixty crescent kick. JP saw it coming, leant back to dodge the foot that came close to his face, then quickly slipped down onto his haunches and pivoted on his left leg, swinging his right out horizontally. He caught Raboud on the heels, the man's legs came up into the air and he went down onto his back.

JP was up again; Haddad was up too and moved in with a lunge with his left hand, which JP deflected simultaneously smashing his left elbow into Haddad's throat and jaw. JP punched hard at the dazed man and heard the bone of Haddad's nose crunch as his fist broke it. Haddad went down to the floor and this time stayed there.

Raboud took out a knife from somewhere and flicked it open, passing it from hand to hand as the two men moved round in a circle facing each other. Probably the same knife he'd killed Keppof with, flashed through JP's mind. Raboud lunged at JP with the knife in his left hand. JP stepped quickly left and turned, catching Raboud's wrist in his right hand, placing his other arm under Raboud's elbow. He pushed down. The man yelled at the pain of counter pressure at the elbow and brought his free right arm up to smash at JP's head and reach for his eyes to gouge them. JP leant forwards and brought his head back up in a violent head butt, smashing it into Raboud and dazing him, and then brought his right foot up behind him to kick Raboud hard in the groin.

The man groaned at the searing pain in his testicles, yet held the knife firm and struggled to get at JP. He tried punching at JP's head and neck, JP gave another violent reverse head butt, rotated to the right and physically pulled the dazed Raboud with him, crashing the man into the opposite wall, and then repeated the movement back onto the other wall, then back again. Raboud tried to bring his left arm in using his bicep but JP was stronger.

JP grabbed the thumb clutching the knife and began to force it loose. He pushed hard, forcing the thumb away, and then the knife was loose and it fell to the floor. He twisted the thumb more, levering Raboud's arm out and down. JP felt the growing weakness of his opponent and took the moment. He locked his left arm, still under

Raboud's, onto his right in a vicelike grip, gave one final hard push downwards and broke Raboud's arm at the elbow. There was a hideous crackling of bone and tearing of ligament and tendon as the joint was destroyed, and Raboud let out a ghastly screamed gurgle. JP released his grip, turned round quickly and smashed Raboud's face with a powerful left punch, catching a quick view of Raboud's bulging eyes and mouth stretched wide in agony. Raboud went down, and was unconscious.

JP straightened up and took a deep breath, and looked at the two men on the ground. "That's for my friend, Dr Keppof," he said. But neither of the men could hear him.

JP took out four nylon tie cords from his jacket and quickly bound the two men at their feet and hands behind their back. He had a little difficulty with Raboud, since his elbow didn't want to go where he needed it to go, but he forced the destroyed arm anyway. He took out a small roll of duct tape and wound some round the mouths of both men so that they couldn't speak when conscious again, and cut a small slit in the tape over Haddad's so he could breathe. They were secure.

JP looked at his watch. Eight minutes had passed. Christ. He picked up his C8 carbine, and put his gun back into its holster. He opened the door, dragged the two unconscious bound bodies outside and left them in the darkness up against the wall of the corridor. He might want something from those two later.

JP deftly ran back round the corner and then along to the other end of the building following the covered pathway, looking at the door as he went by - it had a keypad on it, which didn't surprise him at all. He carried on to the end of the wall and peered round, and could see the steel stairway to the top level. There was nobody in sight. He ran down along the wall, past the stairway, to the end.

He peered round the last corner to check that side of the building, that he had not been able to view except with the satellite feed. Half way down, the pathway turned left to the residential section of Cuttle Cove. He ran stealthily beyond it, hugging the wall past some waste bins to the final corner. There was nobody around.

He turned back, and was going to head to the stairway. He thought that the door at the top would be the entrance probably to some kind of observation control room. He had watched several people go in and out from there both from his vantage point on the hill and more recently on the satellite feed. He would next deal with the people in there. He would have to shoot his way through the door, and that was going to make a noise, but there wasn't time or option to devise any alternative.

Eighteen minutes left.

A door opened at the building opposite. JP immediately dropped to the ground and lay crouched in the darkness and shadows of the waste bins. A man came out in a long white coat and walked towards the missile hangar. As he passed in front of JP and disappeared from view, JP quickly shouldered his C8 and followed the person round the corner. He was ten feet from the stairway when JP's arm reached the man's throat and the silencer of his handgun was thrust against the man's temple. JP cocked the gun so the man could know how close he was to dying.

"One sound and you're dead," he said in the man's ear quietly.

JP pulled the person back around the corner down to

the additional cover of the bins, and spun him round. He placed the gun at the man's forehead.

"Do you understand English?" asked JP.

The man nodded.

"Good. Answer me immediately, and you will live. If you don't, I'll kill you where you stand. Do you understand?"

The man nodded again. His eyes were wide and terrified. He looked into JP's eyes and could see only cold heartless steel. And he didn't want to die.

"Is there a keypad lock to the door at the top of the stairs?"

"Yes," replied the man, with a shaking voice.

"What is the combination?"

"Four, six, three, two."

"Is that the same number for the door on the other wall?"

The man nodded quickly. "Yes," he said, "it's the same."

"Good," said JP. "There was a girl brought here; she was kidnapped and brought here. Do you know her?"

"Yes, she's here," he said. "She's here."

"Good. Thank you. Where?"

"I don't know."

JP was ready to fire the gun. The man realised it, and he spoke again. "I don't know. I don't know. I swear it. But she is here, I know she's here. But I don't know where she is. That's the truth, please, please don't kill me."

JP thought for two seconds. He didn't shoot the man. Instead he de-cocked the gun, spun the man round and smashed his gun against his head, knocking him unconscious. JP caught him as he fell. He brought out two more ties, secured the man, taped his mouth and left him in the shadows at the waste bins.

JP opened another zipper pocket on his jacket, and brought out a black circular object three inches in diameter and an inch high. He moved out round the corner to the foot of the stairs, and climbed them silently. At the top he entered the code, opened the door just enough to slide the gas canister in along the floor and closed the door again. Immediately there was a quiet soft explosion, as the clear invisible nerve gas reached every part of the small elongated control room. The occupants were first instantly paralysed and then knocked out by it.

Sixteen minutes.

JP was already at the bottom of the stairs running quietly to the corner to get round to the entrance door. He stopped when he heard the door open. Someone walked out. JP waited, ready to take them if they appeared. He heard the door close, followed by the sound of a lighter. JP was close enough to smell the smoke from the burning tobacco as it drifted along in the air.

He would have to risk a quick glance. If the man was looking his way, he would shoot. JP peered silently round, bringing his gun level at the same time. The man had his back to him. That's a bit of luck, thought JP. He quietly holstered the gun and brought out his knife from his belt. He went round the corner and walked silently up to the man. In one quick motion JP put his left hand round the man's mouth and plunged the six-inch black steel blade into his neck, cutting his carotid artery and his vocal cords almost simultaneously. He pulled back and down, pushing away to the front with his knife.

Colonel Anatoly Linchuk was dead before he reached the ground. He would never meet with Vashinsky to collect his fifty million US dollars.

JP wiped the blade on the man's jacket and sheathed

his knife. He dragged the body off towards the darker area of the storage buildings that he had first visited when he scaled the wall, and tucked it up alongside the base in the shadows.

JP ran back to the door. He pulled on the entrance handle. As he had guessed, the lock had been put on the latch by the smoker to get back in easily. JP pulled his C8 from his back and put it on full automatic. His watch said 10.41pm. He had fourteen minutes before the laser guided bomb would arrive and blow the place to pieces and him with it, and release lethal radioactive material into the Cyprus air that would kill thousands. He opened the door, took the lock off the latch and stepped quietly inside, closing and locking the door behind him. He ignored the almost overpowering hypnotic sight of the nuclear weapon and focused on what could kill him first. He levelled his C8 at the people inside.

There were seven of them. Two women in burkas and a man in a military uniform stood to the left of the Spider. In front of the launch vehicle was another woman in a white coat and further right of her were three men also in uniform, although JP couldn't tell what uniform or country. The Spider was at right angles to him in the centre facing a large sliding door, which obviously led to the wide corridor where JP had encountered Haddad and Raboud. The missile was slightly raised from its launch vehicle; its nose pointed ominously off right. At the top of the building left and running the length of the wall was the glass observation block. He could see the heads of people slumped forwards, disabled. He knew they had been put to sleep.

Just then one of the three men to the right noticed him and shouted out something in Arabic, and drew a gun from his waist holster to fire at JP. JP was quicker. He swivelled round and pulled the trigger. His carbine spat out a series of quiet pop, pop, pop sounds as a short burst of automatic fire left the rifle. The man was hit squarely in the chest and the force lifted him up into the air and threw him back five feet. The other six people in the room spun round at the noise and faced JP, who levelled his gun at them.

"Don't move, anybody," he said in a loud voice. He had no idea if anyone spoke English, but at that moment the weapon was acting as a universal translator and they knew what he meant. He gestured with the gun at the other two men standing by their dead colleague, to make them move over closer. "And let me see your hands, all of you."

"And what are you going to do now, young man," said the girl in the centre in the white coat, shocked but who was recovering her composure remarkably quickly. "Are you going to kill us all? Are you insane?"

"Coming from you standing in front of that nuclear missile, that's an interesting choice of words," said JP.

"We all have guns," she said. "The next time you try to shoot us, one of us will get you. You hear, everyone?" She spoke the last sentence louder, as a command to the others in the room, and repeated it quickly in Arabic. She said again in English, "We are now six against one. You can't get us all. And there are fifty men here in this place, armed, and they will be here soon and you will be dead," she added.

"Be quiet." JP spat out the words. "If you co-operate, you can live. Otherwise, I am going to kill you all. And make no mistake about it, I can kill you as easily as I could swat a fly, it won't worry me one bit." She might be right though, he thought. I might not be able to get them all. He could see the hands of all of them except the burka woman in the middle. Maybe they didn't all speak English. But anyway if any of them moved even an inch, he was going to open fire.

The woman in the white coat hesitated; he could see she was thinking about drawing a gun. He could feel it, and see it in her eyes. He would ask quickly, and then probably have to shoot.

"I'm looking for a girl," he said. "The one who was kidnapped. Where is she?"

He looked around at them, waiting for a reply.

The girl in the white coat started to laugh, a sneering, sarcastic laugh.

"You've come for a girl?" she said incredulously. "There is this weapon here that can kill millions, and you are asking about one single girl?"

"I won't ask again," said JP. "You have ten seconds, and then I will shoot."

"Be ready," said the girl in a loud voice to everyone in the room. "Just make sure one of you gets this pathetic pig."

JP knew that as soon as he opened fire they would all dive for cover, and there would be six guns on him against his one. He had no protection, standing with his back, literally, against the wall. JP glanced at the two men to his right, and the girl in the coat; and then to the three people to the left of the missile, looking at them one by one. He was just about to take his eyes away from the middle one, a girl in a burka, when she did something odd. She closed her right eye, and winked at him. JP frowned slightly. What the hell was that for? I'm about to shoot her, and she's...

JP's mind raced back in a series of nanosecond flashes, back through the events of the last weeks, through the travelling, back through London, to Zimbabwe, to South Africa, to Gracie and Thomas in St Lucia, to the beach, the sun and the sea... His memory found it.

I know those eyes. *"Whenever you want, boy,"* she had said to him, and had given him an inviting slow wink with her right eye. I know those eyes.

It's Stella.

JP swung round to the men to his right and shot them both. The pop, pop, pop came out again and belied the ferociousness of the gun. One man got three rounds in the stomach and with a scream doubled up in agony, falling to the concrete floor in a spate of blood and intestines and gurgling another scream as he died. The other almost had his gun out when four rounds hit him in the chest and killed him outright. He reeled backwards without a sound.

The girl in the white coat made a grab for her gun from a shoulder holster and the burka girl and the other man reached for theirs. JP had been counting on Stella's doing something to hinder the two people either side of her and gain him a few seconds, and he was right. With all her might she shoved her shoulder into the man to her left making him lose his balance, and then turned to the burka girl and head-butted her viciously, just as JP opened fire again on the white-coated girl that had done the talking.

Aisha died as two bullets cut into her neck and another two into her chest, whipping her backwards off her feet. Her lifeless form crashed down onto the floor.

The girl in the burka was dazed and on the ground, and Stella levelled a kick straight at her head, just as JP shot the man dead with a single burst of fire straight through his heart.

JP moved swiftly to Stella, who was letting out a loud moaning sound. He lifted off the top of her burka. She had duct tape wrapped around her mouth and was handcuffed behind her back. He loosely shouldered his C8 and pulled off the tape.

"Where the fuck have you been?" shouted Stella at him. "What the hell took you so long?" she screamed, shaking her head wildly.

"Well I thought I'd been rather quick, actually," said JP, somewhat taken aback, and with a hurt expression on his face. "It's been a little tricky, you know."

"Get these things off me," she said, "the keys are in that one's pockets somewhere." She gestured towards Shurafa on the ground. JP went over and found the key, and released Stella from the handcuffs. As soon as she was free, she turned round and put her arms around his neck and pushed her body close to him, and squeezed him, and cried out aloud; no words, just a loud long cry. JP put his arms around her and hugged her and held her, rocking her to and fro gently. She felt his strength, his protection, his love. She tried to fight back the tears, but couldn't, and they were streaming down her face.

"I knew you'd come," she said quietly. "I knew you would. Thank you. Thank you."

"You're welcome, darling," whispered JP back. He said nothing else. He just held her, just waited for her.

"So where's the cavalry?" she asked, as her breathing calmed a little.

JP took her hands down from around his neck, and wiped her tears from her cheeks with his thumbs. "Well, er...," he said, "actually... Well, actually, there isn't any. There's just me."

"*What?*" she said. "What do you mean? Just *you?* Malekka's got forty or fifty men out there, and I don't know why they aren't here yet. What do you mean there isn't anyone else?"

"Look, there's no time to explain now," said JP. He knew he had had to give her a few seconds, but she had regained a little composure, and he had to move on. Now he needed her to concentrate and work with him.

"Listen to me. We need to disarm this weapon, and we need to do it right now. Are there explosives around here too?"

"Yes," she said. She was breathing better now and was in control of herself more. "There are explosives all over the place; the launcher, and the walls of the hangar."

"Right," said JP. "Now I need you to handle the disarming of the Spider, and I'll do the explosives, ok? Can you do that?"

"Yes," she said to him. "Just a second." She went over to Shurafa, who was beginning to stir on the ground back to consciousness, and gave her a massive kick in the head again.

"You bitch," she said. Shurafa shot off into unconsciousness again. She turned to JP.

"You see that metal chair there, just behind the end of the missile?"

JP followed her gaze. There was a metal chair that was bolted into the concrete floor.

"They were just about to tie me into it. They were going to put me in it and let me roast in the flames as the missile launched. Fucking bastards."

She started to take off her clothes. "I've been in this stinking burka straight jacket for too long," she said. "I detest it."

JP continued to glance around the building, ready for the assault he knew could come at any time. Stella was quickly in her bra and panties, and high-heeled shoes; all that she was wearing, and had been permitted to wear, under the burka. At any other time, JP would have enjoyed the vision of the beautiful half-naked woman, but he remained cold and totally focused. Their lives, and the lives of countless others, depended on it. She only took a few seconds, and JP smiled at her when she was ready; she made a little smile back.

"Right," he said, "come here," and with that he picked her up as she walked over and in two strides he was adjacent to the Spider. "Ok, here you go." He all but threw her up onto the top of the launch vehicle. She landed safely and moved over towards the top end of the missile. "Jimmy, I need a couple of screwdrivers," she said, "there, at the base of the table."

He ran over and grabbed the whole toolkit, quickly stuffed a couple of heavy steel spanners into a pocket, ran back and lifted the toolkit up onto the launcher too. She rummaged around, and found what she needed. He brought his carbine down from his shoulder and looked around for more cameras. Shit, he thought. There were two, one at each end of the wall at the base of the observation room. He destroyed each with a single shot. It can't be long now. His luck has held for a long time, Malekka's people have to be here in any second. He looked down at his watch. It said 10.46pm. They had nine minutes left. And then it wouldn't matter about Malekka anyway.

He ran over to the large sliding door that opened into the corridor where he had encountered Haddad and Raboud, and forced the two large spanners under the wheels of the door, jamming them so they couldn't move and so locking the door closed. He didn't want Malekka's men in from that route. He ran back to the Spider and found the explosives around the launch vehicle quite easily, and it was a simple matter for JP to disarm them by disconnecting the firing mechanism, a mobile phone.

JP then checked the perimeter of the building, found the explosives at the base of the walls and began to disarm them. He glanced briefly over at Stella. In nothing but a skimpy bikini, or bra and panties anyway, she was sitting open-legged astride the five hundred kiloton nuclear ballistic missile, with her long blonde hair curled around her neck and her heels raising her legs and shaping her calves. He turned back to the work, filing the erotic image away in his mind for later, if there was a later. He knew he would remember it for as long as he lived. Which, he said to himself, at this precise moment looked as though it would be about six minutes.

Around thirty thousand feet above, two Israeli jets had the hangar in their sights. The target lighting plane at a slightly lower altitude turned on its laser. The plane above confirmed target acquisition and then released its ten thousand pound bomb. It extended small wings as its nose tipped towards the earth, following the guiding line of the invisible beam bouncing off the roof. From thirty thousand feet the bomb would take two minutes and forty seconds to impact.

Suddenly there was a yell from Stella. "JP, it's started a countdown. The thing's going to detonate," she said. "Shit."

"How long do we have?" he shouted back.

"Two minutes, less some seconds."

"Then you'd better get the thing out soon."

"Are you done there, Jimmy?" she asked, the stress clearly in her voice. "Can you help? I don't think we're going to make it in time."

"Nearly done," he replied. So they know we are here now, and Malekka has gone for detonation. What took him so long, he wondered? But then it's only been twenty-five minutes since he was lying on his stomach on the hill at his observation point, and he's been inside the perimeter for twenty, he said to himself. The element of surprise. And twenty minutes can be both a long time, or then again hardly any time at all. He disarmed the final explosive, and then ran over to the

Spider. He leapt up onto the launcher to help Stella. She had removed the outer casing covering the Alpha unit which he could see sitting neatly inside the missile just below the area containing the bomb's radioactive components that would create the huge five hundred kiloton explosion. Further below that was the propellant of the missile itself. He could now see the digital clock on the Alpha counting down, its red digits changing with terrifying consistency as the count got lower and lower. She was taking out one stubborn screw, which left one more. JP grabbed another screwdriver from the kit, and started to undo the one above at the other end of the Alpha, the last of the six. He pulled it out just as Stella got her final one released too.

Just then there was an explosion and the door of the building through which JP had entered minutes ago was blown off its hinges and lock and smashed to the ground in several pieces twenty feet away. Before the smoke cleared, JP had his C8 in his hands again and had whipped round, running to the other end of the launch vehicle, firing at the doorway as he went. He could hear the screams and shouting of the people on the other side who caught the hot copper-coated lead rounds his weapon was spitting out. He fired again, there were more screams. He quickly changed his empty magazine and crouched low on the launcher waiting for the inevitable assault through the door.

The smell of gunfire and explosives and heated blood and burnt skin filled the air. JP glanced up at Stella. She was just pulling the Alpha loose and clear of its position. She levered it up with her fingers, but then it dropped back in again. She could see that the red digits were down to eight seconds... seven... six... She tried again, and couldn't do it with her nails. JP fired again as two more came through the door from the outside, and they fell to the ground dead. She picked up the screwdriver again and levered it into position, lifting the Alpha up, at last this time she was able to hold it and raise it in its casing... Another three centimetres and the unit was finally clear of its shackles. As the digits reached zero, there was a click, and four shiny silver-like bolts shot out, two at either side. That was the detonation. Instead of causing the nuclear explosion, the bolts just punched harmlessly into the air.

She looked over to JP.

"Got it," she smiled.

Another two men had charged into the hangar now. JP fired again, and killed them both. JP quickly unzipped and reached inside one of his jacket pockets.

To cover all eventualities JP had also been trained to disarm the Spider by removing the Alpha unit. Now he took out the small communicator box Melton had given him. It had two buttons. The green one he was to press when he had found Stella. The red button was in case for some reason he had to deal with the Spider himself. He really didn't want to get shot by the home team, he had said. The signals would be immediately picked up both by satellite above and relayed to London and by the SAS on the ground, who would then know his location within Cuttle Cove. He switched it on, pressed the red button, then the green one.

He ran along the top of the launcher over to Stella. She was leaning forward, after the effort of just managing to get the Alpha out. She looked up at him, and said again, "I got it, Jimmy."

"Good," he replied with a smile, and then added, "What the hell took you so long," mimicking what she had shouted at him just a few minutes ago. She smiled at him as he jumped down from the launcher, and she jumped off into his arms. He set her down.

"That way, over to the corner," he shouted and they both ran over to the corner of the wall below the glass control room on the opposite side of the blown door. Another two men came running through and he fired his C8 but was out of ammunition again. He drew his gun from his holster as they fired, and leant over Stella. He felt something hard and hot in his back, but was able to get two shots off from the Sauer. Both men dropped to the ground.

"Here, take this," he said, handing her the pistol and slamming another magazine from his jacket into the C8. He pulled the pin on a hand grenade and tossed it over in the direction of the door. It blew the legs off one man who had just come through and flipped the other following him head over heels and back into the doorway. He smashed to the ground, and lay still.

The signal JP had sent was relayed at once to the Israelis, and thirty thousand feet above the two Israeli jets received orders to abort. The two pilots and navigators cursed aloud. It was too late. All they could do was to try to move the target. The plane lighting the target quickly shifted the position of his laser beam, away from the roof of the missile building off to the north, in an effort to make the bomb they had released two minutes and thirty seconds ago reach the quayside instead.

JP looked at his watch. It was time. He shouted at Stella to get down to the ground, he pulled her tighter into the corner and then lay on top of her, trying to protect her as much as he could.

The final seconds ticked away. There were bullets hitting the wall randomly around them as loose gunfire was shot blindly through the open door and the smoke, but JP knew what was coming and just kept low and over Stella. As the bomb struck there was an enormous explosion. The whole building shook violently, and part of the roof above them was blown off and came crashing down in the centre of the floor, much of it onto the Spider. The glass of the control room above smashed and dropped down around them, although thankfully it was reinforced and fell as rounded chunks that didn't cut, just hurt with the impact.

The bomb had been diverted from the building. The navigator above had been able to move the beam onto the quayside and although the bomb hadn't had enough time to divert fully it had deflected away from the Spider 2-3. Instead, it had hit the far end of the residential building to the north-west, destroying it almost entirely and killing most of its occupants. The blast had also seriously damaged the quayside hangar, which now could not open its sliding exit door, trapping the *Excelsior* within.

Gradually the sound from the explosion and its aftermath lessened, and JP raised himself up. The firing from outside had stopped. He let Stella up too, and said to her, "Are you ok?"

"Yes, I'm fine," she replied. "Are you ok?"

"There seems to be something in my back, that's hurting like hell," he said. He turned round to show her. "Can you see?" he asked.

"Yes, I can, shit it's three bullets. You've been hit." She realised he had just saved her life. Again.

"Well, Amen for bullet-proof vests," said JP. "Come on, quickly, we have to get out of here before they come again."

The explosion had shocked the men outside, thought JP, but it was only a matter of time before they recovered and made another attack through the door. He knew they had to get out, and get out soon. He didn't know how long he was going to be able to hold them off, and he only had a limited supply of ammunition. He got to his feet and pulled Stella up with him. He thought they should try to get out through the large corridor, and was just making a start towards it when he heard a different sound. A sound that he had been hoping for. Waiting for. The sound of the whirring blades of helicopters.

He stopped their move, and stayed at the corner. He smiled at Stella, and then his smile broke into a laugh.

"Do you hear that?" he said to her.

"Yes, what is it?" said Stella.

"It seems I was mistaken," said JP.

"What do you mean?" she asked. "What were you mistaken about? What is it?"

"It's the cavalry," said JP, and he sat down again in the corner, pulling her down with him and putting his arm around her shoulders. The gunfire started outside, this time not his, nor from others trying to kill him. He laughed again, and squeezed her shoulders more.

"It's the cavalry."

PART FIVE

THE END OF THE BEGINNING

30

SOAR AGAIN

THE GUN BATTLE didn't last very long. The VC-10 carrying the SAS team had followed the same route as JP's earlier in the day. Once airborne its Captain did all he could to coax more speed out of the aircraft, to gain a more time and land ahead of schedule.

The RAF had wisely insisted upon using the venerable VC-10. It was the fastest transport jet they had; the majority of the transport fleet had long been replaced by the slower Airbus A330-200, but as they had one left the VC-10 got the job. The Captain's effort shaved a full fourteen minutes off the flight time. The SAS landed at Akrotiri at 10.30pm.

At 10.27pm on the way in the SAS was told of the cyber attack and the Israeli response, and that JP had disregarded the abort order from Melton, against all sane odds. The extra time saved would now be put to very good use. The assault plan, named Operation Waterhole, was revised on board in a last inspired three minutes of brilliant improvisational planning.

Waterhole was the job of the fifty-four men from SAS 'A' Squadron. Durford's Bravo Alpha Troop of twelve and Bravo Alpha Troops 1 through 4 each with eight men would tackle the inside of the complex; Bravo Alpha 5, four men, would seal the harbour; and Bravo Alpha 6 with six men would secure the gate and boundary wall outside. As soon as the VC-10 came to a stop at the end of the runway the SAS disembarked and ran straight over to the five powered-up Bell 412 helicopters, designated Hotel 1 through 5, waiting thirty yards away. The Bells, now without doors for easy boarding and exit and their use as a shooting platform, were in the air within one minute. The pilots had full orders to disregard all other normal flying rules and get the SAS to their destination fast.

Sir Donald had just had time to advise the pilots to expect a change of orders in flight. Mike Durford issued his helicopter pilot with the new instructions; the other pilots were briefed in the air by Troop leaders similarly. The helicopters flew faster and lower, and more time was saved.

Just as the SAS were taking off from RAF Akrotiri to head north over the mountains and execute Waterhole, the British diplomatic service was going into overdrive once more. The Prime Minister spoke in turn to the Government Heads of the Republic of Cyprus, the Turkish Republic of Northern Cyprus, Turkey and Israel. This was followed by similar calls from the American President.

So it was that, once the Israelis heard of the receipt of the signal from JP confirming he had secured and disarmed the Spider 2-3, the message to abort was flashed immediately to their jets over Cyprus, and the crews acted at once to divert the laser bomb in the last seconds of its flight. In addition, the diplomatic telephone activity that included, perhaps rarely, some very frank and direct talking resulted in the establishing of a solid united and cohesive front from all Governments.

As they flew in the SAS could see the enormous destruction caused by the laser bomb. The flames of the burning buildings lit up the sky for miles around. Hotel

2 swung wide to the east and dropped Bravo Alpha 5 into the water at the harbour entrance. Their Zodiac boat inflated within seconds and the four men were quickly on board, then up onto the two concrete ends of the harbour entrance, ensuring that no boats could escape. They would take out any high-speed or larger water craft with their LAW rockets.

Hotel 2 landed south-east of the quayside hangar, and the eight men of Bravo Alpha 1 were out immediately. Two men guarded the helicopter and six quickly blasted a hole in the hangar to enter and secure inside.

Hotel 1, with OC Mike Durford and his Bravo Alpha Troop of eleven other men, put down twenty feet south-west of the missile hangar. They fired from the helicopter on approach killing or wounding men at the entrance who, before the shock explosion of the Israeli bomb, had been trying to kill JP and reclaim the Spider.

As he ran to the hangar with his men Mike Durford heard in his earpiece, "Bravo Alpha, Bravo Alpha 5, harbour secured."

"Roger," was Durford's calm reply.

Much of the machine gun fire that had broken out as the helicopters began their landings soon ended. The explosion had disorientated and shattered the moral of Malekka's men, and it very quickly became clear to them that they weren't going anywhere. Bravo Alpha blew two holes in the hangar and Durford and his men entered fast, shouting for JP as they went, quickly finding him and Stella huddled in a corner. They ringed the Spider 2-3.

The gate at the perimeter wall had been flung open as soon as the airborne firing began, but Bravo Alpha 6 quickly rounded up those who came through. Durford's earpiece came to life again. "Bravo Alpha, Bravo Alpha 6, wall perimeter secure."

"Roger."

The other two helicopters landed at the west part of Cuttle Cove, Hotel 3 just to the south of the aircraft hangar, and 4 to the north-east of it. The twenty-four men of Bravo Alpha Troops 2, 3, and 4, leaving two men protecting each exit aircraft, quickly went after their targets.

The Airbus 318, readied earlier to transport the majority of the people off the island, as well as three other smaller aircraft including a Learjet, were easily captured and secured. Durford soon got the confirmation in his earpiece. A considerable amount of gunfire was coming from the northern part of the residential complex, where some stubborn men were holding out. Suddenly there was a louder voice in Durford's ear.

"Bravo Alpha 3, man down, man down."

Shit, thought Durford.

There was gunfire for another thirty seconds.

"Bravo Alpha, Bravo Alpha 1, quayside hangar secure. There's a bloody big ship here but seems deserted."

"Wait on the ship, Bravo Alpha 1. Hold quayside hangar secure for now." They'll need more men to go inside that bugger then, thought Durford.

"Wilco."

"Well Jimmy, my lad," said Durford, walking over to JP and Stella, "quite a body count you've been stacking up I hear."

JP smiled. "Am I glad to see your ugly mug, Mike," said JP as the two shook hands. "Thanks for coming in."

Durford smiled back, a broad-shouldered heavy-boned bear of a man instantly in command. Hard dark eyes, brown mottled skin and a jutting jaw sat under wiry black hair and long sideburns.

"Did you really think we weren't going to, after you went in?"

"No, I didn't," he said. "I was pretty sure you'd be here. I just didn't know when."

"And you, Miss," said Durford to Stella. "Well done. Very well done, Miss."

"Thank you," said Stella. Some clothes were quickly found for Stella from the residential complex, to replace the jacket JP had put round her shoulders. She was shivering with a combination of cold, lessening adrenalin and exhaustion. The jeans, T-shirt and thick pullover soon warmed her thoroughly.

Then Mike got the final call he'd been waiting for.

"Bravo Alpha, Bravo Alpha 3, target secure."

"Roger."

"Boss, there's a lot of people here, we have thirty men, several women."

"Roger, tag the lot."

"Wilco."

"Who's down?"

"Dave T. He won't be dancing for a while, he got it in the leg. He's fine."

"Roger."

The mopping up of Waterhole began soon after. JP was given a little medical aid to patch up his split lip and cuts and bruises to his face. Now that the present action was over the rest of his body ached again from the torture, and his burns in particular needed attention. That would have to wait for now. The shot man from Bravo Alpha 3 had taken a nasty hit in the right thigh, luckily not life-threatening. Waterhole had been a well-executed operation for the SAS, but the work which JP had done himself was beginning to become clear to Durford as his men searched through the entire complex thoroughly, both in the grounds and then inside room by room.

"Well, JP m'lad," said Durford, "before we took our popguns out, we make it so far that it's three dead on the outside wall, one outside the building, another five inside and then eleven more by the door just inside and outside it. There's one person tied up by some rubbish bins round the corner and six people still unconscious in that observation room up there," he said pointing to the control room above them. "There are also two sorry looking large fellers trussed up like chickens round the other side of the building, one with a broken nose and the other with a broken arm."

"That's twenty dead, and nine unconscious or tied up or a combination of the two. Oh, make that ten, there's one girl in here in a burka. Add to that one entire complex virtually destroyed, I'd say you've had a busy evening. That's not bad going for twenty-five minutes."

Stella's mouth had dropped slightly open. "You did all that, JP?" she said. "In twenty-five minutes?" She was now genuinely in awe of this man.

JP smiled. "Not quite," he said modestly. "I didn't drop the bomb. And you got the one in the burka."

Stella laughed.

"And she's going to have one hell of a headache when she wakes up," said JP smiling.

"That's a good job, Jimmy" said Durford. "True to your nickname again. Well done, lad."

"Thanks, Mike." Nickname? wondered Stella.

"Excuse me, Mike," interrupted another soldier. JP knew him. "Charlie Melton's on the line for JP."

"Thanks, Roy," said Durford and JP nodded his thanks too as Roy handed over the lightweight headset, adding, "Fucking good job, JP."

"Thanks," smiled JP and put the headset on. He had been standing with his arm round Stella, but now he left her and walked slightly away for the conversation.

"Hello?"

"Oh good, you aren't dead then," said Melton.

"Not yet, Charlie. The vest helped though."

"We saw the whole thing on television, from the satellite, except when you were in the corridor, and the hangar itself of course. We even had sound until the explosion blew the electronics in the dish. Outstanding leap over the wall, by the way. Well done, JP, from all of us here."

"Thanks, Charlie, and for sending the guys in. I wouldn't have been able to hold it for much longer I don't think." While JP couldn't be ordered by Melton to abort the mission, since he was technically a civilian, the SAS crew certainly could have been, and then there wouldn't have been any cavalry.

"Well we couldn't let you go and mess around there all on your own, could we?" said Melton. "You did good, Jimmy."

JP smiled. Melton couldn't have ordered JP in either, but knew he wouldn't stop.

"Well I had a bit of luck," JP said. "They put Stella in the same building. They were going to burn her there, literally, as the rocket launched, so, although they didn't know it, they had put another player on our side right in with them close to the weapon. She disarmed the bomb while I did some shooting. I couldn't have done the two I don't think. Things were getting rather hot just then."

"How is she?" asked Melton.

"I think she's ok. Physically fine it seems; but she's gone through some pretty nasty things, I've been hearing, as we knew right from the outset would probably occur. But I'm going to go and help do something about that in a couple of minutes."

"Is there any sign of Malekka?"

385

"No nothing yet, but it's still early. It's a big place here, and there's still quite a bit of area to go through. The place is a bit like a labyrinth, there are corridors and rooms all over the place apparently. Charlie, is the other plane there?"

"Yes, it's on the tarmac at the Base."

"Ok, good thanks. I'll finish up, and then move on."

"Copy that, JP. I'll talk to you in the air."

"Roger. Out."

JP walked back over to Mike Durford and Stella, and to Roy, to whom he handed back the headset with a nod of thanks.

"Mike, there's just one thing more." Durford could see that JP wanted a private word and so he walked a few paces away with him. Stella watched as the two talked in earnest for a few seconds. She saw Mike nodding his head at the end of the conversation, and then JP walked back.

"I have to leave you for a while," he said to her, "but it will only be for a few minutes, forty at the most, and then I'll be back," he added quickly as he saw concern on her face. "These three lads will be with you," he added nodding his head to the three men now standing behind him, that Mike Durford had called over, "and all you have to do is just wait here, and relax."

"Ok," she said, "will it be long? What happens now?"

"The lads have to continue the mopping up but you and I can get out of here pretty soon. He started to leave, but paused to add, "Don't worry. It's safe now. It's all safe now. And I'll be back before you know it." He kissed her quickly on the lips, and then turned and walked out through the gaping hole in the wall where the door had once been.

Two other SAS men arrived promptly on the outside

of the hangar. They had Shurafa between them, still in her burka but with her head now uncovered, her hands securely bound behind her back. JP first spoke to one of the men who then spoke curtly to the girl in Arabic. At the same time JP drew his Sauer from its shoulder holster and placed the end of the silencer to the front of her forehead. Ten seconds later the four of them went off towards the quayside and the hanger.

Inside, JP saw the *Excelsior* for the first time. She looked magnificent in her moorings, sleek, cosy and comfortable, at least from the outside. Stella had confirmed the ship as where she had been held captive, tortured and abused; that one helicopter had left to raid the Fincrest Centre, and another had returned with the Alpha, taken with her to Cuttle Cove. And a few things began to fall into place for Stella, too, with JP's explanation of the *Excelsior*'s journey, that they were on Cyprus; especially of why the ship had slowed from its previous speed down to a crawl for twenty-four hours as it passed through Suez.

One of the SAS teams had already cleared the upper decks of the ship of all personnel. They were now awaiting more men before going below, although their infrared and sound detecting equipment showed no other persons on board. In fact, everyone left the ship once the huge explosion occurred and the sliding hangar doors to the Mediterranean had jammed. They tried to escape either by light boats at the quay or by land through the gate at the wall. The SAS rounded up the lot with only the minimum of gunfire, and no casualties, at least not on their side.

Shurafa led the three men as directed up the ramp to the ship, and then inside to the area that JP wanted to see. He returned outside quickly, and Shurafa was given to some other SAS men to be placed back with the other captured personnel, whom the SAS were now interrogating in order to establish who was who and find out more about the activities carried on at Cuttle Cove. JP went off again with the other two lads, and twenty minutes later he was back with Stella.

"Stella," he said gently to her, "I want you to do something for me."

"Ok," she replied at once, "what is it?"

"I want you to come with me onto the ship."

"Oh," she said reluctantly. "Do I have to?"

"No, you don't have to," said JP. "But if you do, I think you'll find something that you will like. And it's quite safe, you'll be with me, and Roy and Sean here as well." JP jerked his head back to the two SAS men, still standing some feet behind him waiting for more instructions.

She let out a little sigh. "Ok then," she said simply.

The four walked out of the building, with Stella holding onto JP's arm with both hands and her head on his shoulder, or as high up towards it as she could get. They walked to the quayside hanger, up the gangway onto the ship, then down into its heart, to the rooms where she had been tortured and held a prisoner for the best part of ten days. She didn't know why JP wanted to take her back there but she trusted him.

They didn't go to the room she had been held in; they stopped at the adjoining one.

JP punched the four numbers that Shurafa had given him earlier via the interpreter into the security keypad. She had given the numbers freely and without hesitation. But then, telling her to do something, or otherwise JP was going to shoot her through the head in five seconds, was an added incentive to make her co-operate, and she yielded up the information easily.

The door to the torture room opened. JP told the two

SAS lads to wait outside this time, and he and a hesitating Stella passed through the doorway. Stella clung tightly to JP, who had his arm around her.

At first her face showed revolting terror as the room quickly brought back horrible memories, of her torture by Aisha and the men, her use by Malekka at night, how he had earlier that very day suddenly, shockingly, discarded her and given her to Haddad and Raboud to rape and use in a particularly violent way, to be killed later. But then after a couple of seconds, she saw something against the far wall; she relaxed, and her face broke into a small wry smile. JP was watching her closely, and saw that she was fine. She looked up at him, and nodded approvingly. The smile widened.

On the other side of the room, the two men that JP had brought aboard the ship one by one had been trussed up and placed into the arm, leg and ankle restraints cemented into the wall opposite, that Stella herself had been shown with great malice some days before. The men were spread-eagled. Additional metal restraints were around each of their thighs, neck and chest; hoods were over their head. It was quite impossible for them to move. Raboud was moaning because of his broken arm. Haddad's smashed nose made his breathing rough. JP walked over to them, and yanked off the hoods. The duct tape that JP had placed around their mouths earlier had been removed.

As their eyes adjusted to the light and they could see JP, their faces began to snarl and a stream of obscenities came from their mouths. Raboud in particular was in no mood to be reconciliatory and he said, after cursing at JP, "What the fuck are you doing, you pig, you can't treat me like this. You are British police or army, and you have to let us go. We have rights, we..." The sound of his talking was interrupted as JP's right elbow smashed into his jaw. The man coughed and spat out some blood. The swearing from Haddad also now ceased.

"Now that's enough of that," JP said firmly. "And there will be no more swearing. There's a lady present."

They hadn't noticed Stella. She walked a few paces towards them and stood looking at them from the middle of the room, with her arms folded in front of her. As they realised their predicament, and that JP was totally in command and didn't seem inclined to take any nonsense from them, they stayed quiet. The blood began to drain a little from their faces.

"Gentlemen," said JP, as he walked back towards the wall and the men pinned securely against it. "This is going to come as a little bit of a shock to you. So get ready." He held out his arm. "Let me introduce Miss Stephanie Raughton. Miss Raughton is a member of the British MI6, is an extremely brave woman, and I am proud to say is also my friend."

There was now a look of astonishment and horror on Haddad's and Raboud's faces, as they looked first from Stephanie, to JP, and then back again to her, combined with utter and complete confusion.

"You see, gentlemen, without knowing it, you and your master, Malekka, have been played, right from the start," said JP. "Stephanie here bears an almost uncanny resemblance to the real Miss Stella Fincrest, who I am pleased to say is secure in a CIA safe house in Miami and with whom Stephanie traded places once the real Stella had left Cape Town and arrived in Miami, so say to join me on holiday in St Lucia. It had been announced and well publicised in the South African media for some time that the rich heiress Miss Fincrest had a new love interest - er, that would be me," he said smilingly and with a slight pause for effect - "and would be holidaying with him in the Caribbean."

He paused again, and looked at the two men.

"Are you two getting this?" he asked with a slight hint of humour in his voice. "I wouldn't want you to miss all the details of where you went wrong."

The two men nodded, in silence, dumbfounded at what JP was saying.

"Stella took a flight to Miami to meet me and supposedly change planes to fly on to St Lucia, and the CIA whisked her off as soon as she arrived there, and the lovely Stephanie took her place. And then Stephanie and I flew on to St Lucia.

"Your master, Malekka, saw the holiday on a deserted beach in St Lucia as the ideal perfect opportunity to grab Stella. And then force her to reveal all the codes and use her fingerprints and retina details to enter the secure room so that he could get his hands on the Alpha unit that he needed to launch his missile.

"But the codes and fingerprints and retina information had already been altered at the Fincrest Centre to match those of Stephanie. And the Alpha had had a little alteration made to it too - a little micro transmitter had been inserted, which Stephanie here would activate once the Alpha unit was with the Spider 2-3.

"You see," he waited slightly, almost enjoying himself as he told the two lowlife specimens on the wall how they had been tricked, "we didn't know where the bomb was. We knew it was going to be taken from somewhere in Russia but we didn't know when or where or how. Dr Keppof was going to tell me that, but you killed him first. But, what we did know was that you needed the Alpha. We had already concocted this little plan to follow the Alpha, and once the Alpha and the bomb came together, Stephanie activated the micro transmitter and then we knew the location of the weapon. And here we all are."

The two men looked as though they were about to throw up.

"And you had underestimated Dr Keppof," continued JP. "His brilliant mind had spotted some internal notification about the bomb as well as the interest in the Alpha unit. He put two and two together, and then told me about his fears, as he didn't know whom he could trust within Russia.

"And then, that's where the two of you came in." JP looked at them coldly now, with all hint of humour gone from the tone of his voice. "But you made a mistake."

"We only did what we were told," said Raboud, almost shouting out the words, and crying them out.

"Yes, we just followed orders," said Haddad, his voice sounding very nasal. "It was business, it was just what we were told to do."

"Actually," said JP, ignoring the words from the two men, "you made two mistakes. The first was when you killed Dr Keppof. He was my friend. You killed him, cold-bloodedly, and I saw you do it. Oh - I was dressed as a tramp, across the Kurfürstendamm, do you remember?"

He could see that they did. Their faces were sweating profusely now, and their eyes were already wide with fear.

"That was your first mistake," said JP. "And the second mistake you made, gentlemen," continued JP, "was when you tortured Miss Raughton here, and touched and hurt her again today. That, you should not have done. She didn't like it one little bit. And I didn't like to hear about it either."

"We're sorry, Miss," said Raboud, and it was echoed by Haddad. "It was a *job*... It was just what we were *told* to do..."

They were whining now, pleading to be released.

All through this, Stephanie had just stood and looked at the two men. How she hated them. What evil these people had. How she wanted to be gone from them. And have them gone from her.

"Anyway," said JP, "I thought you might like to know of what had actually happened, and how good and right had triumphed over evil and your vile efforts to kill three million people."

JP stopped talking. He turned and walked over to Stephanie. He looked down at her, straight into her eyes, and smiled. She gazed back up at him.

"Thank you," was all she said.

"Shall we drop the Stella bit now?" he said quietly to her, still with a smile playing on his lips. She nodded again.

"I thought it might help, to change the image, the memory of this... place... for you, to see them like this. To know that you won, and that they lost."

Stephanie looked at JP, and then at the two whimpering men against the wall. She turned back to JP.

"Thank you. It has helped, will help." They embraced, holding each other for a few seconds.

"Come on, let's get out of here," said JP.

She pushed JP away gently. "No. It's helped. But, it's not enough."

They stared into each other's eyes. JP nodded slowly. He understood.

Stephanie reached inside JP's jacket and pulled the Sauer from his shoulder holster, its suppressor attached. She held out her other hand. He took another magazine from his pocket.

Haddad and Raboud looked on in horror. JP started

to walk towards the door.

"What are you doing?" shouted Raboud, "Let us out of here. Are you crazy? Come back, don't leave us here."

"Please," shouted Haddad, "don't leave us alone with this woman." There was real panic attached to their voices now. "We were just following orders... *Please...*"

At the door JP turned and said, in a voice suddenly as cold as frozen nitrogen, "Oh - you're wrong about something else too. I'm not MI6, or military. Me, I'm just an ordinary citizen, and I'm not under anybody's rules or orders. Or control. Today, for Great Britain, I am the bearer of the Fifth Rubric. Today, I answer to no-one."

And with that, JP turned on his heel and left the room. The terrified whines and shouts of the two baffled petrified men could be heard in the corridor. As the door began to close behind JP the screams gradually lessened like a fade-out audio edit on a recording, until finally the door clicked shut and the sound was cut out by the efficient soundproofing of the room.

Revenge is sweet, said JP to himself. And, sometimes, necessary, as now for Stephanie.

To repair and save the mind, and let the spirit rise free and soar again.

31
SORTING OUT

BEFORE LEAVING THE corridor, JP spoke briefly to Roy and Sean. He had seen action with them in Afghanistan once and had actually saved Roy's life, and it was good to see them again. He asked them to stand guard, and bring Stephanie back up to Mike Durford when she came out of the room, and only that. If they didn't know what was happening in the room, they couldn't talk about it; not that they would if he asked them not to, he knew, but he wanted it that way anyway.

"Sure, JP. It'll be a pleasure," said Sean. "You've done a fucking good job here tonight, mate. Well done."

"Thanks, Sean," replied JP.

"And Miss Raughton's done one hell of a job too, from what we hear," added Roy. "The lads are getting to know more and more about what's been going on. That's one hell of a lady."

"That she is," said JP. "A very brave girl." They shook hands. "Thanks, lads. When this is all finished, we'll meet up and have a few drinks."

"That sounds a good idea," said Roy, smiling. "But, aren't we done now?"

"Yes, or is there more, Jimmy?" said Sean.

"No, not for you. You're done now," said JP. "You'll get the recall soon enough once the regulars are here and take over. But, I'm not done. Not just yet. I've still got a little more to do."

JP left his two comrades and ran back up to the deck. He found Mike in the hangar where he had left him. They went and spoke quietly together in a corner away from the many other people that were now inside and outside the hangar.

"Mike," said JP, "I've left Stephie down there. Once she's back up here, it would be handy if you don't discover that room for, say, another two hours. Is that ok?"

"Yes. Don't worry about that, laddie," he replied. Mike never tolerated any nonsense, thought JP; he was a good man, very direct, and true.

"And that's just between us."

"Yes," said Mike, smiling. He was pleased to be able to do a favour for this man. He had always liked JP, and now was very proud of him, as was the entire SAS team. "You'd better be getting off, hadn't you?"

"Yes," said JP. "Which chopper am I in?"

"You're in mine," said Mike. "It's the first one just outside away from the hangar. The pilot's waiting, just go when you're ready. You'll be in the Meridien hotel in Limassol, right on the beach, about ten minutes' drive from the Base. A car will take you there, and wait and bring you back when you're ready."

"Great, thanks," said JP. "Will you explain to Stephie that I had to go, I haven't told her yet. I'll see her in London. Take care of her, ok?"

"She'll be with me, and Roy and Sean. She'll be well looked after and protected, don't worry, and yes of course I'll talk to her. She'll rest up in the same hotel, after you've gone, and then come back on the Vickers flight with the lads to the UK at around 7am."

They started to walk back to the centre of the hangar, and JP had one more look at the Spider 2-3.

"Bit of a bugger, isn't she?" he said to Mike, viewing

the awesome weapon that had nearly killed more people than he wanted to think about, perhaps even wiped out a nation. He held out his hand. Mike Durford took it in his and shook it firmly.

"Thank you again, Mike. We'll have drinks in the UK. They can all be on you," JP quipped.

"That'll be my pleasure, lad," Mike smiled.

JP turned to walk towards the open doorway, through which less than two hours ago he had been engaged in a gun battle while Stephanie had been disarming the nuclear weapon.

Suddenly, Mike roared out, "Lads."

JP turned round at the sound. All the SAS men in the hangar, on hearing the shout of their Commanding Officer, had come smartly to attention, and were facing towards JP. Mike led the salute. JP smiled, and stood to attention himself, accepting the salute from the SAS and the great compliment it represented, bringing his right arm up smartly to his head in return. As his hand went down to his side again, he nodded, still with a grateful smile on his lips. He turned, and walked off to the doorway.

JP went straight over to the first helicopter. The pilot was standing beside it. "Are you ready to go?" said JP.

"Yes, sir," replied the young pilot. "Back to Akrotiri?"

"Yes, that's it. Let's go, as quickly as you can please."

JP climbed in behind the pilot. The helicopter took off, turning round to the south and moving off fast. He would be back at the Base in around thirty minutes.

Once he was in the air, JP didn't say much. He was thinking deeply. There was only a limited amount of time left in which this part of his plan could be carried out and he had to make sure that everything fell into place properly. And much of it depended on what he would find once he reached his private laptop computer back at Akrotiri.

It was now 12.15am. The next few hours would decide the destiny of the lives of several people. Including his own.

The helicopter landed at Akrotiri twenty-five minutes later. JP was personally welcomed by Sir Donald Gaunchon, who wanted to give his own congratulations. JP thanked the Commander British Forces Cyprus, and then said that his job was not quite finished yet.

"No, so I gather," said Sir Donald. "I take it that you would like to go to the hotel now and rest a little, before going off again? By the way, the aircraft is fully fuelled and waiting."

"Yes, please," said JP. "I will only be a couple of hours, but I could do with a little rest. I haven't slept for a while, and it's been rather physical recently."

"So I see, Mr Peregrine," said Sir Donald with a slight smile. JP's face had a number of cuts and contusions and much of the bruising had now swelled. And his burns in particular were hurting badly. "We'll get you over straight away. Your stuff's already there. And just call me when you're ready to have the Doctors over to attend to your injuries from Zimbabwe, I've heard all about that too from Charlie Melton. They just need ten minutes to get there, so whenever you're ready, and I'll get them straight over."

"Thanks, Sir Donald," said JP, "I'll do that."

"And well done, once more. On everything."

JP was whisked over to the Meridien hotel at Limassol. He was taken up to a very large comfortable suite overlooking the sea which under other circumstances he would have enjoyed fully. As it was, he needed rest, but he put his tiredness out of his mind for now. The first thing he had to do was get onto the internet and find out what had occurred during the day. He knew the Meridien would provide a relaxing quiet environment, which was one of the reasons it had been selected. He sat at the desk, took out his laptop, plugged it in to the power to ensure it was fully charged for the next leg of his journey that night and booted it up. He took out the satellite phone and got a fast secure internet connection, linking it wirelessly with his laptop. The system quickly stabilised. JP opened up one particular programme on his laptop, sat back and waited.

Then it was all there, in front of him. He smiled; and then laughed out loud. He pulled out his personal mobile phone and turned it on too, and then once it had roamed and found the right network he sent a simple text. It read, *'Are you ready.'* Within a minute he had a reply back. *'Yes.'*

Good. Now he could get to work. He put on some protective gloves. From his kit bag he pulled out some paper and the small portable laser printer that he had brought with him, turned it on and loaded the paper into the machine. He linked it wirelessly to the laptop, and then printed out four pages from the programme. Using the stapler from the stationery set he clipped the two sets of two pages each together, and laid them on the table, adjacent to the desk workstation.

Then over the next thirty minutes, JP typed in several codes and sets of numbers and letters. When he had finished, he sat back in the chair.

Wow, he thought.

He next opened a pdf file of one page that he had scanned a few days ago in London, and printed out two copies of it. He added one page to each of the other two sets he had printed minutes before, and used a paper clip to keep the two sets of three pages neatly together. He sent three names and addresses to the printer, for three envelopes.

Now he opened the word processor and started to write. He typed fast, smoothly, and without much pause for rearranging; it wasn't necessary. He knew the details of what he had to type well enough, and the words flowed easily. Half an hour later, he printed off the two pages of text, clipped them together, and added them to one of the other sets, making it five pages in all. After a little further thought, he printed the two pages out again, and added them to the other set.

Finally he opened a small silver box, and took out three business cards. He attached one to a blank sheet of paper with a paperclip, folded it up, put it into an envelope and sealed it. He added some sellotape to give a little extra security. Then he attached another of the business cards to each of the two sets of five pages, folded them and placed them into the two other envelopes. One was addressed to Major Charles Melton in London.

JP repacked everything into his kit bag. He called room service and ordered a quick meal, removed his bandages carefully and took a shower, which was a little difficult and rather painful, and a shave. By the time he was out of the bathroom, the meal had arrived. He called Gaunchon, then ate, and true to Sir Donald's word the doctors were there very swiftly. Creams and sprays went on followed by more dressings; the doctors went. By 3.30am JP was back downstairs. He bought stamps, mailed his letter to London at the hotel box and left.

JP was taken back to Akrotiri, said his goodbyes to Sir Donald and Group Captain Williams, who was also there now, and boarded the private Learjet that had been waiting patiently on the tarmac for him.

The plane started its engines and the pilot obtained taxi clearance. The Learjet rolled along to the end of the runway, and then took off. It reached Larnaca International Airport to the north-east twenty minutes later, and then took off once more almost immediately, once the pilot had filed a Civil Aviation Authority flight plan.

JP relaxed in the comfortable aircraft, and looked out of the window as the lights of night-time Cyprus gradually fell away beneath him.

The plane gained height and levelled off at thirty thousand feet, settling steadily onto its course, north, towards Moscow.

≈

Just as the helicopter with JP in it was lifting off from Cuttle Cove, Stephanie was coming back into the hangar. She had been down in the ship for about forty-five minutes. She walked up to Mike Durford with Roy and Sean either side of her, and, with its handle pointing away from her and its muzzle towards the ground, held out the empty Sig Sauer P226 to him, together with a second magazine, which had no rounds left in it either.

She started to speak, but Durford interrupted straight away.

"Oh thank you, Miss, you found this on the floor where JP had put it, I presume? He told me he had left it lying around somewhere."

"Er, well...," said Stephanie, confused. She was about to say more, to explain what had just happened, what she had just done, what she had had to do; but Durford continued.

"Yes, JP said he thought he had left it on the ground just as the explosion happened, in the middle of the gunfight. You must have found it over in that corner there. Isn't that right, Miss?" he said, nodding over to the corner where the SAS had first found JP and her, huddled together.

Then she understood.

"Yes, Mike," she said calmly, with a grateful smile on her lips. "Yes, that's quite correct."

Two hours later, the SAS discovered the various rooms on the lower deck of the *Excelsior*. They broke into the two of them that had secure keypad locks on them. In the first, they found a bedroom. In the other, they found a torture chamber, with two men pinned up against the far wall. They had both sustained gunshot wounds in the area of the groin, which had been completely shot away on both men, and they had bled to death.

When the bulk of the SAS team finally left Cuttle Cove at 3am, they handed over the control of the complex and captured personnel to the combined armed services of the regular British, Turkish and United Nations forces based on the Island who by then comprised the newly-formed Cyprus Coalition Force, although a small number of the SAS would stay behind for another day or so to help the transition take place smoothly. As Durford walked out with Stephanie, Roy and Sean to his new helicopter along with the other SAS men, he said, "Let's not wake up any more people on the Island. We'll fly out over Morphou Bay and skim around the edge of the Island, and get back to Akrotiri that way."

The helicopters promptly took off and headed out south-west over the water to follow the OC's order. Two minutes after departing Cape Kormakitis, Mike Durford, with Stephanie Raughton seated to his right, leant forward and picked up the bag at his feet, and lobbed it through the open doorway.

The bag contained JP's Sauer with its attached suppressor, and the second empty magazine.

He turned his head to look at Stephanie, and smiled. She returned the smile, then put her head back. She breathed a deep sigh, relaxed down into the seat of the aircraft and closed her eyes.

The bag fell away quickly through the one hundred feet at which the helicopter was flying and splashed into the water. It sank harmlessly into the depths of the Mediterranean Sea below.

32
FALLING DOWN

GENERAL VASHINSKY ARRIVED at the Lubyanka in an exceptionally good mood. He had seen the additional five hundred million US dollars arrive into his Swiss bank account the evening before. He was now a very rich man indeed. He could do anything he wanted, go anywhere he wanted. He would wait for the explosion and he knew there would be an investigation. But he would just decide to resign and leave the service, saying that the demands of a heavy investigation and international activity and interest around it were going to be too much for him.

He had given his mother Russia enough years of his life, and had been a dedicated servant in her armed forces, the KGB and then the FSB for almost forty years. Nobody could complain, not the Director of the FSB, not even the President himself. Now he wanted a complete change in his lifestyle and be free to enjoy his money.

He sat back in his thick leather chair, and put his hands behind his head, tilting the chair back and swivelling around in it like a school kid. He didn't know why there hadn't been a report of the bomb going off, but it would come and come soon, he knew. He turned on the TV to the right of his desk, and flicked through the channels; even CNN wasn't carrying anything yet. Oh well, it was just a matter of time. And anyway, he said to himself, he didn't care. He had his money.

Maybe Malekka would just blow himself up by mistake; it wouldn't matter to him. He had fulfilled his part of the deal, and been paid already. He was rich.

The time passed 10am, and as usual there came the knock on the door. He said, "Come in," and he looked up, ready to receive today's traffic from Director Bortnikov. He was surprised and a little disappointed that it was not Praporshchik Tchepikova who was delivering it. He enjoyed the sight of the pretty girl entering his room each day and they had become a little familiar with each other; he was almost on the point of asking if she would like to have dinner with him one evening. But today, it was Praporshchik Belov, who was older, much more serious and not at all interesting to him in any way. It seemed as though she belonged to the former era of Russia; the one he was shortly to be getting away from. He let out a little concealed sigh.

"Good morning, Deputy Director," said Warrant Officer Belov.

"Good morning, Praporshchik."

"I have the personal traffic for you today from the Director," she said, walking over to him at his desk. She held out the usual data stick.

"Thank you," said the General as he took it. He plugged it into his laptop. "And where is Praporshchik Tchepikova today?"

"Oh she's left, sir," said Lucya Belov.

"Left?" said the General. "Left where?" He didn't understand what this woman meant.

"Gone, sir. Resigned."

"Gone... Resigned?" He was surprised, and also rather shaken. This wasn't expected. Vashinsky didn't like surprises. Especially not today.

"Why did she do that, she didn't say anything to me about it?"

"No, sir, well nobody knew, it happened really quickly. She just met with the Director yesterday, took the compassionate leave she'd apparently arranged earlier, and resigned her commission. I think that there were a lot of personal problems."

"Oh, dear," said General Vashinsky. "But I didn't see any of that at all, she seemed fine yesterday when she brought me the traffic."

"Yes, sir, I know what you mean," said Praporshchik Belov. "I don't think any of us saw it really. I know that someone she was terribly close to died recently, and I think it was all based around that. He had an awful accident."

"How terrible. Who was it, do you know what happened?"

"Well, apparently, well of course relationships within the office are rather frowned on, aren't they, and tend to be kept a secret when they happen, but when she left it all came out. Apparently it was someone who worked for you. You know, the one who died in the subway station. Your driver."

"*What?*" said Vashinsky. He didn't know about this at all.

"Yes, apparently they were very much in love, virtually engaged. Such a shame really."

"Yes," he was almost stammering the words out, " a great shame, of course."

"Is there anything to go back, sir?"

"Er, yes," said the General, "here's the data stick."

"Thank you, sir," said Praporshchik Belov. "Oh and a courier brought something for you downstairs at the main gate, one of the entrance staff was just coming up to you with it and I took it from him for you just now in the hallway, sir."

Warrant Officer Belov handed over a white envelope

to Vashinsky, who took it, rather in a daze.

"Will there be anything else, sir?" she asked.

"No. No, that's fine, thank you Praporshchik." Vashinsky was trying hard not to sound as confused and dazed as he was. "My regards to the Director, and have a good day."

"Thank you, sir, and you too."

Praporshchik Belov left the room, closing the door quietly behind her.

Vashinsky didn't like what he had just heard. How could something like that have happened right under his nose, and he didn't know it? How the hell was he supposed to know she was in love with Corporal Baskov. He had arranged for him to be killed, as an accident, so that there was no link to him or the meeting with Malekka. He wasn't at all worried about the killing. That sort of thing didn't matter to him at all. He was worried that he hadn't known about the association. Those sorts of things can be trouble.

He diverted his thinking away for a minute to the envelope. It had come by courier so it was probably urgent and he thought he had better open it at once. There were degrees of urgency of course, and what was urgent to someone else was rarely urgent to him. But, he opened the envelope then anyway.

Inside was a blank sheet of white paper. Is that all, he thought? And it had a business card attached to it. He took it off the paper clip and looked at it. No name. No writing. Just a picture on one side, and nothing on the reverse, he said to himself as he turned it one way and then the other. He didn't understand what it meant. He stood up from the desk, put his hands behind him and walked slowly across the room and back, thinking through what had just occurred.

That was four strange things that had happened, this

fine day that had started off so excellently. Vashinsky had a sixth sense that had served him very well indeed over the years, and he knew when something wasn't quite right. No explosion; no Praporshchik Tchepikova; now a link to his dead driver that he knew nothing about; and now a blank piece of paper hand delivered just with a card attached, and not one word of writing?

Suddenly he froze. He spun round and stared at his desk, a horrified look on his face. He turned a little white, and went briskly over to his chair and sat down again. He ploughed through the screens. He got where he wanted, and his eyes started to bulge open. Just then the door to his office was flung open, and six armed guards marched in, followed by the Director of the FSB, General Alexander Bortnikov. He quickly slammed his laptop shut, and looked up in astonishment.

Bortnikov stormed along right up to Vashinsky's desk, and glared down at the General.

"General Vashinsky, would you mind telling me why there is an SS-23 Spider nuclear weapon sitting in Cyprus pointed at Israel?"

Vashinsky's mouth fell open. *"What, sir?"*

"I said, would you mind telling me why there is an SS-23 Spider nuclear weapon sitting in Cyprus and pointed at Israel? And why is there a report from someone called P. Keppof about an unauthorised SS-23 movement in your files, and not reported to me? And why do you have a numbered Swiss bank account and why has it received one billion US dollars into it?"

Vashinsky looked pale. He slumped into his chair, and put his hands onto the desk.

"I don't know, sir," he said. "I... I..."

"General Vashinsky, you are under arrest, for high treason." Bortnikov turned to four of the armed guards. "Take him out. He is not to be addressed as an officer any more. Get him out of my sight."

"But I can explain. It's a mistake. It has to be a mistake...."

"Be quiet, Vashinsky," said the Director in a loud harsh tone. "You will have ample time to explain, and explain *everything*, to us very shortly."

General Vashinsky was marched out of the room by the four soldiers.

He turned to the other two guards. "You two," he said sharply, "I want you to seal this office, and do not let anyone else in. I want absolutely nothing touched. And we will want his computers and all of his files."

"Yes, sir," said the guards in unison.

"I'm going to get to the bottom of this," said the furious General Bortnikov as he stormed out of the room.

In the space of less than thirty seconds, General Evgeny Kutuzov Vashinsky had fallen from one of the highest positions of power and influence within the Russian Federation to being an unfortunate tenant about to take up occupancy in a cold, dark and damp cell, deep in the Lubyanka basement.

33
ONTO THE STAGE

IT'S STRANGE HOW much chance can affect things in life, thought Jim Peregrine as he stared out over the calm blue waters of the Caribbean Sea.

He was sitting on the end of a wooden jetty with his feet dangling in the water, enjoying its soft warmth and gentle movement. Sometimes he kicked out like a kid and watched the churned-up water travel a few feet and then splash back in. JP's bruises had gone, his burns had healed and he was back to full good health. The Caribbean sun was just what he needed, after the mad world of terrorists and bombs.

It had been very decent of his uncle, the British High Commissioner of St Lucia, to lend him the official seaside residence while he went on vacation. His mother's brother hadn't been involved much in JP's plan, but Sir William had played his part well and vouched for JP when needed so he could leave for South Africa after Stephanie had disappeared.

The Residence was on three floors a hundred yards from the water's edge, set into a gentle hill. There were five extremely comfortable independent suites, used regularly for entertaining heads of state. There were a few domestic staff, and JP had brought a couple of his own men as armed guards, though they were never in sight. The premises was securely fenced in, with iron railings that reached discreetly into the water at either end of the beach, giving solid security. It was perfect.

Stephanie and he had arrived the previous evening.

Things had come pretty rapidly to a conclusion once he had arrived in Moscow. He had known he would have to make the trip if all went well. When he returned to London from South Africa after the Fincrest raid he visited the Russian Embassy for a tourist visa. He wasn't in Moscow long; the private Learjet MI6 provided landed just before 6am local and the waiting limousine went straight to the Marriott in Petrovka Street. He checked in and, first, had some breakfast.

JP arranged two separate couriers for the letters. The one with the blank paper and his business card went first, to General Vashinsky. The second one, containing the details of what had transpired and the substantiating evidence, went to General Alexander Bortnikov. The short and friendly, but deadly serious, telephone call placed by Sir Alastair Crewe to Bortnikov at 9.30am, suggesting that the General might care to look at the letter being specially couriered to him that morning, was very effective. The two SIS heads, although on opposing sides, had known each other for almost thirty years and such an unusual call had warranted and received full attention. By 9.30am JP was in the limousine heading back to the airport and in the air soon after 10.00am, just around the time Bortnikov was bursting into Vashinsky's office to place him under arrest.

The problem of just how the Russians would retrieve their stolen theatre nuclear ballistic missile from the holiday island of Cyprus was an additional problem for the diplomats and the Cyprus Coalition Force to solve. It was deemed paramount that secrecy should be maintained, otherwise there might be panic in some countries; all that was released to the media was that an Al-Qaeda cell had been discovered in Cape Kormakitis and a terrorist had blown himself up as security forces moved in. The formation of the Coalition was reassuring for the international community, a fine example of how governments were working together to defeat the evil madness of terrorism.

JP left Moscow and flew on to London, arriving at 11.30am. In his debriefing with Charles Melton and Alastair Crewe he told them everything that had happened. Well, everything except one, he said to himself. Or was it two... And so it was that, three days later, MI6 had happily dispensed with him and he could set up the holiday in St Lucia. He made a quick day trip to Geneva. At the end of the week he was off with Stephie to his uncle's home.

There were a few loose ends that JP had wanted tied up, too, and the debriefing had done that. The SAS found Malekka's escape tunnel three hours after JP left Cuttle Cove. JP had, frankly, just not been able to see Malekka staying if he had to detonate the nuclear bomb on Cyprus. Malekka could happily kill everyone else; but Malekka the suicide bomber? No. Not him. Malekka had too good a life and lifestyle to throw it all away. So, JP thought, Malekka must have a way out. In fact, JP had been counting on it. Once his incursion into Cuttle Cove had been discovered, there would be some time, a little time, before the place went up in smoke one way or another. Fortunately, his calculation had been right. The escape tunnel from Malekka's suite at Cuttle Cove went down a hundred feet by elevator to an underground harbour with, it was thought, a small submarine. That was why the bomb hadn't detonated instantly but had a two minute timer, which fortunately Stephanie and he had been able to beat. If it had gone off, Malekka would have been quite safe by then, several metres under water, heading steadily away from

Cyprus.

JP had been lucky, too, he realised, over the CCTV cameras. As they were taken out one by one by the laser gun, purely by chance there was only one man on duty in the CCTV control centre. When the man couldn't reboot the system, he left the centre, apparently rather sleepily, to make a physical check on the cameras. He couldn't see their tiny burn holes from the narrow laser beam and so returned to his post to try another restart, but by that time two more cameras were out. Fortunately the man hadn't bothered to replay the last images from those two - playback from the others had revealed nothing, so why should they be different? Therefore he had not witnessed JP's entry into the hangar, nor seen him confront the seven people by the missile, nor seen him shoot the hangar cameras into inactivity. So, JP had not been discovered, then.

However Malekka, too, had also had some luck. Just after 10pm Malekka had apparently left the glass control room at the top of the missile hangar to start what JP now knew to be the sophisticated radar jamming system operating in tandem with the cyber attack. The initiator for the stretched parabolic dishes hidden on the quayside hangar roof had been built into Malekka's own private suite, presumably so only he could have the pleasure of starting them; JP had heard the humming from around 10.15pm that evening. It was apparently one of three jamming radars (one was believed to be in Syria and the other on a ship) that with the intense cyber attack from Iran had brought down the Arrow and Patriot systems and left Israel crippled. Had Malekka not left he would have been paralysed by the gas and captured.

The missile hangar's thick soundproofed walls had smothered the sound of JP's already-suppressed C8 carbine. His incursion was only discovered when the body of Colonel Linchuk was found, after which the alarm was immediately raised. Malekka first sent two men up to the glass control room. One entered and promptly collapsed from the remnants of the gas; the other, outside, ran to report the occupants were either unconscious or dead. The door on the ground was then discovered to be jammed locked. Malekka realised, to his horror, that he had somehow been discovered and judged he should immediately make his escape. He told his men to blow the door, get inside to take the hangar and kill whoever was in there. The battle started, he headed for the escape elevator and pressed the detonator as he entered to blow the bomb where it lay in two minutes, and take half of Cyprus with it.

But by then JP and Stephanie were already disarming it.

As JP had said to himself once before, twenty-five minutes can be a very long time; or just no time at all. It could have gone either way. As luck would have it, it went his way.

Stephanie had her own separate debriefing. It lasted a couple of days longer than JP's, in part because MI6 had provided some much-needed professional help. Her counselling would necessarily continue for some months.

Now the two were virtually inseparable. Sadly, though, it was not the same. Stephanie was withdrawn, non-sexual and dressed down. Even though she told JP everything that had happened to her, the sheer invasive brutality of her rape by three men remained a huge problem for her to deal with, even more so than the torture.

And, as it happened, for JP too. Though he had difficulty in understanding it, of why her use by other men should impact so much on him. It just did. But that would pass. And it was already a wonderful partial cure that two of the three men were now dead. Revenge for her, and for him, was indeed sweet. However, there was still Malekka. JP had been appalled at the things Stephanie had suffered, which although expected were nevertheless not easy to reconcile, even though the operation had been successfully concluded.

The net result was that JP and Stephanie had not been physical together again. She was just not ready. They occupied separate suites at the villa, and for now this was for the best. JP realised, and had also been told by the professionals, that what she needed most was love, understanding and, above all else, time.

So they just clung to each other, two people in love, helping each other; and waited.

Although JP switched off his sexuality as best he could, he found it impossible to turn off his sense of humour, which perhaps was just as well. They laughed together in each other's company more than ever before. That, he thought, was good at least.

His thoughts were interrupted by the sound of footsteps on the wooden walkway. He turned round. Stephanie came towards him, in a bikini with a white sarong tied around her hips, open to one side. She sat down with him, and placed her feet in the water too. She had brought sandwiches and cold bottles of water. She quietly laid her head against his arm, and he tilted his head over to hers. They sat there for a few minutes.

It was she who spoke first.

"Jimmy, there's still something I don't understand."

"Yes," he said softly back, "what's that?"

"Well, we've spoken about a lot of things that happened to me, I mean I've told you everything; and I know a lot of the details about what you did in South Africa and Zimbabwe, the attack on Cuttle Cove, you and Mike and the lads. But there are still some things overall that I don't understand."

"Ok," said JP. "Then just ask, if you're ready, and I'll fill you in."

"Well, the person that's coming here today," said Stephie, "I don't understand how that all fits in."

"Then I'll tell you." He added, "But it's a bit of a long story, so it will take a few minutes. Are you sure you're ready for it?"

"Yes," she replied. "I have all the time now, plenty of time to digest things." Stephanie was on three months' leave but was considering leaving MI6. She sounded rather melancholy. It was a good sign though, thought JP, that she had asked for more information about the Operation. With her head still on his shoulder she put both her arms around his naked chest and gave him a hug. She left her arms there, as though wanting to hold tight to him for safety while the happenings of the last weeks were brought to the forefront of her mind again.

"Well, it all stems from Dr. Keppof," said JP. "You see, after he had come to see me the first time, in February, about his discovery and worry that someone was going to steal a Spider and an Alpha unit, he did, eventually, put in a report to his superiors but much higher up the chain, thinking that would be safer. He put it into the headquarters of the FSB at the Lubyanka. Unfortunately, direct to General Vashinsky."

"Ok," said Stephanie.

"He signed his report, 'P. Keppof'. That's when Vashinsky made his first mistake. He was horrified when he read the report and realised that someone, this P. Keppof, had discovered the plan he and Malekka had been hatching together. He panicked a little and thought the best answer to the problem was to kill Keppof immediately to silence him. So, he sent Malekka a message, and Malekka had Keppof killed in Berlin by those two men, who we gather had been trailing him for a while and followed him to Berlin from Stavropol in Russia where he worked. A perfect opportunity. Vashinsky thought it would seem just an unfortunate death of someone during a weekend break abroad. A good solution.

"Well, Vashinsky should have known his enemy better before doing that," continued JP. "Had he looked at Keppof's file in detail, or maybe even at all, he would have discovered that Keppof wasn't a German working in Russia and who had a German ancestry, as his name suggests; but that he was a Russian, who had changed his name to a German one when he first worked in Germany for the KGB decades ago, and who then had returned to work in Russia but just didn't bother to change his name back.

"The clues were all there in front of him to see. But Vashinsky missed them."

"Ok," said Stephanie again, intrigued. "But how does all this fit together?"

"Before you came out here and sat down, I was thinking over what had happened, and of how chance plays such an incredible part in people's lives."

"Are you going all philosophical on me now?" ribbed Stephanie a bit.

JP smiled back. "No, not really. But, it is strange.

"You see," he continued, "Vashinsky's boss, the Director of the FSB, General Alexander Bortnikov, every day sends some internal traffic to his number two, Deputy Director Vashinsky. It's on a coded and secure data stick; and Vashinsky sends his own confidential items back the same way to Bortnikov. So in this way they can send each other highly confidential memos and information that they don't want left or to appear at all on the mainframe computers. Every day it's simply walked down the long Lubyanka corridors by someone from Bortnikov's own private staff, usually various praporshchiks, or warrant officers as we would call them. One of those was a girl called Praporshchik Tchepikova."

He paused. "Do you get it yet?" he asked.

"No," she replied, with a little laugh. "I don't."

"Well, in Russia, the women, both wives and daughters, take the man's surname but usually add an 'a' on the end, making it feminine. Both in the Cyrillic script of the Russian language, which I don't speak much of, and in the Roman text equivalent that we and the western world use. So, she's Tchepikova but the family name is actually Tchepikov. Tchepikov can be written either ending in a 'v', or with a double 'f', rather like you can spell the pianist and composer Sergei Rachmaninov with a 'v' at the end, or a double 'f' so it becomes Rachmaninoff, with two 'f's at the end. So, Tchepik*ov* becomes Tchepik*off*.

"When Keppof changed his name, he changed it from his Russian name of Tchepikoff to the German name of Keppof."

Stephanie let out a little gasp. "So they were related?"

"Yes," said JP. "Dr Keppof dropped the extra 'f' at the end to make it more German and less Russian. His first name was Filipp, with an 'F' - F I L I P P - which in German became Philipp, spelt with a 'P' - P H I L I P P. The 'F' disappeared, and became a 'P', so both his first and last names changed. The report which he filed was signed P. Keppof. Had Vashinsky looked at Keppof's file in detail, instead of just ordering the man killed, he might have found the name change, and found the link and thought differently both about killing him and on how to handle the matter. Praporshchik Tchepikova was Dr Keppof's daughter."

JP paused for a while, taking some more water and grabbing a bite of the sandwich.

"Wow, that's amazing," said Stephanie, as she thought through what JP had just said. "Ok, so carry on?"

JP swallowed his mouthful.

"Keppof wanted to send in his report about what he had discovered. He discussed it with me in February, but also with his daughter. She said why not send it to her boss, Director Bortnikov; Keppof didn't want to do that in case, if it was all nonsense and he ended up looking a fool, it might reflect badly somehow on her. He said he would think about it. Apparently, later, he sent it not to Bortnikov, but to the number two, Vashinsky; unfortunately the one person he shouldn't have. And it got him killed.

"But the daughter didn't know her father had sent the report in," said JP. "Keppof had told her that if anything should happen to him suddenly, that she should come and see me - I had met her once before, so she knew me but not well. Then, her father died in what appeared to be a senseless mugging. But his death really could have been just an accident, and in her distress she delayed. That was almost the end of it. Vital days could have gone by."

"Then what?" said Stephanie. She was sitting upright now, looking across at JP waiting to hear the rest of the story.

"Well Vashinsky very nearly got away with it. That's the chance part; if he'd done nothing more, he would have, it would have been too late. But Vashinsky made another mistake, and altered fate, including his own."

"What?" said Stephanie. "What?"

"He had his driver, Corporal Sergey Baskov, killed, by having someone push him under a train at the subway in Moscow. Vashinsky was trying to cover up a meeting he'd gone to that same day, probably with Malekka; we'll never know. But anyway, office relationships at the Lubyanka are frowned on and it wasn't widely known that for quite some time Sergey Baskov had been dating Anna Tchepikova, and that they were very much in love. In fact, virtually engaged to be married. Baskov had sent Anna a text just before lunch on the day he died saying he had driven his boss somewhere on the outskirts of Moscow for an important meeting, was waiting for him to return; just chit chat. They exchanged a couple more texts, and were set to meet up that night. But, on the way home, Sergey met with an accident and died."

"Oh my God," said Stephanie, "How terrible. And the poor girl. She lost them both."

"Yes. So you see," said JP, "two apparent accidents, to the two people who were the closest in the world to her. Of course, they couldn't possibly both have just been accidents, the odds were stacked against it. So it was now clear to Anna that her father had been murdered and that Vashinsky was the connecting point, the common denominator. Her father must have sent the report in, but to him; and Vashinsky also had the man she loved killed. Vashinsky killed them both.

"That's when she came to see me. There was obviously something going on, she was sure it was Vashinsky but she couldn't prove it, and so what should she do? I met her in London at Claridge's when I saw Charlie Melton just after you had been taken on St Lucia, and I was en route to South Africa. She told me that now Sergey had just died too, murdered she was sure, and that Vashinsky was behind it all. Not surprisingly she was in a terrible state, but wanted to bring Vashinsky down if she could. I didn't have time to talk much then. We arranged that she would come back to London, depending on what happened. She returned to Moscow, and waited.

"I wanted to find a way to Vashinsky and establish, for certain, he was the one betraying his country and selling a nuclear weapon to terrorists. I came up with a plan. Anna met me in London again, when I returned there after the Fincrest raid." He paused for a moment, and then added, "That time was awful... trying to stay focused, and wondering how you were and what was happening to you."

She put her head onto his shoulder once more and her arms around him, and squeezed. He hugged her back.

"Anyway, like I said, I came up with a plan. I figured that if Vashinsky was selling a nuclear weapon, he was going to be getting a large amount of money. We knew by then that Malekka was fabulously wealthy and backed by Iran too, so money wasn't a problem. I figured the best way of proving Vashinsky's involvement was to find the money. Which meant I had to get into his computer in his office.

"Anna had told me about the data sticks for the daily confidential traffic. That seemed a possibility. So I suggested she brought me a blank one, and, although it was a big risk, she did. I took it to a friend, Steve Montague, who owns Stemont, an electronics computer firm handling sensitive military systems contracts all over the world. He's a real computer wiz, a total genius. A couple of days later, after my Zimbabwe jaunt, he gave it back to me. He was a bit worried about it actually, poor guy; he said that what he had given me was totally illegal. Which without doubt it was. You see, the data stick now contained an extremely subversive, well-hidden rogue programme that once plugged into a laptop or mainframe would copy itself over and erase itself from the stick. The thing would then go to work, searching for bank details and files, security numbers, keystrokes, passwords… without anything visible or anyone knowing. It would then email everything out direct to me, and erase itself. No-one would ever know it had been there."

"No wonder your friend was so worried then," said Stephanie. "It really does sound totally illegal. Imagine what you could do with that in the UK."

"Yes. But then, it was all for a good reason. I had to have that little programme to get at Vashinsky. So, Anna came to London again, I gave her the stick back the same evening and she went back to Moscow. I told her to wait for my signal, I didn't want her to plant it too early, since something might go wrong; she might get discovered, then questioned, maybe even tortured. And Malekka could then be warned. No, I had to wait for the right moment. Anna made sure she was the one taking the data sticks down to Vashinsky, and spent a little time getting friendly with him - you know, like you girls can when you want to."

They both smiled. Stephanie knew all about that.

Once we'd heard from you, I sent her a text as I left for Cyprus. Anna gave the stick to the Director for the day's traffic when he asked for one, activated the programme afterwards by putting it into her own pc and typing the space bar four times, then walked it down to Vashinsky. She flirted with him a little, he took the data stick as usual and put it into his laptop. And that was that. The programme did the rest.

"She went back to her office, saw the Director in the afternoon, and resigned. She left that day, stating it was because of family reasons, the death of her father. She left Moscow that evening, flew to London and waited for me."

"Wow, what a story," said Stephanie. "It's amazing. And she's so brave to do that. That took a lot of guts."

"Yes," agreed JP. "Her father, whom she doted on, had been killed; and then her fiancé was murdered too. Her life was in total turmoil. She has nobody else in Russia.

"And, that's why I asked her to come here, to spend some time with us. She's a little younger than you, Stephie, but she has spirit, and real guts. I hope you'll like her, and maybe the two of you get on."

"Well I can't wait to meet her," said Stephanie. "She sounds an incredible girl."

"Yes, she is," said JP. "Just like you." He looked at her, and she looked back into his eyes, and smiled. He looked at her lips, and knew the moment was right. He gave her a gentle soft kiss, which she accepted, and which he could tell she was ready for and pleased to have. They pulled back, and she spoke again.

"Ok, Mr Peregrine, the master planner," she said softly. "So now tell me, I want the end of the story?"

"Yes, ma'am," he said back to her. "Well, after the action at Cuttle Cove, I went to the hotel at Limassol for a couple of hours, and checked on my laptop. The programme had worked just as Steve said it would. There were the details of the codes to a numbered Swiss Bank Account. I went in. He'd been paid one billion dollars."

"God, that's a lot of money," said Stephanie. "That's really a huge amount of money."

"Yes it is," agreed JP. "No wonder he was turned. Although he was obviously ready to be turned. Anyway, I printed out the statements of the account and wrote up a note of what had happened and what you, I and MI6 had done. I enclosed a copy of Keppof's report that I'd already scanned in London that he had given Anna for safekeeping, although, as I said, when he gave it to Anna he wasn't sure he was actually going to send it in or, if he did, to whom. Then I put it all in an envelope. I got on a plane that Charlie had laid on and went to Moscow, and had it delivered. Sir Alistair placed a call to Bortnikov and told him to read his couriered mail, which he did.

"Bortnikov immediately arrested Vashinsky. He was taken down to one of the cells of the Lubyanka that they had left over from the old days. They went to work on him, and three days later, apparently, they had everything out of him, the whole plan, the bank details, a full confession. And that was that."

"Good," said Stephanie. "Bloody madman. What happened to him?"

"I gather they discreetly put a bullet into the back of his head. And that was the end of General Vashinsky."

They didn't talk any more. The two of them looked out to the Caribbean sea, and for a few minutes just watched the birds diving into the water, and the odd fishing boat that every now and again crossed the waters.

Later that day, Anna Tchepikova arrived. They took the large Rolls Royce to the airport driven by Sir William's own chauffeur to pick her up. It was at once clear that Anna and Stephanie were going to become good friends. They were female soulmates almost from the first sentences; and had a very similar sense of humour too.

A little later they were all chatting on the beach with a cool drink. The umbrella over the table gave some respite from the hot sun. JP sat back, thinking, and looked at them both. Two very beautiful young women, very sexy, very shapely, lovely people; from different parts of the world, both immensely brave, who had both suffered tragically in the course of the last weeks. The three of them, thrown together by fate.

At dinner that evening in the house, which JP had decided was going to be a formal affair as it was their first, he produced two envelopes from his dinner jacket while they waited for dessert, and placed them down on the table in front of him.

"Ladies, I want to tell the two of you something," he said, pushing his chair back and crossing his legs. "It's a little bit serious, and so I have to ask that we stop laughing for a while, and concentrate. If we can, that is. I think you'll find it interesting."

JP was putting on a serious mode, and he needed his two guests to listen just for a few minutes. Not easy after so much laughter and a few glasses of wine.

"Ok, Jimmy," said Anna, who spoke beautiful English without any accent. What a wonderful job his friend Keppof had done on her, he thought. "What are we going to talk about?"

"Yes, Mr Peregrine, what do you want to say to us?" said Stephanie with a twinkling smile, taking the cue from her new found friend, adding, "We're both all yours."

Was that a flirt?! Just at that moment, he knew Stephanie would be ok. It would take time, and care, but she would be ok. And he would be there, waiting for her to come back. He smiled at them both.

JP opened his mouth to speak again but just then the butler appeared at the door to the dining room.

"Excuse me, sir," said Nawson. "There is a telephone call for you. A Major Charles Melton. He says it's urgent."

"Oh, ok thank you, Nawson," said JP. "I'll be right there."

He turned back to the women. "Girls... I have an enterprise that I would like to talk to you about. Just have a look here. It's all in the envelopes. And tomorrow we're going to take a plane ride."

JP slid an envelope over to each of them and stood. The look of relaxed laughter on their faces had given way to intrigued confusion.

"Just a couple of minutes," he said again, "and I'll be back." He turned and left the room. As he walked he smiled at the thought of the one or two little things that he hadn't told Charlie Melton or Sir Alastair during his debriefing.

One of them was the involvement of Steve Montague and the data stick. He hadn't seen any reason to do so, and it was better that Steve was kept out of it. The assumption was that somehow Praporshchik Tchepikova got hold of the bank information, perhaps by just lifting a statement from Vashinsky's desk; she copied it and got it over to JP. Perhaps.

The other thing was what he had done at the Meridien Hotel in Cyprus after he had printed out the statements of Vashinsky's bank account that showed deposits totalling one billion US dollars.

What price can you put on the life of a woman who gave herself to her country and a cause to find information, save millions of lives, who opened herself up to torture and rape, and physical and mental abuse from which it would probably take her years to recover fully, if indeed she ever could?

And what price can you put on the destroyed life of a woman whose beloved father had been stabbed to death, whose future husband had been pushed under the hacking wheels of a train and killed, but who then produced great strength and courage to bring the murderer to justice?

JP didn't think there was really any price that one could put on it. But he thought that the $200m that was now sitting in each of two numbered Swiss bank accounts, one in the name of Stephanie Raughton and the other Anna Tchepikova, would go some way towards helping. They would travel to Geneva tomorrow to complete the account verification process.

JP had smiled as he had transferred the money out of Vashinsky's account after printing the statements. He thought it was a stroke of genius. For two reasons. First, it would for sure seal the fate of Vashinsky. The people who doubtless would interrogate him and eventually get the account access details out of him would, once they had gone into the account to verify his answers, thereby also further confirming his guilt, discover that the money had been moved. They would think Vashinsky had moved the money on to himself, elsewhere. The interrogation would doubtless continue some more as a consequence. The billion dollars had left Vashinsky's account in various tranches and gone to JP's own numbered accounts, disappearing in the Cayman Islands, the Virgin Islands and then his account back in Switzerland.

Second, who else was going to want the money anyway? Russia? They wouldn't pursue it. Vashinsky wouldn't be able to spend it, and a traitor selling a nuclear weapon stolen from the heart of Russia and almost blowing up Israel from the Mediterranean was a subject best kept quiet and quickly forgotten. It could provoke worldwide condemnation and outrage against Russia costing her billions of Rubles in sanctions and aborted trade contracts.

Iran or Malekka? Iran wasn't going to be admitting

anything and Malekka had disappeared, and neither the country nor the man needed the money anyway. Not that they would try to get it back; why would they? It was payment for services fully rendered.

The money would otherwise be wasted. And at that moment JP was the bearer of the Fifth Rubric and immune from any international laws. He had his own ethics code of right and wrong, his own laws by which to live. On that day Jim Peregrine answered only to himself and the Almighty.

The money could instead be put to very good use. Fighting evil instead of funding it.

It was indeed a stroke of inspired genius.

$200m for each of the ladies, he thought; and he would make very good use of the remaining $600m. The world was full of criminals, terrorists, and evil people trying to harm others. And that included Barakah Malekka, who was still at large; JP was certain that at some time or other in the future their paths would cross again.

JP knew he had much work to do. And $600m would help him. As he hoped the girls would decide to do, too.

Stephanie and Anna opened their envelopes. When they saw the account details, and the amount of money, their mouths opened in astonishment, and each soon had tears in their eyes, from a combination of amazement, gratitude, comfort, relief and a knowledge of a solid future. In addition to the forms, and the statements from the bank confirming the transfers, that JP had obtained in his brief day trip to Geneva, each envelope contained one of his business cards, the same business card he had sent to Vashinsky and General Bortnikov. There was no writing.

Through the tears, Anna said to Stephanie, "But I don't understand the card. What does it mean, Stephie?"

Stephanie blinked through the tears too, and smiled.

"I understand it," she said. "I can tell you what it means."

One side of the card was blank. On the other side, was a picture. It was of a bird. Of a Falcon. The fastest Falcon. A Peregrine Falcon.

JP reached the drawing room. He sat down, and picked up the telephone.

"Hello, Charlie?" he said. He started to listen. His face went grim. There was something new for him to do. For them to do.

He would begin his planning, his chess moves, his calculations, and find the way forwards to defeat the other side. He had the resources, both financial and human, to deal with the evil.

This was what he wanted to do, and was able to do. He was good at it.

And soon, more people would know it.

The Falcon had come onto the stage.

* * * THE END * * *

The Falcon will return

in

Decoy 17

AUTHOR'S NOTE

Although *Spider 2-3* is a work of entertainment there are parallels to much of its story in the real world; the actions of Muslim extremists continue, while despite the joyful Sochi Winter Olympics the Russian Bear remains on the prowl.

I have always been a great fan of Alistair MacLean's novels, and in particular his gripping story *Where Eagles Dare* and the movie of the same name, from filmmakers Elliott Kastner and Brian G. Hutton, and starring Richard Burton and Clint Eastwood. Full of excitement and twists and turns, the full plot isn't revealed until the very end. Great storytelling.

This was my inspiration for this book.

In writing *Spider 2-3* I used some outline diagrams. These appeared first as doodles on napkins and then I upgraded them with backdrops in Quark and Photoshop. I found I referred to these images regularly.

Before you finally close the cover of *Spider 2-3* or lay down your Kindle or tablet I thought I would share them with you.

The working images on the last four pages are:

1: Southern Africa, Musina, Fincrest Centre.
2: Europe, Sochi, Western Caucasus, Krasnaya Polyana.
3: The Second Asset.
4: The Cuttle Cove complex.

I look forward to seeing you again with the next adventure for The Falcon, *Decoy 17*.

Robert Vallier

www.robertvallier.com

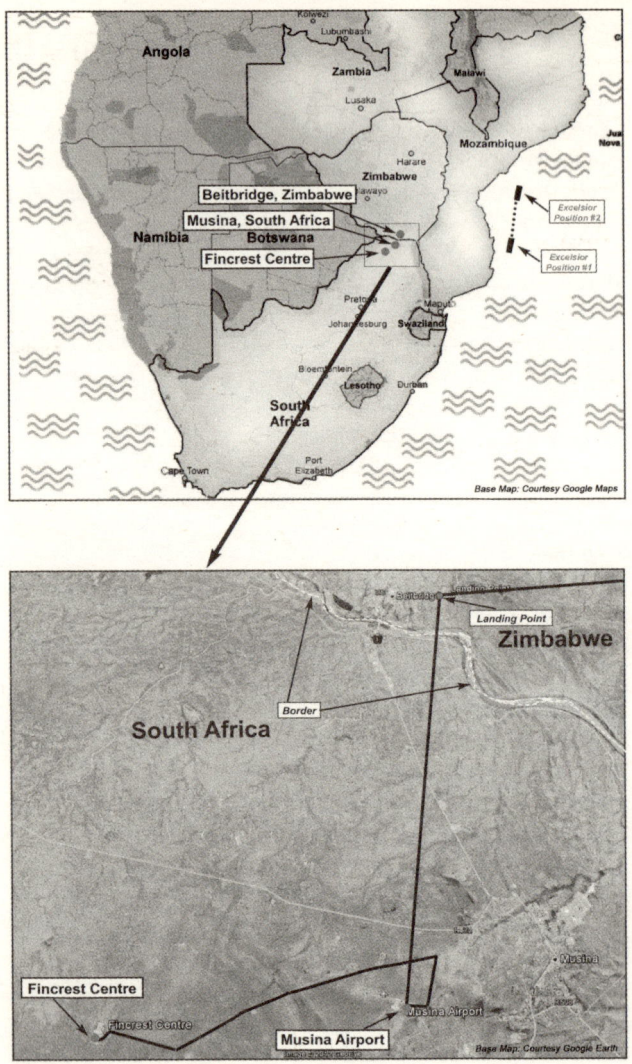

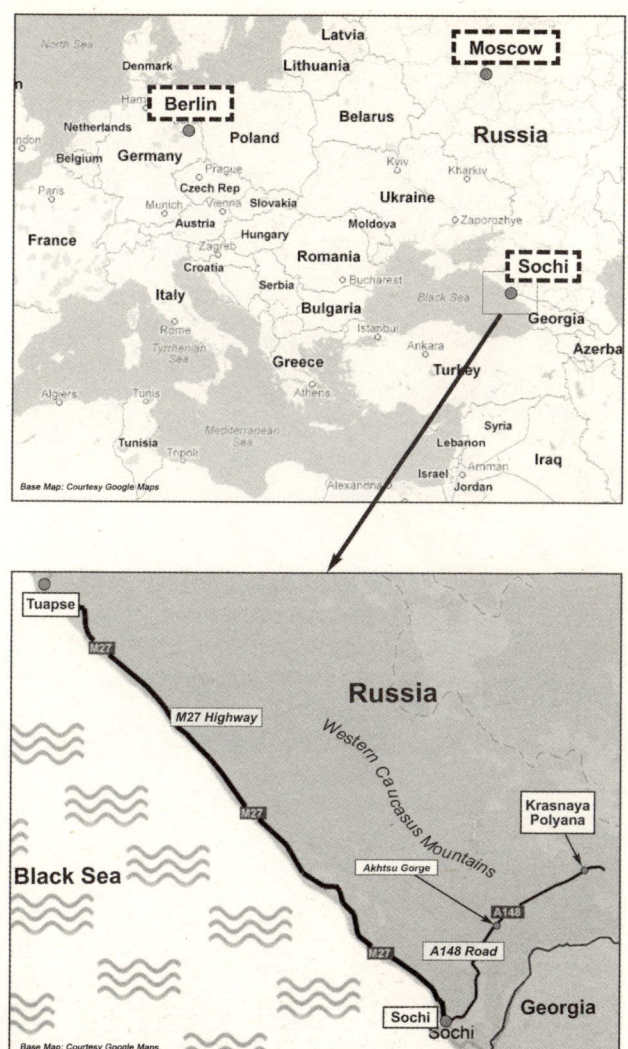

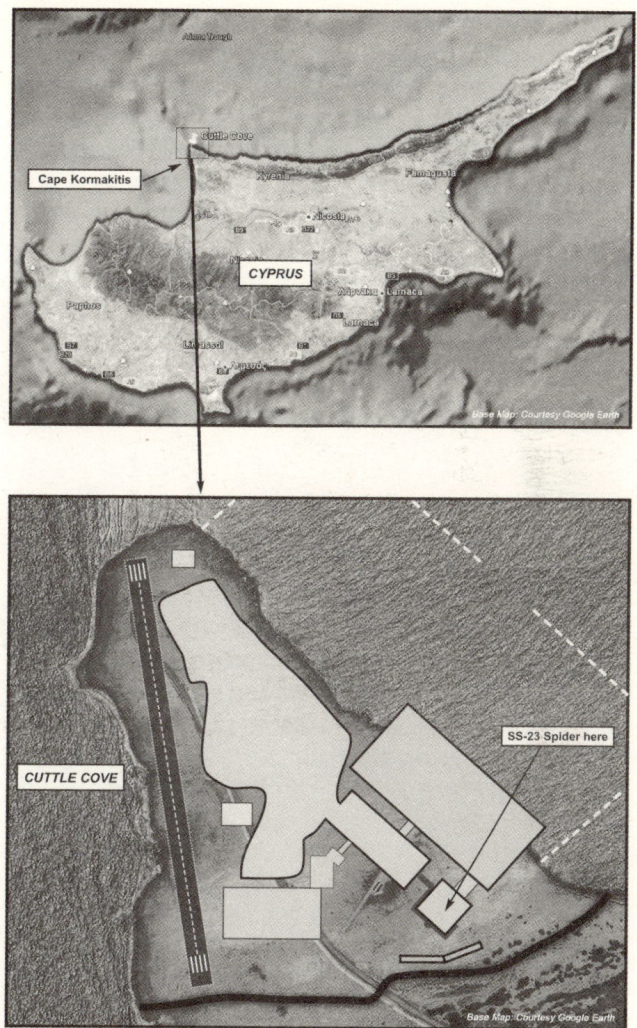